PROVIDENCE

THE MCBRIDE CHRONICLES
BOOK ONE

"It was clear to me as I glanced back over my earlier life, that a loving PROVIDENCE watched over me, that all was directed for me by a higher power."

Hans Christian Andersen.

VALERIE GREEN

a novel

THE MCBRIDE CHRONICLES
BOOK ONE

Copyright © 2022 Valerie Green

Cataloguing data available from Library and Archives Canada
978-0-88839-739-3 [paperback]
978-0-88839-740-9 [epub]

FRONT/BACK COVER DESIGN: J. RADE

FRONT COVER ARTWORK: ALAMY & ISTOCK PHOTOS

PRODUCTION & DESIGN: J. Rade, M. Lamont

EDITOR: D. MARTENS

We acknowledge the support of the Government of Canada through the Canada Book Fund and the Canada Council for the Arts, and of the Province of British Columbia through the British Columbia Arts Council and the Book Publishing Tax Credit.

Hancock House gratefully acknowledges the Halkomelem Speaking Peoples whose unceded, shared and asserted traditional territories our offices reside upon.

Published simultaneously in Canada and the United States by
HANCOCK HOUSE PUBLISHERS LTD.
19313 Zero Avenue, Surrey, B.C. Canada V3Z 9R9
#104-4550 Birch Bay-Lynden Rd, Blaine, WA, U.S.A. 98230-9436
(800) 938-1114   Fax (800) 983-2262
www.hancockhouse.com   info@hancockhouse.com

PROVIDENCE
Is dedicated to
SARAH COTTON-ELLIOTT
The bravest, most resilient woman I will ever know, with abiding love.

"Nothing is stronger than a broken woman rebuilding herself."

AUTHOR'S NOTE

When I first began writing *The McBride Chronicles* and it was still called *House of Tomorrow*, I did not purposely set out to write about strong women.

However, as my female characters developed and grew, I soon discovered they were leading me in directions I never could have imagined. In each book in the series they were showing me the resilience of women when life seems to be at its very worst. Looking back now, I think perhaps all my female characters were inspired by the strong women in my own life. For that reason, I have dedicated each book to one of those women.

I would be remiss if I didn't add that there are also many strong male characters in the *McBride Chronicles* and, on their behalf, I acknowledge with love the strong men in my own life who have inspired and supported me, especially my father, my husband and my son.

The house "Providence" in this story is purely fictional, but I have placed it in an area along the Gorge Waterway, in British Columbia's capital city, Victoria, which does indeed exist and is on the unceded Coast Salish territory of the Lekwungen First Nations. At one time many large mansions were built by white colonial settlers on both sides of the Gorge Arm. Only Point Ellice House remains, now a Heritage Museum open to the public. I would like to think that "Providence" would also have survived in some capacity, so I have taken literary license by embellishing this industrial area in keeping with my fictional story.

I hope you enjoy Jane and Gideon's story in *Providence* (Book One) and want to read more in the forthcoming books. I promise you more adventures and compelling family dynamics to come.

Valerie Green, 2021

TABLE OF CONTENTS

McBRIDE FAMILY TREE

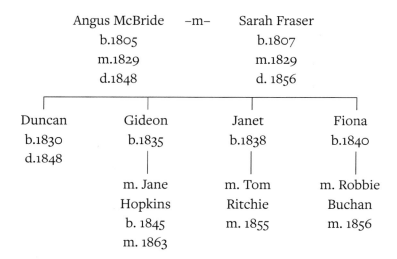

Angus McBride   –m–   Sarah Fraser
b.1805   b.1807
m.1829   m.1829
d.1848   d. 1856

Duncan	Gideon	Janet	Fiona
b.1830	b.1835	b.1838	b.1840
d.1848			
	m. Jane	m. Tom	m. Robbie
	Hopkins	Ritchie	Buchan
	b. 1845	m. 1855	m. 1856
	m. 1863		

CALDWELL FAMILY TREE

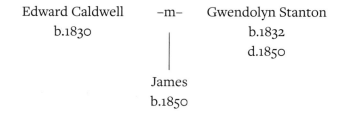

Edward Caldwell   –m–   Gwendolyn Stanton
b.1830   b.1832
                             d.1850

James
b.1850

PROLOGUE

By the time the woman reached her destination, her steps slowed by the basket she carried, the snow was falling heavily. Tears rolled down her cold cheeks.

Three final steps took her up to the front door of the Home. She banged on the door with frozen fingers. Taking one last look down into the basket, she drew the well-worn blanket away from the baby's face. The child's eyes opened for a moment, and she began to whimper softly, as though she understood what was happening.

"I'm so sorry," the woman whispered as the door creaked open and a large woman gazed at her.

"Are you the matron?" the woman asked.

"I am! And what have we here?"

"This ... is my baby. Please take care of her for me until I can come back for her. This letter for you will explain everything. There is also a letter for her to read when she's older—if I can't return." The woman thrust the two letters at the matron.

"Well, we're full right now, but I suppose I can make room," she said harshly. Placing the basket on the step, the woman turned quickly and ran off into the dark night.

The matron hesitated before picking up the basket. Her eyes swept over the two letters, especially the one addressed to "Jane Hopkins Sheridan." The handwriting was elegant and appeared to be written by an educated person. No one ever knocked on the door or left letters. Unmarried mothers usually just deposited their unwanted babies on the step and ran away.

"These mothers never return. But that one seems to be different," the matron mumbled to herself as she took the basket inside. "Maybe I'll take a look at her letter—and find out who she is."

The door slammed behind her, and the baby's fate was sealed.

PART ONE

ENGLAND, *six years later*

JANE – The Orphanage
(1851–1860)

CHAPTER 1

I loved Sundays.

It was the day we went to St. Mary's village church and could watch all the posh people in the front pews without being scolded about staring. The only problem with Sundays was Reverend Erasmus Lloyd, who scared me half to death with his loud sermons and talk about hell and damnation. Thin as a pole, he was, with skin the colour of gray leather. He towered over the pulpit and would grip both sides with his long hands, unless he was marching up and down the aisle.

That Sunday in early February, I was sitting in the back of the church with the other children. I was six years old. My feet didn't quite touch the floor and I could barely see over the pews. Weak winter light filtered through the windows as a woman from the village played a hymn on the organ.

Sixteen of us orphans from Field House, ranging in age from five to fourteen, huddled together on the cold, hard wooden seats. The infants and younger children always stayed back at the home, under the dubious care of one of the village girls.

I stretched as tall as I could to peer at the gentry sitting on their soft velvet hassocks near the woodstove. The ladies wore long leather gloves and fancy hats with feathers. Their sparkling pearl and diamond earrings always caught my eye. I made up my mind that someday, when I became a lady, I would wear clothes and jewelry like that. Yes, I would. I'd sit all careful like, in one of those elegant crinoline dresses. Mine would be colourful and shiny and made of the very finest material. Everyone would be jealous of me.

One of the little rich girls, the one wearing a bonnet tied with bright red ribbons, turned around and stared at us. She raised her chin and narrowed her eyes, the way the gentry did whenever they looked at us. That pretty bonnet would look much better on me than it did on her, I thought. Oh, how I longed to be up front, sitting with them, and then to go home in an elegant carriage to a magnificent mansion.

The wealthy families always entered the church first, and we were brought in once they got settled. After the service ended, they would leave first, and as they passed by, all of us children had to keep our heads bowed. If curiosity ever got the better of us and we raised our heads, Mrs. Creed would whack our hands with her stick. Cursed with an inborn curiosity, I had experienced the pain of her stick across my knuckles and legs on many an occasion.

Agnes Creed was the matron of Field House, the one who had found me on the front step when I was a baby. Someone had knocked at the door, and when she opened it, there I was, lying in a basket, covered by only a thin blanket. "You were no more than a month old," she told me. "And you were crying. I couldn't very well have left you there in the bitter cold, though we were already quite full." Her voice always clucked with annoyance and her double chins wiggled to and fro in the retelling of the story.

On the note pinned to the blanket, someone had scrawled the name "Jane Hopkins" and the message, "Please take care of my child." I so wanted to see that note and my mother's handwriting, but Mrs. Creed said it had been thrown into the fire. I wondered if it had ever existed. Perhaps she had lied.

She would wag one of her thick, fat fingers at me and say that she, the home, and its board of governors had been more than generous to take me in and provide for me ever since. She repeated this again and again, telling me I should be eternally grateful to them all. I was, however, hard-pressed to find anything in her manner I should have been grateful for.

From this scant knowledge of my background, I had decided to make Christmas the day I was born. Not that anyone ever acknowledged birthdays at the home, but when Mr. Lloyd came over to Field House for our devotionals, he would talk to us about baby Jesus, who was born on that day, and I rather liked the idea of having the same birthday.

Once the organist stopped playing, Reverend Lloyd pounded on the pulpit, and a hush fell over the congregation.

"From James, chapter 4," he said, his booming voice filling the church. "What causes wars, and what causes fighting among you? Is it not your passions that are at war in your members? You desire and do not have, so you kill. And you covet and cannot obtain, so you fight and wage war."

In two long strides, the reverend was in the aisle, pacing up and down. His black robes swish-swished as he swept past us. His gray skin and hawk-like features melted into a black blur.

"He who does not seek after righteousness and true holiness, let him pretend what he may, he is dead while he lives! You must heed the word of the Lord or risk eternal hell and damnation!" he shouted, his fist waving in the air.

His words blasted through me, sending shivers down my spine that added to the effect of the cold draft already biting at my ankles.

Reverend Lloyd might have sounded scary, but he was never unkind or mean, like Mrs. Creed. We called her "Old Sourface." My friend Dory Evans had made up that name.

When Mr. Lloyd swept up the aisle again, Dory nudged me. "Look over there," she whispered. I grabbed the back of the pew in front of us and pulled myself up. A boy in a blue sailor suit had turned around to stare at us. He wiped his runny nose with the back of his hand. "See, Scrap, even the rich have snot," Dory snickered under her breath.

We giggled and were rewarded with Old Sourface's stick firmly across our hands. Mine were already red and sore from hours of scrubbing floors. I couldn't help but laugh at Dory's cheeky sense of humor, but it usually got us into trouble, and we'd have to suffer extra chores and a clip around the head.

Dory was two years older than me. She wasn't a complete orphan, because her mother was still alive. Her father had died when Dory was a baby, and her mother had tried to raise her alone. But when Dory was four years old, her mother contracted something called *consumption*, and within a year, she was too ill and weak to take care of her daughter, so she brought Dory to the home.

At least Dory knew who her parents were. I knew nothing about mine, except that Mrs. Creed had told me I was left by a woman of *loose morals*. Whatever that meant, it didn't sound good. I preferred to believe that my mother had merely fallen on hard times and had been forced to give me up.

As for my father, I felt certain he was a courageous sea captain sailing around the world, like Gulliver in the stories Mr. Lloyd read to us during our lessons. My father had most likely set off to sea, unaware of my existence. One day soon, he would return and rescue me from this miserable life. He would find my mother, and all of us would live together in a grand house with lots of servants and delicious food.

And soon, Dory's mother would get better and come for her, too. It had been almost four years since Dory first arrived at the home, so surely her mother would recover any day.

"And if your dad still isn't back from sea, we'll take you to live with us, Scrap," she would tell me. "I'd never leave you here with Old Sourface."

Dory always called me Scrap because I was so small. I hated it when the others teased me about my size, but I never minded Dory's pet name for me, because she was my friend.

As Mr. Lloyd closed his sermon, he bid all his parishioners to end their day wisely and well in the work of the Lord.

"Ah, yes, and I would like to see all the children from Field House in the sanctuary at the end of the service, Mrs. Creed. We will close now with hymn number eighty-one."

My stomach fluttered with excitement, and I reached out to squeeze Dory's hand. We were never invited into the sanctuary other than for our lessons.

As the organ bellowed, we raised our heads slightly—no doubt, Mrs. Creed would have liked to punish sixteen pairs of hands with one stick at the same time. Instead, she muttered angrily to herself and indicated to us all to stand with the rest of the congregation to join our voices in unison, each verse becoming louder as the tenors drowned out the basses until we reached the end:

> *Grant us grace to see Thee, Lord,*
> *Mirrored in Thy holy Word,*
> *May we imitate Thee now,*
> *And be pure, as pure art Thou,*
> *That we like to Thee may be,*
> *At Thy great Epiphany,*
> *And may praise Thee, ever blest,*
> *God in man made manifest ...*

I sang my heart out on the final verse, followed by a resounding *Amen.* That morning I felt as *pure as Him,* and I knew I would be made manifest, whatever that meant. It must be something good. Dory always laughed at me when I said such things. She told me I had some funny ideas.

The gentry finally left the church, including the boy with the runny nose and the snooty girl wearing the bonnet with red ribbons. She stuck out her tongue at me as she passed by, and I did the same back. Thankfully, just then, Mrs. Creed glanced down at her dress to straighten it and didn't notice.

In the sanctuary, Mr. Lloyd stood by his desk—not smiling, but then, he rarely did. He had discarded his black Sunday robe in favor of a dark gray one that matched the color of his hair. Inclining his head toward Mrs. Creed, he motioned for her to sit down.

"Children," he said, I have asked you here today instead of waiting until lesson time tomorrow because, with your permission, Mrs. Creed, I have a special presentation to make."

He paused, and I looked up at him without fear of Mrs. Creed's stick. She didn't use it in his presence, always pretending to be a good, kind, and loving woman, taking care of her brood of orphans. We children knew better.

She nodded to Mr. Lloyd to continue. "I have been extremely pleased with all of you in your daily devotionals and learning of the Holy Scriptures and have decided that one among you who has worked particularly hard shall receive a book as a gift for those labours. I intend to present a Bible catechism to that person this morning."

He held up a small leather book, and I gazed at it in awe. Like most of the Field House children, I had never received a gift before. So for one of us to be presented with a book, even one that we would undoubtedly have to study, would be nothing short of a miracle.

Mr. Lloyd focused his dark eyes directly at me. "The book is being presented to you, Jane Hopkins," he said. "Come, child, come forward and accept your gift with good grace."

My insides shook as I walked toward him, my head high. Mrs. Creed had always told us never to show pride. Pride would be our downfall, she said, for only the meek would be rewarded in heaven. Maybe so, but I had never felt prouder than I did at that moment. Mr. Lloyd had chosen *me* for this gift!

He handed me the small book and told me to open it. "There you will find your name inscribed, Jane, and the date. Continue to read the Scriptures well. Go forth now, and may God bless you always."

"Thank you, Mr. Lloyd," I whispered, my voice trembling. "Thank you very much. I will take great care of this gift."

He placed his hand on my shoulder. I couldn't remember anyone ever touching me in such a gentle way. I was sure then that I must at last be as pure as the one who had died on the cross, the one whose birthday I'd decided to share.

"Come, come, children, it's time to get back." Mrs. Creed rose to leave, her back facing Mr. Lloyd.

She held her stick low in front of her, tapping it softly against the palm of her hand, staring at me as we turned to file out of the room.

A chill shot down my spine.

CHAPTER 2

The snow was falling hard as we left the sanctuary and walked the short distance back to Field House. I held the Bible catechism close to my chest, my heart about to burst with happiness. Distracted, I stepped into an icy puddle, jolting me back to the present. My shoes and the bottom of my smock were soaked, and they would have to stay that way for some time. I had nothing else to wear.

How I wished I had lots of pretty dresses like the rich people, but we girls at Field House had only two gray uniforms, one for winter and one for summer, plus a pair of black laced boots, and a thin over-smock passing itself off as a coat. Underneath the dismal gray smocks, we wore black stockings and a shift. Depending on how we outgrew things, we received a new uniform every year, but because I was so small, my uniforms lasted longer. They were usually threadbare before they were finally turned into rags. But on that Sunday, even being soaked to the skin couldn't spoil my excitement.

Following behind Dory, I had just stepped inside Field House when Mrs. Creed grabbed my arm and yanked me into the corner. "You think you're something special now, don't you, missy? Well, you can wipe that silly smile off your face and stoke all the fires by yourself today."

"But Mrs. Creed—"

She raised her hand and struck me across the head with her stick, nearly knocking me off my feet. "Don't talk back to me, girl. Get to work."

Usually on Sundays after church, all we were required to do was read the Bible in the common room while we took turns stoking the one stove there. For those precious couple of hours, I would read the scriptures while daydreaming about another, better life, where I had a family that loved me and we always had plenty to eat.

The common room was the only heated area in the entire house. The girls' and boys' sleeping quarters were always cold because they were well away from the stove, separated by a long corridor in each direction.

"Jane, I repeat, today you will tend to the fire by yourself while the others sit and read. This will strengthen your character as well as your body. It will teach you not to be proud, child, for pride, as you well know, is a sin. A terrible sin!"

My bottom lip trembled, but I held my breath to hold back the tears. Looking up at her ugly face, I decided that hatred was perhaps an even greater sin than pride. Later in my prayers, I would ask God for forgiveness, but for now my belly was hot with anger.

As I went about hauling in the heavy, snow-covered logs from the pile out back, the others watched me with pity in their eyes. I told myself that my life could have been worse. At least we had Mr. Lloyd, who came every day to teach us our letters and the Scriptures and read us stories. Most orphans and the village poor were sent to the workhouse at the opposite end of the village, and the children were not even taught to read or write.

By the time Mrs. Creed sent me to bed that night, I was so tired I thought I would surely fall asleep immediately. Instead, I lay in the dormitory on my hard wooden cot under a thin blanket, hugging my Bible catechism gift.

I wanted to read my name inside the book one more time, but it was impossible in the darkness. All the candles had been extinguished.

"Are you awake, Dory?" I whispered to the bed next to mine.

"Yes." I heard her turn over to face me. "Are you looking at your present?"

"I'm trying, but I can't see it."

As my eyes adjusted to the dark, a faint light filtered through the one small window, and I passed my fingers over the inside page:

A gift from Reverend Lloyd to:

JANE HOPKINS
5 February 1851

"I can't imagine why Mr. Lloyd chose me," I whispered.

"'Cos you're smart, Scrap," Dory said. "You can read so much better than the rest of us, and you're only six."

I smiled. Then my stomach growled. I was always hungry, but even more so that night because I'd had no supper, the usual bread and soup. It was quite unfair. Nothing was ever saved for children who might be absent from a meal, even if they were doing chores or were ill.

That's all we ever had. A small piece of bread and watery soup with a stray piece of meat or a vegetable floating around in the murky liquid, but mostly it was a yellow-colored gruel that did little to appease my hunger. Still, I would have gladly had some right then.

Now I'd have to wait until seven in the morning for the usual serving of lumpy porridge that would have to last me until supper. Groaning, I turned over, pulled the thin blanket over my head, and drew my knees up to my chest in a feeble attempt to get warm.

I had to learn all I could now, because one day, God willing, I would leave this place and become someone special. Now that Mr. Lloyd had presented me with a gift, I was sure my time would come.

*   *   *

The first bell came at five. Mrs. Creed walked up and down the hallway, swinging the bell back and forth, and when she opened the dormitory doors, she swung it even harder and longer, making my head hurt. We jumped out of bed, hauled in water, washed our faces, dressed, and made our beds. Then, we scrubbed the floors in our dormitories, the corridors, and the common room, where we also stoked the fire again. By the time we sat down to eat, my whole body trembled with hunger. I gagged, nearly throwing up, but there would have been nothing to spew out.

Certainly the gentry didn't have to wake up to the bloody awful sound of bells. And certainly, a maid would haul in water and scrub the floor.

After breakfast, Mrs. Creed customarily took roll call, but I don't know why she did this. We were always there, because there was nowhere else to go. Then, another bell rang. Between eight and ten o'clock, we had prayers to read and the Bible to study, followed by our schoolwork with Mr. Lloyd. Around noon, we were allowed outside. We wandered in circles and played imaginary games, but the girls didn't mingle much with the boys.

In the afternoon, we did more sweeping and scrubbing, followed by more study time until supper. After we ate, Mrs. Creed, who dined in her own room, came to take roll call again in the common room, and we read our prayers once more. At seven o'clock, we got ready for bed, and at eight, all candles were extinguished.

Tomorrow, we would do it all over again.

On the following Saturday, we got to take our weekly bath. Dory and I and the other eight girls dragged the large iron bathtub into the common room and filled it with buckets of lukewarm water we had heated on the stove.

Standing in line, we took turns, from the oldest to the youngest, getting into the water and cleansing ourselves of our "sins." Infants were bathed by the village girls separately, but that didn't happen much because Mrs. Creed said that babies weren't sinful. That's why the nursery smelled even worse than the rest of Field House. Being one of the youngest and definitely smallest of the girls, I was always the last to enter the tub, by which time the water was filthy and stone cold. I felt the iciness deep in my soul. On that particular Saturday, I shivered so violently I thought I was dying.

We were never allowed to remove all of our clothing. Mrs. Creed instructed us to take off only our smocks and black stockings and then step into the tub in our shift.

"Gazing upon one's own naked body is vain and sinful," she said.

But I had learned a few tricks, like sitting low in the water, lifting up my shift, and then placing the soap on my skin underneath and scrubbing hard. I made sure Mrs. Creed wasn't watching, because she would have gone after me with her stick.

The light in all this dreariness was Mr. Lloyd's lessons, without which I surely would have gone mad.

* * *

It snowed nearly every day that long winter, and the strong, biting Cotswold winds blew through the village, creating enormous drifts. Some days we couldn't leave Field House even to cross the lane to go to church. And Mr. Lloyd could not leave the sanctuary to teach us.

To pass the time, Dory and I often made up games to play in our dormitory before the candles were extinguished. "Let's pretend we are a lord and lady of the manor," she would say.

"And we have ten servants each to wait on us," I added. "My maid will curl my hair before dinner. Tonight, we are having roast beef and potatoes."

"Oh and how beautiful you would look, Lady Jane, with your curly locks and pretty green eyes."

"And you, Lady Dory, will be so—magnificent." I tried to think of the most wonderful word I knew. "Your black eyes will shine, and the most handsome man in the room will beg you to marry him."

We giggled boisterously.

At last, the temperatures began to rise and the snow stopped, signaling spring, though it always remained icy cold inside Field House.

One morning, Rose, a village girl, came running into the common room while we were crowded together, reading the Bible and whispering among ourselves.

Rose pointed at Dory. "Mrs. Creed wants you in her room right now."

"Why?"

Rose shrugged. "Blimey, how d'yer 'spect me to know?"

Dory stood and stretched.

"Better 'urry," Rose said. "Mrs. Creed is in a right tizzy, let me tell you."

"She always is." Dory followed Rose into the hall.

What could have happened? It must have been something awful, because no one was ever invited into Mrs. Creed's room. I tagged along in case Dory needed me.

Rose hummed to herself as we walked down the hall. She was always singing or humming a jaunty little song. How could she possibly be so happy all the time?

She tapped gingerly on Mrs. Creed's door and was greeted with a shrill "Enter!"

As she followed Rose inside, Dory threw a quick, worried glance over her shoulder at me. I sat down on the bench in the corridor outside, straining to hear.

A moment later, Rose shot out the door, luckily in such a hurry she left the door ajar.

"I have news about your mother, girl," I heard Mrs. Creed say.

She must have recovered! I almost jumped up and ran in. Dory would be leaving Field House, and if she left, that meant I might also be on my way out of this terrible place.

"Oh, is she better?" Dory sounded excited. "Has the consumption gone, Mrs. Creed?"

"No, she's dead," was the coldhearted reply.

"What! But she can't be!" Dory's voice dropped to a whisper. "My mother said she would come and get me when she got better, so she can't be dead."

"Stop your sniveling, girl. Your mother is dead. Can't be helped—just one of those things. You are now an orphan, and you belong to Field House until we decide it's time for you to leave."

"No, please, tell me that isn't true."

"Get hold of yourself, Dory Evans. You must learn to face your misfortunes with fortitude. Your mother is dead. Be a good soldier—accept it and move on." I could hear that wretched woman rustling some papers on her desk. "Now, go back to what you were doing—off you go. And shut that door behind you, child. It's letting in a draft."

When Dory came out, her face was deathly white and her shoulders sagged. I knew she was holding back a fountain of tears, because Mrs. Creed had taught us never to show emotion. It did not become us, she said.

"I'm so sorry, Dory," I whispered.

She took a deep breath. "Oh well, that's it, I suppose. I'm stuck here in this hellhole with you, Scrap!"

She sank down onto the bench beside me, and we both fell silent. Then I remembered how Mr. Lloyd had placed his hand on my shoulder in a comforting manner and how it had made me feel better, so I slowly raised my arm and put it around Dory's shoulders. I patted her gently.

"We'll make the best of it and get through it, won't we?"

She nodded. "You bet we will, Scrap. I'm never letting that old bitch upset me. She can make my life as miserable as she wants, but I'll never let her know. Never! And when I'm fifteen, I'll leave this place forever, and that's not too long to wait."

I didn't contradict her, even though she was only eight years old, and I knew from learning my numbers that she had another seven years to go.

We sat on the bench for a while, my legs swinging back and forth. Dory sniffed and wiped her nose on her sleeve while my arm went numb as I stretched it around her shoulders. Her mother was dead, yet neither of us dared shed a tear.

We were two pathetic, stoic little souls. Dory should have been crying for a mother she barely remembered but had once loved. I should have been crying for a dream of mine that had disappeared.

But I wouldn't stay at the home forever. Like Dory, when I turned fifteen, and the board of directors placed me out in the world, they would either put me in service at one of the neighboring estates, working for the toffs, or send me to the hiring fair in the village, where the local farmers could look me over and hire me for manual work. The two options weren't much, but they'd be better than life here with Mrs. Creed.

I was just six, though, and fifteen was a lifetime away.

CHAPTER 3

As the years went by with boring regularity, a day never passed without Mrs. Creed scolding or hitting me. Whenever I finished scrubbing my part of the floor, she would come up behind me.

"Bleeding hell, in all my born days, I've never seen anyone so useless. Jane, you call this floor clean? Scrub it again—and do it right this time." Then she gave me a whack on the back of my head with her stick.

When I got down on all fours again, she would stand over me. "You are worthless and always will be—a person of no consequence, abandoned by your own flesh and blood. Doesn't that tell you something?"

Creed yelled at all of us and wielded her stick, but she singled me out for the harshest beatings. Maybe she was right—perhaps it was because I was worthless. Why else would my own mother have left me in this terrible place?

One morning, shortly after I turned nine, she grabbed me by the hair and dragged me down the corridor to the dormitories. All the beds were made except mine—though that wasn't how I'd left it.

"So, now you think you're above the rules, is that it, Miss Uppity?" she shouted to me in a fury. "How dare you, you miserable creature. Your mother was nothing but a whore. Do you understand? She got herself in a fix and you were the result—a bastard—and then she left you."

Creed threw me on the floor. "And it all started with that book."

I looked up to see a corner of my precious Bible catechism showing from beneath my pillow, where I always kept it hidden. She grabbed it and waved it at me. "This has turned you into a haughty young miss! It now belongs to me."

"But, Mrs. Creed, it's mine—my very own gift."

"Nothing is yours. This lesson will teach you to understand that you must never take pride in material things."

The next day, she assigned me more chores, this time at the church. Twice a week, while the others played outside, I was to scrub and sweep the floors, and every Friday I was to help one of the girls from the village prepare for the Sabbath. We would lay out Bibles and hymn books and the hassocks for the rich people to kneel on.

I dreamed about someone adopting me and taking me away, but I was getting too old for that. Besides, Rose had told us stories about evil people who bought children from orphanages and treated them like slaves. On really bad days, I thought about running away. But where would I go? How could I survive on the streets?

Then one day, in the summer of my ninth year, everything changed.

*   *   *

It was a Wednesday afternoon, and I had gone over to the church to do my usual cleaning chores. As I hurried to set out Bibles and hymn sheets, I noticed a thick book on the front pew. *Plays by Mr. William Shakespeare.* The pages were filled with the tiniest print, and I couldn't make out many of the words. No doubt the book belonged to Reverend Lloyd, and he'd be missing it.

The door leading to the sanctuary at the rear was slightly ajar, but when I knocked and no one answered, I pushed it open and went inside. Mr. Lloyd wasn't at his desk, so I placed the book there among his papers and turned to leave—but not before his piano caught my eye. I had seen it before, but that day, it seemed different. The ivory keys sparkled in the late-afternoon light streaming through the window. I looked around and listened. No one was about.

As soon as I sat on the piano stool and laid my fingers on those keys, beautiful music started playing in my head. But what actually came out was a cacophanous clatter as my hands flitted wildly over the keys.

So lost was I that I didn't hear the footsteps. When a shadow appeared over me, I kept my head down, fearing the worst. Mr. Lloyd would be furious. My throat went dry. Why had I done such a foolish thing?

"Little Jane Hopkins, what are you doing?" His voice sounded angry.

I jumped up and turned to face him. "I was admiring your piano, Mr. Lloyd."

"Were you, now?"

"Yes, I love the sound it makes."

"Would you like to learn how to play, Jane?"

I raised my head but kept my voice low, almost a whisper. "Oh, yes, sir, I would like that very much."

"Hmm ... perhaps. I will give the matter my consideration, child."

"Really, sir? You mean I might be able to have lessons?"

"Let's not get ahead of ourselves now. First I would have to ask Mrs. Creed."

"Oh she would never let me," I blurted out.

His eyebrows shot up in surprise. "What makes you think that?"

I remained silent. I could be in awful trouble for criticizing Mrs. Creed. After all, Mr. Lloyd probably thought she was a kind, generous woman.

"Jane, answer me."

"I ... er ... I don't think she would let me play, Mr. Lloyd, 'cause only a person of consequence would play this instrument."

"And what makes you think you are not a person of consequence?"

"Because I'm an orphan, sir. I'm a nobody."

He tutted. "Dear me," he said. "In God's eyes, even the smallest sparrow is important, Jane."

I remembered a quote from the Bible about that. Perhaps he was right. I might have been small, but I *was* bigger than a sparrow.

"I will speak with Mrs. Creed soon." He looked out the window, then back at me. "On second thought, perhaps I won't speak to her, Jane. Perhaps we should keep your lessons to ourselves. You could come for a lesson on the days when you clean the church and the others are outside. That would give you two or three lessons every week. What do you think of that?"

His face lit up with a smile. I'd never seen him look so happy.

Lying was a sin and he was a man of God! But I was not about to argue. I smiled back at him. I was going to learn how to play Mr. Lloyd's beautiful piano. It would be our secret, and I didn't care what Mrs. Creed thought.

The joy of being able to learn to play the piano would far outweigh everything else.

*   *   *

Now I could hardly wait for the days when I had to work at the church. After flying through my chores, I'd slip into the sanctuary to play the piano. I didn't tell anyone, not even Dory. Although she was my friend, she did have a bad habit of gossiping to everyone about everything, and I didn't want Mrs. Creed to find out somehow.

In the beginning, when I returned from a lesson, I was out of breath, the excitement of the music pouring out of my hands. Mrs. Creed would study my face with suspicion in her beady eyes, though that wasn't unusual. Still, I lived in dread that she would discover the truth and my piano lessons would come to an end.

So, after every lesson, I would race back to the Home, stopping just short of the door. Turning my thoughts to more serious matters, like getting caught by Old Sourface, I'd take a deep breath and change my expression so she couldn't see any trace of the joy I felt.

At first, Mr. Lloyd taught me simple scales and theory, quickly advancing to short pieces. After six weeks, he said I had a talent for the piano, and in the months that followed, we moved on to more challenging pieces, like Mr. Beethoven's *Für Elise*, then to a bagatelle and a rondo.

One day, Mr. Lloyd told me I reminded him of someone he knew long ago who also had a special musical gift. He sounded sad. To me, he was no longer the fearful reverend who ranted and raved on Sundays in church. He had become a much kinder man, more like how I imagined a father would be.

Within that first year, I had mastered Mr. Beethoven's *Sonata Number 8 in C Major (Pathetique) Adagio cantabile.*

"You are a wonderful student, Jane," he said.

I replayed those words in my mind again and again, but I feared that if I showed the slightest pride in myself, something terrible might happen.

After a year of secret lessons and still undiscovered by Mrs. Creed, something terrible did happen, though it didn't concern the piano.

* * *

Mrs. Creed discovered the intruders first.

Standing in the dormitory over Agnes Marsden, one of the younger girls, she spotted lice crawling around in her hair. She yelled for everyone to come to the common room immediately and ordered us to stand in line. Then she poked and prodded through our heads.

"Now, children," she said, after examining the last head, "Agnes Marsden is not the only one with lice, so I will deal with all of you." She glared at us all with her hands on her hips, above which drooped her ample bosom. "All of you will have your hair chopped off." She paused. "And to make absolutely sure we have disposed of the lice, every head will then be shaved."

Everyone gasped. She was going to chop off our hair! "No, Mrs. Creed," I said, my anger stronger than my common sense right then, "we don't all have lice, so why should we all have our heads shaved?"

Her hand whizzed through the air and struck my cheek. "There will be no arguments or exceptions. Do you hear me, Jane? Get in line and wait your turn."

Even though God had made me small and somewhat insignificant, he had not overlooked my hair when creating me. It was thick and reddish-brown with tints of gold—at least the part I could see hanging down over my shoulders. We weren't allowed any mirrors at Field House because Mrs. Creed declared it was vain to look upon ourselves at any time—not just when we bathed. But Dory had once told me my hair was pretty, and that was good enough for me.

Unlike the boys, the girls never got their hair cut at Field House, so most of us had hair down our backs that we tied back with a piece of string. When I saw the rich ladies in church on Sundays, I imagined one day having my hair styled like theirs, piled high on my head, with small, wispy little curls flowing over my ears and around my face.

But now, all around me, long tresses slowly fell to the floor, my own included. Snip, snip ... chop, chop. It was the first time I had seen all my hair at one time, and I felt like dying.

The worst was yet to come. With the help of one of the village girls, Mrs. Creed passed a long straight razor over our scalps until we were bald and then washed our nicked and bruised heads with a nasty, strong-smelling soap. I decided I would never look at myself in a mirror as long as I lived, even if I had the opportunity.

The boys snickered and giggled and walked back to their dormitory, their shiny heads leading the way like beacons. But the girls whimpered and cried most of the day, until Mrs. Creed issued each of us a bonnet. The boys were given caps to cover their baldness, but they didn't seem bothered by it at all.

In weeks past, their occasional winks and smiles had made me feel special, but now, without my long, curly hair, I must have looked very ugly, like the toad I had once seen outside, or the baby bird without feathers that had fallen from its nest. I wanted to hide from the world.

"Children," Mrs. Creed said, "these caps and bonnets are to be worn at all times when you leave Field House, so your appearance will not offend the gentry when they see you in church on Sundays."

"And in your daily ablutions," she said, "you will pay special attention to your heads. Scrub them religiously. Dirt breeds these bugs. I will not have it said that my orphanage is dirty."

How could that have been possible? We spent most of our lives cleaning it for her.

I flashed to a passage in my Bible catechism: *What is beauty when made an object of pride?* And the answer: *Favor is deceitful, and beauty is vain; but a woman that feareth the Lord, she shall be praised.*

And another question: *How are females cautioned against pride?*

I was sure the answer had been written especially for me: *Whose adorning let it not be that outward adorning of plaiting the hair, and the wearing of gold, or of putting on of apparel which is in the sight of God of great price.*

Well, I might not have plaited my hair or worn gold or have been dressed in finery, but I had wished for those things in my heart, and wishing was as bad as doing. So God made me pay a great price. He made us all pay a great price because I, Jane Hopkins, was proud, and I was vain.

I wore my bonnet night and day, indoors and out, over the next year. My hair did grow again—first a peach fuzz, then a rough stubble, and finally ordinary short hair covering my scalp. Eventually it would grow long once more.

Once again, we would all look like human beings.

*   *   *

The morning Dory told me her news, I forced myself to be happy for her.

"The board told me I'm being hired as a scullery maid at the Sinclair estate, Scrap," Dory said. "Imagine! Me in service! I'll be mixing with the toffs up at the big house. Who knows, I might even meet some gentleman up there who'll want to marry me." She giggled.

"I'm sure you will, Dory. You'll be living in style before you know it."

"I'll put in a good word for you too, Scrap, when your time comes, and you'll be up there with me, I promise." Dory loved to make promises, most of which, through no fault of her own, she could never keep.

I nodded, trying to hold back my tears. At thirteen, I still looked no more than ten, while Dory already looked fifteen. They wouldn't hire me if I didn't look big or strong enough to work. I had a lot of growing to do. My size had never stopped Mrs. Creed from giving me the hardest, most menial of jobs around Field House, but working for the toffs was different. We had to look our age.

Dory and I had never shown much affection toward each other over the years, so when the time came for her to leave, she patted my arm awkwardly. "Take care, Scrap," she said in her usual chirpy voice. "Don't let Old Sourface get to you."

As she walked away, I rubbed my arm where she'd touched it. There was no point in talking about how much I would miss her, how lonely I would be without her. No point in prolonging the agony. It would be a waste of time.

I called out a cheery "Bye, Dory." After a moment, I shrugged my shoulders and went over to the window. Carrying her few belongings in a brown paper parcel, Dory walked down the path away from Field House. She would pass through the village and up the hill leading to the Sinclair estate. None of us orphans had ever gone that far, so I could only imagine what the big house must be like. Dory would soon know. I would have to wait at least two more years to find out.

Mrs. Creed appeared beside me. "Lost your little friend, eh? No one to go crying to now, Missy?"

I scurried away from her to return to my daily chores, thankful I still had Mr. Lloyd's piano lessons to look forward to.

Sometimes, when I had the regular church chores to do, the reverend would arrange for one of the village girls to do mine for me, so we could have a longer lesson. So far, no one appeared to suspect anything, even Mrs. Creed, and because the church was far away from the main house, no one had ever heard me playing. If they had, they would no doubt have thought it was Mr. Lloyd.

His smile and his welcoming face whenever I arrived made me think he enjoyed our secret as much as I did.

But how much longer would we be able to keep our secret?

CHAPTER 4

It was a sunny Friday afternoon in May. The dogwood trees along the hedgerow and the apple tree blossoms outside the church bloomed bright pink and white. When I entered the sanctuary, Mr. Lloyd smiled and signaled me over to the piano, as he always did.

"I have a special piece for you to play before you leave today," he said kindly.

I returned his smile as I started with the usual scales to limber up my fingers. Once my hands touched the keyboard, I instantly forgot about Mrs. Creed and her cruelty. I forgot about my loneliness. I forgot about everything but music.

I moved into a piece by Mr. Chopin I had learned the week before. Mr. Lloyd stood facing the window, his hands behind his back. When he turned around, his face beamed, and he began to tap his foot with the melody.

"Good ... good ... beautiful expression," he muttered.

I closed my eyes as my hands moved over the keys, the music flowing through my body. Surely I had died and gone to heaven.

When I finished, I played a few notes of something I had been composing in my head.

"Hmm. That's lovely, Jane. Where did that come from?"

"It came to me while I was scrubbing the floor."

"Not only can you play magnificently, but you can also compose? Brilliant." He touched my shoulder gently. "Now for that special piece I promised you—"

Just then the outer door burst open, and a gush of air hit my back. I felt as if I'd been struck. "Aha! So this is what you've been up to," Mrs. Creed's voice screeched from behind.

I dropped my hands and kept my head down, hardly able to breathe.

The reverend coughed. "Good afternoon, Mrs. Creed."

"And just what might be going on here, Mr. Lloyd?"

"Jane is having a piano lesson," he said, his voice calm.

"By the sounds of her playing, she has obviously had more than one lesson, Mr. Lloyd."

"Yes, yes, she has had a few."

"And by whose permission has this come about?"

I looked up at that horrible woman, her hands waving about as she stomped around the room. I felt sorry for the reverend, for his part in our deception. But my fear of her and what she would do to me far surpassed anything else.

He paused. "I took it upon myself to allow Jane this privilege, knowing that you would not object, not when a child has such obvious talent."

Oh, Mr. Lloyd was smart. He was appealing to her intelligence, but he had no idea how much she hated me.

"Mr. Lloyd, as you well know, these decisions are made only by our board of directors. The lessons must stop immediately. We cannot show such favouritism at Field House. The child is an orphan in our care. I would be in a great deal of trouble were this ever to get out."

"I doubt that, Mrs. Creed."

She glared at him. "Jane is *my* responsibility, not yours. I alone make decisions about her." She turned to me and poked me in the back with her stick. "Stand up, child."

I obeyed, avoiding her eyes.

"Get back to Field House. I will deal with you later."

I walked over to the door, daring to take one last look back at Mr. Lloyd, who nodded at me and smiled, as though he would make it all right. Of course, he would fight her on this. His sermons were so strong and full of fire—he would use that fire now to put Old Sourface in her place.

But in my heart, I doubted that even Mr. Lloyd could fix this. There would be no more playing, no more music. I would never hear the piece he was going to share with me that day.

We had lost.

*   *   *

I darted out of the sanctuary and ran all the way back to Field House, tears streaming down my face. I threw myself on my bed and sobbed. Thank God, everybody else was in the common room. I couldn't face them. When I stopped crying, I didn't move, waiting for her. There would be a price to pay—but this time, I vowed she would pay, too.

I heard her footsteps long before she stormed into the room.

"Get up!" she yelled from the doorway.

I jumped off the bed and stood on the other side. "I wasn't doing anything wrong!" I yelled back at her.

Her face turned purple with rage as she leaned across, grabbed me by the collar, and yanked me to the floor.

"It isn't a sin to play the piano!" I scrambled to my feet and began punching and kicking her fleshy body.

She reached for my hair and nearly ripped it out. "Goddammit, girl, you think you're so special. I'll beat that pride out of you if it's the last thing I ever do."

She dragged me along the corridor to one of the supply rooms at the far end and threw me inside. I turned quickly and tried to make a dash for the door before she closed it, but she threw her arms around my waist and tossed me backward like a rag doll. My small size was no match for her enormous bulk, so I scurried around the room hurling pails and brooms and brushes at her.

"You vile child!" She put up her arms to ward off my attack but somehow managed to thrust her fist into my chest, sending me flying against the wall. That's when I caught a glimpse of the leather strap in her hand. I'd never seen it before.

Creed's hair hung in shambles, and her face dripped with sweat. "Raise your smock and bend over," she said through gritted teeth.

"No!" I slipped around her and went for the door again, but she caught my smock and pulled me down hard to the floor onto my stomach, then pinned me there with her knee.

I prayed to God for help, knowing it would take a miracle to save me now.

She lifted my smock and whipped the strap across my back in one swift blow. The pain shot through my body, knocking the breath out of me, but I refused to make a sound. I kept my eyes closed as she beat me over and over, screaming at me with each swipe of the leather cutting into my skin.

"Cry, you stupid little bitch. Cry! What made you think you were special enough to play a piano? You're nothing, do you hear? Nothing. The offspring of a whore, a prostitute. Cry! Damn you, cry!"

"Never! Never! Never!" I screamed back. I would never cry—even when her voice seemed to fade into the distance. My ears started ringing before peaceful darkness descended and I passed out. When I came round, she kicked me in the side with her heavy boot, but still I didn't cry.

"Remember this day, Jane Hopkins, if you ever decide to play the piano again. Now, get up!" she yelled, her voice coming at me in waves.

I was far too weak to stand. Seizing my arm, she hauled me back to the dormitory, my legs dragging on the floor. She threw me on my bed, and I lay there on my stomach, unable to move.

"Tonight, there will be no supper or prayers for you," she said, breathing hard. "You will stay in bed and contemplate your sins. If you ever go near Mr. Lloyd's piano again, the punishment will be far worse." The door slammed behind her.

Then, blessed silence.

*   *   *

When the other girls came to bed hours later, they spoke in whispers, carrying their flickering candles. No one addressed me or asked what had happened. No doubt, they had been forbidden to talk to me, Jane Hopkins, the Sinner, the Outcast.

Throughout the night, whenever I tried to move, lightning bolts of pain shot up my back and down my legs. My stomach heaved with nausea.

When the first bell rang the next morning and all the girls started getting up, I stayed still. Someone called my name, but I didn't respond. Maybe they would think I was dead. It didn't matter anymore if Mrs. Creed was angry and came for me herself. What else could she do to me? She had taken away the one thing I treasured most—my music. The physical pain was secondary to the ache in my heart. Obviously, Mr. Lloyd hadn't been able to make it all right.

Somewhere in the distance, a bell rang. It was time for devotionals. Needing to relieve myself, I tried to sit up. The room spun around. At the same time, I felt a warm, wet stickiness between my legs. I twisted slightly and looked down. My smock was bunched up, showing my under-smock and a red stain spread across it. Mrs. Creed had beaten me across my back and buttocks. How could there be blood between my legs? I rolled over again on my stomach. What was happening to me?

Soon I heard footsteps and a soft humming. "Mrs. Creed sent me to get you, Janey," a kind voice said.

It was Rose from the village. Now a young woman, she had worked at Field House for years.

I turned my head to one side. "I can't move, Rose," I whispered.

"Well, I 'spose not. I hear she beat y'er real good, eh?"

"I'm bleeding, Rose ..."

"Let's take a look now." She rolled me gently to raise my clothing and I heard a sharp intake of breath. "Cor blimey, what a mess your poor back is. That needs some ointment. Wait, I'll be right back."

She ran off, and I dozed again until I heard her voice once more and felt her gentle hands on my back. I softly cried as she cleaned my wounds and put on ointment.

"I think I'm bleeding down below, too," I said.

"Down below, where?"

"Between my legs," I murmured.

Sighing, she rearranged my clothing to take a look. "Poor little innocent. That's just your monthly."

"My what?"

"Your monthly curse, that's what. Aint y'er never had it before?"

"No, never."

"Well, you'd better get used to it, 'cause it'll come every month now. I'll get you some rags."

"What is *the curse*? Did Mrs. Creed give it to me?"

She laughed. "No, luvey, she didn't give you no curse. But God knows what that wicked woman did to your back. Crikey, I ain't never seen the like. What got into her?"

"I was playing the piano."

"That ain't nothing bad, Janey. Lots of people play the piano, so I've heard."

"Yes, but I kept it a secret." Talking made me feel bad again. My head spun. The pain came and went in waves of agony so fierce I almost blacked out.

Rose continued to gently rub ointment on my back, then fetched some rags and placed them inside my drawers, fastening them with safety pins. She turned my head and wiped my face with a wet cloth, humming the entire time. Her kindness calmed me.

"I'll tell Mrs. Creed you're too ill to move, Janey. I'll say you should stay in bed."

"She won't let me. She'll make me do my chores."

"Over my dead body—not in your state, she won't."

Where had Rose suddenly managed to find this resolve against a woman she had also feared and detested for years? Was it the sight of my back?

"But what is the monthly curse, Rose?"

"God's gift to women, Janey. Every month we get the curse. It means you're a woman now, and you could make a babe inside you."

"Oh, no. Am I going to have a baby?"

She laughed again. "'Course not, silly. You 'ave to 'ave a man poke you first. Having the curse just means it's possible now, so make sure no man pokes you, see."

What on earth was she talking about? My head ached so badly I couldn't think straight. I just wanted to escape into sleep again and make this incredible pain go away. I no longer had my gift from Mr. Lloyd or my music, my back was cut to shreds—and now I had something called *the curse*.

Could anything worse ever happen?

* * *

Mrs. Creed gave me one day's grace, during which I drifted in and out of sleep. Occasionally Rose visited me and gently rubbed more ointment on my back. She also brought me water to sip, and while the others were at supper, she crept into our dormitory with a bowl of soup for me. I didn't think I was hungry, but the first spoonful she fed me tasted so good it made me realize I was ravenous. Somehow she had also managed to find me a slice of bread.

This respite could not possibly last. I could well imagine Mrs. Creed being made more and more furious by my absence. The next morning, after ringing the bell as she paced up and down the corridor, she entered the dormitory and marched over to my bed.

"Well, Jane Hopkins," she said in a loud voice so everyone could hear, "I trust you have learned your lesson."

I turned my head slightly toward her. "Yes, Mrs. Creed, I've learned my lesson."

She bent down and whispered, "And never, ever strike me again, Jane Hopkins, do you hear me?"

As much as I hurt, my only regret was that I hadn't fought back harder.

She glanced around the room. "Let this be a warning to all of you. No one disobeys or lies to me. No one is allowed to make their own decisions. If any of you choose, as Jane Hopkins did, to try something underhanded behind my back, you will be treated as she was. Thirty-nine lashes with the whip."

She looked back at me. "Now, missy, I expect you to be dressed and ready for prayers this morning."

As soon as she left the room, everyone started whispering. Some of the girls stood around my bed.

"Did it hurt, Janey?"

"Were you really having piano lessons with Mr. Lloyd?"

"How did you keep it a secret?"

One of the girls offered to help me put on another smock. She even said she would wash the blood-stained one for me.

They all seemed to think I was very brave to have carried out such a daring plan for so long without Mrs. Creed finding out. They also wondered, as I did, what would happen to Mr. Lloyd. Would the church dismiss him for disobeying the rules of Field House? If that happened, I would feel doubly guilty.

In the coming days, as much as the pain swallowed me whole, I never let Mrs. Creed know. She had destroyed my back but not my spirit.

Although I immediately had to join in all the daily functions and chores at Field House, she would not allow me to attend church or Mr. Lloyd's lessons in the sanctuary for two months. The other girls told me he was still there and had even asked about me.

Once things returned to normal and I could take part in lessons again, Mrs. Creed walked me over to the church when I was working there and then escorted me back. She and Mr. Lloyd didn't speak.

To my relief, I didn't have another "monthly curse" for three months. Rose told me it was normal. The curse would take a while to settle down, she said. I wished it would stay away forever. When it eventually became regular, I had the extra chore of having to wash out my rags. I hated it. Only one other older girl had the curse, but it was too private and shameful a thing to discuss with her. Thank goodness I had Rose.

I never played the reverend's piano again. I was afraid to even look at it when we did our lessons in the sanctuary. Mr. Lloyd did not speak to me privately or make any reference to that awful day when our secret had been discovered. I missed him so much, but I missed the piano even more.

CHAPTER 5

Rose approached me in the hallway one December day while I was scrubbing the floor in the dormitory with the others.

"Janey, luv," she whispered. "You're wanted in Mrs. Creed's room. Now, now, don't be worried, 'cause I think this might be good. The board of directors is having a meeting, and you will be fifteen soon, so I 'spect they're discussing you leaving."

My heart lurched. Yes, I'd be fifteen in just three weeks—at Christmas—and I had yearned for this day for so long. But it might be another disappointment. I had not grown much in size or stature over the last couple of years.

Nodding to Rose, I stood and pulled myself to my full height, trying desperately to make myself look taller by drawing back my shoulders and keeping my head erect. Following her down the corridor, I waited as she knocked on Mrs. Creed's door.

"Enter!" replied that familiar, dreaded voice.

We both went in, and then Rose quickly left. The first thing I noticed was how warm and cozy the room was, not a bit like the rest of the drafty, cold house. An enormous fire burned in the hearth, and comfortable-looking furniture filled the room. Mrs. Creed's desk stood to the left, and over by the window was a long trestle table where four gentlemen sat, together with Mr. Lloyd, who was wearing his long gray robes. He smiled at me. The others did not.

Sitting at the head of the table, Mrs. Creed spoke first. "Stand over here, Jane Hopkins." Her eyes scanned the group. "Gentleman, I present Jane Hopkins to you," she said in her sweetest, sickliest, la-di-da voice, the one she only used in front of the board. "She will be turning fifteen years of age in less than three weeks, and a decision must be made about her future." She paused.

"As you see, she is small for her age. I doubt she would be capable of doing agricultural work, so placing her in the hiring fair next spring would be to no avail. No farmer would hire her, and—"

One of the directors interrupted at this point. He had a long nose and several gold teeth. "Placing her in service would be more appropriate, then?"

Mr. Lloyd nodded. "Yes, yes, Jane would do fine in service, I feel sure. She would be a good worker."

I smiled at him gratefully.

Mrs. Creed narrowed her eyes at Mr. Lloyd and thumped her hand on the table. "The child is far too small for service. She'd be incapable of carrying hot water or scrubbing floors."

And what exactly did that bitch think I had been doing for the past ten years at Field House, if not the very same thing? So why would I not be able to do it elsewhere?

"In any case," she continued, "I hear that Lady Sinclair at Noxley Manor isn't looking for maids right now."

Mr. Lloyd leaned forward. "But surely there is always room for an extra scullery maid or even a dairymaid on the Sinclair estate."

She grunted and glanced down the table to another gentleman on the board who had not yet spoken, a gray-haired fellow with sallow, wrinkled skin. He kept fingering a pocket watch resting on his paunch, as though in a hurry to have this whole procedure over and done with. Mrs. Creed beamed her sickly smile at him. "Mr. Finch, I am sure *you* would concede that this child is far too skinny and small to be put in the outside world to work. Would you not agree that she should stay at Field House at least one more year?"

"Yes, I would, Mrs. Creed. I think we are all of one mind on the matter."

"But, Mrs. Creed—" It was Mr. Lloyd.

"Sir," she snapped, "as you well know, we must always obey the wishes of the board."

I was losing my case, which meant I'd have to stay here. I clenched my fists, screaming inside.

"So," Mrs. Creed said, gathering her papers and clearing her throat, "it is agreed then. Jane Hopkins remains with us. Her case will be reviewed again in one year."

They all raised their hands, even Mr. Lloyd, though slowly and somewhat reluctantly. "The matter is passed, then," she said.

No one said anything to me, as though I wasn't even in the room. They had decided my fate. Mrs. Creed waved at me in dismissal. "You heard the decision, Jane Hopkins. You may leave us now and go about your business. Go. Out with you."

I turned, catching a watery smile on Mr. Lloyd's face. His sad eyes and slumped shoulders told me all I needed to know. She had defeated us again.

I left the room and closed the door behind me. Walking back to the dormitory, I realized that Mrs. Creed had more control over the board of directors than I had imagined. To beat her, I would have to gain equal power. And to do that, I would need to find her weakness, the chink in her armour.

I flashed back to the first day I played the piano, when the reverend said to me that "in God's eyes, even the smallest sparrow is important, Jane."

I wasn't a nobody. At that moment, I had no idea how I would defeat that wicked woman, but by God, I knew that one day I would.

*   *   *

Now that I was the oldest of her orphans, Mrs. Creed made me her personal servant. I had to clean her quarters, including emptying her slop bucket every morning, sweeping her floors, dusting, and setting her table for all her meals, which I was called upon to serve. She went out of her way to think up extra, ridiculously minor tasks for me to do so I would never have an idle moment, scolding me at every turn.

"How clumsy you are, Jane," she would say.

"My tea is always cold, child. You are far too slow."

Christmas came and went like all the others before it, and with it my fifteenth birthday. I still had found nothing to give me power over Mrs. Creed. I constantly prayed to God for help.

One day in late March, I woke up, as usual, to Mrs. Creed's bell at five o'clock. As the oldest, I was now responsible for making sure everyone in our dormitory washed, made their beds, scrubbed the floor of the dormitory, and read their Bibles before going for breakfast. I also had to serve Mrs. Creed her breakfast before I could eat my own.

That morning, Cook had made her a soft-boiled egg and toasted and buttered her bread. In all my years at Field House, I had never eaten an egg, soft-boiled or otherwise, or seen any butter. Mrs. Creed actually smiled and thanked me as I set her tray in front of her. She even looked brighter, not as dark and mean, and today her graying bun was neat and tidy for a change. Her face had some colour to it, powdered with rouge. The board of directors must be coming later, I thought. She was always sickly sweet then.

After our morning lessons in the sanctuary, we walked back to the house without her hovering presence, a rare occurrence. Approaching the front door, I saw the horse and carriage that belonged to Mr. Finch, one of the directors, that despicable chubby fellow with the pocket watch from my interview who had quickly agreed with Mrs. Creed about keeping me at Field House.

Rose met us in the hall. She had been bathing the three new babies now part of Field House, and her apron was still wet. Smiling at me, she said, "Janey, luv, Mrs. Creed has a visitor today and doesn't want to be disturbed, so you won't have to see to her lunch. But maybe, you should serve her tea later this afternoon."

I smiled back with relief. Now I'd be able to join the others for lunch right away and then rest for a while. I was ravenous and already tired.

By mid-afternoon, when all the others were reading in the common room, I slipped outside. The carriage was still there. Sometimes Mr. Finch stayed late after a meeting to finish going over the books with Mrs. Creed. By now, Old Sourface would want me to serve them tea.

I boiled a kettle in the kitchen and, with Cook's help, prepared an elegant tray for Mrs. Creed and her visitor. Carrying it carefully along the hall, I arrived at her door with my usual trepidation. I tapped gently, but there was no answer. When I put my ear to the door, I heard no voices. Perhaps they had stepped outside for a few moments. I could leave the tea so it would be waiting for them when they returned.

Opening the door slowly, I entered the room and placed the tray on her table. No one was around. Could this finally be the chance I'd waited for—to look through her things and find something I could use against her? A pile of papers sat on her desk. Would I have time to look through them?

As I headed toward her desk, I heard strange noises coming from another room off to the side, which must be Mrs. Creed's bedroom—sort of small grunts and sighs. So, she was there after all. Maybe the old bitch was ill.

The door was ajar, and I nudged it slightly and poked my head in. On the bed were two people—with a great deal of skin showing. The gentleman—whom I presumed was Mr. Finch, though his naked rear end was all I could see—was lying on top of Mrs. Creed, whose ugly flesh spilled out all over the bed, reminding me of a whale I'd seen in a picture book. Her eyes were closed, and she was panting and puffing as Mr. Finch's rear end rose and fell above her.

I stood, open-mouthed, unable to move. Was he attacking her? But Mrs. Creed was giggling. Indeed, it sounded like she was enjoying herself.

Just then, her eyes popped open, and she saw me. Screaming my name, she thrust her body up, launching Mr. Finch off the bed.

"What the—?" he yelled.

He peered over at me as he reached for his clothes, his face crimson. Mrs. Creed's was purple. She threw the crumpled sheets across her naked body. No wonder she had always insisted it was a mortal sin to gaze upon one's bare body. Hers, with its numerous layers of fat, was grotesque.

"I ... er ... brought ... you ... er ... some tea, Mrs. Creed," I stammered.

"Get out! *Get out!* How *dare* you intrude into my bedroom. How *dare* you. You little sneak. Leave. Do you hear me? LEAVE AT ONCE."

I ran all the way back to the common room, where I dropped into a chair, my heart thumping, then opened my Bible while trying to wipe the sight I had just witnessed from my mind.

What had they been doing? I knew it was a sin to look upon your own skin, so why had Mrs. Creed been naked, and why had she allowed Mr. Finch to gaze upon her? It made no sense. I had to ask Rose.

Undoubtedly, I would now be in trouble. Another beating? She could try it, but this time, I would fight back a lot harder.

But nothing happened all afternoon, and when Rose came back that evening to help Cook make supper, I told her what I'd seen.

She laughed so long I thought she would never stop. "So, that's what the wicked old bitch gets up to, eh? And with old Finch, too. That's 'ow come she gets favours from the board—from giving her favours to them."

"Favours?"

"He were poking 'er, Janey. Having a good old go by the sounds of it."

"Does that mean she'll have a baby now?"

"Not likely. She's too smart—and probably too old—for that." Rose kept laughing. "Well, well, well. I wonder what the church officials would think if they knew about this. Maybe Mr. Lloyd would even tell the bishop and get back at her. She'd be in big trouble, I can tell y'er. She might even lose her comfy job here at Field House."

My heart soared as her words slowly sank in.

Power! I finally had it—the dirt on Mrs. Creed I needed to escape this awful place. I could tell Mr. Lloyd, and she would be sent away.

The next morning, before I could do anything, Mrs. Creed called me into her room. This time, I held my head erect and stared her boldly in the face.

She cleared her throat and kept looking around the room, avoiding my eyes, her mouth pressed into a thin line. My God, was she actually afraid of me?

"What you saw yesterday, Jane Hopkins, is never to be repeated. Do you understand me?"

"Oh, of course not, Mrs. Creed," I said innocently. "I saw nothing."

"Umph, that's as may be, but in any case, you will be leaving Field House next week."

"I will?" My mouth opened wide. "Where am I going?"

"A position as scullery maid has suddenly opened up at the Sinclair estate. Arrangements are being made as we speak for you to take it as soon as possible."

"Oh, I see. But ... er ... am I not still too small, Mrs. Creed?"

Glaring at me, she opened her mouth, about to shout at me by force of habit, but stopped herself in time. Instead, she muttered under her breath and said with a forced smile, "You'll grow—you'll grow ..."

I leaned over her desk with new confidence. "In that case, Mrs. Creed, if I'm leaving, I want my book back. NOW!"

She unlocked a drawer, pulled out my book, and threw it across the table to me.

Power is such a beautiful thing!

God, in His wisdom, saw to it that I would find a way out of there. I smiled to myself all the way back to the dormitory.

The following week, I said my farewells to Field House, especially to Rose, who was always so kind to me, and I left for good, determined never to think about that terrible place or that evil woman ever again.

SCOTLAND

GIDEON – Growing Up in Scotland
(1845–1849)

CHAPTER 6

Only God and I knew how much I hated fish!

I hated the smell of them as we hauled in the day's catch. I hated the slimy feel of them as I emptied the nets alongside my father and brother. And most of all, I hated the taste of them when Ma cooked them for dinner.

"Gideon, help your brother haul in another net," my Da called to me. "We have to move fast to get all these gutted and packed in crates. Duncan and I had *gud* luck today. In fact the luck was with all the McBrides and Frasers."

He smiled at us both. "We should make some big money, lads, but we won't get the best price if the fish are not fresh, so be quick."

I obeyed Da without question and returned to help my brother haul in another net and empty the herring out. Duncan and Da worked fast, which meant that soon we'd be gutting all the fish, the part that always made me gag.

It was bitter cold that day, so at least the fish didn't stink as much as they did when the weather was warmer. I had been helping them both every day except Sundays since I was strong enough to use a knife. But in all my ten years, I had never seen so many fish as they had caught today. It would be a big celebration later for us all.

As we worked, my thoughts went back to earlier that morning. I'd no idea then that the catch would be this big. My cousins and I, and the other lads from our village of Rosehearty, about four miles away, had waited for the boats to return from the high vantage point on the Kinnaird Head. The Head is where the North Sea meets the Moray Firth.

As soon as we had seen the boats on the horizon, we took off running towards the harbour, like bolts of lightning. On that particular blustery November day, we ran extra fast, trying to keep ourselves warm.

While waiting on the pier for the fleet to arrive, I had studied other vessels already anchored there. Most were large, elegant, sailing ships far bigger than the fishing boats, all of them with different flags. I saw two new flags that day. I'd look them up in one of Da's books later to see which countries they came from. I pointed them out to my cousin, Jamie, who was a year older than me—but he wasn't particularly interested.

"Hey, Gid, look at that young lassie over there," he said. "Take a peek at the size of her bosoms."

I shook my head. "You never change, Jamie." I returned my attention to the other vessels, more interested in ships than lassies right then.

The wooden crates being unloaded were labeled in strange languages I didn't recognize. What might they be trading, I wondered—spices or silk? On one ship, I had seen black men in chains coming up from the hold. I'd heard about slavery from stories Da had read to us, but I doubted that Scotland bought slaves. Why would you need a slave here? The black men looked quite thin, their clothes in rags. Once they had unloaded the cargo, they were sent back down below. I had decided that morning that the large ship I would someday captain would never trade in slavery.

Now my thoughts returned to the work we were doing, filling up crate after crate. Da and my two uncles, along with the dozen other fishermen on the pier, and some women who were there with their husbands, all began to sing as we worked. Ma would be there with us one day too, when my two little sisters, Janet and Fiona, were older.

Usually Uncle Gordon led by singing the refrain, and we all joined in with the chorus:

It's early in the mornin' and it's late into the nicht
Your hands aa cut and chappit and they look an unco sicht,
And you greet like a wean when you pit them in the bree,
And you wish you were a thousand miles away ...

The next song was the old English shanty I loved the best, especially when we all joined in with the "Hey ho and blow the man down" bit.

Come all ye young fellows that follow the sea,
To my way haye, blow the man down.
And pray attention and listen to me,
Give me some time to blow the man down.
Hey ho and blow the man down . . . .

I rubbed my own chapped hands together to warm them, so frozen were they now from the biting winds. My back was aching too, and I stretched as I took a sip of water from the pouch Ma had given us.

In five years, I'd be going out to sea with these men. I did'na want to think about that. It wasn't the life I fancied for myself. But the men in our village rarely did anything else and certainly never left home.

Toward noon, Da, Duncan, and I hustled uphill to the market in town, our cart loaded with gutted, packed herring. Da said we'd get a shilling a crate, but Duncan disagreed. "We'll get at least double that, Da," he said.

At sixteen, my older brother was already a head taller than Da. His long legs were soon a full stride ahead of the rest of us. He took after Ma's side of the family, the Frasers, who had settled here three generations ago. I was more like Da and all the other McBrides. Da had told me that most of them had large hands and broad shoulders, and their hair was darker, with just a whisper of red, as Ma would say.

Da had come from the Isle of Skye, off the west coast of Scotland. As a young man, he had made his way to the Broch, north of Aberdeenshire, when the herring fishing industry was doing well. He'd had some education but he was looking for adventure, too. He decided to stay here after meeting my mother at church one Sunday. I loved to hear the story about how Ma's flashing blue eyes and beautiful smile had immediately captured his heart.

After Da finished bartering with the fishmongers that day (Duncan was right—we did get two shillings a crate), we took our cart back to the harbour and locked it up in our storage shed. We then headed over to Ye Olde Galleon tavern to celebrate. I'd never been inside a tavern before. It was loud, dimly lit and smoky, and I gagged at the overpowering smell inside of beer, fish, and men's sweat.

Da ordered meat pies and whisky for everyone at our table. Ma's two brothers, Uncle Hector and Uncle Gordon, were there with us, with my three older cousins. While we waited for the order to come, I looked out the dirty window at the large ships down in the harbour. The sea captains were now talking to well-dressed gentlemen who had driven up in fancy carriages.

"Da," I asked, "those men down there must be rich traders, right?"

"Aye, indeed they are. They have a wee bit more money than you or I will ever see."

Everyone laughed. I thought of the rich people I'd read about in Da's adventure books. Surely not everyone was poor like us. Why couldn't we be rich?

A girl brought our order and, as she bent over, Jamie's eyes were wide with delight at the sight of her ample bosom. I was too busy tucking into my meat pie. I'd never tasted anything so delicious. But when I picked up my glass of whisky and took a gulp the way Duncan did, a fire roared down my throat and I nearly fell off my chair. Everyone laughed heartily as I spat out the rest.

"It'll be a while a'fore you try the demon drink again, I think, laddie," Da said, as he ordered another round for everyone else.

Maybe I would get a taste for it one day—but I'd never get a taste for fish, never in a million years.

* * *

As we walked back to our village of Rosehearty, the men began singing again, but this time they stumbled over the words and leaned on one another for support, all a little the worse for wear.

By the time we reached home, the light was fading fast. Black clouds were rolling in and dark smoke rose from the chimney. We called out our goodbyes to the others as Da opened the door to our small house. Yet another fish stew was bubbling on the stove.

"Oh *gud*, you're all home," Ma said as we came in. "I was getting a wee bit worried."

Da wrapped his arms around Ma's waist and kissed her fondly. "Aye, lassie, you should not worry so much. It was a very gud day at sea and we were all a-celebrating."

"Why, Angus, you've been drinking, haven't you?" She sounded stern, but she was smiling, too.

"Aye, I might have had a wee dram or two." He laughed as he pulled her close and began dancing her round our tiny, one-room house, the way he did when Uncle Gordon came over and brought his fiddle. Watching them smiling and having fun made me feel safe, like nothing bad could ever happen to any of us. As they danced, Ma's dress kicked up dust from the earthen floor.

"Ach, Angus, what a mess we are a-making," said Ma, but she smiled at the four of us children clapping time as they danced. Janet and Fiona also began to jig around the room while Duncan and I continued to beat time.

When they stopped, Ma went to the stove to pour the fish stew into our bowls. We all crowded around the small table—my two younger sisters, along with Duncan, Da, and me. Once Ma sat down, we all bowed our heads and Da said grace.

"God grant us all gratitude for what we have here in our small house—a roof over our heads and clothes on our backs. We have space for our fishing gear and my books. We have fish a-plenty, with onions drying on hooks, and a rush-pit for wicks for our *eeley dolly* lamps. We have pots cooking on a warm fire. And most of all, we have each other. What more can we ask? Thank you, Lord, for all the blessings you have given to our family."

"Amen," we chorused.

I had to work hard to swallow the fish stew, remembering the large meat pies I had relished earlier. My parents were happy and grateful for everything, though I knew that Ma had lost two babies between my brother's birth and mine. No wonder they were glad when I was born and they now had two healthy sons to follow in Da's footsteps and become fishermen.

After supper, Da took down a book from the blackened beams to read us a story, as he did every night. He told us all that we should read and learn so we could better ourselves.

Always seeking answers, I asked Da a question that night. "Da, why were you content to just be a fisherman if you say we can better ourselves?"

He looked at me for a long time before answering. "Ah, laddie, I fell in love with your ma and was happy to remain in Rosehearty and have the life of a fisherman. It was my right place to be in the world. We all have to find our right place."

He opened the book *Historical Tales of the Wars of Scotland: Border Raids, Forays and Conflicts.*

"While his army was on the march," he began, "the Earl of Angus pursued them with a strong body of cavalry, captured two of their cannons, and slew their general—"

"Goodness me, Angus," Ma said, interrupting him. "These are not suitable tales for the wee girls." She raised an eyebrow in protest.

But the tales were exciting to Duncan and me, and I soon lost myself in the adventures of the clans while gazing around our small room. I loved hearing about other places and other people's lives and learning the history of the Highlands over a hundred years ago. It was a grand time when Bonnie Prince Charlie was everyone's hero, until the famous battle at Culloden when all the Jacobites were wiped out because of the Prince's poor military judgment.

When Da stopped reading, I begged for another story, but Ma would have none of it and sent us all to bed. After saying our prayers, Duncan and I climbed into the bed we shared with our sisters, but Fiona couldn't settle that night, so Ma took her into theirs.

"I told you, Angus, that the girls would be scared by your stories," I heard her whisper.

I was glad that Fiona wasn't in our bed, because now the rest of us had more room. But despite being able to stretch out some, I couldn't fall asleep, my head still full of lairds and clansmen and the rich merchants in Fraserburgh who had fine carriages and clothes and plenty of money to sail around the world.

Maybe Da was right. I had to find my own right place in the world. Perhaps it wasn't here.

* * *

Some mornings I would sit up on the Head, daydreaming about those things as I looked out towards the sea. I also thought about Ma's favorite saying, which she often quoted to us:

"Cod and corn dinna gaun the gither."

She was right. Cod (the fisherman) and corn (the farmer) didn't go together or mix. The farmers lived inland and we fishermen visited them only to buy eggs and milk; most of the time each kind kept to themselves. It seemed strange to me that we didn't mix more. I wished we did, because I wanted to meet other people and experience other ways of life.

Whenever I was up at the Head looking out at the wild North Sea, I also couldn't help but think about all the fishermen who had been casting their nets off the northeastern coast of Scotland since long before the Vikings came ashore. From what I'd read in Da's books, many men had lost their lives to that cruel sea—all the stones in the cemetery inscribed with brief lifespans were proof of that. We had often attended funerals for people we knew, and Duncan told me most bodies were never found and the coffins were empty. That seemed strange to me and somewhat scary.

It made no sense to me that everyone accepted this as a way of life. There might well be other cruel seas in the world, but I refused to believe that my life had to be tied to this one. The far horizon tugged at me, and I longed to be out there. I wanted to travel the world, see other places, and sail other oceans. Surely that's what Da had wanted before he fell in love with Ma and settled here.

Sometimes after church on Sundays, my Da, Duncan and I went out in our small boat, but only along the coastline, where it was calm and the scenery was bonny. I loved the smell of the ocean and it made me realize again that there were other parts of the world I wanted to see.

"Eeh, laddie, I can see passion for the sea in your eyes already," my Da would tell me.

That at least was true. *But not to be a fisherman*, I wanted to scream at him. But I said nothing because I had no desire to hurt his feelings.

I couldn't tell Ma or Da how I really felt. The hurt in their eyes would be too much to bear. How could I tell Ma that I hated it when she patted me on the head and said, "Gideon, your turn to go out to sea to fish with the men will come soon enough."

Like Da, she assumed I was as eager as every other lad in the village to follow in the footsteps of generations of fishermen.

But she was wrong.

CHAPTER 7

In the wee hours of one sultry August morning in 1848, we were all woken up by the wind smashing against our tiny house. A storm was brewing and soon shook the walls and screamed through the rafters—like nothing I'd ever heard before. Ma and Da talked back and forth, and I heard the fear in Ma's voice.

"Angus, maybe you and Duncan should stay home today. It's a wild one out there."

"Remember how calm it was when we set the nets last night, though? It will soon calm down again and we can retrieve our catch," Da replied.

Brutal storms pounded the coast throughout the year and fishermen still went out to sea. But this was the first time I'd heard Ma ask my Da not to go.

"We'll be fine, Sarah," Da said. "God will watch over us. It always sounds worse in here than it is once you get out there."

I heard Ma get out of bed and walk to the stove, where she began to cook some breakfast. It was not easy with the house seeming to sway to and fro.

Just then a loud clap of thunder boomed above us, followed by flashes of lightning. Da tried to open the door, and a strong gust almost blew the door off its hinges before he slammed it shut again. Some books fell off the shelf above us, and my little sisters and I dove under the covers. They were crying, and I felt my own tears close.

This storm was very angry. *Oh please Da stay home*, I prayed. But Da and Duncan were already eating at the table, after which they knelt down to pray, as they normally did before leaving. I wanted to ask Duncan if he was afraid.

"Lord, protect us this day and bring us home safely," Da said as he kissed Ma.

"Amen," she whispered.

Da then placed his hand on the Bible and touched the cross hanging on the wall, which my mother kissed reverently. She hugged Duncan to her bosom and told them both to stay safe.

Da looked across at the three of us in bed. "Gideon, lad, take care of your Ma and sisters this morning. By noon we should be back, so we'll see you at the harbour as usual. If we are a little late, don't worry. All will be well. The storm will calm down soon, I'm sure. They usually pass quickly."

I nodded. Just at that moment, another crack of thunder shook the house with such force I thought it would collapse. Rain was now pelting down hard on the roof. Why did Da think this would calm down?

After they left, Ma spoke to me. "We have to keep the faith, Gideon."

"But this storm sounds extra bad out there," cried Janet, as another gust violently rattled the windows. Her tousled red curls were all awry, as she had tossed and turned most of the night. She and Fiona both had their eyes open wide now with fright.

My mother, her own face twisted with worry, hugged us all. "We trust that God is watching over them. Now, up you girls get. You too, Gideon. We must all eat some breakfast, and then we'll do some drawing to pass the time till Da and Duncan return. They will be in the harbour by noon and you'll be meeting them as usual, Gideon. Mark my words."

But the storm worsened during the morning and I could see her anxiety growing. Everything in the house was creaking. Once I ventured outside to see if we had been hit by something, but the wind took my breath away. Debris was flying around everywhere. Nothing had hit our house, but some neighbours were not so fortunate. The roof of the cottage next door had collapsed.

I prayed that Da had decided not to go out and was now still sheltering in Fraserburgh harbour. I usually left well before noon to meet the fleet, and as the morning wore on I couldn't stand it any longer. I was scared, but I needed to know what was happening.

"Ma, I'm going to walk up to the Head to see if I can see the boats on the horizon or down in the harbour like usual."

She grabbed my arm. "Oh, please be careful, Gideon."

A wall of rain and wind pushed against me as I fought my way up to the Head. Other lads were there already, huddled together in a circle. Black clouds hung low, and sheets of rain beat down on the churning sea. Waves rose to heights I'd never seen before. The noise was too deafening for anyone to be heard over it.

There was no sign of boats. My stomach clenched. They must have gone out, but how would Da and Duncan ever make it back to shore?

When I stumbled back home, soaked and weary, Ma jumped up and hugged me. "What news?" she whispered. "Did you see them?"

"No, not yet—but I'm sure they will make it back." I couldn't bring myself to tell her anything else. She nodded.

For the rest of that day, we listened to the waves crashing and the wind howling. Ma forbade me to leave again, so instead I read some stories to my sisters to take our minds off the storm.

Later, I tried escaping into one of Da's books myself, but even the wild Highland tales couldn't ease my mind.

* * *

Da and Duncan were still not back by dark, so that night, all four of us lay in the same bed for comfort. But sleep was impossible as the storm continued to rage. When the dawn light seeped in, the rain and wind suddenly stopped. The silence felt eerie.

We threw on our jackets and boots and raced out of the house down to the Rosehearty beach. Many of the other women and their older children hurried on to Fraserburgh. That way, we had the entire coastline covered.

But pieces of wreckage were already floating ashore and scattering on the rocky beach, and each wave brought in more, causing our hopes to dwindle. Broken boards tangled in fishing nets, rubber gumboots and yellow sou'westers were scattered everywhere.

I heard a woman near us screaming. "Thirteen boats from our village left yesterday and each had at least two or three men aboard. Can they all be gone?"

"Perhaps they made it back to the harbour in Fraserburgh," Ma shouted back.

But once news reached us from those returning from Fraserburgh, we knew the worst had happened. By then, the sun had started breaking through the clouds as Ma and I pored through the debris on the beach. *Please, God,* I kept praying, *please make them all right.* Surely, Da and Duncan would show up soon. I kept gazing down towards Fraserburgh harbour, but there was still no sign of any boats.

Then Ma called to me. She had been combing the beach further north and was bending down to pick up something shiny on the sand.

"It's Da's pocket watch!" she screamed.

She dropped to her knees on the wet sand and began sobbing violently. My sisters and I gathered around her and hugged her to us, all of us crying now.

"Maybe Da is still safe on another boat. He and Duncan might have been rescued and are in Fraserburgh now," I whimpered.

But I knew in my heart this wasn't possible, and the sound of other women and children weeping everywhere only made it worse.

Had Ma really lost a husband, a son, and a brother, my uncle Gordon? Was it possible?

Uncle Hector had stayed home because he'd been sick with the ague for days. He'd had a very high fever and sickness of the stomach. Now he wandered the beach, aimlessly shuffling along and looking like he should still be in bed. He was cursing to himself. "I should have gone too. I should have gone too."

In the days ahead, no bodies were ever recovered. The cruel sea had claimed them all—over one hundred men and one hundred twenty-four boats had all gone to the deep. Rosehearty alone had lost thirty men in that violent storm.

I felt numb. My Da gone. Duncan gone. Uncle Gordon gone. I wanted to scream at the sea and at the heavens and, most of all, at God, who hadn't answered our prayers to keep them all safe. There seemed no point in going to church, because it was always empty. Families began erecting wooden markers in the cemetery where later would be headstones.

"Why, Ma? Why? Why did they have to go out that day?" I asked her over and over.

"'Tis the way of the fishermen, lad."

That sounded so foolish to me. Surely they were smarter than that. They knew the sea and all its moods. Yet, she was right. That *was* the way the fishermen and their wives felt. They accepted that one day it might be their own fate.

But I would never accept it. I wanted to explore the world first. Maybe other seas were also cruel and would claim me one day, but not here, like this. I was even more determined now that being a fisherman and accepting death at sea in a flimsy fishing vessel was not going to happen to me.

I intended to sail the world in larger, stronger vessels.

*   *   *

Overnight, I became the man of the house. I was only thirteen and I was scared to death.

But I had no time for tears or grieving, and all I felt in the days to come, I kept inside me. I could not express my anger or sorrow and most certainly could not allow my mother to see my fear. I had to take care of my family now.

I wasn't yet old enough to go to sea, so Ma was forced to become a fish wife, like many of the other widows in our village who had young children to provide for. I helped her scour the shoreline day after day for the smallest of the catches which had been cast aside when the boats returned. Every morning, as the North Sea winds cut through our bones, we would fill wicker creels and hoist them on our backs. We then walked many miles to barter for butter, eggs, and vegetables at the farms and crofts. The older women in the village took care of Janet and Fiona while we were gone.

Most days we returned home tired and hungry, with not much to show for our efforts. We were lucky to make enough for a few eggs and a slab of butter. Occasionally we traded our scraps for some *neeps* (turnips) and *tatties* (potatoes), and that night Ma would make us a feast of a stew. Once I captured a wandering chicken from one of the farms, just so we could have some meat.

But Ma never complained. "Gideon," she'd say, grabbing my shoulders, "when you're fifteen, you can go to sea with your Uncle Hector, and then we'll make a good living again."

Did she consider *a good living* to be the way we had scratched and saved for years, only truly happy when the catch was big? There had to be something better.

I had no intention of deserting her or failing in my duty as provider, but I couldn't go to sea as a fisherman with Uncle Hector. My mother's oldest brother was a brute of a man who had no patience for children. He was always angry and had a rough tongue on him, whereas Uncle Gordon had had a kind word or joke for everyone and had been my favorite. Not so Uncle Hector.

I remembered again how often Da had told me that reading books was important. "An educated man can achieve great things in life," he'd say, "as long as you also have the smarts."

After his death, I continued to read and learn as much as I could, which was difficult since there was no schooling in Rosehearty then, but I read and reread all the books my father had brought with him when he first came from the Isle of Skye.

I liked to read about the brave men of long ago, like Rob Roy, my favorite hero, and I delighted in the poems of Robbie Burns. I also learned about other places in the world, other continents and other oceans, and it made me even more determined to see them for myself one day.

Eventually, I would also have the smarts to do just that.

CHAPTER 8

One Sunday afternoon, not long after I turned fourteen, Uncle Hector appeared at our door.

"Gideon, lad," he said gruffly as he stared hard at me from beneath his bushy eyebrows, "your ma needs the money, so I'm going to take you out with me tomorrow and teach you a thing or two about fishing, even though you're not yet fifteen. I'll pay you well to help your family. But you must listen to me and do as you're told."

He scared me, but for Ma's sake I went with him anyway in the early hours of the following morning and obeyed his every order. I had to pull my weight like the other fisherman. After a week at sea, he grudgingly admitted he was grateful for my help.

"You've done well, lad," he said as he paid me a good wage. My time with the other fishermen made my love for the sea grow—but it didn't improve my love of fish or the life of a fisherman.

One Sunday after *kirk* I walked up to the Head and gazed out to sea as I sat down on a large rock. I was trying to work up the courage to tell my mother what I wanted to do with my life. I knew I couldn't wait much longer.

Suddenly I heard Ma's voice. "Gideon, there you are," she called out as she puffed her way up the hill. "I thought I'd find you here."

Out of breath and with her hair escaping from the bun she always wore, she sat down beside me and put her arm around my shoulders. "Eh, laddie, y'er have a face that wid soor milk. Something's been troubling you. What's the matter?"

"Nothing's the matter, Ma ... just makin' plans."

"Plans, is it? Well, laddie, don't fret yourself. It'll all come oot in the wash. I know you're sad sometimes, but everything passes, the soor along wi' the sweet."

My dear mother had an answer for everything. She thought I was missing Da and Duncan—and I was—but I had to talk to her about something else now. I wriggled around on the rock, avoiding her eyes.

"Gideon, you're fussing like a hen on a hot griddle."

"Aye, ma, and wi' good reason. I made a decision, but I'm afraid to tell you."

"Oh, no need to be afraid, lad. Just spit it out."

"Well, I've decided I don't want to be a fisherman forever and trawl the North Sea. I want to sail around the world instead."

She leaned her head back in shock. "Good Lord above, 'tis big ideas you have?"

I did have big ideas, but I believed I now had the ability and the wit to carry them out.

"I'm serious, Ma. I'm gonna go into Fraserburgh and find out about the Hudson's Bay Company. I overheard someone say they're hiring cabin boys. They sail to North America, to Rupert's Land—so it would be a beginning. I've read about the company and how I could rise quickly working for them. I would make good money, which I'd send home for you and Janet and Fiona to live in a fine hoose away from the village. We won't always be peer as a kirk moose. I promise I won't let you and the girls starve. And before I leave, I'll make sure that Uncle Hector takes care of you until I can send back money, which might be a while. Meanwhile, the girls are big enough now to help you look for discarded fish scraps in the harbor and along the shore for extra money. But I promise that won't be forever."

By the time I finished talking I was out of breath, anxiously waiting for her reaction.

"We're fine, laddie, wi' this life, for fit we nivver hid, we nivver miss. The bit I earn as a fish wife gets us by. And yes, soon the girls will be able to help me. And with you now going to sea with your Uncle Hector, we'll all be fine. We need you here, Gideon. You canna leave us. Surely you can't be serious aboot this idea. I think all those books your da read to you have put some wild thoughts in your head, lad. You must stay with us, and we'll all be fine."

"But I'm *not* fine, Ma. I want a better life for all of us. I may even find it far from here. Da told me once that I have to find my own happy place in life, and when I do, I will send for you and the girls, and we could all live in style."

She paused for a moment when I mentioned what Da had told me.

"But Gideon, lad, ya ken that *the girse is aye greener.*"

"Maybe so. Maybe so. But I have to discover for myself whether it seems greener or it really is. When Da told me he had found his rightful place here with you, I knew I needed to search for my place in the world. He loved the life of a fisherman—but I don't."

"Gideon, I am shocked and hurt that you want to leave Rosehearty."

"But Ma," I said. "I canna bear for you to lose another son to that cruel North Sea in a year or two. 'Tis an awful inevitability, I fear."

She stood up then, and I knew she was far from happy. With her hands on her hips, she finally spoke.

"There is danger everywhere, Gideon, not just in the North Sea. But I still blame myself for not stopping your Da and Duncan from going that morning. I should have been firmer. It has been such a heavy burden to carry. But if a storm like that happened again, I would not let you and Hector go out."

"But you couldn't stop Da and Duncan that morning, so what makes you think you could stop us? You said yourself that it was the way of all fishermen."

"Aye it is —but ... "

"Well I don't want it to be *my* way. Can't you understand that?"

Maybe I was being selfish by wanting to leave. But I reasoned that Ma was also being selfish, expecting me to stay when my heart wasn't in it.

"Well, laddie," she said, "whatever you decide, you must always be ready to sidestep trouble when it comes knocking. And in times of stress, do not lose your head." These were two of her favorite sayings.

In that moment I knew she would never give me her outright approval, but this was her way of accepting my decision. I stood and hugged her to me, noticing a tear running down her cheek.

"I always had the fear inside me that you would want to leave one day. It's just hard to accept, that's all."

"It's hard for me too, Ma."

She turned quickly and walked down the slope. A brave woman, my Ma was, and I loved her dearly.

Nonetheless, as soon as possible I would head into Fraserburgh and make some enquiries.

* * *

It still being early in the year, the sun offered little warmth on the April morning I set off on foot for Fraserburgh.

The herring fishing industry in the area had grown even more in the last few years, and the harbour was always a hive of activity these days. There were far more people and ships in town, and many companies, including the Hudson's Bay Company, had set up businesses along the main street.

The air tingled with excitement. Men were trading on the street, striking bargains with other traders for their wares. I paused to listen to their conversations above the screech of the gulls. My pulse quickened as I heard them talking about their merchandise and other shipping lines and foreign places.

I asked one of the shopkeepers nearby for directions to the Hudson's Bay Company office and picked up my pace as I headed off in the right direction.

Knocking on the door, I stepped inside. A large man with red whiskers and small spectacles propped on the end of his nose sat behind a desk, looking over some papers. He ignored me, even though I had caused a considerable draft when I opened the door, knocking some of his papers off the desk. I coughed and he finally looked up, his face scrunched in irritation.

"What d'yer want?" he said as he removed his spectacles.

"I've come about a job, sir," I said. "I've heard you're hiring cabin boys."

"And what makes you think you'd be a good cabin boy, laddie?"

"I know the sea, sir. Me da, me brother, and all me uncles were fishermen."

"And do you not want to be a fisherman too?"

"Naw, I'd rather work for your company, sir."

"Would you indeed?"

"Yes, sir. I want to travel to the New World, work at the company posts in Rupert's Land, and make lots of money."

The red-whiskered man sat back in his chair, studied my face for a moment, and then burst into laughter.

"Well, young laddie, I'll give you this much. You have a mouth on you, and a confidence that'll take you far. But how do I know you're telling me the truth?"

"Because I was raised to never tell a lie, sir. I stand by my word."

He almost sounded impressed when he replied, "Well, a ship is leaving port on Tuesday next, sailing for Hudson Bay. They have need of a cabin boy, and the wages will be ten pounds a year. But why should I hire you? What's so special about you?"

"I'm a hard worker, sir, and I know the sea well, but I was hoping for more money. I have a mother and two sisters to support in Rosehearty."

His eyes narrowed. "Cheeky young brat!"

I feared for a moment that I might have gone too far.

"Hoping for more money, are you? Well ten pounds is all we're paying. Take it or leave it."

He paused as though considering the matter further. "But if you work hard for the company you'll be promoted one day. Then you might see more money."

"Aye, I will that, sir. Thank you. So am I hired?"

He grunted his approval with a nod.

"And where shall I report, sir?"

"Tuesday at dawn at the harbour. The ship is called the *Jonathan*." He wrote something on a slip of paper. "What's your name, laddie?"

"Gideon McBride, sir."

"Well, young Gideon McBride, you give this paper to the boatswain, Simpson, and he'll sign you aboard."

He handed me the note, and I stepped forward to shake his hand. He pulled back in surprise, but then reluctantly offered his beefy hand in return. "Good luck to you, laddie. And come back one day when you're a rich man."

"Oh, aye, sir. I plan to."

It was as simple as that. I was now a Company man.

* * *

I now had to tell my family and then say goodbye to everything that was familiar to me. My heart raced at the thought of it.

After I made my announcement and told them I would be leaving the following week, Janet and Fiona clung to me tightly.

"Please don't leave us, Gideon. We need you here," Janet cried.

"I have to go, little one, but one day soon I'll return a very rich man."

On the night before I was to leave, Ma cooked a special dinner of roasted chicken and vegetables she must have bargained for at one of the farms. Seeing it there on my plate brought tears to my eyes. I realized then that she knew all along that I didn't like fish, even though I had tried to disguise it. This was her way of showing how much she loved me. She also gave me three books to take with me—the Bible, a book of poems by Robert Burns and a small book called *The Broch.*

"You must never forget your roots, son," she said. "However far you travel or however rich you become, never forget where you came from."

I knew that I never would.

Next morning, Janet and Fiona cried as though their wee hearts would break. My mother stood stoically beside me, blinking back the tears already forming in her blue eyes.

"I'll send you back money as soon as I get it, Ma, I promise."

"I know you will, Gideon lad. I know you will. Just be safe and come back to us soon. Remember too all the lessons your Da taught you, so put your writing skills to gud use now, and write to us regularly."

"I promise, Ma, I promise," I whispered, trying hard to hide my own tears. I was a man now, and men didn't cry.

Then she rummaged in her apron pocket and laid something in the palm of my hand.

"Gideon lad, you must take this wi' ye'r, and keep it always close to your heart on your grand adventure. Your father, God rest his soul, always wore it around his neck, except for the night he was lost at sea. He left in such a hurry that morning that he forgot to take it, but it would have saved his life, I'm sure of it. It will always keep you safe and remind you of your roots."

I looked down at the piece of flat, shiny metal attached to a leather strap. I inspected it closely and saw the words on the metal were written in Gaelic, from the area of Scotland where my father had grown up. In this part of Scotland, on the northeast coast, we spoke only Doric or English.

"What do the words say?" I asked my mother as I placed the leather strap around my neck, vowing never to remove it.

It says "destiny will always bring you home," she said sadly.

I hugged them all one last time. Suddenly I no longer felt like a man. I was a young lad who still needed the comfort and love of family and home.

As I walked away, I fingered the piece of flat, shiny metal on the leather strap hanging around my neck and hoped with all my heart that destiny would indeed bring me home again one day.

ENGLAND

JANE – In Service
(1860–1862)

CHAPTER 9

The long brick driveway leading to Noxley Manor stretched before me in the afternoon sun.

Daffodils and snowdrops pushing up through the cold soil dotted the flower beds on each side of the driveway. They were as determined as I was in their quest to find spring and a new beginning. Pulling back my shoulders, I lifted my chin and walked toward the house, my palms sweaty and my heart thumping with nerves and excitement.

I had left Field House with nothing but a brown paper parcel containing my meager belongings—my one other gray shift and the book from Mr. Lloyd. As I passed St. Mary's, I wondered whether to go in and say goodbye to the reverend but decided against it. He knew I was leaving, yet he'd made no attempt to visit me or wish me well.

Mrs. Creed had instructed me to go to the back door of Noxley Manor and report to Mrs. Rowlands, the housekeeper. On no account was I to present myself at the front door. She could have spared me the warning—Noxley Manor was far too imposing and grand for me to have dared walk up the steps leading to the massive oak front door. Instead, I hurried around the side of the house to the back, where I found a small door at the foot of three steps.

I knocked, holding my breath. The door creaked open a crack, and a young woman in a black dress and white apron peeked around it.

"I'm Jane Hopkins, the new scullery maid," I said, clutching the parcel to my chest.

The girl eyed me up and down. "Yes, we heard you'd be 'ere today. Come on in."

She led me down a narrow passageway that opened into a large, bright kitchen. "I'm Molly. You'll be taking my place down 'ere because I'm being promoted to upstairs maid." She said this all haughty-like, jutting out her chin and raising her nose skyward, the way the gentry did in church. "You'll be sharing a room with me."

I nodded, wanting to ask the one question that had been on my mind since leaving Field House, but I was afraid of the answer. "Is the work hard?"

"No, not too bad, but it'll keep you hopping. You're a bit small, though, ain't ya?"

I bit my bottom lip. "Yes, I 'spose, but I'm very strong."

She squinted at me, tilting her head to one side as though she doubted that very much. "How old are you, Jane Hopkins?"

"Fifteen—and a half."

"I came here two years ago when I was sixteen. Me family lives over in Great Tew. Me dad is a laborer there on the estate. I started here when Dory Evans did. She was from the Home, too. Did you know 'er?"

I smiled for the first time. "Oh yes, she was my friend. Is she still here?"

"She left about a month ago—sent up to the Sinclairs' London residence, she was. She's to be an upstairs maid to Lady Penelope, the oldest daughter."

The London residence! How grand. Good for Dory, but I had so looked forward to seeing her again.

Molly laughed. "Dory is quite a case, I can tell y'er. Got herself in a pile of trouble with Mrs. Rowlands when she started courting our Tom. Tom's me brother and one of the footmen 'ere. Mrs. Rowlands caught them one day canoodling right here on the kitchen floor, and I can tell you that put the cat among the pigeons, did that." She leaned in closer. "That's why Dory was sent up to London, though Mrs. Rowlands wanted to get rid of her completely. Her ladyship was too kind, in my opinion. She told Mrs. Rowlands to just send Dory away from temptation instead, and yet still keep her in the family's employment because she was a good worker. Don't you believe that, though!' She sniffed. "Our Tom wants to marry Dory one day, though, and do the honorable thing

by 'er—more fool, 'im. Now sit you down there, Jane." She pointed to
a chair in the corner. "I'll let Mrs. Rowlands know you're 'ere. She's in
'er room right now, working on the menus for tonight."

After Molly disappeared, I glanced around the kitchen, comparing
it to the small one at Field House, which had very little in it. This kitchen
had three enormous stoves taking up one complete side of the room,
and the long counters and tables had been scrubbed until they shone.

I heard voices in a room nearby, which I assumed was the pantry,
and I listened for footsteps, but there were none, so I took a chance
and opened some of the cupboard doors to peek inside. All the shelves
were stacked with jars of fruit and vegetables, and an unfamiliar but
pleasant aroma filled the room. Later I learned Cook was baking cherry
pies in one of the stoves.

At the far end of the kitchen, I opened a door that led into a cold
larder. Never in my life had I seen so much meat. Large sides of beef
hung from a rod alongside other light and dark meats I didn't recognize.
And there were baskets full of potatoes on the floor. So this was what
it was like being rich—having so much food you could feed the whole
village for a year and still have some left.

I heard a door opening farther down the passageway and scurried
back to the chair.

Molly was back. "Mrs. Rowlands wants to see you in her room
now," she said. "Follow me."

* * *

The housekeeper's room was cluttered with little angel figurines
and fancy teacups of all kinds. The sofa had puffy cushions, and several
small paintings hung on the walls.

Sitting in a large armchair, Mrs. Rowlands smiled at me, her
bright eyes and rosy cheeks making me feel welcome. She wore a
gray dress with a large, white lace collar. A white apron covered her

rather expansive middle, and a white cap perched jauntily on top of her head. She stood to greet me as I walked toward her, unsure if I should curtsy in return.

"Thank you, Molly. That's all for now. I'll ring for you when we're done." She studied me with a kindly expression. "Jane Hopkins, eh? Well now, you look a wee bit small, but we'll soon fatten you up, and maybe you'll even grow taller." She laughed.

What a relief. She was nothing like Mrs. Creed. I smiled back at her and stood as tall as I possibly could, clasping my hands together in what I hoped was a respectful manner. "I can work hard, though, Mrs. Rowlands."

"I'm sure you can, having come from the orphanage." She sat back down in her chair. "The work is hard here, too, but once you learn everything, you'll manage."

I felt a moment of panic as I thought of what would happen if I couldn't manage. Would I be sent to the workhouse? Or even back to Field House? No, I couldn't let that happen.

"Your job will be to keep Cook's kitchen spotless. You will scrub the pots, pans, counters, and the floors every day and sweep the back porch every other day. In wintertime, the grates down here need cleaning out every day, and you'll need to wash out all the servants' chamber pots every morning. You'll also carry up the milk from the dairy. Fanny, Cook's assistant, will show you what has to be done."

I nodded. Most of that sounded like the cleaning I'd done every day at the orphanage. But I wasn't so sure about carrying the milk. I'd only ever seen milk for Mrs. Creed at Field House.

"My husband, Mr. Rowlands, is the butler here, and he looks after all the male staff on the estate, and I look after all the women. The governess, Miss Spring, teaches the two younger misses. There are two upstairs ladies' maids, Hannah for her ladyship and now Molly for Miss Julie and Miss Anna. Miss Penelope, the oldest Sinclair daughter, is at the London residence at present with her aunt, and Dory Evans is her personal maid. Dory came from Field House, too—you might have known her."

"Yes, I—"

"Mr. Rowlands supervises his lordship's valet, Mr. Benton, and the two footmen, Tom and Simpson, as well as the groom, Harry, who takes care of the horses in the stables, and Jones, who drives the carriages. Harry does odd jobs around the house, too. There are twelve of us here—the staff at the Sinclairs' London residence is much larger."

I stared at her in horror as I tried to keep track of the flurry of names.

Mrs. Rowlands then rang the hand bell on her desk. For a brief moment, I thought back to Mrs. Creed. But this bell had a far gentler sound.

"Lady Sinclair enjoys spending the summer months down here in the country," Mrs. Rowlands continued. "They'll return to London for the winter. She's a grand lady, I can tell y'er, always working on her charities and the like. His lordship is a grand gentleman too, but I don't suppose there will ever be need for you to meet either of them. Just work hard, and you'll do well." She smiled again.

When Molly returned, Mrs. Rowlands told her to take me to our room. "Your shoes and two uniforms will be there, Jane, and it's your job to keep them spotlessly clean. You'll get one day off a month. You can go now."

Out in the hallway, I followed Molly down another small flight of stairs at the far end of the corridor. Our room had only enough space for two cots and a cupboard in the corner, for hanging our uniforms. A small shelf sat above each bed for personal belongings.

The tiny window provided scant light, and the poky room would probably be cold and damp in the winter, but compared to the dormitory at Field House, it was paradise.

* * *

Once I learned the routine, the work wasn't any harder than it had been at Field House—and I didn't have to worry about being beaten if I did something wrong.

But I had other concerns.

One morning I went into the kitchen looking for Cook and found Molly by the stove, preparing a tray of tea and toast for the two young misses.

"Why, Jane," Cook called out, as she hauled a bag of flour from the cupboard, "you're a speedy little thing. Got all your chores done already? God bless you, my dear, you are a hard worker."

"Thank you, Cook. What do you need me to do now?"

"You can start by cleaning my counter here, so I can make some pies."

When Cook returned to the pantry, Molly rolled her eyes upward. Out of earshot of the older woman, who was somewhat deaf anyway, she said, "Quite the little apple shiner, ain't ya, Janey?"

I shook my head. "I'm only trying to do a good job."

"You better be careful. We don't take kindly to people who make the rest of us look bad."

Barely a week later, Cook called to me as I was about to leave for the dairy.

"Jane, what happened here?" she asked sharply.

The counter I had finished scrubbing a few minutes earlier was now streaked with a dark, sticky liquid. "Did you miss this area?"

I looked at it in alarm. "No, Cook, it was spotless a moment ago."

Molly was behind this, I was sure. I had just seen her dart out of the kitchen as I was going in. But without proof, what could I say? Being in service meant we all had to know our place and follow instructions from our superiors without question, so I kept my mouth shut and apologized to Cook as I cleaned the counter again.

Later that same day, as I was about to go down the hall to sweep the back steps, I overheard voices, so I stopped and listened for a moment. Miss Spring and Mrs. Rowlands were having a heated discussion around the corner.

"I refuse to be treated like one of the lower servants, Mrs. Rowlands," the governess was saying. "If I choose to eat in my room or with the children, I should be allowed to. Why must I eat in the servants' hall with the likes of a lowly scullery maid—like Jane?"

"Jane eats in the kitchen with Fanny and Cook, Miss Spring—which I know you're fully aware of—and the rest of us eat in the servants' hall. You should be no different. This must not happen again."

"But my position here is different. I am part of the family. Please remember that."

"Stop that high-and-mighty attitude with me right now, Miss Spring, or I will report you to her ladyship."

I decided I'd better stop eavesdropping, so I moved around the corner and continued down the hall, attempting to squeeze by them.

Mrs. Rowlands turned to me, her face in a scowl. "Jane, please go about your business quickly. This doesn't concern you."

"Yes, yes, of course." I bowed my head and hurried on my way, trying to ignore all that I had heard and the fact that Miss Spring poked me in the side as I passed by. Now it seemed that she also disliked me. I was an outsider among the staff.

I went on my way and began to sweep the back steps in preparation for one of the footmen to scrub them later, after the front steps were done. Sweeping was so much easier than washing dishes until my hands were raw, or emptying the chamber pots of all the female servants every morning and then rinsing them with that nasty vinegar, a smell I couldn't get out of my nose. Sweeping also gave me the rare opportunity to get some fresh air outside.

"Hello, Janey."

I looked up to see Tom, Molly's brother, a tall, lanky fellow with thick black hair, striding toward me from the stables. He gave me his usual crooked grin.

"You're looking very pretty this morning," he said with a wink. "Almost pretty enough for me to steal a kiss." He removed his cap and bent close to me, his lips poised.

I pushed him away and wagged my finger at him. "I thought you were betrothed to my friend Dory. She might have a thing or two to say about you kissing me!"

He took a step backward. "You know Dory?"

"She was my best friend at Field House."

"Oh ..." He shuffled his feet and twisted his cap in his hands. "Well ... er ... it was only in fun, Janey. Dory is my girl, so let's forget about it, eh?"

Smiling, he whistled as he hurried inside, leaving me to wonder if I would now need to keep an eye on both Molly and Tom. And Miss Spring wasn't on my side, either.

I slammed the broom down with a flourish. To hell with them all!

CHAPTER 10

One Saturday in early June, we got up at the usual time of five o'clock, but that day everything felt different.

There was hustle and bustle everywhere. The Sinclairs were holding a dinner party that night for over fifty guests, which meant a lot of extra work for everyone. It would be at least eighteen hours before we saw our beds again.

After I finished emptying all the chamber pots, I hurried to the kitchen to help Cook with morning tea for the servants. Mrs. Rowlands was already there, giving instructions to everyone.

"Good morning, Jane," she said. "I'd like you and Fanny to help Tom polish all the silverware today. We'll need much more cutlery for dinner tonight, so everyone must pitch in, especially now that Hannah is still too sick to work. If you do a really good job, you can come up to the dining room with me and Fanny to help set the table. It will be a good lesson for you."

It was too bad Hannah had taken to her bed with a stomach ache, but I was secretly not all that sorry. I trembled with excitement at the thought of going upstairs and could not imagine the sights I might see.

But every time Molly came into the kitchen and passed by the table where I was sitting with Tom and Fanny cleaning the silver, she brushed past me and managed to knock a knife or a fork to the floor, making Tom laugh.

"Molly!" I yelled. That made Cook look across at me, so I lowered my voice to a whisper. "Why do you keep doing that?"

"Doing what?"

"You know you keep knocking things on the floor and I have to clean them again."

"Gosh, Janey, sorry if I'm giving you extra work." She giggled.

I felt like knocking her to the floor, along with the cutlery. Tom continued to laugh with his sister, and I glared at them both. Tom had perhaps learned his lesson about flirting with me, but he was still becoming a nuisance, just like his sister.

I had to stop midway through our task to go and wash the breakfast dishes in the scullery. As I went about my work, I overheard a conversation between Molly and Tom coming from the kitchen.

"Why do you keep teasing Janey, Molly?" Tom asked.

"Well, she deserves it."

"Why?"

"Don't you get it, Thomas Jenkins? She's so damn perfect. She always does a good job at everything and speaks better than us. Won't be long before she'll take my job as the young misses' maid, and I'll be back down 'ere again scrubbing floors, you mark my words." She sounded like she was crying.

"You worry too much, Molly."

"And you don't worry enough, Tom. We both came from nothing and had to fight to get these jobs. I ain't going backwards again for anyone."

Cook was back in the kitchen, so their conversation stopped. But I felt sorry for Molly. She was really just like me—worrying about her job. I thought, maybe I should be a little kinder to her in future and even try to be her friend.

By the time I returned to polishing, Tom was down to the last few knives and Fanny had returned to assist Cook. Molly was called to serve sandwiches to Lord and Lady Sinclair in the drawing room because the dining room was being prepared for dinner that night. After we finished the cutlery, Cook, Fanny and I quickly climbed the servants' back stairs to the dining room and set about preparing the table for the evening.

I gasped in amazement. An enormous chandelier with candles ready to be lit hung above the long table, which sparkled with glassware and all the best china—and now the knives and forks we laid at each place setting. A white napkin fashioned in the shape of a rose sat on every plate, and a colorful profusion of fresh flowers in glass vases ran down the middle of the table.

"Be quick, girls," Cook told Fanny and me as she instructed us on how to set the table. We had precious few seconds to admire our work before Cook hurried us back down to the kitchen to start preparing for the feast that night, leaving the two footmen to adjust the seating around the table.

"I'll run through the menu with you all again," Cook said back in the kitchen. "My special turtle soup is simmering on the stove. That will be followed by curried lobster and sole with a main course of roasted chicken, lamb, squash, peas, and potatoes. Fanny, you can start preparing the vegetables now."

I listened, wondering how people could possibly eat that much food at one meal. But Cook wasn't finished. "All of that will be followed by a choice of puddings—marmalade, gingerbread, or jam roll—and, of course, my special cherry pie."

Cook turned to me. "Jane, I want you to bring out all the chickens from the larder and three legs of lamb. They need to go into the oven soon. Then you can begin to scrub the counters so I can make the puddings and pies. You must keep up with washing all the dishes and pans in the scullery as I finish using each one."

I nodded and began to do her bidding, and by seven o'clock that evening, the air in the kitchen was thick with the delicious smell of roasted meat. My stomach rumbled with delight. Oh, how I would love to sample the roast beef covered in thick gravy. I watched with envy as Tom and Simpson carried one platter after another upstairs.

"Some of the gentlemen wanted two or three servings, Cook," Tom said when he returned to get another platter of lamb.

When dinner was all over and I was in the scullery working on all the pots, pans, and dishes, I could hear music from upstairs. Mrs.

Rowlands had told us that morning that the Sinclairs would be bringing in a small orchestra from Oxford to play waltzes and reels.

Molly flew down to the kitchen periodically, bursting to tell us the latest news. "I've put the young misses to bed and now the adults are dancing. My, you should see those dresses. I swear I've never seen anything so beautiful."

I longed to see them for myself, but I would not be allowed upstairs again. Instead I had to be content with washing dishes and helping Fanny scrub all the counters once again. Poor Cook was worn out and had already collapsed in a chair, fanning herself with her kerchief before dozing off.

* * *

It was close to ten o'clock when Mrs. Rowlands came back into the kitchen to thank us all for our hard work before heading off to her room.

Molly turned to me. "Jane, if you want to see the dancing upstairs, follow me. I know a spot where we can watch it all."

"No, Molly, I couldn't do that. Cook would not allow me upstairs again."

"Don't be such a little milksop, Janey. She's so worn out she won't even know you've gone. It'll be safe. And Mrs. Rowlands has probably gone to bed now, as she's tired. No one will see us. "

I glanced over at Cook, who was still asleep in her chair, and after I'd washed the last plate, I crept out of the kitchen with Molly, remembering my earlier resolve to try to befriend her.

We climbed the back stairs, and at the very top we slipped down underneath into the stairwell where, above us through the open door, we could see the whole dining room. It had now been cleared, and the sliding doors had been opened to extend the space into the great hall. A three-piece orchestra was playing at one end of the enlarged room, and couples were dancing. I recognized the violin, cello, and viola from pictures in a music book Mr. Lloyd had once shown me.

How wonderful it would be to be a part of a scene like that, dining and dancing in splendor, being able to have servants wait on me. How elegant everyone looked—the ladies in their spectacular full gowns and the gentlemen in their dark evening suits and bow ties. And the music was so sublime I couldn't help but tap my foot to the beat and sway to and fro.

All of a sudden, I felt something sharp poking my shoulder and heard the housekeeper's voice above me. "Jane, what on earth do you think you're doing, hiding down there?"

I turned to see her foot through the gap between the stairs. "Oh Mrs. Rowlands, I'm so sorry. We ..." I scrambled up through the stairwell and looked around for Molly, but she was nowhere to be seen.

"Get back downstairs at once. I will deal with you in the morning."

Molly had set me up—again! She probably knew Mrs. Rowlands wouldn't have gone to bed yet. I returned to the kitchen knowing I would be reprimanded tomorrow, by both Mrs. Rowlands and Cook.

But when we finally finished all the remaining chores, Cook stirred herself from her nap and asked Fanny to put on the kettle. She seemed unaware I'd ever left.

"I think we all deserve a well-earned cup of tea," she said.

I was about to sit down when the door opened and a handsome, fine figure of a man with graying hair and a warm smile strode in. Cook and Fanny shot up from their chairs. I froze. It was Lord Sinclair himself. For a moment, I wondered if he had personally come down to reprimand me, but he seemed too happy for that.

"Oh, your Lordship, how nice to see you. What can we do for you?" said Cook.

"Excellent job, Cook. I just came down to thank you all for your hard work today. But I also have a small confession to make." He paused. "I was hoping to sneak away with one more slice of that delicious cherry pie now that everyone has gone home. Would that be possible, Cook?"

"Why, of course, sir," Cook said, obviously delighted with herself as she cut another slice and handed it to him on a plate.

"Not a word to her ladyship," he teased, patting his stomach. "She complains I am putting on weight, so I'll take this to my library."

"It's our secret, m'Lord," Cook said.

Everyone joined in the laughter as he left the room with his cherry pie.

* * *

Once we finally got to our room, Molly started in right away about all the women guests and what they were wearing that night.

I was still furious with her for leaving me in the stairwell, my anger boiling up in my stomach. "Molly, why did you trick me into going upstairs, knowing that Mrs. Rowlands would probably find me there? And you mysteriously disappeared."

She giggled. "Well now, Janey, you were enjoying yourself so much that you probably didn't hear me say I was leaving to check on the young misses."

"Probably because you never said it. You just left me to be found there and get into trouble."

"Janey, why would I do such a thing?"

"Why indeed!" I tried to go to sleep, but Molly kept jabbering on.

"I even spotted that gentleman from Oxford here tonight. He was the one who was courting Miss Penelope, and he was the reason she was sent up to London before you came. Her ladyship did not approve of him. He has a bad reputation with the ladies, so I hear."

"And lucky for Dory she could go to London with her," I murmured.

"Yes, but I'm wondering if those two together could be trouble. Dory is full of cheek, I can tell you. Mind you," she added, more seriously, "Miss Penelope's aunt, the Countess, will be keeping a very strict eye on them."

I turned over, desperately needing sleep. It was already well past midnight, and we'd have to get up in less than five hours. But I decided to indulge her that night to prevent her from making even more trouble for me.

Her voice faded in and out as I tried to doze off. "... and of course, their son got himself into hot water lots of times."

"Hmm?"

"Mr. Philip. He's an officer in the army and has been all over the world. He was back on leave early this year when the family was all in London, and he'll not be back again until this winter. He's so good-looking, but he has an eye for the ladies too. Even some of the servants, like Clara, the young misses' previous maid. He got her in the family way. That's why she had to leave."

Family way? What was she talking about? But I had no energy to care. They were all strangers to me. As she chatted on, I conjured in my head my favorite piece of music by Mr. Chopin: *Nocturne Op. 9 Number 2 in E-Flat major.*

Eventually the music drowned out her voice completely, and I fell into a deep sleep.

CHAPTER 11

I was standing at the bottom of the servants' stairs, trembling with fright as I gazed upwards.

That morning, Hannah had been sent back to her family's farm to recover from what had been diagnosed as a serious case of dysentery. Mrs. Rowlands had asked me to take care of her ladyship until a new personal maid could be hired. Cook had refused to let Fanny leave the kitchen because she needed her assistant there, so that left me and Molly to take on the extra chores. After what had happened under the stairs with Molly, followed by Mrs. Rowlands' reprimand the next morning, I didn't think I'd ever be able to leave the kitchen again. She must have been desperate to allow me to attend her ladyship.

I took a deep breath and started climbing. Apart from seeing the dining room and the great hall on the night of the party, I had never entered the domain of the upper class before. The cups on the tray rattled so much from my nerves that I had to stop halfway up the stairs to keep from dropping everything.

C'mon, Jane, I said to myself, taking a tentative step. *You can do this.* I flashed to the last time I had delivered tea to someone and smiled to myself, remembering Mr. Finch flying off the bed and Mrs. Creed's horrified face.

"No more breaking the rules, Jane," Mrs. Rowlands had warned me. "Her ladyship is entertaining a very important guest for tea in the drawing room. When you get to the top of the stairs, go down the hall to the first door on the right. Then knock gently before entering."

I dared not make another mistake. At the drawing room door, I placed the tray on the floor and tapped lightly. At that very moment, the grandfather clock across the hall chimed the hour and I nearly jumped out of my skin, letting out a startled cry.

"Come in," came a voice from inside. As I stepped into the room with the tray, Lady Sinclair continued speaking to her guest without looking in my direction, thankfully oblivious to the noise I'd made outside the door. I stood in the center of the room, my knees knocking, not knowing what to do next.

When Lady Sinclair turned to me, I was struck by how beautiful she was. I recalled seeing her in church long ago, her auburn hair styled fashionably upwards. Today she wore a green satin gown and a long string of pearls around her neck. Her smile was what stood out the most. It made her face light up and her eyes sparkle, showing off her natural beauty.

"Ah, you must be Jane Hopkins. Please set the tray right here. We can serve ourselves." She waved a graceful hand toward the small mahogany table between them. "Thank you, Jane."

My mouth dropped. One of the gentry had actually spoken to me, and thanked me, no less. I managed to bob as gracefully as possible and choke out, "Yes, ma'am."

My eyes took in the rest of the room—the blue and beige sofas, high-backed wing chairs, and polished tables, along with Lady Sinclair's guest in a mauve dress. I stared a bit too long at the box-shaped hat perched high on the other lady's head. It appeared to be the nesting place for two small birds. Before me were all the riches and elegance of life above stairs.

As I turned to leave, my breath caught sharply and I could scarcely move for a moment. In the far corner was the most magnificent piano I'd ever seen. It was polished to a high sheen. Oh, how I would have loved to play such a grand instrument! I had sometimes heard the two young misses struggling with their scales during their lessons or whenever they practiced. Of course, upper-class ladies were expected to be accomplished at the piano, but it was an impossible dream for people like me.

Suddenly remembering my duties, I left the room and raced back downstairs. But my glimpse into that other world had left me dazzled.

*   *   *

Over the next month, Mrs. Rowlands often asked me to attend to her ladyship.

Every time I returned to the drawing room, the piano beckoned to me, just as Mr. Lloyd's once had. One afternoon in the middle of the summer, when the whole family was visiting friends in Oxford, I had my usual one free hour before Cook and Fanny would need me in the kitchen. Perhaps I should have gone to the laundry room and washed out my uniform, as Molly was doing. But instead I crept up the stairs. As her ladyship's temporary maid, I was allowed above-stairs now anyway.

After quietly closing the drawing room door behind me, I tiptoed across the thick carpet to the piano and sat on the padded bench. I gently raised the lid and brushed my fingers across the keys. My whole body tingled with excitement.

Before I realized it, I was playing again—one of my favorite piano sonatas by Mr. Beethoven. I remembered all the notes. I played as softly as I could, gracefully moving my hands across the keyboard as Mr. Lloyd had taught me. I was so caught up in the music again that I had completely forgotten Mrs. Rowlands' warning. "One more mistake, Jane," she had said, "and you'll be dismissed!"

When I moved on to a Chopin piece, I realized I wasn't alone. I jumped up and turned to see Lady Sinclair herself standing there.

"Oh, your ladyship ... I'm so sorry ... I had no idea ... please, please forgive me," I stuttered out my apologies, not daring to look up, my face burning with embarrassment and fear. How did I think I'd get away with it? Mr. Lloyd had discovered me the same way at his piano many years before, but I was no longer a child. This time there would be severe consequences. Why had I been so reckless?

Lady Sinclair said nothing for a moment, and I didn't dare speak again. Surely I would throw up on the beautiful carpet, worsening my crime. But peering up, I saw only amazement in her hazel eyes, not anger.

"As you can see, Jane, I didn't leave with my husband and daughters. I decided to stay home because I have a terrible headache. I was resting upstairs when I heard you playing."

"Your ladyship, please forgive me for disturbing you."

"Hush, Jane. I was enjoying your music, and I want you to continue while I sit here and rest. I find your playing so soothing. It helps my headache."

She lowered herself to the couch, put her feet up and arranged her green velvet robe around her, all so casual and familiar, and not what I expected from a lady.

"How in the world did you learn to play the piano so beautifully?" she asked, her striking auburn hair cascading over her shoulders.

"Reverend Lloyd taught me—until Mrs. Creed at the Home found out and she became very angry and she ... she . .. . er ..."—I couldn't tell her about the beating—"she stopped the lessons."

"What a pity. You have a great talent, my dear."

"Thank you, your ladyship, but I must get about my duties now. Mrs. Rowlands will be very angry with me, and I'm so sorry I disturbed you."

"Not for a little while, Jane. I want you to stay. I'll explain to Mrs. Rowlands. Please go back to what you were playing."

I sat back on the bench, wobbly with relief. She had every right to be furious with me—a servant touching her beautiful piano.

When I began to play again, everything Mr. Lloyd had ever taught me about adding feeling and expression poured forth from my hands. The music sounded the best it ever had. Whenever I paused, thinking that maybe her ladyship had grown tired of my playing, she waved her hand at me to continue. Her trance-like, peaceful expression seemed to bring out an excellence and a new dimension to my playing.

I could have played forever, but I finally stopped and turned to her.

"That was delightful, Jane," she said, smiling. "I would like you to come every afternoon to the drawing room and play for me like this. I must confess my headache has completely disappeared."

"Thank you, Lady Sinclair. Thank you for allowing me to play again. I have missed it so much."

"Then we will both gain something from this afternoon's encounter. Now run along, my dear. I will see you again tomorrow at the same time. And I will explain to Mrs. Rowlands."

"Yes, yes." I almost tripped over myself backing out of the room.

*   *   *

Mrs. Rowlands was in the kitchen when I got back, so I immediately explained where I had been.

"I disobeyed and went upstairs without being called, but now her ladyship wants me to play the piano for her every afternoon in the drawing room, Mrs. Rowlands."

Her eyes widened. "What! Was that you I heard playing a little while ago?" She put her hands on her hips. "I thought it was her ladyship, since she had chosen to stay home. But you disobeyed the rules yet again. What am I to do with you? And how did you ever learn to play like that?"

"Well ... I ... you see ..."

She waved her hand. "Never mind that now. Whatever her ladyship wants, we must do. Just make sure you still get all your chores done as well."

I breathed a sigh of relief.

Later that night, as Molly and I prepared for bed, she couldn't hold her tongue. "My goodness, Janey, you certainly know how to toady to the gentry, don't you? I hear you are to be playing the piano for her ladyship, no less! Goodness me."

"It helped her headache."

"Who taught you how to play?"

"It's a long story, Molly, and I don't want to talk about it."

"Imagine a person like you, allowed to play a piano? You must have done something very special for someone. Maybe you're not as coy and innocent as you pretend to be."

This time, I refused to take the bait. Ignoring her, I pulled the blanket over my head, remembering the horror of the beating Mrs. Creed gave me.

But I also remembered the satisfaction of fighting back.

*   *   *

A few weeks later, I was about to start washing all the pots from supper in the scullery when Mrs. Rowlands called me into the servants' dining room. Everyone was sitting around the table finishing their tea and kidney pie.

Mrs. Rowlands said she had an announcement to make.

"Sadly, Hannah will not now be returning to us. She's too weak and not likely to recover for a long time. Her ladyship has decided she will need a new permanent maid, so she wants Jane to fill that position."

My mouth dropped. "Me?"

"Crikey!" Molly screamed. "No one moves up in the world that quick. Jane's just a scullery maid. That's not fair, Mrs. Rowlands. Jane, what have you been up to?"

"That's enough, Molly," Mrs. Rowlands said, glaring at her. "We do not question or comment upon the decisions made by our betters. Her ladyship must have good reason for appointing Jane to this position.

Molly, now you will have only the young misses to attend to, so this arrangement should help you out. We will be hiring a new scullery maid instead."

I glanced at Molly across the table, and her dark eyes glared back at me, her lips pressed in a thin line.

That night in our room, I could not stop from smiling as I undressed, humming to myself.

"How did you manage it?" Molly said. "You came here only a short while ago as a scullery maid, and an orphan at that."

"You are still personal maid to the two young misses, Molly, and you rose to that position from working as a scullery maid too, so why begrudge me the same chance?" I turned my back on her.

But I knew I would have to watch her even more carefully now.

*   *   *

Every morning I went to Lady Sinclair's bedroom to brush her hair and attempt to style it.

"You have a particular knack for making me look good, Jane." She smiled.

"Thank you, your ladyship. But I'm afraid I have few skills in styling hair. It is simply that your hair is so beautiful and easy to manage."

I also had to bring up her breakfast tray every morning and prepare a bath for her, but I was grateful that one of the footmen always carried up the hot water. I simply had to lay out her ladyship's clothes and help her dress.

Sometimes I accompanied her when she went out for a drive in the carriage. We often took trips into Oxford to visit her dressmaker.

But the very best part of my new position was playing the piano for Lady Sinclair every afternoon. Whenever she experienced one of her frequent headaches, she asked me to play my most soothing pieces for a longer time. I began to pray she would have many more headaches.

I wanted that delightful summer to last forever. But soon the days grew shorter and a nip came to the Cotswolds, though even the month of October at Harvest Festival time proved pleasantly warm. Farm workers on the estate were given the day off to enjoy the fruits of their labours. St. Mary's Church was decorated abundantly with fruit and flowers, and we sang hymns of praise and thanksgiving.

One morning in late October, two months before my sixteenth birthday, while helping Lady Sinclair get dressed, she casually mentioned that everyone would be moving up to London in just a few weeks.

"Of course, you will come too, Jane," she said. "Mr. and Mrs. Rowlands always stay at Noxley Manor year-round to keep an eye on the estate here. Cook and Fanny will also stay, as will the new scullery maid, but you and Molly, Miss Spring, Mr. Benton, Tom and Jones will accompany us to our London residence for the Christmas and New Year's holidays. We may possibly stay until the spring for the London season next year."

Christmas in London! I had no idea what the London season was, but it sounded exciting. And I would finally meet up with Dory again.

"That's wonderful, my lady. I look forward to seeing London for the first time."

"Oh yes, Jane, you will adore it. And next spring will be a constant round of parties and entertaining. It will be a busy time for everyone."

My heart sang. I wouldn't let Molly or anyone else spoil this grand adventure.

CHAPTER 12

The day before we left for London, I went for a walk during my free hour.

I wanted some fresh air and exercise, so I walked down the hill to the field next to the church, where I found some wildflowers still blooming despite the chill in the air. Those tiny pink and yellow flowers seemed hardy, inspiring me to be equally strong, so I picked a bunch to bring back with me.

In my room, I took out one of the flowers and pressed it in my Bible catechism to remind me of Mr. Lloyd and my piano lessons. Then I went to the kitchen and handed the rest to Cook.

"Bless you, my dear. I will miss you when you're away in London."

"I'll miss you too, Cook."

I suddenly felt sad, as though I'd never see her again, even though we would all return the following summer.

"You'll enjoy the train trip, Jane," Cook told me. "Before 1855, the family always travelled to London by carriage, but in August that year, his lordship paid for a single-line branch railway to be opened up near the estate, and this line now links up with the Great Western Railway line from Oxford to London."

I barely slept that night, thinking about us all travelling by train from the small station at Great Noxley, and the next morning those of us who were leaving for London said our farewells to Mr. and Mrs. Rowlands and the other staff. No doubt the Rowlands rather enjoyed this annual departure of the family. They could now run everything and act as the lord and lady of the manor themselves.

* * *

Until that November day in 1861, I had never seen a train, let alone ridden on one. We servants were even allowed to join the family, at a discreet distance in first class, where the seats were of red velvet and softer than the wooden ones on the rest of the train.

I stared at everything in wonder. I loved the clickety-click of the train on the tracks as we journeyed through fields and meadows and passed the occasional village. Closer to London, I gawked in wonder at all the tall, gray buildings and a few elegant homes with neat gardens, as well as the broken windows, caved-in roofs, and squalor of the slums.

There was so much hustle and bustle at Paddington Station! Everyone moved at a fast pace, darting here and there, porters carrying luggage, whistles blowing, people calling out to one another.

We rode in separate carriages from the station to the Sinclairs' London residence in Belgrave Square. As we journeyed towards the west end of the city, we passed shops with large windows displaying elegant, expensive-looking dresses.

These buildings were much cleaner, most of them painted white with black front doors sporting brass door knockers. They were a far cry from the slum area we had passed through, nearer the station. Many buildings were situated in pleasant squares where the grass was green and well-manicured, and shade trees lined the avenues. This was where the rich lived.

As we approached the Square, my heart beat with excitement. The Sinclairs' London residence was a tall, elegant brick building surrounded by a black wrought-iron railing. To the left of the main entrance, steps led down to another door, which Molly informed me we would be using to get to the servants' quarters.

"Tradesmen also use that entrance," she said. "Along with the likes of us servants."

Up ahead of us, the Sinclairs were alighting from their carriage at the front door, opened wide by two imposing figures standing on the top step.

Molly nudged me. "That's Mr. Leighton and Mrs. Sanders," she whispered. "She's the housekeeper, and he's the butler. Have to mind your p's and q's around them, like with the Rowlands back at Noxley Manor—only *they* think they're even more important."

As we unloaded our limited baggage, two footmen rushed in all directions to unload the Sinclairs' considerable luggage. Saying nothing to us, Miss Spring walked away to join the family, no doubt seeing herself as part of the family entourage.

But then Lady Sinclair also called out to me. "Jane? Jane, come here a moment," she said. "I want you to help me get settled in my room. You can get acquainted with everyone else downstairs later on." She waved an elegant, gloved hand toward the basement entrance. "The girls won't need you right now, Molly, so you can head downstairs."

I stood there motionless, my feet stuck to the pavement. Molly gave me a push. "Go on," she whispered. "Get moving. You're going in by the front entrance today! Ain't you the special one."

I climbed the broad front steps of Enderby House behind her ladyship and entered through the open doorway, with its polished brass handles glistening, into a black-and-white marble-floored great hall far more magnificent than anything I could ever have imagined. If Noxley Manor had been grand, Enderby House was ... *opulent*. I'd heard Lady Sinclair use that word once, and it seemed to fit the scene around me perfectly.

Servants were everywhere—maids, footmen, the butler, the housekeeper—and they all spoke differently here in London than we did in the country, with posh accents. The servants appeared to be trying to imitate their employers, but their speech sounded forced and unnatural.

I knew I could do a better job. I vowed not to drop my h's the way the other servants did. That way, when the opportunity arose for me to take my rightful place in society, I would be prepared.

Mr. Leighton was a staunch, upright man, and Mrs. Sanders a short, buxom woman with a prominent brown mole on her chin. As they welcomed the Sinclairs, a young woman with flaming red hair rushed down the grand staircase and flung herself first into Lady Sinclair's arms and then into Lord Sinclair's.

"Mama, Papa, it's so good to see you."

"Penelope, my darling," murmured Lady Sinclair. "How pretty you look."

Miss Anna and Miss Julie also hugged their older sister and then their aunt Charlotte, the countess. Tall, like her brother Lord Sinclair, the countess was an imposing figure, but her eyes were cold and her mouth pinched. She seemed the perfect chaperone for Lady Penelope in London. But oh, to be part of a family like that!

The three daughters ran ahead up the large staircase, and Lord and Lady Sinclair smiled at their departing figures and constant chatter.

"Now, Charlotte," Lady Sinclair said, "you must tell me all that has happened while we've been away in the country. I do hope all went well."

The countess looked down her long nose at all the servants hovering nearby. "I'll have tea served for you in the drawing room, my dears, and we can discuss matters privately."

"Of course. Now come, Jane. Help me with my things. You can also lay out my clothes for dinner."

Along with Benton, Lord Sinclair's valet, I followed Lord and Lady Sinclair up the enormous staircase as people scattered in all directions. Benton carried his lordship's valise, and I carried her ladyship's smallest valise.

Lady Sinclair turned to me with a smile. "Jane, Enderby House was built in the 1830s by Lord Sinclair's father, the Earl of Sutherland, and it is one of the last aristocratic homes to be built in the west end of London. It's such a beautiful house. I always love coming back here."

It was indeed spectacular. The grand entrance hall showcased the upper floors, the first of which separated in two directions, left and right, into long corridors. A portrait gallery on the first floor contained paintings of Lord Sinclair's ancestors.

We could still hear the girls' happy chatter fading from down another long corridor as we entered her ladyship's room. Lord Sinclair and Benton slipped into an adjacent room.

My mouth dropped when I saw an actual bathroom with a gold-plated claw-foot bath and a private water closet in a separate room. It was even more elegant than the one at Noxley Manor.

Soon after I helped Lady Sinclair with her attire and laid out her gown for dinner, his lordship returned from his room. His thick head of gray hair had probably once been red, judging by his daughters' hair color.

"Come, my dear," he said," let's go down and join Charlotte for tea while the girls catch up on their gossip."

Lady Sinclair laughed at him as she turned to me. "Thank you, Jane. That will be all. You may join the other servants now. One of the footmen will show you the way downstairs to your quarters. I'll ring for you later when I need you."

Dutifully dismissed, I bobbed and left the room. I stood for a moment on the landing, gazing upward at nymphs and cherubs carved onto the ceiling and the pillars. I peeked again at the portraits of earlier family members and the glistening chandeliers hanging from the ceilings. Below me was the elegant black-and-white marble flooring of the great hall. I had to pinch myself to believe that I, Jane Hopkins, an abandoned orphan, was really here in this magnificent setting as personal maid to a grand English lady and earning twenty-five pounds a year!

I slowly descended the stairs, hoping I would find someone to show me where I needed to go. As I arrived back in the foyer, one of the many footmen appeared from a side entrance. "Can I help you, miss?"

"I'm looking for the servants' quarters. I'm Lady Sinclair's personal maid."

"Are you now?" He grinned. "Well, la-di-da. And what might your name be, Miss Personal Maid?"

"Jane Hopkins," I said, my face growing hot.

"Follow me, Jane Hopkins."

I knew he was teasing me, and even though I was shaking with fear at all the grandness around me, he somehow made me feel at ease. I followed him to a back hallway, where he pointed to another set of stairs. "Head down there, and you'll find the kitchen and servants' common room."

"Thank you ... er ..."

"William," he said. "Just call me Billy."

"Thanks, Billy."

"Don't mention it, Janey, and good luck to you."

I soon found myself peering into a large room with a long, wooden table, around which sat several Enderby House servants having tea. There was a great deal of chatter and laughter, and I had to cough to make my presence known.

A scream of delight came from the end of the table.

"Scrap! My goodness, if it's not little Scrap!" Dory Evans bounded toward me and threw her arms around me, nearly lifting me off the floor. I wasn't used to such emotion from anyone, let alone Dory, but it felt good to be made so welcome. She looked a little different now. Her dark hair was pinned back under a maid's cap, and her cheeks wore a healthy rosy hue. Like me, she had also filled out, obviously thanks to better food.

"You made it!" she said. "Everyone, this is my little friend, Jane Hopkins. We were in Field House together. So you finally got out of Old Sourface's clutches, eh? And you grew, Scrap. You actually grew!"

I nodded. "I've been at Noxley Manor since early spring, and then her ladyship made me her personal maid because I played the piano for her one day and—well, there's so much to tell."

"Gosh, there must be. Playing a piano? We'll talk later. This is wonderful, Scrap. You looking after her ladyship and me looking after Miss Penelope. And my Tom has come up from the country, too."

Tom was sitting beside Dory, looking very pleased with himself.

Molly interrupted our conversation with a sly look at me. "He's been pining away for you, Dory, ever since you came up to London, so now perhaps we'll see a smile on his face again. Right, Janey?"

Before I could reply, Mrs. Sanders came in, looking cross. "What is all the noise about?" she said. "Goodness me, Dory Evans, I could hear your voice from upstairs. We don't want to set a bad example for Jane. We must all conduct ourselves with dignity in London, if you please, and only talk about our personal affairs when we are not on duty. Now, I'm sure you all have chores to perform. Tea is over."

The maids scurried in various directions, including the *two* scullery maids. Wow, what I wouldn't have given for help with all those pots and pans at Noxley Manor! Dory and Molly stayed behind, offering to show me my room, which I would be sharing with them and one other maid named Flora, an upstairs chambermaid, who was a quiet little mouse.

"Only one of you need do that," Mrs. Sanders said. "Dory, you can show Jane, and the rest of you will all go about your duties. Less noise, please."

Dory was still the same girl I remembered, with the happy nature, the willingness to help, and the determination to never give up in times of despair. I was sure she must be doing a good job as maid to Miss Penelope, despite what Molly had said.

Our room had four cots and two small dressers, but I barely noticed its sparseness. It was larger than the one I had shared with Molly at Noxley Manor, and it was wonderful to be with Dory again.

As we headed back upstairs, she prattled away about life in London and how she intended to marry Tom one day soon, and they'd own their own house in London and have a pack of children. Before that, they wanted to get positions as housekeeper and butler somewhere, like the Rowlands or Mr. Leighton and Mrs. Sanders, so they could make enough money to make all their dreams come true. She seemed so happy, and I would never spoil that by telling her that Tom had tried to kiss me once at Noxley Manor.

As soon as we returned to the kitchen, Lady Sinclair's bell rang, and I was summoned to duty once again.

CHAPTER 13

I loved working at Enderby House.

Lord and Lady Sinclair were kind people who cared about those less fortunate than themselves. And they treated all their servants with respect. But the best part of working for Lady Sinclair was the fact that I was still allowed to play the piano every afternoon in the drawing room for her. This piano was even grander than the one at Noxley Manor.

One day, her ladyship said to me: "I'm considering having you give lessons to Miss Anna and Miss Julie. Would you like that, Jane?"

"Oh yes, my lady, I would love it."

But later that day, I heard Miss Spring talking to Mrs. Sanders and Lady Sinclair in the grand hall as I stood on the upstairs landing. She had obviously been told about this decision and strongly disapproved.

"That can simply not happen!" I heard her say. "I was hired as the governess, and that includes ALL the education the young ladies need. I am proficient enough in music, I am sure."

But you can't play the piano as well as me, Miss Snootyface, I thought to myself.

"It seems I have insulted Miss Spring," Lady Sinclair told me that night with a smile. "Between you and me, I think you would make a far better music teacher, Jane, but perhaps we should leave things as they are for now. I don't want to lose her. She is a very good governess, and they are so hard to come by."

Her confidence in me made me think that one day I might also rise to the position of governess.

Throughout the day, Lady Sinclair devoted much of her time to her many charities. I admired her for promoting Mr. Charles Dickens and his Ragged Schools Scheme, by working tirelessly to improve the deplorable conditions of the London slums.

One frequent visitor to Enderby House was a lady called Miss Coutts. She also devoted her life to charity work. A striking woman with a stern expression, she wore her hair severely pulled back from her face and sported no jewelry other than a cameo brooch pinned on her high collar, beneath her chin.

According to Billy, who often confided in me, she had inherited a vast fortune as a young woman from her banking grandfather, Thomas Coutts. She could quite easily have squandered it all, he said, but instead she gave a good deal of her money away to the less fortunate.

She lived most of her time in Torquay in Devonshire, but she also had a residence in London on Stratton Street. I often accompanied Lady Sinclair to her London house and listened to other wealthy ladies discussing fund-raising for the relief of the poor or for building homes for "fallen women."

Every time I heard those words, my stomach knotted. They were talking about women like my mother—a *fallen woman*, as Mrs. Creed had once described her. It pained me to think that my mother must have been desperate enough to leave me at the orphanage. What had happened to her? Why didn't she ever return for me? Was she really just a prostitute who didn't care about me? Sometimes when I lay in bed at night, a rush of emotions would flow over me—shame over where I might have come from, mixed with so much despair and longing to know the truth about my past.

I hardly had time to think about her, though, or much of anything else. Preparations for Christmas soon began in earnest, and the Sinclairs entertained or attended functions almost every night, which meant all the staff at Enderby House were busy from before sunup to way after sundown.

All of us servants helped decorate the house. We hung wreaths of holly and strung laurel and greenery over the bannisters as the footmen carried an enormous tree into the foyer so that we could decorate it with coloured baubles and candles.

The Sinclairs hosted several musical evenings, banquets and parties, and the kitchen staff had to be on their toes at all times. I was equally busy attending to Lady Sinclair, but I didn't mind. I enjoyed all the hustle and bustle in the house.

One morning, as I was dressing her ladyship, she told me they would be going to the opera that night—*The Magic Flute* by Mozart was being performed..

"Jane," she said, "I'd like you to accompany me tonight. I know how much you appreciate music and especially like Mozart."

My heart skipped a beat. Was she really inviting me to the opera? "Oh, your ladyship! I would so enjoy that."

"You will, of course, be sitting in the servants' seats in the auditorium below, but first you will be required to help get us seated in our box."

I would actually get to see the famous new Royal Opera House and hear all the beautiful music by Mozart being performed. It would be a night to remember. Could this possibly be true?

Billy winked at me as we all gathered in the grand hall to await our carriages that evening. Molly was scowling at me because she had not been chosen to go. I almost felt sorry for her.

Her ladyship was dressed in peach satin. The countess wore an elegant purple gown, and Miss Penelope and the two young misses were in various shades of pink and blue chiffon. His lordship was in evening attire with black tie and looked very handsome. Jewels sparkled and thick fur wraps covered bare shoulders.

I was thrilled to see the lighted streets all the way to the opera house as the carriage rattled over the cobblestones. Was I really riding in a carriage in the west end of London at night as part of the Sinclair party?

When we arrived, I walked dutifully behind her ladyship, taking in all the splendour around me. My senses were aroused by exotic perfumes and bright colours and the occasional aroma of a gentleman's cigar. I accompanied the party to their box, where I settled her ladyship and helped her remove her wrap before going back downstairs to the seats allocated to the servants at the rear of the auditorium. Before I left their box, I overheard a gentleman in the next box talking to his companion.

"This location seems odd to me, old boy,' he said. "Building it in a back street in Covent Garden indeed! Pity the old building burned down. This is nothing compared to the grand opera houses in Paris and Berlin."

But to me, London's Royal Opera House would have been elegant wherever it had been built. The balconies, decorated in creams and golds, were embossed with garlands of angels, a fitting backdrop to all the beautiful gowns and sparkling jewelry on display everywhere. I wished my plain black dress were more striking.

And the music was sublime! I was lost in another world, and I wanted the evening never to end. Later that night, after her ladyship retired, I lay in my bed in our little room, reliving the evening and imagining that I had been the one in the peach gown sitting in the box listening to Mozart.

*   *   *

Christmas festivities continued. A week before the actual day, while I was serving afternoon tea in the drawing room to Lady Sinclair, the countess, and Miss Coutts, Billy entered the room with a telegram on a silver tray. He bowed and handed it to Lady Sinclair, who quickly ripped it open.

Billy smiled at me before he left. He always seemed to make a point of sitting next to me at mealtimes. I liked that. He was very jolly and kind to me.

"Oh, this is wonderful, Charlotte!" Lady Sinclair said as she read the telegram. "I must let James know immediately."

She turned to me. "Jane, please go and ask his lordship to come at once." And then to the ladies, she added, "Philip has four months' leave from his regiment and will be arriving home tomorrow. He will be with us for Christmas, after all! Hopefully, he will have mended his ways."

I scurried away to the library, where I found his lordship smoking his pipe and going over some paperwork. "Sir, her ladyship requests your presence in the drawing room. She has some good news."

"Oh, bother those women, Jane," he said, leaning back in his chair. "Just when I was enjoying some peace and quiet." But he smiled. "The news had better be really good."

"Oh it is, sir, yes, I'm sure."

It wasn't until much later that I wondered what her ladyship had meant about hoping her son had mended his ways. But then I recalled the gossip about him that Molly had delighted in telling me.

* * *

After the arrival of Captain Philip Sinclair, son and heir to the Sinclair fortune, Christmas was in full swing.

I would stop as often as I could to gaze at the enormous fir tree in the foyer, transfixed by its beauty. I had never had a real Christmas before. One day, Billy came up beside me in the foyer while I was staring up at the tree. "It's beautiful, isn't it, Janey?"

"Yes, it certainly is. I believe Prince Albert introduced this custom of bringing a tree inside a house. In Germany, it is quite commonplace, and trees are now displayed at Windsor Castle and throughout the nation."

"How smart you are, Janey."

"Not really, Billy. I just read it somewhere. But I've never seen anything quite as lovely as this one."

Billy looked at me for a long time. "I think I have, Janey," he said kindly.

I felt my face redden. "Oh Billy," I muttered as I hurried upstairs to Lady Sinclair's room.

Two days before Christmas, Lady Sinclair called me to her private sitting room, where she had a second, smaller piano.

"Play something Christmassy, Jane," she said.

I obliged with some Christmas carols I remembered from St. Mary's Church. Soon Lord Sinclair joined his wife, and together they sipped sherry while I continued through my repertoire. I moved on to Mozart, and at the end of one piece, I heard some slow clapping and turned to see a handsome young man in uniform leaning idly in the doorway.

"So this is the lovely creature that makes such enchanting music," he said. "Mother, where have you been hiding her all this time?"

"Philip, this is my maid, Jane Hopkins. She is a sweet child and works very hard for me, but she also has this incredible talent as a pianist. She often plays for us."

"Well, well, she certainly is talented," he said, his eyes looking me over.

They talked about me as though I weren't there. I turned back to the piano, uncertain what to do, a chill running down my spine. Captain Philip was a tall, handsome man, but his lazy smile didn't quite reach his eyes.

Lord Sinclair came to my rescue. "A few more carols, Jane, and then my son and I are leaving for the club."

"Yes, please, Jane, play some more," her ladyship added.

I continued playing but could still feel Captain Philip's eyes boring into my back the entire time, and I hurriedly made my exit when her ladyship dismissed me.

As the door closed behind me, I heard Lord Sinclair say in an angry tone, "Philip, you must satisfy your sexual appetites elsewhere—*not ever* in this house again, and certainly *not* with that young girl. She is an innocent child."

"Listen to your father, Philip," her ladyship added.

"Oh, really, dear parents. Give me some credit, please. I can see she is merely a child. Nonetheless, a very charming one."

Despite their warnings, and Captain Philip's dismissal of me as "merely a child," I was still afraid of him. Molly's words came back to me about Philip putting another maid in "the family way."

Every time we met, which, thank goodness, was not often, I felt the same frightening chill. I couldn't read the expression in his dark eyes, but I sensed it was evil.

Regardless of these undercurrents, and even a warning from Dory to beware of him, Christmas at Enderby House that year was the happiest I had ever known. Food was plentiful, even for the servants. I had never seen so much meat or so many pies, vegetables, cheeses, and desserts in my entire sixteen years.

All of us received presents from the Sinclairs. Mine was a set of embroidered handkerchiefs with the Sinclair emblem in the corner. I treasured my gift, placing it with my small leather-bound book from Mr. Lloyd.

*   *   *

On New Year's Eve, the Sinclairs held another lavish party. Earls and countesses attended, along with lords and ladies, and even a Russian princess. The large dining room table had been set with white linen, sparkling silverware and shining crystal glassware. It was a spectacle to behold.

After I finished helping Lady Sinclair dress for the evening, my duties were over until she would ring for me again in the early hours of the morning to help her prepare for bed. The two formal drawing rooms, usually separated by dividing doors, had been opened up into one large ballroom, where an orchestra was playing and couples could dance after dinner and herald in 1862.

I spent most of the evening down in the servants' quarters, talking with Dory and listening to her plans for marrying Tom. He and Billy were on duty all evening in the main foyer, attending to the arrival and departure of guests. Dory and I also helped Flora carry linen upstairs after she had finished her ironing, and we listened to the music flowing throughout the house. The laughter became more raucous after midnight as guests drank and ate liberally.

I volunteered to make the final journey upstairs with a pile of linen for the large linen cupboard, allowing Dory and Flora to finish ironing the downstairs linen. The linen cupboard was located in an offshoot corridor on the second floor. Having deposited my load inside, I turned quickly—and stepped right into the path of Captain Philip Sinclair.

"Oh! I'm so sorry, sir," I said.

"Little Janey," he said, his voice slurred. "I've been watching you. You shouldn't be working so hard on New Year's Eve. Come now." He took my hand and pushed me back toward the room, housing the linen cupboard. "Why don't we go inside here and relax for a while, eh?"

"I'm sorry, sir. I still have things to do.'

He pushed me firmly against the door and placed his finger under my chin. "No, you have nothing to do until Mama rings for you at bedtime, and that won't be for hours. Just come and make me happy for a while."

His finger ran slowly down my neck toward my high collar. Then he traced the line of buttons on my dress all the way down to my waist.

His hand rose again, but this time paused midway. It strayed there, and touched my small breasts.

I could barely breathe and my heart was beating wildly. Should I scream? If I complained, would I lose my job?

As though reading my thoughts, he said, "Come now, Janey, just relax. I will be most upset if you don't oblige me. You are so sweet. I need you tonight."

"But sir ..." I tried to push him away.

"Charming girl. Charming, innocent little minx. A virgin, no doubt."

His body pressed against mine, and I could smell his stale breath, a mixture of alcohol and tobacco, as his mouth leaned toward mine. At the same time, he slowly began to unbutton my dress at the top, and his fingers began to caress my neck.

"Sir, I still have work to do. I must go. I really must."

"Nonsense, Janey. Come, we can find a nice warm spot in the linen room here."

"No! Please stop."

And then, mercifully, I heard voices from the direction of the main corridor. Some guests were using one of the two upstairs water closets provided for visitors.

Captain Philip pulled away from me roughly. Putting a finger to my lips, he said: "Not a word, Janey. We will continue this later."

He turned and stumbled away, leaving me shaking with fear.

I ran down the two flights of stairs and flung myself into Dory's arms. Between my muffled, garbled, out-of-breath words, she finally understood what had just happened.

"He's had his eye on you all along, Scrap. Just like he did with Clara, back at Noxley. Wouldn't leave her alone, and then finally got her in the family way and abandoned her."

"The family way?"

"Oh, Janey, you really are so innocent. Got her pregnant, of course. Then, off he went, back to India or wherever, and poor Lady Sinclair had to sort out the mess. I think she is paying for the child's upbringing, so Clara was more fortunate than most. Some houses just kick the servant out after the lord and master has had his fun."

"Oh, Dory, what am I to do?"

"Just be careful never to be alone with him. If things get worse, you must tell her ladyship."

"But maybe she won't believe me," I cried.

"I'm sure she would. She must know what he's like."

Things did get worse. Captain Philip always seemed to visit his mother in her private drawing room when I was there attending to her. He made a point of brushing against me as I left the room or he entered.

Once, he whispered in my ear: "I want you so much, Jane!"

I knew he was talking about sex, that peculiar coupling of a man and a woman, but it scared me. I could not imagine ever becoming excited by a man touching my body. I still believed such things were sinful and would forever connect sex with the image of Mr. Finch rising and falling as he sweated on top of Agnes Creed.

If *that* was what Captain Philip Sinclair wanted with me, he could think again! I vowed I would have no part of it—or of him.

* * *

But over the coming weeks, Captain Philip's attentions became more and more challenging to avoid. I had to pass his bedroom door on my way to Lady Sinclair's room, and I always prayed he was either still sleeping or had left the house already.

One early morning in mid-February, as I hurried past, he suddenly appeared, grabbed my arm, and pulled me inside.

"Now, at last, I have you, Jane." Kicking the door shut behind him, he turned the lock with one hand and began to pull me toward his unmade bed with the other.

"I am due to leave with my father for the club in twenty minutes, so let's be quick, my little innocent." He started to pull up my skirt, running his hand up my leg as he pushed me backward on the bed.

I began to scream, but his other hand covered my mouth. "Just relax. I promise I won't hurt you. You'll like this." He grabbed my most private parts and I shuddered with revulsion.

"Ah, you like that?"

My head was pounding. I couldn't imagine liking anything that entailed such feelings of dread and disgust. My biggest fear was making a baby. I would *not* let that happen. I would not be like my mother and create some poor unwanted bastard who would become an orphan like me in this cruel world. So I began to kick and fight and bite, finding a strength I never knew I had, but my resistance seemed merely to excite him more.

"Feisty little devil, aren't you? All the more fun to conquer you." His breathing became heavy and laboured. A part of his anatomy down below had grown and was pressing against my stomach. I remember Rose telling me about that after I had seen Creed and Mr. Finch on the bed. She said that once that enlargement occurred, it was often too late to stop a man.

Well, too bad for him! And so, with a mighty effort, I raised my knee and jammed it hard against his enlarged anatomy. He screamed in agony and rolled away from me.

"Bitch—you little bitch," he gasped, doubling over in agony and clutching at himself. I jumped off the bed and ran to the door just as someone rapped firmly on it from the other side.

"Everything all right, sir?" It was the captain's valet, Sergeant Brooks. "His lordship is waiting for you in the library, sir."

Still purple in the face, Captain Philip held on to his crotch and choked out that he would be there in five minutes.

I could have called out to the valet, but would he believe me? Maybe he was used to the captain having women in his room. So, once I heard his footsteps retreating, I gingerly unlocked the door and made a hasty retreat, adjusting my clothes as I ran away.

Now I knew exactly what Captain Philip Sinclair had in mind for me. I also knew his leave would not be up until May, when he would return to his regiment and a posting abroad.

Maybe I would have to speak to Lady Sinclair. But would she side with me against her only son? If I complained, would I be dismissed?

She was a generous, kind woman, but Dory also told me that most of the gentry accepted the indiscretions of the male members of their families. If the son and heir decided he wanted to take his pleasures with one of the servants, most of the gentry tolerated such behavior, dismissing it with a chuckle and a wave of the hand.

Would this be the case in the Sinclair household? Would they help a servant a second time, having once experienced his misbehavior with another girl? I *had* to make sure I would be protected. I had to find another escape, should things become worse. I was determined that my life would not follow this path.

I had far better dreams and plans for myself.

CHAPTER 14

As time went by, I saw less of Captain Philip, which was a blessed relief. Perhaps my attack on him had subdued his passionate pursuit of me.

By the spring, the London season was already in full swing. The whole event seemed ruined for me because of my constant fear of the Captain. Dory worked extra hard because Miss Penelope was being launched into London society, to find her a suitable husband. This meant numerous teas, parties, afternoon dances, and balls she had to attend, and Dory was required to dress and coiffeur the eldest Sinclair daughter to her best advantage.

Meanwhile, I often accompanied Lady Sinclair on her charitable outings, and when not doing that, she called upon me to play the piano for her. Miss Coutts occasionally brought pamphlets and literature with her concerning the work the ladies were doing in the slum areas of London. I glanced at some of these when tidying Lady Sinclair's private drawing room, but it was the one about the Columbia Mission Society that caught my eye.

When serving tea on one occasion, I overheard Miss Coutts telling her ladyship about a meeting of this society on February 27 in a London tavern. She spoke about the emigration of young women to a place called Columbia in the far west of the North American continent, where women were needed to help populate the colony. The women would join in Christian marriages with men who had gone there searching for gold.

During tea on another day, Miss Coutts told her ladyship about the Anglican group called the Columbian Emigration Society. She said it would help solve the problem of the large number of young girls in England who were left destitute after being abandoned as orphans and then at the age of fifteen turned loose into the world. It would be far better to emigrate than to end up as prostitutes.

I listened carefully to every word. There would be jobs available as governesses in the New World, where no one needed to know my past. Maybe I might even invent a whole new history for myself. I could be someone completely new. It wouldn't be a lie, would it? Just a new life.

At the beginning of April, Captain Philip began watching me again whenever he visited his mother. It seemed he was becoming restless again, and in his restlessness, he resumed his pursuit of me.

"Miss Penelope told me he has been courting a young woman from a nearby respectable family," Dory told me one day. "But it seems he has now become bored with her."

Dory, like Molly at Noxley Manor, seemed to know everything. "He could always visit a prostitute," she told me. "But I think he prefers a challenge, Jane, so watch out."

So, true to form, he began looking in my direction, while I began looking for a way out of this predicament.

It was worse when he had been drinking, and he was drinking more frequently. I spent my days constantly trying to avoid him, and my nights in dread that he would come below stairs looking for me, or would simply ring for me to come to his room.

I felt lucky to have Billy as a friend. He always sought me out and sat next to me at mealtimes, and although I sensed his interest in me, he never pressured me. Maybe there were some good men in the world. However, I still could not share my fears with him about Captain Philip. I was far too embarrassed.

One morning, as I was brushing her ladyship's hair, she looked up at me in the mirror.

"Something is troubling you, Jane. Can you tell me what it is?" she asked gently.

I was still afraid to complain about her only son. "No, ma'am, there is nothing wrong."

"I sense you're hiding something from me, Jane. You seem jumpy these days. Is there something ... or perhaps *someone* ... you're afraid of?"

This would be my opportunity. "Well, your ladyship, I ..."

At that moment, a tap came on her door, and the object of my fear entered.

"Mama, dear," he said, "Father and I are taking breakfast in the conservatory together. Won't you join us this morning? My time here is getting shorter now, and soon I will be off to foreign parts once again. All the girls will miss me, right, Jane?" He laughed. "Even my dear mother."

"Of course, Philip. I would love to join you both."

"Well, I'm sure Jane has made you beautiful by now." He gave me a wicked grin.

Lady Sinclair glanced up at me. "Thank you, Jane, that will be all for now," she said, but then added, "We will talk again later."

But that night, Lady Sinclair was tired and went to bed early, so I didn't bring up the subject again. As I left her bedroom, further along the corridor Captain Philip barricaded my path once again with his large frame.

"Jane, come with me now. I won't wait any longer."

"No, sir, I still have some chores to finish."

"I will take the blame for delaying you, my dear." He took me firmly by the arm and pushed me into a dark corner. His hand took mine and guided it down his body, to his enlarged member. "I want you to touch me here, Jane. Tell me, now—don't you feel the same excitement I do?"

I wanted to tell him I simply felt sick—sick with fear. My insides screamed while my voice got lost somewhere inside my pounding head.

"I'm sorry, sir," I whispered. "I don't want to do this ... please let me go."

"Sweet child. You can, and you will. Come to my room with me, and this time I will take it slowly, and you will enjoy yourself. I promise."

Finally, I found my voice. "NO! NO! I won't!" I screamed.

His hand immediately covered my mouth and I bit him hard, but he dragged me into his room and kicked the door shut behind him. He let go of me for a moment as he locked it and I ran to the other side of the room, frantically searching for something to attack him with. Laughing, he chased after me. "Aha! It's to be a game, is it? "

"NO! Let me go—"

But he easily caught me and threw me down onto the bed. Then he was on top of me, tearing at my clothes. I struggled desperately, waving my arms about as I tried to strike him and push him off me.

"Stop. Stop!"

"Keep quiet, little bitch." He raised a hand and struck me firmly across the face. My head spun and I saw stars. And for a moment, everything went black and I grew weak. When I recovered slightly, he was speaking in a lower tone.

"Just lie back and enjoy."

He had already lifted my skirt and pulled down my drawers. One hand was touching my private parts while the other was caressing my breast through the material of my bodice.

I attempted again to push him off me, but his weight made me weary. He was strong, and I had no more fight left in me, and this seemed to please him. He removed his hand from my breast and slapped me again across my face. This time, it almost knocked me senseless.

"That's much better, Jane. Relax."

He was panting hard, and now his enlarged member was thrusting inside me. I was being torn in two with each thrust. He was ripping my insides out, and I was helpless to stop him.

Eventually he rolled off me, obviously satisfied and exhausted. I wanted to crawl into a hole and die.

After a moment, I slipped off the bed, pulled up my undergarments, and pulled down my rumpled dress. This loathsome man had already collapsed into sleep and was snoring.

I swear if I'd had a knife, I would have killed him right there and then. Instead, I gazed down and spat on him in disgust before creeping to the door and escaping.

And then I ran—oh, dear Lord, how I ran.

Down the corridor, down the main staircase and the stairs to the servants' quarters. I don't know where I found the strength to move so quickly. Thankfully I passed no one on the way.

Entering my room, I threw myself onto my bed and wept. A few moments later, Dory came in.

"What's wrong, Scrap?" she asked.

How could I possibly tell her I was spoiled, damaged for life? Maybe even pregnant?

"Jane, you have to tell me. What happened?"

Between convulsive sobs, I finally told her. She tried to hold me, but I shook her off. I couldn't bear to be touched, even by her.

"Jane, you have to tell her ladyship now. You must."

"What if I'm pregnant?" I whispered.

"Her ladyship will help you."

She helped me undress, tutting as she noticed my face. "Did he hit you?"

I nodded.

"I'll do the rest of your jobs tonight. You must wash yourself down below. Hopefully, he didn't make a baby inside you. Then you should try and rest. Tomorrow you must tell her ladyship."

I moved mindlessly, obeying her. As I washed the stickiness from my legs, I felt sick. I was unbearably sore and convinced I was damaged beyond repair. Once undressed and in my nightgown, I lay down, but sleep escaped me for many hours.

The next morning, Dory and Molly woke me up. I think Dory must have told Molly overnight, but I didn't care. I felt weak when I stood up and I was still very sore, but I went about my early morning chores before her ladyship rang for me.

As I helped her dress, I prepared in my mind exactly what I would say to her. I no longer cared about whether I lost my job or not. But before I had a chance to speak, she made a particular point of telling me her son would be returning to his regiment very soon in early May, and he would most likely be posted abroad. Later in the summer, after the Season was over, we would all be leaving for Noxley Manor.

"I'm sure you'll enjoy being back in the country, Jane," she said.

"Yes, ma'am, I will." Just a couple more weeks, and I could breathe again. It was almost May, and if my monthly curse came and I wasn't with child, maybe I wouldn't need an alternative plan to escape. Maybe. So once again I didn't say anything about what had happened.

Later that evening, Lady Sinclair called me to the dining room during dinner to bring her shawl, as she felt an evening chill. Retrieving it from her room, I walked in as Captain Philip was telling everyone he had some news.

"It appears that I'll be stationed in London at St. James Barracks throughout the summer after all. My regiment won't be posted abroad for another six months."

My heart plummeted.

"So you'll all have me around for a while longer," he said, flashing his dark blue eyes in my direction. "Maybe you all might extend your stay in London also. I know my sisters would love it." All three sisters readily agreed and immediately began making plans for a summer of fun with their brother.

"Pen, dear, I can take you to the ballet or the opera next week," he said lovingly, sounding nothing like the despicable man who attacked me. "There is something on that you will enjoy, I know."

Penelope hugged him with delight. "I will see if I can fit you in." She laughed. "My card is so full of engagements."

How could they possibly approve of a brother who chose to treat women with so little respect? But would they even care if they knew what he had done to me?

I turned to leave the dining room. Earlier in the day, I'd seen a pamphlet left by Miss Coutts on the hall table. When I prepared Lady Sinclair for bed that night, I asked her about it and about the Female Emigration Society to Columbia.

"Why, Jane, I had no idea you were interested in our work," she said.

"I ... er ... it sounds intriguing, ma'am," I said, helping her into her nightgown. "Though not the part about becoming wives for the starved male population out there," I added hurriedly. "But aren't some of these women being sent to positions as governesses or teachers? I thought, that is, I wondered if I might be able—if the fare is not too expensive—to start life in a new world."

She studied my face. "Oh, Jane, why would you want to leave us?" She paused. "Is this to do with my son?"

I nodded ever so slightly, my eyes welling, unable to say the words.

"Has he hurt you or taken advantage of you?"

I nodded again.

"What did he do? Jane, you must tell me."

"He violated me, my lady." Finally, the words were out. "I swear I didn't encourage him."

"I'm sure you didn't, Jane. Damnation!" She muttered to herself. "What is the matter with that boy?"

We looked at each other, and I felt a sympathy and understanding pass between us.

"Jane, are you all right? Did he—hurt you?"

"I will be all right, my lady, but I need to get away from here."

"I'll inquire on your behalf through the society, but I really don't want to lose you, my dear. If only I could think of another solution."

"That would be so kind of you, and I will be eternally grateful for the job you've given me here with you, but ... I cannot stay any longer. I want to better myself in life, and maybe a new country and a new start in life will be the way to do it, as long as ..."

"As long as what?" she said in alarm.

"I am not—with child."

"Oh dear God." She paced the room, stopped, and walked back to me. "Jane, I do understand. I will have my physician examine you. If you are pregnant, I will help you, my dear. Never fear. We will not talk of this anymore today. I will ask my physician to come here to examine you. You are indeed meant for better things."

She patted my hand gently. "I'll see what I can do. I believe the new London Female Middle-Class Emigration Society might be more suited to what you have in mind. They are organizing two sailings next month, both to a place called Victoria on Vancouver's Island in Columbia. They are indeed looking for governesses in the new world. Leave the matter to me, my dear."

"I can't thank you enough, my lady."

She shook her head in despair. "I will miss you so much, Jane, especially your beautiful piano playing."

And I would miss her. But at that moment, without the need for more words, we had somehow settled the problem, although I did sadly wonder if I would ever have another opportunity to play the piano.

Two days later, her personal physician from Harley Street arrived at Enderby House. He was taken to her ladyship's room on the pretense of her experiencing another headache. Meanwhile, she had already rung for me, and I was waiting with her.

They told me to lie down on the bed and I had to face the humiliating experience of being internally examined. The whole time her ladyship held my hand.

"There is some evidence of abuse, your ladyship," the doctor said. "Some internal tearing, but the young lady should heal and recover."

Lady Sinclair nodded. "Thank you, doctor. What about pregnancy?"

"It's too soon to be certain, but once her monthly cycle returns, we can be sure."

A week later, my monthly cycle did return, and I gave thanks to God for this small blessing. Now I could continue my life.

What had happened to me was just one more loss in my life, one more thing taken from me. My body had been abused and violated, but I vowed my dignity would always remain intact.

I would not let him win.

SCOTLAND

GIDEON – Heading West
(1849–1856)

CHAPTER 15

"Get your ass over here, boy!" Simpson yelled.

The boatswain had been yelling at me ever since we set sail the week before. He was a brute of an Irishman, tall and broad, with long hair hanging down past his shoulders. He reminded me of Samson in the Bible. What would happen if he ever cut his hair? Would he lose his strength too?

He spent most of his time shouting and swearing at me and all the crew. As boatswain, he was in charge of everything—rigging, cables, sails and anchor. There was no one above him other than the captain, but I hadn't seen him yet.

"He stays in his cabin most of the time," one of the crew told me. "Simpson is the boss around here. We take our orders from him."

And each time Simpson told me to do something, I fairly trembled at the power of his loud voice.

"Have you gone deaf, boy?" he shouted again now.

"Coming, sir." I dropped the rope I was mending and raced over to him. Running everywhere was a cabin boy's life.

"Take this message down to Captain Rodney," Simpson said. "Tell him we're changing course to the north. And don't pound on his door. He hates being disturbed, but this is important."

Finally, I was about to see the captain! I headed below to his cabin and knocked softly on the door. A gruff voice inside answered: "Enter."

Immediately the thick smell of booze and sweat hit me so hard I almost gagged. The room also stank of urine, because his piss pot by the bed was full. Captain Rodney was sitting back in a chair with a bottle in his hand, his disheveled, black jacket stretching over his large gut. A thin slice of light from the small porthole fell across his red face and bleary eyes. He reminded me of the drunks back at the tavern in

Fraserburgh, when I'd gone there with Da and Duncan long ago. He looked nothing like what I had imagined of a ship captain. The sheets on his unmade bed in the corner were yellowed with stains, and his table was overflowing with papers and maps.

"Message from the boatswain for you, sir," I said.

He squinted at me. "Who the hell are you?"

"Cabin boy Gideon McBride, captain."

"So what's the message, cabin boy?" he slurred.

I relayed what Simpson had told me about changing course. The captain waved his hand in the air. "Changing to a northerly course, eh? Well that's fine with me ... tell Simpson to carry on ..."

Grunting, he tried to stand. I was surprised to see how short he was. Seconds later, he fell back in his chair and closed his eyes, and I scurried away, thanking the good Lord that Simpson was running the ship and not this drunkard. I badly needed some fresh air.

When I surfaced on deck, Simpson barked at me again. "Cook wants you in the galley to prepare dinner. Get going!"

After I peeled the potatoes and Cook had made dinner, I hauled buckets of beef stew up from the galley, along with a basket of bread. The crew gathered around in the fo'cstle as I ladled the stew into their bowls and handed everyone a chunk of bread. Back and forth and back and forth to the galley I ran, until I could finally sit and eat my own meal. I was so starved by then that my stomach had even stopped growling.

Just as I was about to stuff a piece of meat into my mouth, Simpson yelled at me again, "Boy, climb the mast and fix that sail up yonder. It got tangled up in the wind."

As hungry as I was, I didn't mind doing that, because it was the only job I liked. Up so high, I could look out across the vast ocean. It was far better than emptying the crew's piss pots every morning, swabbing decks, hauling food, mending ropes or any of the thousand other jobs Simpson and the crew made me do. Remembering what

I'd seen in the captain's cabin, I wondered who was responsible for emptying his piss pot every day. I was just glad it wasn't me.

Next morning, when I was hoisting two of the piss pots to the upper deck to throw the contents overboard, one of the crew put out his leg and purposely tripped me up. As I fell down hard, all the contents spilt everywhere and everyone laughed at me.

"Poor little boy, he will have to clean the deck again. He must love the smell of piss."

I hated being teased, and I hated the way they made me work.

By the time I got to bed every night, I collapsed onto my hammock, so homesick for Ma and my sisters that I thought my heart would surely break in two. My only comfort was to hold on tight to the trinket around my neck that had once belonged to my Da.

Not long after that, I began to hear strange rumors about a member of the crew called Kendric, an evil-looking man with eyes the colour of coal.

"He has a fancy for young lads like you when he's been at sea too long, so make sure you're never alone with him—unless you want to be," said Simpson.

I didn't fully understand what he meant, but I took his advice and tried to avoid Kendric as much as I could. Nonetheless, at night as we slept in our hammocks, I often woke with a start to see him looking down at me. I glared back at him in the gloom and then he was gone.

Had I imagined it, or was he really there watching me?

Another time, when we were eating our grub, he sat down next to me and placed his hand on my leg. He began to stroke my knee, but then his hand moved up inside my leg. I jumped up and moved away to another bench. He leered at me in a disgusting way as he played with his own private parts, but no one else seemed to notice.

One afternoon, after I finished helping Cook with the midday meal, I went up on the upper deck, looking for a quiet moment to myself away from the rest of the crew, when I heard a sound behind me. I turned to see Kendric behind a pile of sacking. His pants were down and he was lying on top of Pierre, a younger crew member only a few years older than me. Pierre's pants were also pulled down. Kendric was humping and heaving hard on Pierre's frail body. At first, I didn't realize what they were doing, but then I remembered seeing horses on the farms doing that. I shuddered. I thought those things only happened between males and females and not that way between two men.

Pierre had once told me his mother had abandoned him in Glasgow when he was thirteen, and he'd had to make his own way ever since. Like me, he had signed on as a cabin boy at first, but now he was a somewhat reluctant crew member. He was pale-skinned and almost feminine looking and seemed far too feeble to be a sailor.

I quickly ran off before they saw me and told Blair, one of the crew, what I'd seen.

Blair just laughed. "Well he's found his fancy boy for this trip, laddie. Pierre must enjoy being sodomized if he hasn't complained or fought him off."

"But what if he doesn't like it? He's just a young lad and wouldn't be able to fight off Kendric."

Blair shrugged. "It happens all the time, lad. Men are at sea far too long. Those *marys* will poke their dick into any hole they can find, and men like Kendric take their pleasures with young, innocent boys. You're safe now he's found Pierre."

"What's a *mary?*"

"Homos, lad. Men who do it with other men."

I was shocked because it still bothered me. What I'd witnessed disturbed me greatly and I'd wanted to save Pierre, but I would have been no match against Kendric if I had tackled him.

But I swore that if he ever came near me and tried something like that, I would fight him to the death.

* * *

Three weeks after we had set sail from Fraserburgh, the heavens opened up and blasted us with one storm after another. Even with another change of course, we couldn't avoid them.

Simpson set this latest course up at the helm, where he explained his decision to all the crew, shouting above the wind. "Now that you've adjusted the mainsail, foresail and mizzen, men, we are setting our course nor'east. That way I hope to avoid the worst of this weather."

Nonetheless, gigantic waves towered high into the sky before crashing against the ship, threatening to slice the ship in two. Was this what Da and Duncan had faced the day they died? Was the Atlantic even more brutal than the North Sea? And worse still, had I been wrong to leave home? Maybe I'd die at sea anyway.

We hadn't even had time to take the three cows and two pigs down below with the other animals. They were still penned on the top deck when the first violent gales hit. I watched in horror as they were all swept overboard, disappearing into the raging waters. Thank the good Lord we still had those other animals down below deck.

The gales persisted for two more days, continuing to sweep away anything that wasn't tied down. We all spent a lot of time on the top deck fighting the elements, and no one slept much.

I realized then that all seas could be cruel and angry. I even began to rethink my plan to sail around the world. Had I made the right decision to leave my family for this life, which was so uncertain and no better than being a fisherman in Rosehearty, where at least the men were friendly to one another?

On the third day, the rain and wind continued to thrash against me as I helped Simpson hold down the rigging. Above the deafening noise of the wind, Simpson, with water dripping down his face, shouted at me again. "I have enough help up here now, lad. Go on down below."

But as I turned to leave, a huge wave slammed onto the deck and knocked down three of the crew. The bow of the ship heaved high into the sky, and the men started sliding along toward the violent sea.

"Help them!" I screamed to no one in particular, as I let go of the rigging and stretched out to grab one man's leg. Over the roar of the crashing waves and thunder, the other two men were flung overboard into the raging water.

Simpson grabbed the other leg of that third man—Forbes was his name—and as the ship righted itself, we crawled back along the slippery deck toward the steps leading down below, where we held on to the beams to stay upright.

"Jesus Christ, Gideon," said Simpson. "That was a brave thing you did."

Forbes, who was visibly shaken, grabbed my hand. "You saved my life up there, son. I will never forget that."

Then he flung his arms around me, which momentarily alarmed me. Was he another Kendric? But even in my state of shock, I could see his gratitude and affection were different. He told the other men what had happened and they all clapped me warmly on the back.

I sat down with them, but I was still shaking and bringing up dry heaves as the ship continued to rock. Da had said it was always best to stay up on deck during a storm and stare at the horizon. It helped the sea sickness. But now, there I was, sitting below, trembling like a baby and wishing Simpson would let me go back up. By then, he had returned to the upper deck himself, but he insisted I stay below with the other men who were taking a break before going back up to relieve the others.

I kept picturing Ma and how much I missed her arm around my shoulder and her soothing voice. I missed the taste of sweet tea she made for us when we had a fever or were upset over something. The pain of those memories seemed to sever me in half right there, a feeling so much worse than seasickness. Instead of being at home with those comforting thoughts, I was now a lonely boy sitting among rough, hardy men who were nothing more than strangers—even though they were looking at me differently now.

"You're a strong young lad," one of them muttered, maybe regretting how he had often teased me.

"Aye, not many a boy would have done what you did up there. You risked your own life for Forbes." This was from the man who had tripped me up.

Once the storm diminished a wee bit and the *Jonathan* was once more on an even keel, Simpson joined us again. He came over to me immediately.

"Gideon, I know what it's like to see men swept overboard." His voice was a little softer than usual. "But remember, the sea will take you if it has a mind to. Damn well nothing you can do about that. Just have to accept it, boy. As long as we save the cargo for the company, that's all that matters."

"And what is our cargo, sir?" I asked for the first time.

"Mostly grog, laddie. It's safely down below in the hold. Captain Rodney made sure of that before the storm started. The company loves its whisky as well as trading it for the pelts and furs. We also trade knives and tools. We'll still be trading the grog this time, unless the captain drinks all the cargo himself before we land," he added with a smile.

Simpson was certainly gruff and always shouting orders at me, but now he had shown me some kindness. The rest of the crew had either made fun of me or sworn at my ineptness before, but now they, too, were different. They were being kinder to me and making me feel like one of them. They were looking at me with respect. It was the difference I needed, the comradeship I had missed.

So somehow, through all the misery and hard work that came my way over the next few days, I still loved the sea. I savoured the smell of the salt air and the biting winds across my face. And once Simpson allowed me to stay up on deck with him in the roughest of seas, holding fast to the masts, my seasickness went away and I laughed when the waves pounded the vessel, making it creak and groan.

I also relished calm seas, knowing from my Da that the sea spoke many different languages, some angry and some peaceful. It didn't take me long to learn them all.

I wrote my first letter home the night after the storms subsided. I wouldn't be able to mail it until we reached land, but it made me feel better to talk to Ma that way. In part of that letter I wrote:

I am now loving the life of a cabin boy. I remember all that Da taught me about the moods of the sea, and I have quickly learned many things about sailing the ocean. Of course, I often make mistakes, and whenever I do, I try to listen to the wisdom of the old salts on board who have sailed many an ocean and know far more than I do. Their words of wisdom have become my Bible.

The men seem to like me now although they had teased me in the early days. I promise I will send my wages back to you once we land. Meanwhile, I hope you are managing.

Please give my fondest love to Janet and Fiona and of course to you, Ma. Your beloved son, Gideon

I thought she would especially like the reference to the Bible.

The day after the last storm, Captain Rodney finally surfaced from below. He was a little steadier on his feet now and dressed more smartly, wearing a different jacket and a captain's black hat. I watched him and Simpson up at the wheel discussing the charting of our course, and I listened with keen interest, trying to learn as much as I could.

The captain was asking most of the questions. "Why have you reset our course to west by sou'west now, Simpson?"

"Look over to the east, sir. Could be another storm on the horizon, so I'm trying to bypass it."

"Good man, good … yes, very good idea. Carry on."

From their conversation, Simpson still appeared to know a lot more than Captain Rodney about sailing a ship, and I wondered again how he had ever become a captain.

When the seas were calm, one of the crew was allowed to stand guard as helmsman. I loved those days, because when it was my turn I could pretend I was the captain at the helm of my very own ship as I caressed that polished oak wheel.

And it felt so good.

*   *   *

I sensed his presence long before I saw him, because my skin began to crawl.

Kendric crept up behind me and grabbed me around the throat as I stood alone on the upper deck one evening. He tugged at the leather strap I wore round my neck and pushed his body hard against mine. I smelt booze and another overpowering odour of sweat.

As he squeezed his hands tighter, he whispered in my ear. "It's finally gonna be your turn, laddie. I know you want it as much as I do."

I somehow managed to turn sharply, and in that moment I became a violent maniac.

I fought Kendric with a force I didn't know I possessed. I screamed and scratched and kicked him hard in the bollocks with a new confidence I had gained from saving Forbes and all the respect the crew had given me. My screams, together with his yells of pain, attracted the attention of other crew members, who all came running.

"Hey, what's going on here?" someone shouted.

"Bloody little whipper-snapper went crazy on me," said Kendric, clutching his lower regions in agony.

"He grabbed me first," I yelled back. "He had his hands around my throat and he tried to get me to do what he does with Pierre. It's NOT happening 'cos I'm not a *mary*."

Out of nowhere, Simpson lunged at Kendric.

"Get away from this boy, you damn son-of-a-bitch," he spat the words at Kendric. "If you don't heed my words, I'll clap you in irons and put you in the hold for the rest of the voyage. Might do it anyway."

Kendric was still doubled over in pain, but Simpson shoved him hard until he limped away, while everyone cheered.

The men were all looking at me with respect again. Despite his enormous size, I had fended Kendric off and they seemed to enjoy that. They were all laughing heartily as he scuttled away.

"Shiver me timbers! Never seen anything like this boy when he's fighting mad," said one of the crew. "Wouldn't want to take you on, lad."

They all gathered around me. "Well done, Gideon lad. Old Kendric won't even be able to play with his fancy boy for a while."

"You got that cocksucker good," someone else added.

I realized then that Pierre must be enjoying Kendric's attention; otherwise, he too would have screamed and the crew would have come running to save him.

And although such violence was against my nature, in that moment I felt very special.

I believed I was indestructible.

*　*　*

Blair, who was also the son of a fisherman, cornered me the next morning. "Gideon, would you care to join us all in a poker game tonight?"

"But I don't know how to play." To be asked to join them in a poker game was an honour. It proved they now thought of me as one of them.

Blair was a short, funny little fellow. He was always smiling, showing off his mostly toothless mouth. His remaining teeth were stained yellow from booze and tobacco.

"We'll teach you, Gideon," he said.

The crew loved to play cards, especially poker. That night, I was allowed to join them around the table as Blair dealt out the cards. Kendric and Pierre were nowhere to be seen.

Blair explained to me the difference between a straight, a royal flush, four of a kind, and a full house, which outranked everything else.

"Bluffing is the secret to a good poker player, Gideon," he told me. He was a good teacher, and I was a good student. It didn't take me long to catch on. And I could bluff with the best of them.

In the next three weeks that it took to reach Hudson Strait and head into Hudson Bay, I became a skilled poker player. I was soon winning much more than I was losing. Poker was a game I found easy. One night, I won a particularly large pot of money and the crew began to complain, half-heartedly.

"Goddamn it," one of them said. "This young fellow is taking all our money. You taught him too well, Blair."

"I guess I did," he admitted.

I felt very pleased with myself. For during those weeks at sea, I had not only become a seasoned sailor and shown a fierce strength I had never realized I possessed, but I had learned another very valuable skill.

I had become a gambler!

CHAPTER 16

As we entered the Hudson Strait, large masses of floating ice appeared, slowing us down. Simpson shouted out orders to all the crew.

"Up on deck, men, and keep running from one side of the boat to the other to make the ship tilt. You know the drill."

Soon the ice began to break up as the ship tilted back and forth in an attacking motion.

"Look at the birds up there," I shouted with delight as we kept running between port and starboard. They were seabirds, but quite unlike the gulls or sea ernes I was familiar with.

"Aye," said Blair, who knew everything. "They're snow petrels. They're only found in Arctic waters. They live up north here and only go ashore to breed."

"I've never seen anything like them before."

"You'll only find them here, Gideon. Those odd tube-nosed birds were given the name *petrel* to honor St. Peter the Apostle."

I stored this information away, and before I settled down to sleep that night, I wrote another letter home.

> *Dear Ma,*
>
> *I write you these few lines hoping to find you and the girls in good health as this leaves me at present, thanks be to God.*
>
> *I am still getting along very well on board ship. We get good grub. I especially like the pork and bean soup which the cook often makes, although we lost a couple of pigs in a storm a few weeks ago so our pork supply is getting low now.*
>
> *We'll be reaching land in two days and I will be able to mail you some money with these letters. We have already seen some*

strange-looking birds called petrels that were given that name to honor Peter the Apostle who walked on water. What do you think of that?

What joy I have found aboard this ship, Ma! We have had the most horrible storms and sickness, but all is forgotten once the sun breaks through the sky and the sea calms again.

I know now that this is what God wants me to do. I hope you will be happy for me in my chosen life.

I am confident that Uncle Hector is taking care of you and my sisters as he promised.

I send my love to you and to Janet and Fiona.

Your beloved son,

Gideon

I hoped the letter sounded convincing, because I still had moments of doubt and feelings of immense homesickness. I continued to question whether I had made the right decision about leaving home.

On our last night at sea, as we sat below deck playing cards again, I asked Blair what he knew about the Hudson's Bay Company.

"How do I make more money?" I said.

"Sign on at one of the company posts first, and eventually you can rise to a position of clerk, trader, factor or even a chief factor, and be in charge of the whole trading post." He smiled. "It's a good time for you to have joined the company, lad, because since the 1820s, the Hudson's Bay Company has enjoyed some of its best years."

I listened, enthralled, as he told me more stories about the history of the Hudson's Bay Company, but I knew that I wanted to work for the company only until I had made enough money to be independent.

Then I would be able to buy my own ship and get back to the sea as a captain, to sail the world on my own terms.

* * *

On a sunny but bitterly cold day in early September of 1849, we dropped anchor at Fort Rupert in James Bay, within the reaches of Hudson Bay.

At last I was in Rupert's Land. I was just fifteen years old, but very tall for my age. I didn't tell any of the crew my age because I didn't want anyone to know when I went looking for a job.

After we weighed anchor, Simpson headed over to the trading post and returned with our wages, which he handed out to us as we all stood around on the dock.

"Good luck to you, Gideon. Head to the trading post over there," he said, pointing to the building he had just come from. "They'll be in need of a strong boy like you."

I shook his hand and thanked him. "Where can I mail some letters, boatswain?"

He smiled at me. "Ah, good lad. Send news home to your family and let them know that you're safe. Your dear Ma will be thankful. Take your letters to the schooner over yonder. She is sailing back to Scotland tomorrow and will be carrying mail in her cargo."

In my latest letter to Ma, I placed all my wages as well as some of my gambling wins, leaving only a few shillings for myself to allow me to survive for a while. I knew that the money I sent home would see Ma and my sisters comfortably through the winter—that is, God willing, if the ship safely reached the shores of bonny Scotland in the next six weeks.

I shook hands with all the crew and said my goodbyes, realizing that I had formed a strong bond of friendship with these tough men after all. They all wished me well as we disembarked and headed in various directions.

I soon found the schooner and the mail depository, and for a brief moment I wondered if I should sign on and return to Scotland. *No,* I told myself firmly. *I have come this far and I won't give up on my dream now.*

After that, I headed over to the trading post. The man inside looked up at me without interest.

"I'm looking for a job, sir," I began.

"How old are you?"

"Sixteen," I lied. "I've just arrived on the *Jonathan* from Scotland, where I signed on with the company in Fraserburgh. I have a lot of experience at sea and I'm a hard worker."

He nodded but looked bored, as though he had heard that same story many times. But to my surprise, he replied: "I'll hire you on as a labourer at a shilling a day." That was the same lowly wage I had made as a cabin boy.

"Report to the chief factor," he said, pointing to another building next door.

As I left, I saw Pierre walking off with Kendric. I waved to him, but he bowed his head and kept walking. I hoped he would be all right, because I cared about his safety.

I passed many strange-looking women sitting cross-legged on the ground doing beadwork or weaving baskets and blankets. I realized they must be aboriginal women. Their long, black hair was greasy, and their dark-skinned faces were round and fat. As I stopped to admire their work, some looked up at me and smiled a toothless grin. Did all the women here look like this?

The chief factor, a middle-aged man by the name of Jefferson, told me what my duties would be. "You'll be cleaning out the room where we keep the furs and beaver pelts and making sure they are kept in an orderly fashion, listed and numbered. Trading with the natives is very important to the company, and we have to keep on good terms with them. Remember that. You'll also be helping the carpenters when they need it. Do you have any other skills, young man?"

I thought about my reading and writing abilities. "I'm knowledgeable about the world, sir. I've read many books, and I can write."

He looked at me with surprise.

"Can you indeed? Not many lads we get here can write—most can't even read." He paused. "Perhaps labouring is not for you after all. We could use your skills here as an apprentice clerk. You will be paid one pound every week, with the possibility of advancement if you prove your abilities."

Thank you, Da, for your advice about education, I thought to myself as I wandered back outside to find my accommodation with the other men at the trading post.

I now truly had become a company man.

* * *

A few days later, I discovered that Jefferson was married to one of the native woman himself. She was a little more attractive than the others I had seen, and they seemed very happy together.

One of the traders, a Frenchman named André, sat me down one night after supper and explained these marriages to me. I had noticed there were many Frenchmen at the trading post, which I hoped would make Pierre feel more at home, unless he had already left on another ship with Kendric.

"It's hard for the white man in these remote posts, young man," André said. "The only women we see are the natives, so some of the company men marry them."

"Is it because there aren't any white women here to marry?"

"*Oui*, and the arrangement is called *à la façon du pays*, or 'in the custom of the country.' Not a real marriage because ... how you say ... no clergy, no church, but good enough. You don't have to marry them, though, if you want a woman."

"What do you mean?"

"How old are you, Gideon?"

"Sixteen."

"Are you still a virgin?"

"Er ... no ... I'm not a virgin," I certainly wasn't about to admit the truth to him.

"Well if you ever feel like having a woman, I can help you get one. Even though some of them look ugly, they are all pleasant enough in the dark." He laughed in a leering way that made me wish I'd never asked. It all sounded to me like abuse by the white man of these unfortunate women. But I let it pass.

In fact I didn't give it much more thought at all after that, because I had too much work to do—work that was both back-breaking and tedious and yet managed to occupy my mind all the time. I was doing both labouring and clerking.

As the winter set in in earnest, going outside in the below-zero temperatures did not help my state of mind. I had thought Scotland was cold, but living in this frozen northern wasteland was beyond anything I could have imagined.

"It's cold enough to freeze the balls off a brass monkey," one of the other labourers told me. "Your face can freeze in a few seconds."

I heartily agreed. As the temperature plummeted, each time I went outside, my ice-covered eyebrows crackled whenever I touched them.

The first thing I had done with my money was to buy a fur-lined jacket and a pair of heavier boots at the trading post. This meant I had used up all my wages by the end of the first week.

As time went by and the weather became even colder, I began to think about sex again. I had been brought up to honour and respect women, and using these native women simply for my own pleasure did not seem right to me. I wanted to find a relationship with a woman like my Ma and Da had enjoyed.

One day, while walking past the women weaving baskets, I noticed a young native girl sitting with the older women. She was far prettier than any of the others and could not have been more than sixteen. Her long, dark hair was freshly washed and not greasy like some of the others. It framed her small, pretty face and dark eyes. I nodded to her and she smiled back at me.

The next day I saw her again and I introduced myself.

"I'm Gideon," I said. "And you are?"

"Me Anya," she replied shyly.

After that I spoke to her every day, but I don't think she understood all that I said. On one occasion, after I finished work, I plucked up the courage to ask her to go for a walk with me. She said something to one of the older women in her own language. The woman looked me up and down and then nodded. I guess I met with her approval.

As the weather began to warm up a few degrees and winter reluctantly turned into spring, we walked together every day. I talked to her about Scotland and my family back in Rosehearty.

"I don't know whether you understand all I'm saying, Anya," I said on one occasion.

"I understand some, but I do not have all the words to tell you."

"Then I will teach you English," I offered and she squealed with delight.

"And I will teach you about our customs here," she replied.

It was a pleasant arrangement and soon I took her back to my quarters and began to teach her English, which was very motivating for me. First I wrote down the alphabet and then a few words, which she repeated perfectly in her soft, sing-song voice. She was a quick learner and I was a good teacher.

In return she described the life of the Indigenous people. On our walks after the snow had completely disappeared, she showed me some healing plants her people gathered in summer for curing various ailments. These were picked and stored, along with the bark of alder and cedar. I was amazed by her medicinal knowledge, but I wondered about her life, which seemed very hard to me.

"My father trades beaver pelts with the Company men," she told me. "We make good living. My mother died many years ago and my aunt takes care of me. We weave together and now I teach her some English too."

I then told her about how my father and brother had been lost at sea.

"We never found their bodies," I said.

"That is so sad, Gideon," she replied. "It is important in our culture to send those who die on their journey to the Great Spirit in the sky. We have special ceremony for that." She described how the body of the dead one is washed and wrapped in a shroud where it lies for four days before burial.

One night the following winter, Anya came back to my quarters as usual. We had become very close by then and had shared our thoughts and experiences. So it seemed natural that on that night our relationship moved to another level. Before then we had only kissed as friends, but suddenly our emotions became stronger. We were both virginal, but we began to explore each other's bodies and our eventual coupling was innocent as we touched each other in our most private places.

As we lay in one another's arms we learned together the art of lovemaking, in a gentle manner that pleased and excited us both. I tried not to hurt Anya, but the first time we tried, I came too soon so we tried again until we discovered the perfect way to please each other.

I could see no harm in what we were doing, but I was too naïve then to really understand. Now, with the advantage of some years to think on it, I sometimes wonder whether I was just another white man taking advantage of an innocent young native woman. I certainly had no intention of marrying her; I was far too young, I had much more of the world to explore, and I didn't want to settle for married life too soon without following my dream, as Da had. Besides, when my thoughts went to marriage at all, I had to wonder what my mother's reaction would be if I brought Anya home as my bride—even if the company had allowed such a thing, which they probably wouldn't. Then again, my mother would undoubtedly approve if it meant that we stayed in Scotland and gave her grandchildren. But I didn't think I was truly in love with Anya.

And so I let things go on for another year, enjoying Anya being "my woman." She was a pleasant distraction during those cold winter nights and she was a kind, sweet girl who only wanted to please me. She left every morning to do her work, cooking meals for her father and threading beads or weaving baskets with her aunt and the other women, but she returned every night to lie beside me.

Towards the end of our second winter together, I noticed a change in her. Some nights she clutched her stomach tightly and appeared to be in great pain.

"What's wrong, Anya?" I asked her one night.

"It's nothing, Gideon. Just my monthly cramping." But to me it seemed really bad. Some nights she was in obvious agony and I had no idea what to do.

"I will go for the trading post doctor," I told her. "Or your own medicine healer if you prefer?" I knew the Indigenous people preferred their own medicine.

"No, Gideon, I'm all right. The pain always passes."

Mostly it did, but then one night she didn't come to me as usual after work. This was very strange and I became more and more anxious as the night wore on. Eventually I went looking for her. I found her in her father's lodge, a short distance away.

There were many people inside, and at first I could barely see through the smoke from the fires burning. I recognized the aroma of sage and alder bark and older women were circling and swaying around a pallet bed on which Anya was lying, writhing in agony.

I ran towards her, but I was pulled back by many arms, allowing the medicine healer to minister to her. Was she in childbirth? But there had been no indication that she was with child. Her father was standing in the corner of the room, chanting and weeping.

"What's wrong with her?" I screamed. What kind of ritual was this? Was she being healed or was this something else? Her aunt came towards me.

"Anya very sick. Her tumour is growing. She is near end now," she said.

"Her tumour?"

"She has a tumour in her stomach. There is little hope now. Her spirit is leaving us to be with the ancestors."

"No, that cannot be. We must save her. I will go for the white doctor. Perhaps he can save her."

My pleas were ignored, and as the women's singing rose, I realized I was interrupting their religious ceremony. This was the ritual Anya had explained to me long ago, and now I was witnessing it firsthand. But I was an outsider in their culture and not welcome in their midst.

Nonetheless I pushed through the women and knelt down beside Anya's bed, ignoring the hands all pressing on my arm.

"Anya, you must get better."

She seemed to relax as she heard my voice and her eyelids fluttered briefly. "Gideon—thank you. I love ... you."

I squeezed her small hand. Why would she thank me? I had used her for my own purposes without even offering her security as my wife.

"She's gone," her aunt said a few moments later. They were already covering her beautiful face with a sheet.

"NO. NO!" I screamed again and again.

On the far side of the room, her father's sadness was palpable. I had to escape. I could no longer bear it.

And so I ran out of the lodge and into the cold night. I kept running until sheer exhaustion made me collapse in the snow. I don't remember how I got back to my room. I suppose someone must have found me there and carried me back.

But for a long time afterwards, I wished I had frozen to death that night. It would have saved me so much heartache.

CHAPTER 17

For four days I saw smoke rise from the lodge as my Anya lay on her raised pallet inside. But I felt unable to return. Just as when my Da and Duncan had died, I couldn't face death or accept it. I always needed to run away.

So on the fourth day I watched from a distance as a procession carrying her coffin left her home and headed to the Cree burial grounds over the hill, where Anya would be laid to rest. I prayed silently that she had met her Great Spirit in the sky.

Two weeks after Anya's death, Jefferson called me into his office.

"Sorry to hear about your woman dying, Gideon. Rough business."

"Thank you, sir."

"A position as clerk at York Factory trading post has come up and I thought of you. It might be good for you to start again somewhere new. Are you interested?"

I felt a brief moment of excitement, despite my grief. It would be a good move. I'd make more money, and working at the company headquarters would give me opportunities for promotion. Here at Fort Rupert I was still only an assistant clerk.

But then I felt guilty. Anya was gone, and I was only thinking of myself. I'd been so lost without her, not knowing where my path would now lead. My heart constantly ached for her companionship, and now I felt empty.

My original dream had been interrupted for a while, spending time with Anya, but I knew I now had to move on. This opportunity might be the answer.

"Yes, sir, I'm interested," I replied quickly before I changed my mind.

And so, a few days later and with little regret, I left Fort Rupert behind, along with all my many memories of sweet Anya.

Through hard work and determination, my guilt, along with my grief, dissipated. I continued to be promoted from clerk to trader as I moved from York Factory on to other trading posts circling Hudson Bay. The trading posts also provided opportunities to make money gambling. Most of the company men enjoyed playing cards, and I soon became known as a high-stakes poker player. The skills I'd learnt aboard the *Jonathan* were serving me well. I was driven to make more and more money.

But something was missing. I longed for the sea, for I had been on land far too long. Maybe that was what was wrong with my life, I thought. So when another opportunity came up to work as a trader aboard a ship sailing to a place called San Francisco, I jumped at it.

We left from Fort Churchill, sailing first to New York City and then down the east coast of the Americas and around the Horn, encountering a few storms along the way. I felt at home again. My love for the sea returned, along with my original dream to support my family and then resign from the company. The voyage to San Francisco convinced me that this was the right thing to do.

San Francisco was a raw tent town with few buildings, but I could see the possibilities there. Pedro, another trader, agreed with me as we walked around together after finishing up our company trading business on our first night there.

"Even though the gold rush of '49 is over, this town is going places, you mark my words," he said. "And there is still some gold left in the valleys and gulches. Don't leave it too long before you return, if that is what you want to do. I foresee that this will be a boom town in another year."

I nodded. "I agree with what you're saying, but first I need to return to Scotland one more time. It might be many years before I can do that again. I want to make sure my family is all right."

Finally, I had a plan—of sorts. I would return to Rupert's Land after our trading was completed on the west coast and then take a leave of absence from the company. I would be leaving behind a wage of over a hundred pounds a year as a high-grade trader. This would be a gamble—but gambling had never bothered me. I thrived on the risk. I intended to sail back to New York and find a ship sailing for Scotland.

All went according to plan, and I was soon back in the big city of New York, strutting around on the dockside like a young buck in my brand-new coat and leggings. There I purchased a passage on the first ship leaving for Glasgow.

I was twenty years old and full of piss and vinegar.

*   *   *

My sister, Janet, was the first to greet me in Rosehearty. She hugged me tightly.

"Ah Gideon, it is so *gud* to see you." She turned to the man standing beside her. "This is my husband, Tom. I'm sure you will like one another."

Now seventeen, Janet had married Tom Ritchie, a herring-boat fisherman, a few months earlier. In a letter, she had told me they were living in a small house similar to the one we had grown up in. She was content with her life as a fisherman's wife, and Tom was a good man. I could visualize the same future for fifteen-year-old Fiona, who apparently already had her eye set on young Robbie Buchan from Braidsea.

"Robbie has given his heart to me and proposed marriage already," she whispered to me later, when no one else was around. "But I think I will make him wait for my answer." She always was a little tease, but once I met Robbie and saw them together, I knew she would accept his offer of marriage one day.

Fiona and my mother were living away from the village, in a cottage they had purchased with the money I sent home through the years. I felt good about that.

As I walked up to their cottage, I could see Ma at the front door, waiting to greet me. She looked older—but then, we all did. She had tears in her eyes as we hugged tightly.

"Ah, Gideon lad, I have long waited for this day—to see your bonny face again. The *gud* Lord has answered my prayers."

I held her to me, and we did a little jig around the room. It felt so good to be with them all, and a warm feeling of being loved and treasured enveloped me.

That night and in the days to come, I boastfully regaled them with stories about the sights and sounds I had seen in the frozen north during my six-year absence from home. I even told them a little about Anya.

"She was a good friend to me," I said, leaving out the precise details of our relationship. "I was very sad when she died."

I was happy for them all, because I knew I had achieved my purpose and made their lives easier, as I had promised. But at the same time, it didn't take me long to realize that I no longer belonged in the Broch. I felt adrift.

I came to this realization one morning as I climbed up to the Head and looked down at the coastline. A sudden feeling of despair brought tears to my eyes. This was my home, and yet it felt strange to be there, and I hated the fact that I seemed like a foreigner to the people I had grown up with. In the six years I'd been gone, many of the lads I had known as a boy had married or were about to wed. The wife of one of them already had a small baby. I envied them all for their contentment, but I knew it was not the life for me.

It was painful indeed to know I was no longer a part of life in the village. I was not considered my father's son, because I had not, as expected, followed in his footsteps. He and Duncan were long gone, and with them went all the good memories of friendship I had once known with the other fishermen and their families.

So, after saying my goodbyes to everyone, I left Scotland again with an unbearable ache in my gut that almost ate me alive.

I had no idea where I belonged any more.

*   *   *

By the time I reached Rupert's Land, it was late summer.

I severed my ties with the Hudson's Bay Company for good by resigning my position at Fort Rupert, where I had first signed on. With all my back pay, I now had enough money in my pocket to strike out on my own.

After that, I headed back to New York again, to spend a few weeks there enjoying the sights before travelling west. The city was larger than any I had ever seen. After six years of living at trading posts in the cold northern wilderness and then seeing the bleakness of Scotland again, I was overwhelmed by all the sounds and smells around me.

Crowds of people swarmed everywhere on the gravel streets. Some streets were even paved with granite blocks that felt hard beneath my feet, unaccustomed as I was to walking on hard surfaces after years of treading on soft earth, frozen tundra or deep snow.

Jewish shopkeepers, wearing small black caps, were selling their wares on the streets. Some people had black or yellowish skin, and their accents were strange to my ears. There were people all around me of different nationalities, speaking languages I didn't understand. New York seemed to be a melting pot of many cultures.

I eventually found lodging in a quieter part of the city. Still assailed by the noise and chaos everywhere, I asked the innkeeper where I might find some open spaces.

He looked at me strangely.

"Open spaces?" He laughed. "You won't find any here. If it's space you want, you'll have to travel far away from Manhattan Island."

"But isn't there even a green park somewhere?" I desperately needed to breathe some fresh air.

"There are few open spaces, but there's talk of using land for a park in Upper Manhattan. I hear the government has given over 700 acres from 59th to 106th streets to build it. Gonna cost millions of dollars, though."

"Well, I hope it happens," I replied. "With this many people in a city, you need an open space somewhere to be able to breathe."

He nodded and smiled at me, obviously amused by my optimism. "Yes, New York City now has four times as many people as it did in 1821."

That was just too many people for the likes of me. Maybe New York was not the place to stay, and I remembered again the rumours of great wealth on the west coast, especially in San Francisco. I recalled my conversation with Pedro about opportunities abounding, and how he had advised me to return while the city was still growing. I might even be able to make enough money there, I thought, to purchase a vessel of my own to ply the Pacific Ocean and trade in the Orient.

I had big dreams, but now I felt so confident about my ability to do anything that I spent $300 on a first-class passage to San Francisco, aboard a steamer from New York that would sail around the Horn by way of Panama. Steerage would have cost only $100, but I felt sure I could make up the difference by gambling aboard.

Sure enough, by the time we arrived six weeks later, I had won back all my passage fare and a whole lot more cash. I always seemed to find men willing to part with their money at the poker table. I played every night and kept winning. It was such an easy way to make money, and I became even more addicted to the game.

It was now early in 1856, and San Francisco was changing quickly. No longer the tent city it had been a year earlier, it was now a small metropolis, bustling with activity and enterprise. New buildings were going up all around me, some flimsy wooden or sheet-metal structures, standing alongside sturdier brick and stone.

After leaving the vessel and heading uptown, I found the What Cheer House, run by a Mr. Woodward, at the corner of Sacramento and Leidesdorff streets. It was the only hotel that claimed to have bathtubs. I checked in, took advantage of a much-needed bath, and then headed back outside to explore the city.

My boots clomped loudly on the wide wood-plank sidewalks, and my feet soon felt sore. It was a strange feeling for me, similar to how I had felt in New York, and I wasn't sure I liked it. Tomorrow I would buy another, more comfortable pair of boots. Some streets had cobblestones and one or two were paved in brick and stone, but the majority of streets and sidewalks were still made of wooden planks.

I couldn't believe all the changes that had happened in San Francisco, and I remarked as much to a dark-skinned man who walked by me.

"The vigilantes have gradually been cleaning up the city since the gold rush of '49," he said, with a broad smile that showed off perfectly white teeth contrasting with his ebony skin. "Now we're becoming a respectable city."

We both laughed as I nodded to him and walked on.

Indeed, the streets were now lined with respectable-looking offices. I passed a Wells Fargo head office on one corner and the Union Club next door. I felt sure this city would one day be as large as New York, but with all the hills and sea views, there was still a certain charm about it that had been missing in New York.

Back at my lodgings, I wrote another letter home.

Dear Ma,

I have now arrived on the west coast of America. You would'na believe this city of San Francisco! So much different from what it was when I stopped here before with the company. Then it was nothing but a small parcel of land covered with tents and shacks left over from the gold rush of forty-nine.

Now it's like New York, with large brick and stone buildings everywhere and almost sixty hotels, so I'm told. Imagine that! I'm staying at a place called the What Cheer Hotel, right in the center of things.

Like in New York, I have seen many people of different nationalities and different skin colours. Just now I met a man with skin as black as night and we talked. He seemed very pleasant.

I'm enclosing more money for you and the girls and God willing, I'll still have enough to be able to purchase my own ship here soon.

Your beloved son,

Gideon

I did not tell Ma how I'd been making money. She would not have approved of gambling. Later I headed out again to mail my letter. The bustling movement of carriages, horses, and people made so much noise, but there was another sound that was missing.

Although this was a seaport, I couldn't hear the screech of seagulls, so I wandered down Montgomery Street toward the bay, yearning for that familiar sound of gulls to remind me of home.

I walked around the harbour for a while, trying to come up with my next plan of action while drawing comfort from the sound of those birds swirling above my head in search of food before settling for the night. Like me, they were looking for a purpose, a direction.

One week later, I found mine.

ON ROUTE

JANE – The Voyage
(May–September 1862)

CHAPTER 18

The massive ship rose above me, blocking out the morning sun. Miles of rope wound around the deck, and the masts rose into the sky, seemingly touching the clouds. I couldn't breathe, feeling overwhelmed by this giant vessel that would travel thousands of miles to the new world with me aboard.

Had I made a mistake?

In that moment, I wanted to run after Jones, who was heading back in the carriage to Enderby House. Lady Sinclair had insisted on having him drive me to the docks that morning. Soon after dawn, she'd met me outside the servants' entrance to say goodbye. A shawl was wrapped around her nightclothes.

"Jane, I wish you all the best in the new world," she said, hugging me warmly to her breast, the closest thing to motherly affection I'd ever known. "I have a small gift for you, a journal and pen to write down all your adventures."

Tears stung my eyes. I could barely speak. "Thank you, my lady," I whispered.

So there was no turning back now. True to her word, her ladyship had made arrangements for my passage, and the society had paid my forty-five-pound fare, covering my accommodation and food.

I'd said my goodbyes to everyone else the day before. They were all surprised to hear I was leaving. Billy looked very sad and pleaded with me to stay. Only Dory and Molly knew the truth. Dory clapped her hands in delight after her initial surprise.

"I'm truly happy for you, Scrap," she said when we were alone later. "But I will miss you so much. I can't bear the thought of you leaving."

I was thankful that, during the two weeks leading to my departure, Captain Sinclair had not come near me. Dory told me that he spent much of that time either at the barracks or at his club. Although I had no proof, I suspected his parents had given him a severe warning to leave me alone. He'd never listened to them before, though, so perhaps this time they had threatened to cut him off as their heir.

Dory was preoccupied on most days before my departure, as she and Tom were preparing for their wedding. After a quick ceremony with a justice of the peace one day, they spent their wedding night in a local tavern, and then returned to their duties the next morning as Mr. and Mrs. Tom Jenkins. They were lucky the Sinclairs had accepted their relationship and allowed their courtship to proceed. Many upper-class families would have dismissed them both.

"We'll visit you one day in the new world," Dory told me. "I promise, Scrap."

"That would be nice," I said vaguely, but I doubted they would ever come. Since the whole mess with the captain, I no longer felt sad about leaving her. I didn't even experience a longing that we would meet again one day. I didn't feel anything at all about anything—other than impatience to leave England, once and for all. Most of the time, I just felt numb.

If I stayed, I'd never become someone important, someone who would live in a grand house like Enderby House. The highest position I could ever hope for in service would be as a housekeeper. The Emigration Society told me I could have so much more in the new world, and I wanted to believe that was true.

You don't know it, Captain Philip, but what you did to me made me determined to leave England and move to a better place.

No one in that land of Columbia in the new world, so far away, would ever know I was once an abandoned orphan who had worked in service and been raped. That would be my secret. I could start my new life any way I chose.

* * *

But now, as I gazed up at the *S.S. Tynemouth* looming above me, I felt lost and alone. I'd always had people around me, telling me what to do and where to go. Now I would be the one making the decisions.

Other women began to gather at the docks, all part of the "female consignment." Some were heavily made up, similar to the women I saw on the street corners of London. Others looked like children, some younger and smaller than me. Some had walked to the ship or had been brought there by the society in carts.

Two of them turned to each other and whispered, apparently about me. Maybe they wondered why I had arrived at the docks in a fancy carriage yet hadn't gone aboard with the other higher-class passengers.

One girl came over to introduce herself. "My name's Alice," she said. "Are you as scared as I am?"

Although she looked younger than me, she was quite tall. She had a pale face and long black hair that fell over her slumping shoulders. I saw her hands tremble. I felt sorry for her but was glad of some company.

"Yes, I'm a bit scared. My name's Jane."

"Can we stay together?" Alice asked, and I nodded.

"Thank you, Jane. I feel better talking to someone. You are so pretty. I adore your curly hair."

Pretty? Me?

"Thank you, Alice. How old are you?"

"Fifteen. I lived in an orphanage before they moved me to the workhouse. I hated it there and wanted to escape to a new life. I can perhaps work in service in Columbia."

"Perhaps," I replied vaguely. I didn't want to disclose my past, but I did tell her I was sixteen and had worked in service.

We chatted for a while. When the nearby church bells struck noon, a large, middle-aged woman, dressed in black with a shawl covering her hair, separated herself from the crowd and clapped her hands several times to get our attention.

"Girls, girls," she called out. "My name is Mrs. Robb, and I will be responsible for your well-being on this grand adventure. This is my husband, Charles"—she waved her hand in the direction of a stout, balding man to her right—"and these are my three children."

She pointed to two boys and a girl, all of them under the age of ten. They were a strange-looking trio and very ugly, all with the same beady eyes and pointy noses as their mother.

"And here is your other chaperone, Reverend Scott. He will conduct Sunday services for us. Next to him is his wife, Mrs. Helen Scott, and their two children."

A middle-aged man dressed in black with a pinched face stood alongside a chubby, smiling woman and their daughters, both staring at their feet. Mrs. Robb said the Scotts were on their way to the Sandwich Islands to do missionary work.

Although she didn't look like Mrs. Creed, Mrs. Robb had that same clipped, demanding voice and manner that reminded me of that heartless woman, so I didn't take an instant liking to her—or to the Reverend Scott, for that matter. The minister's sour, humourless expression gave the impression of a mean disposition. He made a short speech about morals that made some of the women giggle. Most of it I didn't understand.

"Sanctimonious clot!" I heard one woman whisper.

Our two chaperones led us onto the ship and down a narrow ladder to a below-decks section, mid-ship, a dark, poorly ventilated space far too cramped for sixty women. Bunk-style beds attached to the side of the ship were lined up in rows, six in each group.

Mrs. Robb assigned one bed to each of us. "This is where you will sleep and spend all your time. You will not be able to go to other parts of the ship once we set sail. This is for your own safety. Your meals will be brought to you here, as will your water for washing."

Alice and I made sure we were close to each other, to give us both some comfort. Her bunk was above mine. Mine at least aligned with a small porthole. Even though it was covered in grime and let in very little light, I'd at least be able to distinguish day from night.

I began to feel the sway of the ship already, and it was horrifying to imagine being stuck in this cramped space for weeks on end. How would I ever survive?

CHAPTER 19

We left the London docks the next morning, the 24th of May, and steamed down the River Thames to Dartmouth, where Mrs. Robb had told us we would put to sea four days later. During that short trip, we could still see land on both sides, which I found comforting.

The first night aboard the ship, I couldn't sleep. The bed was hard, and we had one blanket each but no pillow, so I rested my head on my small valise, which gave me a stiff neck. The space was stuffy and seemed much worse than the orphanage, which I didn't think was possible. How would I ever last three months? Alice, who was nearby to talk to, made things a bit easier.

I lay there, wondering again if I'd made a mistake. "Isn't this awful?" Alice whispered on that first night.

"And it's so cramped. I can barely stretch my legs, and I'm short."

"I hope we can survive this," Alice sighed.

I felt like telling her to be brave and just bear it. I had known worse—or so I thought.

At Dartmouth, Mrs. Robb announced that the ship had mechanical problems with the boilers so that we wouldn't put to sea just yet.

The waiting was unbearable. We were not allowed to leave our quarters—even for some fresh air. Having my bunk near a porthole gave me enough light to read. I had brought *Oliver Twist* by Mr. Charles Dickens with me. I also often read passages of comfort in my Bible catechism and fingered the pressed flower inside as I thought about Mr. Lloyd and Cook, both of whom had once made my life bearable. I began to write in my journal while some of the women played cards. Most of the time, Alice just sat cross-legged and stared into space.

We finally put to sea on the ninth day of June. Mrs. Robb told us there were about four hundred passengers on board. Still, the only ones I ever saw were the other fifty-nine women in our group, Mrs. Robb, who slept in separate quarters with her family one deck above ours, and the Reverend when he conducted services for us.

Mrs. Robb visited us a few times every day to distribute our rations and provide us with seawater for washing. Fresh water, handed out sparingly, was used only for drinking. As our accommodations were so cramped, even washing ourselves became difficult. Some of the women didn't bother, but I tried my best to keep myself reasonably fresh and clean. Alice always followed me like a shadow, whatever I did.

Reverend Scott's sermons always emphasized the importance of good morals, but I soon saw that they were a lost cause with many of the women, who laughed and made fun of him after he left.

Soon after we left on that June day, the sky darkened, and the waves rose and crashed against the ship. The water whipped us around like some sea monster. It felt as though we had somehow been swallowed up by a whale, like Jonah, and were now stuck in its swirling bowels. I prayed to God to release us from this hell, just as he had released Jonah from the whale.

I got sick, as did most of the other women. The room filled with the sounds of retching. The foul stench of unwashed bodies mixed with that of vomit. Some of the women were too weak and ill even to use the buckets, so vomit covered the floor. I gripped the side of the bed to keep from rolling off, afraid I'd choke on my own puke.

I gazed upward at Alice, but at that moment she puked over the side of her bunk. Her vomit landed squarely on my face. I screamed, but she didn't hear me above the noise of the crashing sea. I tried to get up to reach some water to wash my face, but it was impossible to stand, and I fell back onto the bunk and prayed for death.

*   *   *

By the second day, the sea had calmed, and I managed to stand and move about. I joined a couple of other women to mop up the mess and clean myself. We had to use the same buckets for relieving ourselves. The sea finally settled down, but the unbearable stench in our cramped quarters continued, and I could hardly go more than a few hours without retching. One morning, after not sleeping most of the night, I couldn't hold my tongue any longer. When Mrs. Robb came in with our usual breakfast of oatmeal biscuits and a gray-brown liquid thinly disguised as tea she carried in a large tin canteen, I spoke up.

"Mrs. Robb, I'm sure the ladies of the Female Emigration Society back in London have no idea we are being subjected to these disgusting conditions," I said. Lady Sinclair would have been horrified to see this, I was certain.

"You are quite the hoity-toit, aren't you, Miss Hopkins," she said. "Just think yourself lucky that you have been given this grand opportunity to start a new life in a new land, and be grateful to those ladies of the society."

Be grateful—I'd heard that before. *Be grateful to the board of directors, Jane Hopkins. Be grateful to the Home. Be grateful to me for taking you in and sheltering you when you were abandoned by your own wicked mother.*

Just as I had at the orphanage, I stood in that dark, dismal, stinking hole and could think of nothing to be grateful for.

"At least we should have more buckets and mops to clean up our quarters."

She looked away and then back at me. "I'll see what I can do."

It paid to speak up. Mrs. Robb got us more buckets. At the end of every day, we placed them outside our door, and a crew member emptied and washed them out with vinegar before returning them to us. That offensive vinegary smell made me think of my time as a scullery maid at Noxley Manor.

Our rations also improved slightly. While the storm had pounded the ship, Mrs. Robb rightly assumed that no one would be hungry, but now she, together with one of her ugly sons and a member of the crew, started bringing us salt beef and pork, canned meat and fish, preserved potatoes, sugar for our tea, and salt and pepper. Mrs. Robb told us that the storm had washed some pigs overboard, so now pork would be in short supply.

I finally grew accustomed to the motion of the rolling sea and the noise of the steam engines. But then, somewhere in the middle of the Atlantic Ocean, on calm, smooth waters, something seemed different.

"The engines have stopped," the woman named Betty called out.

"What's happening?" Alice asked, her voice quivering.

Everything was quiet, as though the vessel had come to a halt.

Then, we heard raised voices above. "Mutiny!" someone yelled.

Mrs. Robb rushed down to our quarters, her face flushed. "The men who load the boilers have refused to work. So the captain put them in irons as mutineers. They're to be confined for the remainder of the voyage. Some of the male passengers, including my dear husband, have volunteered to continue the work of the rebellious coal-passers. We must thank God for their sense of duty. Without them, the unthinkable would have happened."

I assumed that the unthinkable would have meant returning to England under sail and then starting all over again. I doubt I would have survived.

For the next month, until we reached the Falkland Islands, the male volunteers continued to keep the vessel moving, and at the end of every day, they were rewarded with a pint bottle of stout and their meals ready-cooked for them. Their laughter and good cheer reached down to us. I envied them even more when it rained because they could strip down on the top deck and take a "rain bath." Mrs. Robb, who related all this to us, added that such behavior was unseemly, and her husband had not joined in. I thought it was a practical solution. And at this stage, I wished I could have joined them to wipe the grime off my body. By contrast, the complaints and offensive language coming from the mutineers also made it down to our quarters.

Mrs. Robb had gradually become more pleasant as the voyage continued. She enjoyed imparting these snippets of information, which broke the monotony of our lives.

Before we reached the Falklands, a second mutiny occurred among the sailors. "My goodness me," Mrs. Robb said, all a-flap and very flustered. "One of the sailors threatened to throw the captain overboard, but the other passengers managed to subdue the mutineers. It seems that some of the male passengers had previous experience sailing aboard vessels, so they knew what to do."

"Thank the Lord," we all chorused.

"Yes, and sixteen men, including the coal-passers, are now under arrest."

Once we entered the South Atlantic region, with its warmer trade winds, our vessel used sails as well as steam. Sometimes the steam was cut off completely and we cruised entirely under sail. Even down where we were, we could hear the sails flapping in the breeze.

Toward the end of July, and not far from the Falklands, the ocean unleashed more violence. For the next night and day, towering waves again slammed against our sturdy vessel.

Above us, we heard the large iron storage tanks and railway iron rails breaking loose from their moorings on deck. They rattled and rolled back and forth from one side of the ship to the other throughout the night. It sounded like the boat was being torn in two.

Water rushed over the decks above us as the ship rose, fell, and shuddered. Some of it trickled down to us. Once again, no one in our quarters slept. We tried to comfort one another by shouting back and forth, just to prove we were all still alive.

Alice continued to whimper. "I wish I'd never come," she said. "Why did I leave England? Why, oh, why?"

As I again lay gripping my wooden bed for fear of falling to the ground, I felt like agreeing with her, but I remained silent. Instead, I stared out my porthole into the watery darkness and prayed for death to release me from this misery. This must be what purgatory was all about. I had always wondered when Mr. Lloyd spoke about it. Now, I knew. But morning came, and the storm subsided. And I was still alive.

Soon after first light, someone let out a loud wail.

"Elizabeth! Elizabeth!" It was Maisie, an Irish girl. "Oh my God, my God, she's dead ... why? Dear God, why?"

I hadn't spoken more than a few words to either Elizabeth or Maisie during the entire voyage. Still, several of the other women began to cry. Two crew members entered our quarters to remove Elizabeth's body. Mrs. Robb told us she had died during the night of a bad fever and would be buried in Stanley Harbour as soon as we arrived there. I was stunned, knowing how easily it could have been me.

* * *

Two days later, our captain sighted land.

For the next thirteen days, while the vessel anchored in Stanley Harbour, we were not allowed to leave. The other passengers were taken off in smaller boats when the weather permitted, to tour Port Stanley. I found it hard to understand why we could not also take these excursions.

"You ladies have been promised as a 'complete consignment' to be delivered to Vancouver's Island and nowhere else," Mrs. Robb said when I questioned her. "If I allow any of you ashore before our final destination, some of you might decide to stay here and the society would not have fulfilled its obligation of delivering an intact cargo."

Is that what we had been reduced to? A consignment? An intact cargo?

Thank God for small blessings, though. Whenever the passengers and crew went ashore, we were allowed to go up on deck to get some much-needed fresh air. We watched the vessel being loaded with more supplies and the sixteen mutineers taken ashore in chains for trial.

Early in August, after supplies were loaded aboard by some newly hired crew, we finally left the Falkland Islands and continued on our journey around Cape Horn. Talk spread among the women about the possibility of more dangerous storms ahead.

Betty said she had been told back in England that this could be the worst part of the voyage. "I heard that some ships never make it around Cape Horn," she said, her voice trembling.

Of course, this news sent Alice into another panic. "Oh, Jane, I will never survive another storm. I know I will die like Elizabeth."

"Alice, stop complaining!" I replied sharply. "I'm sick of hearing it. We are all scared. But think about what we have already come through, and we are now almost there."

She pulled back as if I had slapped her, and I immediately regretted being so harsh. Like me, she was just a frightened child.

Every night, I prayed with her to calm us both. "God almighty, please watch over us. In your mercy, please keep us safe," I repeated constantly.

And God did spare us. The sea stayed calm as we travelled around the tip of South America and sailed north again. Even the winds subsided, and the vessel enjoyed more gentle breezes.

Because there was so little wind, our coal ran out before we reached San Francisco on September 9, and the sailors busily cut up every available piece of wood to keep the boilers stoked. Again, the women were not allowed to leave the ship. We went up on deck once and got a brief glimpse of the city before Mrs. Robb hurriedly escorted us back down below.

From my very brief glimpse of the city, I saw it was a busy place! Ships were coming and going in the harbour, and houses and buildings stretched across the landscape of rolling hills. But the city looked much newer than London, with all its many ancient buildings.

"Did you hear about the man who came aboard?" Betty told us later. "He was going to offer us jobs here. When we were up on deck, I heard one of the sailors talking about it. That's why Mrs. Robb rushed us all down here so quickly."

"What kind of jobs?" I said.

"It would probably be the same work I left behind, selling myself to make a living on the streets." This came from a woman called Lucy, who had previously told us tales of her experiences as a prostitute in London. I remembered Dory telling me about Captain Philip visiting prostitutes. I wondered if he might have been one of Lucy's customers.

"It might have been offers of marriage," Alice said hopefully.

I felt safe in the knowledge that teaching and governess positions would surely be waiting for me on Vancouver's Island in Columbia—or so I hoped—and this sounded a whole lot more respectable. I had no desire to find a husband, either—I wanted to work and be independent.

Three days later, we set sail once again, and the weather continued to treat us with kindness as we sailed north toward Esquimalt Harbour on Vancouver's Island. I took it as a good omen and felt optimism within my heart as we finally reached our destination on the evening of September 17.

Unlike most of the others, many too weary to bother about their appearance, I changed into my one clean, but very creased, spare dress. A somber gray, it was plain and simple, but at least it made me feel more presentable. I longed to wash my other dress properly, having worn it the entire voyage. I even saved some of my water ration to wash my hair.

I desperately wanted to rid myself of the odours and miseries of the last three months aboard the *S.S. Tynemouth*.

GIDEON

SAN FRANCISCO – GAMBLING AND GOLD
(1856–1862)

CHAPTER 20

The Invincible was anything but attractive.

I had looked at many ships for sale, but they were all far too expensive. Then I spotted that old, neglected clipper high up on a mud bank in the Bay with a "For Sale" sign on her side. Her paintwork was peeling, and barnacles clung to her sides. She would also need a new set of sails, as hers were ripped to pieces. But I was sure that, with a little effort, I could make her seaworthy again, even if it took me a long time.

And just maybe I could afford this one. From the moment I first caught sight of the *Invincible* I felt a strong connection to her and knew I had to have her.

One of the other ship owners in the harbour told me the clipper was owned by Joe Johnson, an old-timer who spent most of his time in his favorite pub, the Olde Sea Shanty. A few minutes later, I found him there, sitting alone at the bar sipping a whisky.

"Are you Joe Johnson? The man who owns the *Invincible?*" I asked.

His long, gray beard was stained with whisky spills and items of food that had lodged there.

"Who wants to know?"

"Gideon McBride, sir." I thrust out my hand. "I'd like to buy her from you."

Ignoring my hand, he studied my face, probably thinking I was far too young to know anything about ships and the sea.

He turned back to his drink. "Okay. I'll sell her to you." He took a large swig. "But for $1,000."

"What! She's worth nowhere near that, and you know it. I'll give you $700 and not a penny more. I don't have that much right now, but I can get it."

"Smart young fellow, eh? Well, you have until Sunday at noon, because after that I'll be selling her for scrap. Don't want to pay another month of dockage fees for that old pile of junk."

"I'll be back on Sunday at noon," I promised. This time he shook my hand.

After mailing most of my remaining money to Ma and paying for accommodation, I only had $100 to my name. How would I get another $600 before Sunday?

The way I'd always made fast money—playing poker!

*   *   *

I roamed around the city that night, looking for somewhere to gamble.

The first place I spotted was the Maison Rouge on Davis Street. The building had a sign outside that read: *Gambling! Girls and Good Whisky!* So I walked through the swinging doors with an air of confidence I didn't really feel. It was my first visit to a gambling den since I'd arrived in San Francisco, and I needed to win big in three days. The warm atmosphere and the music on the honky-tonk piano soon calmed my fears.

A woman with bright red hair, dressed in vivid green, walked towards me as soon as I entered.

"Welcome to the Maison Rouge, *monsieur*," she said as she hugged me to her large, warm bosom, most of which was exposed in her low-cut dress. "I am Madame Fleure Frechette Harvey, the proprietor. Please have a drink or gamble at one of our tables, and later perhaps enjoy the delights of my girls upstairs."

She was very different from the women I had known in my youth, who had little or no colour on their faces, unless from the wind or the sun. And she was very unlike Anya's youthful, innocent appearance. This woman's face was heavily painted and the perfume she wore was intoxicating, but I was most fascinated by her French accent and the seductive smile on her very red lips. I could see how easily she could entice customers into her establishment.

But in that moment I couldn't allow myself to think about anything except how much I needed money to buy the *Invincible*.

"Just the gambling tonight, Madame Harvey."

She linked her arm through mine and led me over to the bar. "But the first drink is always on the house for new customers."

Although wanting to keep a clear head, I accepted the drink. She was simply too hard to resist. "Thank you, Madame."

"Oh please—call me Fleure, monsieur. And you are?"

"Gideon. Gideon McBride."

"Good luck at the tables, Gideon." She patted my hand and floated off in a cloud of perfume to welcome another customer.

I avoided the blackjack tables and walked towards a group of six older men who were playing poker—a motley group who all looked up at me with amusement. They probably thought my youth made me an easy mark. Despite my beard, I still looked inexperienced and young, which was fine with me.

Let them think I don't know anything about poker.

"Come join us, lad," one of the men indicated as he pulled up another chair. He had an eye twitch, which bothered me a bit. I would have to be careful not to let it distract me from the task at hand.

"We always welcome new blood," said another man, who started to deal out cards. He tipped back his wide-brimmed Stetson and began to explain how to play, apparently assuming I'd never done so before.

"Poker is played with a pack of fifty-two cards, which are ranged from high to low," he said. "Ace, king, queen, jack, ten, and so on down."

I didn't interrupt, but I wanted to laugh when he described the four suits as though I'd never seen a playing card in my life.

"There are spades, hearts, diamonds and clubs, and no suit is higher than another. All our poker hands contain five cards. We make our bets depending on the hand we are dealt, and the highest hand wins."

I purposely lost the first two rounds, just to make them think I was a complete novice, but after that I couldn't hold back. It was so easy.

As the air became thicker around us, I used all the skills I'd learned from the old sea salts as a lad. I played each hand masterfully, using my bluffing skills to perfection. No one could anticipate the hands I held, and it wasn't long before I had raked in $500 and then another $300, more than enough to purchase the *Invincible* and still have enough to pay dockage fees for at least a month until I could move her.

My heart was beating fast by the time all the other players had folded. The last hand was played out and the game was over. I was $800 richer, but I could see the men were all boiling with rage at having lost their money.

As I stood up to leave, the man beside me placed his hand firmly on my shoulder, forcing me back into my chair.

"You hinted you had never played the game before, but you managed to take us all. Could it be that you cheated, young man?"

"Certainly not, sir. If you remember correctly, I did not say I'd never played before. You just assumed as much."

He raised his voice. "But you listened when I explained the game to you. Why didn't you admit you knew the game?" I looked down and saw his hand on the gun in his belt holster.

"Perhaps because you never asked, sir."

Fleure, who had been watching and overheard the exchange, headed towards us. "Now, gentlemen, no one cheats in my establishment. And there will be no gun fighting in the Maison Rouge."

"Better tell that to this fellow," the man with the eye twitch replied.

"Gideon, I suggest you leave now. I don't want any trouble."

"Yes, Fleure. I'm off. I don't take kindly to men who accuse me of cheating."

I was only too happy to leave, so I boldly strolled out into the night, whistling as I headed back to my lodgings.

Shortly before I reached the What Cheer House, I felt a sharp blow to the back of my head, which momentarily stunned me, knocking me to the ground. When I came round, I immediately checked my pockets. They were empty. All my winnings had been stolen.

"Damn and blast to hell!" I muttered to myself, rubbing my sore head. One or two of the other players must have followed me and taken back all the winnings I had honorably won.

My youthful inexperience and excitement at winning had made me forget two very important poker lessons: never trust anyone, and always keep your winnings close to you.

How could I possibly have been so reckless?

* * *

I didn't sleep much that night, partly because my head was throbbing but mostly because I knew how foolish I'd been. I now had only two days to recoup my losses.

I finally fell asleep in the early hours of the morning and awoke around midday with a splitting headache. It was Friday, and Sunday was the deadline.

After splashing cold water on my face, I got something to eat and then returned to the Maison Rouge with my last $100, which I had left back at my lodgings under the bed. It was all I had left to my name, and I vowed I would be more careful with it.

Unfortunately, I was not so lucky this time. I won a few games but lost a few others, and the stakes were much lower during the afternoon. No one in there was putting up much money. I ended up winning only another $200.

Fleure must have seen my desperation. "What happened to all your winnings last night, Gideon?"

"I was knocked out cold on the way home, and it was all stolen."

"Better than being shot as a cheater, *mon ami*."

"I don't cheat, and I resent their insinuations that I did."

She bent down and whispered in my ear: "Come back tonight and tomorrow night, Gideon. We have some big gamblers here on Friday and Saturday nights."

I thanked her and decided to confide in her. "I need the money for a ship I'm buying, Fleure, and I have to have it by Sunday at noon!"

"You are a good poker player, Gideon. You can probably fleece those high-stakes players, and I know you did not cheat."

I was grateful for her trust in me, which felt good. When I left, I walked back down to the dock to take another look at the *Invincible*. I knew I *must* have her, and next time I gambled I would be more aware of my surroundings and be a whole lot smarter.

*   *   *

The games that night were indeed played with much higher stakes.

I joined a game with $200 that soon turned into $500. No one accused me of cheating this time, and I was getting closer to my goal, but I still needed more so I'd have enough to make the *Invincible* seaworthy again.

This time, when I left, I made sure to look behind me and keep my money close to my heart. The next day, I also opened a bank account at the Wells Fargo bank, where I deposited $300 of my winnings. I was getting smarter.

I returned on Saturday night with the remaining $200 to play with. This time, my opponents at the table were playing for even higher stakes. When the bets reached the thousands, I felt uncomfortable.

Still, my $200 soon turned into well over $1,000. But instead of leaving, I made the mistake of playing one more game. This time I lost, and I was back down to $200. Although it was by then the early hours of Sunday morning, I knew I couldn't leave. I only had a few hours left to recoup my winnings if the *Invincible* were to be mine.

I tried to remain calm—the first lesson of being a good poker player—but I could feel sweat forming on my brow. Time meant nothing now. I was hooked into a game with a man called Charles Williams, who, according to Fleure, lived in the wealthy part of town and could well afford to lose. But he was not about to give up—and neither was I. We were now the only two players left at the table. All the others had folded.

By eleven o'clock the next morning, I was watching the bills pile up in front of me again. By 11:30, I had won $900 and cleaned out my opponent, so I wisely decided to take my winnings and leave. Having played all night and most of the morning, we were both exhausted.

"Thank you, sir," I said as I stood up. "The game was most enjoyable, but now I'm afraid I have to leave."

"I will look forward to another game with you soon, so that I might recoup some of my losses," he replied.

We shook hands, and Fleure smiled at me as I flew out the door and ran all the way down to the harbour.

When I got there, I couldn't believe my eyes.

Joe and two other men were already hoisting the clipper off the mud bank.

"Hey, wait, wait!" I screamed above the noise of screeching gulls. "Joe, I have your money. We made a deal. It's only five minutes to noon!"

Joe looked up and grinned, showing all his gold front teeth. "So it is, young fellow. I didn't think you were coming back. Show me your money, son, and she's yours."

I quickly counted out the full $700 into his eager hands. Turning to the two other men, I said, "You can leave her here, because I'll be fixing her up right where she is. I will call on you again when she's ready to be put in the water."

I knew now I still had enough money left over to pay them and the dockage fees.

The Invincible was finally mine.

CHAPTER 21

Five months later, I stood at the helm of the *Invincible*, steering her back into San Francisco Bay. The satisfaction and pride I felt was beyond belief. I had achieved the impossible.

"Weigh anchor now, Cap'n?" asked Skiff, my second mate. I nodded, feeling an unfamiliar sting in my eyes. The rest of the crew was busy lowering sails and coiling rigging as I edged the ship alongside the dock. And now we were finally weighing anchor, back after my first trading voyage to the Orient. Best of all, I had money in my pocket as testament to a successful trip.

My cabin boy, Rick, was helping our ten Chinese passengers down the ramp. These men had paid for a passage from Shanghai to come to America in search of a better life. One of them fell to his knees and kissed the ground. I hoped they would find that pot of gold they were looking for.

As I watched the other ships in the harbour, I could not believe how well my crew had turned out. After I'd spent the first weeks scrubbing, scraping and painting the *Invincible* until she shone, my next job had been to hire a crew. But the transients who drifted in and out of town were an assorted group of men who had all laughed at me when I said I needed a crew for the *Invincible* to sail to the Orient.

One had called out to me, "You can't be the captain of that old clipper. You're far too young and she's far too old."

They were beginning to drift away until one black-skinned fellow stepped forward and also began to challenge my experience. "Have you ever sailed before?" he asked.

"Let's get one thing straight right now," I replied angrily. "I have years of experience. My name is Gideon McBride, and I was brought up in a fishing village on the North Sea in Scotland, and I've sailed in many a storm. I also worked for the Hudson's Bay Company in Rupert's Land. I may be some years younger than many of you here, but I know the sea and I understand the import and export trade. If you work for me, you will obey my orders. I am the captain, d'yer understand that?"

The black man blinked and looked at me with fresh respect, and at that moment I recognized him as the fellow I'd spoken to on my first day in San Francisco. I would never forget how his ugly old face had broken into a smile. "Aye, aye, sir," he said, this time without a trace of sarcasm. "You're the cap'n, Captain McBride."

Captain Gideon McBride! I really liked the sound of that.

"Now, are you interested in signing on with me or not?"

"Yes, sir! My name is Sam Skiffington, but everyone calls me Skiff," he'd replied. "I came to California as a free man. Here are my freedom papers, captain."

I was still shocked whenever I heard about a man actually owning another human being.

We shook hands, and Skiff signed on as my first crew member. It was the start of our friendship. After that, I soon had a complete crew of fourteen men and one young boy.

I would certainly have preferred men with more sea experience, rather than those who signed on simply because they needed money to survive. But they had all pulled their weight during our months at sea, and it sent shivers of pride down my spine. And now we were safely back in the harbour and my ragamuffin crew had become like family to me.

I came back to the present, thinking about what I still needed to do, now that we were back.

"I'm going ashore now to make sure the cargo gets to the warehouse," I called out to my men. Once you've finished tying everything down, join me at the Olde Sea Shanty for a meal and a few drinks on me."

"Aye, aye captain," they shouted in unison. They were a good bunch, and I owed them a lot.

I climbed down the ramp and supervised the dock workers unloading my cargo onto carts. I paid them well to take the crates to a nearby warehouse I'd rented. I would easily be able to sell the contents of those crates, because the citizens of San Francisco were quickly developing a taste for the finest goods from the Orient: silk fabric, tea and spices.

Next, I went to the bank to deposit my profits, leaving enough out to pay the crew. One hour later, we were all sitting around a table at the tavern and I was doling out their wages.

Before we'd set sail, Paddy, an Irishman full of blarney, had told us stories of pirates in the Pacific.

"So, Paddy, where were those pirates you told us about?" I laughed. "Did'na see any plying the Pacific Ocean."

"None have been seen since the 1830s," he admitted with a grin. "But there could have been a few still around. You were just lucky, captain, because you had the luck of the Irish with you. I was your lucky charm."

"You weren't much of a lucky charm in that storm, though, Paddy," chipped in Skiff with a grin. "Shivering like a baby, you were."

We all laughed and I ordered a second round of drinks and a meal of roast beef and fresh vegetables for everyone. Cook's eyes were shining. "I've got to learn to cook like this," he muttered as he stuffed a mouthful of beef and gravy into his mouth. He licked his lips as some of the gravy dripped down his chin.

They all shouted their agreement. "Yeah, this meal is far better than the slop you served us, cook."

"Hey, men, he did his best," I said.

"Saints alive! If that was his best, God help us on the next trip," another crew member said.

The next trip! So they wanted to stay with me.

Ho Chi, the Chinese man who had been my translator during trading, now spoke up. "Cook good man. You all good men. And Captain Mac, he the best."

I slapped him fondly on the back. "Remember how we did that excellent trade in Shanghai, Ho Chi? I couldn't have sold all that cotton at such a good price without your help."

He smiled, stood up and bowed to me. By then we were all a little tipsy, so we all stood and bowed to one another.

"And we only lost a couple of crates of tea on the way home, which wasn't bad considering the force of that storm." Paddy was still shaking from the memory of it.

A few hours and many drinks later, we stumbled outside, hugging one another and laughing at everything—even things that weren't particularly funny. I loved to hear their cheerful banter back and forth. It reminded me of Da and his friendship with the fishermen of Rosehearty.

"Here's to our next trip!" I called to them all as I made my way back to the What Cheer House. On my way upstairs to my room, I picked up my mail from the hall table and was surprised there was only one letter from home. I thought Ma would have written more during the three months I'd been gone.

What troubled me most was that this letter was in Janet's handwriting. My hands trembled as I ripped it open. The hazy warmth of many drinks quickly disappeared. I suddenly felt cold stone sober.

I could barely read the words in Janet's letter, which was dated January 1, 1857, for my eyes soon became bleary with tears.

"My dearest brother Gideon,

It is with a sad and heavy heart that I have to write this news to you so far away. Our beloved mother went to meet her Maker two days before Christmas. She had been sick a while, but na'er complaining, as was her way. It has been a bitter winter and the cold she took visited her chest and refused to leave, despite the care we took and the ministering of old Doc McLeod.

*Mother's last words were of you, Gideon. She prayed for your happiness
—where ever you might find it.*

*You need not send more money to us now, dear brother. Tom and I
are doing well and making a comfortable living. Fiona is going ahead with
her wedding to Robbie Buchan in April, as it was Ma's last wish. By the
time you receive this letter, she also will be a married lady at barely 16. But
Robbie is a good man and will take good care of her. So, you need not worry
about us. We will be fine, and we thank you, dear brother, for all the help
you have given us in the past.*

*Our greatest wish is that one day you will visit us again. We miss Ma
so much, as I know you will also. She never stopped talking of the son she
was so proud of, because you had sought out your dream and would one
day captain your own vessel.*

Take care, dear brother. Our love is with you always.

Your loving sister and brother-in-law,

Janet and Tom

*p.s. We will make you an uncle in May. I just wish that Ma had lived
to see her first grandchild.*

My hand shook as I read to the end.

All this had happened in the last few months, while I was at sea
in blissful ignorance. My baby sister was now married. My older sister
was about to become a mother. But, worst of all, my beloved mother
was dead. How could that be? I could still see her face, her rosy cheeks
and blue eyes. I could still hear her voice. Automatically I fingered
the leather rope around my neck with the piece of metal attached. I
could still hear her explaining its inscription to me when I was a lad
of fourteen—"destiny will always bring you home."

She could not be gone from this earth forever.

I crunched the letter in my hand and flung it on the bed as tears
began to escape down my cheeks. But I then smoothed it out, knowing
that later I would want to read it again, as much as I hated its contents.

I needed a drink. Oh God, how I needed a drink.

I headed out the door, making my way to the Maison Rouge. I wanted to see Fleure, as it had been many months since I'd last seen her. The barkeep told me she was working in her office, so I ordered a double whisky, and when it was placed before me, I stared at it for a long time before I finally raised it to my lips. It went down well, warming my throat on its journey. I nodded to the barkeep and told him to leave a bottle there. After my fourth drink, the room looked fuzzy, and the noise of voices and music around me floated in and out of my consciousness. Someone must have sent for Fleure, because suddenly she was standing there behind the bar, looking at me and shaking her head.

"What is it, *mon amour?*" she whispered, her gentle French accent giving me comfort in my distress. "I am glad to see you home safely from your voyage, but you do not look so good."

"Don't feel so good, Fleure."

"Something is wrong, eh?"

"Oh yes."

"Tell me."

"Had a letter." I slurred my words now. "Letter from home. My mother ..."

"She is sick, *oui?*"

I slammed down my glass on the bar. "She's dead."

"Ah, *mon Dieu!* I am so sorry. But this," she said, pointing to the almost-empty bottle of whisky beside me, "this is no way to celebrate your mother's life."

"I said she's *dead*, goddamn it. Dead! I'm na'er celebrating her life. I'm mourning her death."

"I know, Gideon, I know. Come ..." She walked around the bar and gently took my arm. "Come with me, *mon amour*. You need to come upstairs and sleep this off. You will feel better in the morning."

"Na'er feel better. She's gone," I slurred. "I should ha' been there—should' na'er have left them all." She supported my unsteady gait to the back of the saloon, and we slowly climbed the stairs together.

I'd been up there before to visit one or two of her girls, but this time Fleure took me to her own room at the far end of the corridor. As she opened the door, I was confronted by a blur of pinks and greens inside. She led me to her large, fluffy bed and began to undress me, although I wasn't really sure what she was doing, as once I fell onto the bed I passed out.

The next time I opened my eyes, it was morning. The sun was pouring through the window and Fleure was standing beside the bed with a mug of steaming coffee in her hand.

"Ah, he wakes," she said. "Here, drink this, Gideon. It's strong enough to ease the pain in your head."

Suddenly I remembered everything again. "What about the pain in my heart, Fleure?"

"That will take a little longer. But it, too, will ease in time."

"Will it?" I took a sip of the black liquid. "Ma was a wonderful woman."

"Please tell me about her."

I took a sip of the coffee as she sat on the edge of the bed and listened. I told her about my mother—that strong, determined little Scottish woman who had borne the loss of children and a husband, and then seen her only surviving son head off to the new world to make his fortune. That brave woman who had worked her fingers to the bone as a "fish wife" to support us all. The woman I should never have left.

"Ah, you are lucky to have had such a mother and such love in your family."

"Didn't you?"

She shook her head. "No, I grew up in the slums of Paris and never knew who my father was. I had to learn the art of stealing in the back alleys so that my mother and I could survive."

She told me her mother had sold her to a rich man who had brought her to America when she was only thirteen. She never saw her mother again.

"The man turned out to be a sadistic animal, and I was his prisoner for years. Eventually I escaped and met Sam Harvey, who brought me to San Francisco and taught me English. He offered me a job as hostess at the Maison Rouge, and eventually we were married when I was twenty."

"I didn't realize you were married, Fleure," I said. "I haven't met your husband."

She patted my hand. "Nor will you," she whispered. "He was shot two years after we were married. The city was still wild then, and there were few laws. One night, someone accused him of cheating in a game of poker, pulled out a gun, and shot him through the heart. The killer escaped and was never brought to justice."

"Oh, I'm so sorry ..."

"Do not be. Sam was a good man, and I still miss him very much, but he was not the love of my life. I have not met *him* yet." She laughed. "Sam left me the Maison Rouge in his will, and a considerable amount of money, so I am now very comfortable. He also taught me how to be a good businesswoman in this town. That was almost three years ago, Gideon, and today no one gets the better of Fleure Frechette Harvey!"

From what I had seen, she could handle herself and her clientele, some of whom became very rowdy on occasion. Sam Harvey had taught her well.

The more we talked, the more comforted and safe I felt. And for the first time, I looked deep into her eyes and realized how very beautiful she was. I touched her soft, velvety cheek. She lay down beside me and put her arms around me and we kissed. I felt my body responding, and in that moment I wanted her just as much as she wanted me.

She must have known I was using her body to ease my own pain, but she didn't object. She began to seductively remove the rest of my clothing, and our bodies soon joined in an almost spiritual union. On that early May morning in the year 1857, Fleure taught me the many joys of loving in a tender, slow coupling.

Later we executed a far more aggressive and passionate performance, which helped me release all the tension and hurt I felt inside.

After that night, I delayed my second voyage to the Orient. My crew deserved a rest, which was well-earned. Meanwhile, we made short trading trips up and down the coastline, which allowed me to enjoy the delights of Fleure, who was quickly becoming a close friend. Somewhat selfishly, I didn't bother about how she might feel about me.

I also began drinking heavily and gambling recklessly. Night after night, I visited saloons. Gambling and drinking to excess until I passed out seemed to help the pain in my gut. The only truly happy times I experienced were spent at sea with my crew, especially Skiff.

And despite Fleure's earlier warning, I also visited some other gambling dens down by the wharf on the Barbary Coast, all the time increasing my fortune.

I believed I was invincible—just like my ship.

CHAPTER 22

"Nobody can play a hand like you, Cap'n," said Skiff, who was standing behind me at the table one night.

I was playing another poker game at the Crazy Horse Saloon, down by the wharf, with a large amount of money piled in front of me.

It was a particularly cold night towards the end of that year, but it was warm and smoky inside the card room beside the bar. I wasn't about to stop while the odds seemed to be in my favour. My remaining opponents at the table were making too many mistakes. Other players had folded and we were now down to two.

"Not if the captain happens to be cheatin'."

I looked up from my hand at the Southern gentleman across from me. He sported a large moustache and was smoking an expensive-looking cigar.

"Would you care to repeat that remark, sir?" I said calmly.

"I would indeed. I call you on the last card you took, because it is my firm belief that you took two cards at once and carefully slid the other out of sight beneath the table."

I shifted my chair back away from the table. "I resent your remark, sir, and invite you to come around here and look under the table. As you will clearly see, there is no second card hidden."

The room went quiet. Even the piano player had stopped playing and was looking our way.

"Maybe we should leave," Skiff whispered.

"Leave?" I shouted. "Why should we leave? I'm winning this hand, and I'm winning it fair and square. If this gentleman wants to dispute that fact, he'd better be proving it."

A few people were standing behind me now, examining the table as they bent to look beneath it. "No card there," someone said.

The Southern gentleman was not satisfied. "I don't have to prove anything. I saw exactly what you did, and I'm sure there are witnesses who will back me up. I also do not trust the word of a man who would associate himself with a black animal like him."

Now my blood was really boiling.

I jumped to my feet, knocking over my chair. "How dare you! I demand an apology on behalf of my friend for such a despicable remark, and I suggest you give that apology immediately."

Skiff nudged me and whispered, "Hey, cap'n, watch what you say. That fellow, he have big power here, I think."

I ignored him. "And, may I ask, where are these so-called witnesses you mention? Present them to me and I'll take them to task on my behalf as well as my friend's."

The Southerner was laughing. He and the man he had come in with now had their hands on the pistols holstered at their sides. One quick draw and the situation could easily escalate— or come to a fatal end. A good fist fight was one thing, but I would have no part of anything involving a gun. I'd been down this road before, and I also remembered Fleure's story of her late husband.

As I began gathering up the money I had won, I said, "I will not play with a man who insults my friend, accuses me of cheating, and questions my honesty. Skiff, you're right, we're leaving."

"Not so fast, captain," the Southerner said. "The money on this table is mine. Your win is still in dispute."

Not responding, I picked up the rest of my money, all the time watching for trouble from the man and his companion. It came all too soon. The first punch was aimed at me, but Skiff intervened—he always enjoyed a good fight. I retaliated with a second punch aimed straight at the Southerner's face. "That one was for you, Skiff. No one insults my friends."

Between the two of us, and a few others sitting around the bar who decided to join in, we made short work of the Southerner and his companion and sent them packing outside. In the process, glasses were smashed and tables were knocked over. One man fell through a window and bottles went flying over the bar.

By then, Skiff and I were the only two left standing—but not for long. Judd, the bar's big, burly owner, grabbed both of us by our collars and booted us down the steps of his saloon, one at a time.

"Cap'n McBride, you and your buddy are going to be in my debt for a large sum of money to put my bar to rights," he called behind us. "I'd estimate you owe me at least a thousand dollars for this night's work, and I'll be coming after it. I know where to find you."

I landed hard on my back side, rubbed my sore head and protested loudly. "Hey, pal, we didn't start this fracas. You saw how that fellow incited us into this brawl. He started it—not us."

"That's as may be, but you ended it, so you pay."

I sat in the dirt with Skiff beside me, feeling sorry for myself and licking my wounds. My winnings that night, which I'd manage to scoop up before the fight started, were not going to be spent compensating Judd. I could taste blood in my mouth from a thick lip, and I was sure a black eye would soon make an appearance.

Suddenly a voice nearby asked, "My dear chap, is there anything I can do to assist you?"

Chap! Who the hell used words like that with such an educated English voice in this godforsaken part of town? I rubbed my eyes and grinned up at a well-dressed man looking down at us.

"Not unless you have an extra thousand dollars lying around—or you know of a good lawyer," I said.

"Here, let me help you up," he replied as he offered his hand.

"Captain Gideon McBride, sir. And this is Skiff, my friend and first mate on the *Invincible*."

"Pleased to meet you both," he said. "I'm Edward Caldwell, and I think I can help you. I don't have that amount of money, but I do know of a good lawyer."

"Hey, I was joking. Nobody settles these bar brawls with a lawyer. They're usually settled with a fight or a gun."

"Well, maybe it's high time we brought some civilized law to this city. Here, take my card. Now, can I help you both on your way to your place of abode?"

The way he spoke intrigued me. His accent was very high-class and proper.

"Well, Mr. Edward Caldwell, that is very civil of you, and we appreciate your kindness. Maybe you would first care to accompany us to the Maison Rouge and we could buy you a drink. It's a far better establishment."

"I would be delighted to accept your kind offer, but I cannot be gone long. I have to return soon to my boardinghouse on Mission Street to check on my young son. The landlady has been watching him while I conducted some business in this part of town."

"Business, eh?" I glanced at his card for the first time. "Well, I'll be damned. I see that you're a lawyer yourself."

"Indeed I am, but believe me, I was not trying to drum up business for myself over your unfortunate mishap tonight. I simply meant—"

"Aye, I understand completely. And I don't blame you for offering your professional help. In fact, maybe I will hire you. There were many witnesses at the Crazy Horse tonight who would vouch for the fact that Skiff and I did not start this brawl, nor were we the only ones who did the damage. I will happily pay for my share—but not the entire amount —and maybe I do need a lawyer to plead my case. Come, Caldwell, let me buy you a drink and we can talk some more. I promise we won't delay you long."

He was an Englishman through and through, totally out of his element, and I might well have felt the same myself had I not had my early years of experience at sea and with the Hudson's Bay Company. This man looked like he had just arrived in town and was bewildered by all that he saw. He reeked of upper-class England. Probably had come from a wealthy family and attended all the best schools. The wild, raw atmosphere of the American west would be completely foreign to him. But his legal experience might be of assistance to me, and in return, maybe I could help him adapt to this foreign land.

And so, somewhat reluctantly, Edward Caldwell allowed himself to be escorted to the Maison Rouge, a kind of establishment I am sure he would not normally frequent.

*   *   *

"I really can't stay long, gentlemen," he kept saying after we had introduced him to Fleure and she had placed a whisky in front of him. "My son will be wondering where I am."

"A son, eh? And is your wife with you too?"

"My wife died giving birth to James six years ago," he said.

"Oh, I'm so sorry."

"We were young when we married; too young, perhaps, and then when we knew we were to be blessed with a child, we felt very fortunate. But Gwen was a frail girl, not made for childbearing. She died a few hours after James's birth."

He paused before taking another sip of his drink. "My sister looked after my son while I worked in London, but after a few years it somehow did not seem to be enough. Gwen and I had often talked about heading to the New World, and, had she lived, we would probably have left England anyway."

"How brave of you to come here alone with a young boy," Fleure said. "When did you arrive in California?"

"A month ago, after six weeks at sea. God, what a voyage! How can a man love the sea?" He grinned. "You, captain, probably enjoy being tossed about by the elements."

"Aye, it's my life, and Skiff's here, now. Nonetheless, you are in one of the wildest cities in the west, so you probably need a little guidance. How are you finding it so far?"

"Not totally to my liking, I must admit. I wanted a place that was new. A town where James and I could start a good life, but this does not quite seem to be it. I should perhaps have arrived in '49 when opportunities, and gold, abounded! Now, although the laws of the city still need much improvement, San Francisco is becoming more civilized. But I've heard of a place farther north called Fort Victoria, on Vancouver's Island in New Caledonia. As it's under British rule, it might be more to my liking."

"Aye, I've heard of it, too. There is talk of gold on the Fraser River, and Governor James Douglas up there will be having a wee amount of trouble, I'm thinking, trying to keep law and order in Fort Victoria. He's a Hudson's Bay Company man, like I was once. Personally, I don't think I could live under company rules again, as no doubt Douglas thinks himself king in that neck of the woods."

Caldwell was on his second drink now and loosening up somewhat. "Ah, but being a Scotsman, surely even you would prefer to come under the jurisdiction of the more civilized British law."

I laughed heartily. "Have you not heard, man, that the Scots and the English have been warring for centuries?"

"Then we, Captain McBride, must put an end to that war here and now, and form a friendship between us. Maybe eventually, I'll even convince you to come north. I am more than ever sure that that is where James and I will eventually head."

I did not say so that night to Caldwell, but I also had been hearing much about this place called New Caledonia and the gold fever that was slowly spreading along the Fraser River. I admit that it had interested me—the thought of actually mining for gold!

But something else had occurred to me, quite apart from the gold. There would be need for transport upriver, and transport meant vessels. I had read about the sternwheelers and sidewheelers, and perhaps I could own some and become a river boat captain. Could there possibly be more gold to be made that way, rather than actually staking a claim in the gold fields?

I had studied the currents and routes of the mighty Fraser and had read much about Fort Victoria, the arrival port from California, and New Westminster on the mainland, at the mouth of the Fraser. It had certainly intrigued me, but until I met Caldwell that night, it had not stirred my imagination enough to uproot myself from San Francisco. So, for the moment, I said nothing.

We all shook hands as we got up to leave.

"You boys should never have gone to another saloon," Fleure said as a parting shot. "I've told you before, Gideon, you should only patronize my establishment, where everything is run above board." She was probably right.

Skiff and I delivered Caldwell safely back to his boardinghouse after making arrangements to meet for lunch the next day to discuss the incident in the Crazy Horse Saloon.

Edward Caldwell was as good as his word. He managed, on my behalf, to settle the whole matter with me paying only $100 damages. The Southern gentleman and his friend were each liable for $450 apiece, they being the instigators of the dispute.

I decided I liked this lawyer. He was smart. Maybe I'd keep him around.

CHAPTER 23

As time went by, Skiff and I enjoyed Caldwell's company and that of his six-year-old son, James, who was a very bright lad. He'd spent his entire life around adults so acted far beyond his years.

We all spent Christmas together at Caldwell's boardinghouse, relishing an enormous goose with all the trimmings cooked by Mrs. Bunting, his landlady.

Fleure took an instant, motherly liking to James and also joined us for Christmas dinner. As we all relaxed around a roaring fire, she taught James some French carols.

I felt so relaxed and happy that night, considering myself lucky in the choice of my new circle of friends, albeit an odd group—an upper-class English lawyer; a lovable, somewhat precocious six-year-old; a black, formerly enslaved man from the Southern states of America; and a French saloon madam.

Edward, James, Skiff, and Fleure had become my new family. Even Edward, a very proper gentleman, seemed to have grown so accustomed to our friendship that he no longer saw anything unusual or odd about our curious mix of backgrounds.

Early in the new year, my crew and I made two short trips up and down the coast, carrying various cargos at a handsome profit. While in Mission, I even purchased two cheap lots, in case I ever decided to stay and build a house there.

But I continued to hear talk of gold on the Fraser River in the north. On our return to San Francisco, the newspapers were full of it. Caldwell and I had another discussion about the possibilities of heading north.

"Ed, I've read about the sternwheelers and sidewheelers that could be used on inland river routes, and I'm intrigued by it all."

I still had a passion for the open sea and trading, but I could visualize another, even more lucrative means of making money. I also had a hankering to actually go to the gold fields myself.

"I think that might be worth a try—actually mining," he replied, quickly adding, "but lawyers will also be needed up there to settle the inevitable disputes, and I'm sure there will be much legal work involved in setting up claims."

"Cap'n, I hear that this man Douglas up at Fort Victoria is also encouraging black folk to come to Vancouver's Island," Skiff told us. "Lots of work for us there, and a good life where they're not always lookin' sideways at us black folks."

"You'll always have a job with me, Skiff, wherever we go," I replied. "How could I run a good ship without you?"

* * *

And so, full of youthful enthusiasm and ignoring Fleure's earlier warnings, I headed back to the Crazy Horse once again to bolster my savings before making any final decision to head north.

There were always inexperienced gamblers there, men reckless with their money. I was so convinced I could win a large pot that I had withdrawn all my money from the bank to play with. If I was going to leave San Francisco, I was determined to leave with a fortune in my pocket.

That night the saloon was lively and full to capacity. I soon found a table and joined a game already in progress, easily winning the first few games. I probably should have left right then. But as the money continued to pile up in front of me, I was sure I couldn't possibly lose.

"Luck seems to be with you tonight, sir," said the man opposite, giving me a superior sneer across the table. He was well dressed, much older than me, and put on an air of grandeur. We were the only two left in the game at this point.

"Seems that way." I smiled.

"Are you willing to double your last bet, sir? All or nothing?"

The bravado I felt when I'd first entered the saloon pushed me the wrong way. I nodded and shoved all my notes into the center of the table. If I lost, it would be disastrous. But if I won—?

"All or nothing," I said with confidence.

People were watching us now, and the room went quiet.

The cards were dealt. My hand was looking good but, instead of smiling, I tried to look worried in an attempt to bluff him.

Challenged to lay down my cards, I remained confident. I had a straight flush—five clubs in sequence. Only a royal flush could beat that.

Then slowly he laid down his hand, one card at a time. Ace of diamonds, king of diamonds, queen of diamonds, jack of diamonds, ten of diamonds.

A royal flush.

My stomach plummeted. For a moment I couldn't breathe.

"Are you willing to try to recoup some of your losses, sir?" he asked with a sadistic smile.

God, I had to! I had to find some way to win back some money! But how? What did I have left?

I still owned the *Invincible,* but I would never trade her. She was all I had. I was sweating, feeling the tension building in the room and all eyes on me. I wiped my brow with the back of my hand.

Then it came to me: the two pieces of land in Mission. I still had the sale vouchers in my pocket. I dug them out and threw them on the table.

"Here—I stake this land against what I lost to you."

He laughed. "My dear fellow, what is the land worth?"

"Each lot is now worth $1,000—more than double what I originally paid for it."

"So," he said, as he examined the vouchers. "I will agree to put up $2,000 of what I won from you."

It wasn't much, but it was something. The cards were dealt once again, but luck was deserting me, along with my usual confidence. The big loss had shaken me to the core, and now I was making mistakes—not a good way to play poker. I had learned that way back when, from the Company men. Once again, he beat me fair and square: his four of a kind against my full house. I folded and watched him rake in the two land deeds as well as all my money.

I was devastated and totally broke. Should I trade in the *Invincible?* Finally, a small voice in my head knocked some sense into this foolish gambler's head. The ship was now my only means of livelihood! I left the table, barely able to stand in my despair, and stumbled out of the saloon. What a fool I'd been.

I found myself heading towards Edward's boardinghouse, where I banged loudly on his door, no doubt waking the landlady and everyone else in the vicinity He was surprised to see me at such a late hour.

"Ed, I've done something really stupid."

"What now, old boy?"

I sank into the armchair in his room and told him what had happened. "I've lost it all, Ed. Every cent I have, plus those two pieces of land I owned in Mission. I need to get out of this town and try somewhere new, but now I don't even have the money to do that. I'm ready to join you and James to head north, if you can lend me some money to live on right now."

"Do you still have your ship? Or is that gone, too?"

"She's the only thing I have left, so at least I have some collateral. I have to keep her for now and perhaps make some money transporting passengers north. It's all I have left in the world, and I swear to God that I will pay you back."

"Thank God you didn't lose your ship." He patted me on the shoulder. "Perhaps it is for the best, old boy. Stay away from the gambling tables now, and stick to what you know best—ships and the

sea. And yes, of course I'll loan you the money, and you don't need
to pay me back."

I realized in that moment that I certainly had not lost everything.
I still had the one thing left which was far more valuable—friendship.
To me, it was worth all the money in the world.

*   *   *

Within a couple of weeks, I had made a plan to salvage my losses,
and this time it didn't involve gambling.

On April 21, I watched as the *Commodore* became the first of
many vessels to leave San Francisco and head north with thousands of
gold-seekers aboard, all anxious to find the mother lode. I then made
two trips north myself, carrying eager passengers aboard the *Invincible.*
On each trip, I barely had time to take in the bedlam happening in
Victoria because I simply dropped my human cargo and sailed back to
San Francisco to take on more passengers. I made some fast money
and was able to repay Edward, despite his refusal to accept it.

"I insist, Ed. Your trust and friendship mean the world to me."

We talked constantly about when we ourselves would leave. Skiff
was determined to come with me, and we had even talked Fleure into
joining us. She had become very fond of James, and she enjoyed the
friendship of us all. In the romantic sense, I was content with the way
things were between us. But one night, after we'd finished making love,
she looked deep into my eyes.

"I have never felt like this before, Gideon," she said. "Some days,
I even think about having a child of my own one day, and I really ..."

I interrupted her with a kiss because I thought she was about to
express her love for me. I valued her, but I was not in love with her.
I suppose I was being unfair, simply using her for my own pleasure
on occasion, just as I would use any woman for release of my sexual
frustrations. The intricacies of deeper relationships were still beyond

me. I enjoyed the life of a bachelor and had no desire to change that any time soon.

So I replied, "I care about you too, Fleure, and I'm glad you are coming north with us."

It was of course the coward's way out, and I was being selfish. Nonetheless, at the beginning of May, Fleure put the Maison Rouge up for sale. "As soon as it sells," she announced, "I will be ready to leave with you all. I think I will use the money to purchase a respectable hotel in the north."

By July of 1858, it seemed we were all prepared to enter the fray ourselves and begin the new adventure. We were, however, perhaps a little wiser and better equipped than most. The Maison Rouge had been sold at a handsome profit, giving Fleure ample funds to reinvest in an establishment in Victoria. Caldwell had cleared up all his outstanding legal jobs. And I still had a little money in my pocket.

So, early on the morning of July 21, we all boarded the *Invincible*. We were laden down with both freight and passengers, which would give me a respectable income away from the gambling tables. Once we arrived, I intended to anchor the *Invincible* in Victoria, should I ever decide to continue trading.

The voyage itself was a rough one, taking longer than usual as heavy gales and monumental waves suddenly appeared, causing a great deal of discomfort to most of the passengers. Six of my original crew had stayed with me and intended to try their luck in the north. Skiff and the crew helped calm the passengers while I steered the ship. Rough seas were just another challenge for me to enjoy.

Fleure and Edward spent most of the voyage in their cabins, suffering from seasickness, but, much to my delight, young James proved a far better sailor than his father. After one bout of sickness on the first day, his stomach settled down and he began to enjoy the rise and swell of the ocean almost as much as I did.

Valerie Green

Most of my passengers despaired as the cruel sea prolonged the sickness for men, women and children alike. Many had been destitute and hungry before even embarking on this journey, and hoped desperately that the gold fields along the Fraser would be the key to turning their fortunes around.

The conditions on board, to my regret, were not an auspicious beginning for them. I had overloaded the *Invincible* to full capacity, so sanitation was not optimal. The food I was able to supply was poor quality, and the stench from the hold was unhealthy. It made me even more determined to sail passenger vessels under only high-quality conditions in future. I had put down a deposit on three sternwheelers in San Francisco that could negotiate the Fraser, carrying freight and passengers to the gold fields.

As we neared Victoria, I felt a shiver of anticipation in my spine; something about this landing made me feel that I was about to become a part of history. We anchored in Esquimalt and my passengers disembarked. Like us, they walked the rough trail into Victoria because the inner harbor in Victoria could not accommodate larger clippers.

Upon arrival, we discovered thousands of people camped in the town-site circling the fort. It seemed every nationality was represented, and the streets were lined with their tents.

The surrounding fields were full of colorful flowers, and a large swamp to the north was crowded with pond lilies and cattails. To the south and east were dense forests of oak, cedar and fir. There were few buildings outside the fort, so we purchased a tent, some food and other necessities, and then made camp away from the densest area.

Fleure made the tent more comfortable with blankets and pallets and then prepared a meal for us over an open fire.

On that first night, we met David Higgins, a writer who had arrived the day before aboard the *Sierra Nevada* and was camped next to us.

"I was in San Francisco in the early days, too," he told us. "I wrote a lot about the vigilantes who eventually brought some law and order to that city. It will be the same here, no doubt. It takes a while for a town to settle down and grow."

"And is that why are you now here in Fort Victoria?" asked Edward, who was still looking a little green around the gills. "Do you enjoy being in at the beginning?"

"Yes, indeed. It's the start of a new era here in Fort Victoria. I foresee the Fraser River gold rush as something phenomenal. I want to write about it all," he added with passion. "Future generations will remember this time, and I'm going to be here to document it!" He waved his hands around, gesturing at the chaotic scene of the tent encampment surrounding us. "Just look at it all. Don't you find it thrilling?"

"I totally agree," I said, feeling excitement building in my chest.

We were treated to occasional glimpses of grouse and deer, which excited James, though he seemed intimidated to hear that bears also sometimes roamed near the camp. As we sat around our campfire that first evening, while Higgins went off to scribble in his journal, I discussed my plans with Edward, Skiff, and Fleure.

"I have decided it's time to make use of my Hudson's Bay Company connections," I began. "I still have my discharge papers and record of service. Tomorrow I plan on using them and requesting an interview with Governor Douglas at James Bay House, where he apparently lives."

"For what purpose?" Edward asked.

"Well, Douglas has to be worried about the arrival of so many Americans around his fort. His biggest fear is what the Crown fears—seeing this territory annexed to America. Since the first miners came north in April, Fort Victoria and parts of the mainland have been inundated with people, mostly Americans. Look around us, Edward, at this sea of humanity. The so-called pastoral existence of the old Fort Victoria is no more, so one of his immediate problems is what to do with all these people who want to get to the mainland and onto the Fraser. I've heard some have tried to build their own small crafts to cross the Strait and perished in the attempt. Maybe I can help in this regard, for a price."

He smiled. "I'm beginning to see your plan, McBride."

Young James began jumping up and down. "Uncle Gideon, you mean that you will sail the ships across to the mainland."

"That's the plan, James. But I need to build more sternwheelers. They're perfect for negotiating the Fraser, at least as far as Boston Bar or Lytton." I spread out a map on the ground, which we all studied intently. "Later we might even challenge the Upper Fraser, depending on the diggings. And for all that, I will need more money."

"Ah," said Caldwell, "and that will depend on our first trip upriver ourselves."

"That's only part of it."

Edward still seemed anxious to see the gold fields for himself, and his enthusiasm spurred me on. I was somewhat surprised that this very proper English gentlemen was so enthusiastic about exploring the gold fields—but then there was no accounting for the lure of that which glitters.

James looked at his father. "Can I come gold hunting too, Father?"

"No, my boy. You would need to stay here with Fleure. It will be a very rough adventure. Far too rough an undertaking for a young chap like you." James was not happy with his father's answer and told Edward as much.

I listened to their conversation back and forth, but I was thinking of something else entirely. Looking for gold to make my plans come true was risky. In many ways, the dream of gold was a lot like gambling, and I'd learned a hard lesson about that kind of folly.

To achieve my goal, I needed friends in high places.

Come hell or high water, I planned to meet with the Governor tomorrow and persuade him to give me a loan.

CHAPTER 24

The governor's residence stood a short distance from the fort, across the James Bay mud flats. As I walked along the narrow path, his large house soon came into view. James Douglas lived there with his wife, Amelia, and their many children.

I arrived unannounced, which probably was a poorly conceived plan on my part. But I was hopeful that, with my company record papers in hand, Governor Douglas would at least see me and, in the end, readily approve my ideas.

"Do you have an appointment, sir?" a servant asked at the front door.

"No, but I have important business to discuss with the governor," I said with bravado.

"One moment, sir."

He returned a few minutes later and ushered me into the parlor. Douglas was standing by a window overlooking his garden, watching some children playing outside. He didn't turn as I entered, so I coughed softly, but there was no response.

He was a giant of a man, taller even than the leathery old potted aspidistra plant that stood in the corner, which must have been well over six feet.

"Sir," I said, "I apologize for disturbing you at this hour. My name is McBride; Gideon McBride."

There was still no response. Perhaps he was hard of hearing.

I cleared my throat loudly and continued, "I have a proposal to put before you, sir, that I hope might interest you. As you will see from these documents, I was once a Company man myself, and I feel—"

His head whipped around and he glared at me with sharp, penetrating eyes.

"Company man, eh? So why are you not with the Company now, Mr. McBride?"

"It's Captain McBride, sir," I said. "I severed my connections a few years ago in order to go into business for myself as a sea captain and trader."

I immediately regretted the use of the word *trader*. In Douglas's eyes, only Hudson's Bay Company men were traders. I'd heard about his reputation when I first arrived in Rupert's Land. In his opinion, trade on the North American continent ought to be the sole purview of the Hudson's Bay Company.

"And you think you can help *me*?" He pointed his thumb at his chest.

"Well, sir, from my initial impression of Victoria, I see that you have quite a problem here. Too little space and too many people."

He laughed, but it wasn't a happy sound. Seating his large frame in a chair behind his desk, he finally indicated a chair where I should sit down opposite him. "And how long have you graced us with your presence in Victoria, Captain McBride? A day? A week?"

"Two days, sir."

"Ah ... two whole days. And already you're an expert on *my* problem."

"Far from it, sir." I leaned forward and handed him my company records, but he barely glanced at them. "I simply believe that I could help transport some of these people to the mainland and on to the gold fields, which, in turn, would help you regain some semblance of order and that quiet and peaceful existence you once enjoyed in Victoria."

"And what makes you think that I want peace and quiet here again, McBride?"

"I assumed ..."

"Never assume anything."

"No, sir."

He then looked down at my company papers and scanned through them quickly. "Your record with the company is admirable. Why did you leave?"

"I'm an independent man. That's why I've come to you now with this plan to solve your problems and ..."

"And put money in your own pocket, eh, McBride?"

I smiled. "Of course, sir."

"Well, at least you're an honest man. And a fellow Scotsman. Where d'ye come from?" He leaned back in his chair, a softer expression on his face now.

"Fraserburgh, in Aberdeenshire."

"Ah, I myself was educated in Edinburgh. My father sent me there as a young boy."

"Education is very important, sir," I said. "My father insisted on me reading as many books as possible and learning about the world."

"Did he indeed? And did you bring any books with you when you arrived in—I see it was Rupert's Land—when you were sixteen?"

"Yes, I brought books about Scotland, a world atlas and, of course, the Bible."

My reply seemed to please him. His face relaxed for a moment and a small smile curled the corner of his lips.

"All right," he finally said. "I'll hear your plan, Captain McBride, but first, know this. I have no intention of returning Victoria to a pastoral community of five hundred people. We are a bastion of Britain on this coast. I visualize a large city here one day."

"Of course, sir, but right now you have more than three thousand people, mostly Americans, camping on your doorstep, impatient to get to the mainland. Your 'city' is not yet ready to accommodate them, and it's best to get them dispersed before they become troublesome to the Company's interests—or the Crown's."

"True. Gradually, we are disposing of those people."

"I could help speed up the process."

"We need many vessels to do that. How many exactly do you own, Captain McBride?"

"My ship, the *Invincible*, is anchored in Esquimalt harbour. Before I left San Francisco, I placed orders for three steamers, which should arrive by the Columbia River within the month. All four vessels could easily dispose of many of those gold-seekers in quick order."

He nodded. "A mere four vessels! But what of the next three thousand that arrive? I am sure this gold rush won't be over soon. And there are other American skippers about to bring their vessels north to alleviate this problem."

"I agree, which is why I have come to you today for permission to start building more vessels here in Victoria. *British* vessels, sir."

"Do you have the money to build these ships?"

"Well, sir, I ... thought ..."

He leaned forward towards me and narrowed his eyes. "Ah, now we get to the crux of the matter. Are you asking me to *finance* this idea of yours?"

"A loan, sir. All I want is a loan—that I would quickly repay." I couldn't let this opportunity slip by. I had to convince Douglas that I could pull this off if he gave me a loan.

"You have great confidence in your abilities, Captain McBride. I suppose, like all those other fools, you expect to make a fortune from this gold business."

"Not necessarily mining for gold, sir. There are other ways to make money in a gold rush." He grunted, and I took that as agreement. Again, my answer seemed to please him.

He stood up, indicating that our meeting was over, and as he rose, I noticed again the full height of the man. Hardly any wonder he had commanded respect from his men at the fort for so long. I also stood, my eyes never leaving his. I was determined not to be intimated by how much he towered over me.

But he merely turned back to the window. "My children, grand-children, and their children will one day enjoy this place. It is idyllic, you know. I sensed it the first time I saw it back in the '40s. It's a perfect Eden. There is great potential, and many people will settle here eventually and build the city I envision. Perhaps those who find gold on the Fraser will return to Victoria to help build that city one day."

He paused before turning back to me. "You might even be one of them, Captain McBride. We will need men of conviction—English, Irish, Scots. Good men who will ensure this piece of earth remains British. Perhaps you'll have a future in politics. Not long from now, McBride, we will be setting down the new laws of this land."

Was that his way of creating a bargain between us? He would help me if I promised to help steer Victoria's future in the right direction?

"I hope I do make a fortune, sir, and in return I pledge to you that I will give something back to this country."

This time he actually smiled.

"Let me think about your idea," he said. "Come back again in a few days and we'll talk some more. If I think your idea has merit, I will telegraph the London office for approval."

I was being dismissed with a wave of his hand.

As I left James Bay House and crossed the Flats, back to the chaotic settlement around the old fort, my head spun with ideas. I'd leave politics to the lawyers—men like Edward would enjoy shaping the future of this place. As for me, I would do what I did best. Sail the waters of the Northwest and become a man who would be respected, esteemed, and long remembered in these parts.

And the next time I met with James Douglas, he *would* shake my hand.

* * *

Three days later, the governor sent a message asking me to return. He greeted me pleasantly as I walked into the parlour again. This time, he invited me to sit in a comfortable armchair.

"Can I interest you in a whisky, Captain?"

This was a good sign.

"Thank you, sir." I needed something to calm my nerves as I waited patiently while he slowly poured out two tumblers of good whisky.

A grandfather clock was ticking out the minutes behind me. Finally he spoke. "McBride, I have considered your proposal and think it might work. The Colonial Office in London has approved the idea and arranged for a bill to be made out in your name. It is being telegraphed from London for the sum of two thousand pounds as we speak and will be placed in an account in your name at the bank at Fort Victoria."

I exhaled with relief. I could barely speak. "Thank you, sir." The amount was well over four thousand dollars!

"My three sternwheelers, the *Sarah M*, the *Janet M*, and the *Fiona M*, will be arriving from San Francisco in three weeks. Your loan will allow me to build more here."

I didn't mention that I had only put down a deposit on those vessels, so Douglas's loan would also allow me to pay for them in full and then build more.

Douglas passed over a paper for me to sign, stating this was a loan to be used for the sole purpose of shipbuilding and was to be repaid to the Hudson's Bay Company, with interest, within two years. I couldn't sign it fast enough.

"I will not let you down, sir," I said.

And this time, when I left, Douglas stood up and firmly shook my hand.

*   *   *

I couldn't wait to tell my friends the good news.

Things were moving ahead quickly for us all. Fleure had hired carpenters to build a hotel on Government Street, which she planned on calling the Western Star. Edward had also made some connections and was about to set up a legal office.

"Let's go over to the mainland first and see what it is happening in New Westminster," he said. "That is, if you agree to take a trip over there with the *Invincible*."

I readily agreed, as I still had to wait for my sternwheelers to arrive. So the Caldwells, Skiff, and a couple of my crew made the trip over together with me. Also aboard was my first load of gold-seekers—paying passengers.

I immediately realized that the *Invincible* would not be suitable for the kind of work I anticipated. Most of the crafts crossing the Strait and negotiating the Fraser that year were sidewheelers, with one paddle-wheel on each side, but I could see their limitations. Sternwheelers would definitely have a longer life, having only one paddlewheel at the stern, which made docking far easier. I had certainly made a good investment having those three sternwheelers built in San Francisco.

That visit to the mainland was eye-opening. New Westminster was growing even faster than Victoria, and with a house there, I could live nearer the passenger loading point in Hope, where miners and their supplies would embark for the gold fields.

Edward and I both decided to build a home there. His decision was based on the fact that there was opportunity on the mainland for James to attend school. Skiff would follow wherever I decided to lead.

Having hired men to build our two houses on Royal Avenue, we returned to Victoria, where I awaited the arrival of my three vessels. When they finally steamed into the harbour, I set in motion a plan for three more sternwheelers to be built in Victoria immediately. I had to concentrate on building a profitable business. James Douglas would be impatient to see his company money put to good use.

Meanwhile, Edward opened up law offices in both Victoria and New Westminster. He rented some property on Government Street and hung up his shingle, though he had decided, like me, that he would spend most of his time in New Westminster, across the Strait.

The Western Star was soon flourishing. For the most part, the hotel was respectable, but Fleure's background would not allow her to ignore the fact that money could also be made from the oldest trade in the world—especially with all the transients passing through. It was, I guess, in her blood, though she no longer took part personally, because I had long since become her only partner. So whenever we came over to Victoria with James, Edward insisted we stay not at the Western Star but instead in a suite we jointly rented at the Windsor Hotel.

By November, I was in the shipbuilding business in earnest and looking forward to the winter months in harbour before a new season on the Fraser would begin in the spring.

An Act to provide a government for the region previously called New Caledonia had passed in the faraway Parliament in London in August of 1858, and on a cold November day, Douglas was officially sworn in at Fort Langley, on the mainland, as Governor of the Crown Colony of British Columbia, in addition to serving as Governor of Vancouver Island. I witnessed those proceedings with pride, rain trickling down my face.

British Columbia was now my home. Queen Victoria had named it using a pre-existing term for the vast region drained by the Columbia River, with 'British' added to distinguish it from the portions held by the United States.

We were bounded to the south by the United States of America, to the east by the chain of the Rocky Mountains, to the north by Simpson's River and the Finlay branch of the Peace River, and to the west by the great Pacific Ocean. Vancouver Island remained a separate colony.

Deep within my soul, I felt a kinship with this great, majestic, forbidding land, as yet unconquered, and I already had begun to love it with a passion.

CHAPTER 25

Once I had my fleet of sternwheelers in business, I discovered that competition was fierce among riverboat captains. I was exhilarated to be a part of that rare breed of men, all anxious to make fortunes transporting passengers up and down the Fraser.

I demanded much of my crew, but I demanded an equal measure from myself. On occasion, I even demanded a certain amount of help from my passengers.

On one particular trip aboard the *Sarah M*, I shouted instructions to all the passengers when our fuel supply ran low: "It would be of great assistance if you could help the crew chop wood along the river bank so they can keep the boilers stoked." Most passengers were happy to help, so much in a hurry were they to get to their destinations and find gold.

Later on that same trip, we needed help hauling the *Sarah M* over a sandbar because the water level had dropped. One particular passenger, a pompous gentleman who fancied himself an expert on gold mining, refused to comply with my order to go over the side and grab a towline, as the other passengers were already doing.

"My dear Captain," he said, "I paid you twenty dollars for my passage. I do not expect to work like a common crew member."

I turned to Skiff with a grin. "What's the steam pressure right now, Skiff?"

"Close to 180 pounds, Captain," he said, anticipating where my thoughts were going.

"Give her another twenty pounds and let her blow. Maybe then we can get this vessel moving again and won't need this gentleman's assistance after all."

Most people knew engines would blow up under such pressure, causing both vessel and passengers to lose their lives.

The man looked at me in horror. "Surely if you increase the pressure you'll blow us all to hell and back."

"More than likely," I said. "That's why we need everyone to pitch in and haul us off this damn sandbar."

Still grumbling, he nonetheless went overboard to assist the others in hauling the *Sarah M* off the offending sandbar.

On trips back downriver, I sympathized with the passengers I picked up who had suffered weeks in the wilderness and found little gold for their trouble. They were exhausted, hungry, filthy and covered in mosquito bites that had swollen their faces and hands grotesquely.

Edward joined me on one upriver trip, just for the experience. After depositing the passengers, we decided to venture inland to pan for gold ourselves. We found very little but managed to stake some claims, under Governor Douglas's mining licence system, that might prove workable later.

One night, as we sat around the campfire we had built to an enormous height in a vain attempt to deter those miserable mosquitoes, Edward turned to me and said, "McBride, no amount of gold is worth this bloody nonsense." I heartily agreed.

We headed out of there, certain there were far better ways to get rich!

*   *   *

Controlling the freight market on the Fraser River was one way.

Rates between Victoria and Hope rose swiftly, so I usually carried mail and other goods in addition to passengers across the strait and upriver. This was very profitable, thanks to the inflated price of everything. Mailing a letter from Yale to Victoria cost a dollar, and the price of coffee, butter, bacon and beans was much higher in Yale, upriver from New Westminster, than in Victoria. For me, this was another form of trading, and I reveled in it for a time. But competition between the riverboat captains eventually lowered these prices.

Competition continued well into the year 1860. By then, the fare between New Westminster and Victoria, previously around ten dollars, was now as low as fifty cents. All the big money had been made in the first two years, and those days were now over.

"We need another gold rush," I said half-heartedly to Edward over an after-dinner whisky at my house in New Westminster one night in the summer of 1860.

"God forbid!" Edward was by then well-established as a lawyer. In addition to our respective professions, much to our amazement, we had also profited from those mining claims we had staked on our one and only trip to the gold fields. One particular creek was now being worked and offering handsome profits to all its original stakeholders.

On the other hand, many folk were saying that the Fraser gold rush was over. A new word was being bandied about. *Cariboo!* Yet another gold rush was on the horizon.

Thanks to my good fortune, I had been able to pay off my debt to the Hudson's Bay Company. My shipbuilding operation, McBride's Transportation, continued to prosper, and by then I also owned two ship chandlery stores, one in Hope and one in New Westminster, which brought in a steady income. It seemed that, overnight, I had become a very wealthy man.

When not captaining one of my own vessels, I lived most of the time in New Westminster, but I paid many visits over to Vancouver Island and Victoria. On occasion, I was even invited to dine with Douglas and other men of note.

As I had predicted, Edward entered politics as a representative in the Colony of Vancouver Island's new House of Assembly in Victoria and was also a dinner guest at these events. We all enjoyed discussing the future of Victoria, and each of us, in our own way, offered our opinions as to the direction that future should take.

As much as I felt a part of this growing community, sometimes I lay in bed at night, contemplating my life, and thought back to Scotland. I had become so busy that I rarely thought about those early days now, except when a letter arrived from Janet or Fiona, full of happiness and contentment. Those letters always made me wonder whether something was still missing in my own life. My sisters were so satisfied with their simple lives.

Perhaps being rich was not the answer after all.

*   *   *

The winter of 1862 was one of the most severe in living memory. Snow fell waist-high in both Victoria and New Westminster, and patches of ice floated down the Fraser and formed together in enormous floes.

Edward and James stayed in Victoria, as crossings to the mainland were impossible. I remained in New Westminster and missed their companionship. James was delighted to have to stay put, as it meant that until the weather improved he couldn't return to school. But eventually a slow thaw set in and spring arrived, along with the second-greatest gold rush in British Columbia. This meant more business for me.

Cariboo! The word was magic. Once again, many desperate men set off to the goldfields even further north, imagining that area would now be the one paved in gold. I was only too happy that they were booking passages aboard my vessels.

Many came from England, whereas others, known as the Overlanders, came from the East, travelling across all manner of wild terrain to get here.

As a result of all this, my business flourished, because this gold rush was different from the one in 1858. The simple panning for gold in creeks yielded very little gold, but fortunes could still be made by those who joined together to pool their resources and dig deeper shafts.

With the civil war still raging south of the border, there was a smaller American infiltration into this particular gold rush, and James Douglas seemed to relax in the belief that British Columbia would indeed remain British.

Then, in May of 1862, another problem descended upon us all. A virulent disease appeared and spread quickly, almost annihilating the entire native population. Smallpox!

Edward and I discussed this with Douglas, as the disease was posing a threat to everyone in Victoria within a few days. All the native Songhees were told to vacate their huts across the harbour and head north, or see their huts set ablaze by Douglas's newly formed police force. Only the indigenous women living with white men were allowed to stay.

"I don't like this compromise," I said to Edward. "It's not solving the problem—it's just spreading the disease elsewhere."

"I agree," he said. "It's so unfair and very saddening to see these people losing their homes and being forced to leave. After all, this disease was brought here by the white man."

We decided to return to New Westminster to temporarily escape the problem, but in August, we returned to Victoria to witness its official incorporation as a city. A very popular, jovial butcher by the name of Thomas Harris was elected, by a show of hands, as Victoria's first mayor. I felt convinced that, from such simple beginnings, Victoria would become a great city.

But on our return to New Westminster I continued to feel unsettled and on edge. Something was missing in my life—something I couldn't quite put my finger on. I had achieved many of my goals. I had a fine home in New Westminster, plenty of money, good friends, and was well-respected by my peers. So why was all that still not enough? Why did I feel I needed more?

The following month I heard about some land for sale along the Gorge Arm in Victoria, and I spoke to Edward about it.

"Well, we could certainly go over and take a look," he said. "What do you have in mind?"

"Possibly building there also. Who knows? Victoria has grown so much, and it could eventually become the capital city. What d'yer think?"

"I rather think the capital will be New Westminster. But maybe that is for the best. Leave Victoria as the pleasant little city she has become."

"But the legislature is over there."

"True. Are you thinking of living there permanently, then? Remember the land you purchased in San Francisco with the same thought a few years ago—and then you ended up losing it."

"Don't remind me! I haven't forgotten my foolishness, Ed. But I haven't decided what I'll do yet. We could take a look at the land, though. Prices are good."

"Well, Fleure would certainly be happy if you lived in Victoria."

"Um—possibly." I wasn't thinking of Fleure or of settling down with a wife, if that was what he was insinuating.

"Let's go over next week, before James begins school again. In fact, I may have to stay over there myself for some months because of cases I'm working on. Every day brings some new dispute to be settled in the court of law. I will probably have to put James in another school."

"Not much choice of schools over there in Victoria," I said, little knowing how that particular remark would change the course of my whole life.

* * *

A few days later, Edward, James, Skiff and I headed back to Victoria. I wanted to scope out the land I had considered purchasing along the Selkirk Water of the Gorge Arm.

The three of us spent our first evening in town dining at the Windsor Hotel, talking of many things, including the arrival from England of the steamship *S.S. Tynemouth* that evening in Esquimalt Harbor.

"Can we go and see her tomorrow, Uncle Gideon?" James said, his eyes wide with excitement.

"Yes, I'll take you."

Long before her arrival, the *Tynemouth* had already created much interest because of the cargo of women she was carrying. People were intrigued by the notion of bringing women out to the colony as potential brides.

After Edward and James retired for the night, I stopped by the Western Star to see Fleure. Although I would normally have stayed the night with her, I decided not to this time. I drank far too much at the bar anyway, which I hadn't done in a long time. Eventually I stumbled back to my suite at the Windsor to get a good night's sleep. I went to my room, trying not to disturb Edward and James in the room next door.

Hours later, I awoke with a horrendous headache and Edward's voice pounding into my head.

"McBride! McBride! Get your lazy ass out of bed! We have things to do and places to go, man!"

He was shaking me out of a most pleasant dream about my childhood home in Scotland, which I didn't want to leave. I could still hear my dear mother's voice, God rest her soul, telling me something about destiny and fate, and being in the right place at the right time. She used to love delivering oratories on the ironies of life. My siblings and I never contradicted her, because the bonny Sarah McBride always knew what she was talking about.

"Can you hear me, Gideon?" the voice said again. "It's already past ten."

A younger and far gentler voice added, "Come on, Uncle Gideon. Move your sorry ass." He was immediately reprimanded by his father for his cheekiness. I opened one eye and gazed up at the two of them.

"What the hell's the hurry, Caldwell?"

"The hurry is simply that you wanted me to take a look at that land with you this morning, and time is wasting. All the best lots will be sold before we even get there."

I raised my head from the pillow, and the room took a couple of nasty turns.

"And you promised to take me out to Esquimalt to see the big ship later, Uncle Gideon," young James added.

"I did indeed," I muttered. "Well, let me find my sea legs and get myself cleaned up, and then we'll see what we can do."

A splash of icy cold water on my face helped revive me somewhat, and after dressing and working hard to keep down a breakfast that my stomach wanted no part of, I set off with the others to inspect the land.

We hired a carriage and headed out on the road alongside the Gorge waterway, where various lots were staked out. As we rose up over a knoll, I spotted one lot that still had a For Sale on it. The spot immediately stirred something deep within my soul.

My first thought as we alighted from the carriage was how peaceful it was. Nearer to the road, the land was flat, ideal for building on, but then it rolled gently down towards the Gorge waterway. Oak trees and one large Arbutus dotted the area, and an abundance of wildflowers filled the air with a delightful fragrance. Across the water were two other large residences. And in the distance to the south, the snow-capped Olympic Mountains rose high into the sky. Despite the gunmetal-gray clouds above, the land and its surroundings gave me a warm, pleasant feeling, and I drank in the serenity. I knew I had to purchase this land.

"This is the acreage I want to buy," I said to Edward. "Let's head back to the office in town and sign the paperwork before someone else snaps it up."

Edward agreed with me that it was indeed a splendid piece of property, and within thirty minutes I was the proud owner of twenty-five acres of prime land along the Gorge Arm.

*   *   *

By the time we reached Esquimalt Harbour, after walking there from town, the sun had broken through the clouds, and it had stopped raining. James ran ahead to see the *S.S. Tynemouth* anchored in the harbour.

Edward and I joined him and watched passengers being loaded onto a tender that would carry them to the inner harbour in Victoria. A shout rose all around us: "The crinolines have arrived! The women are here!"

"My goodness," said Edward. "How awful for those poor young women to be gaped at that way."

"And it will be even worse once the tender reaches the inner harbour. Not sure I want to witness that. Come, James, you've seen the ship, so now let's head back to town."

"But can't we watch the passengers arriving in the harbour?" he said.

"I'm sure it will be a spectacle, as your Uncle Gideon said," Edward told him. "Let's stroll back into town. By the time we get there, they should all be unloaded and gone."

But when we reached the inner harbour, the tender was still unloading more women, and up on the dockside, some were washing their clothes without any privacy.

It seemed pretty damn demeaning to me. Some naval personnel arrived, and the women were told to walk past the gathering crowd. One by one, they went by, their eyes downcast.

And then I saw her.

She was so small and fragile, yet she pulled back her shoulders, tossed her long hair behind her, and lifted her chin proudly as she began to walk with the other women through the crowd of gawking onlookers.

When she dropped her valise and stumbled, I rushed forward to help. She looked up at me, her eyes wide with indignation, and my heart nearly stopped. I wanted to drown myself in those beautiful green eyes forever.

Despite her distress, she obviously wanted no part of my assistance and paid little attention when I introduced myself, Edward and James. She merely thanked me and walked on without a backward glance.

After all the women had passed by, I elbowed Edward. "Can you find out more about these women?"

"What do you want to know?"

"Their names."

He cocked an eyebrow. "I suppose you could find out their names at the barracks. Why?"

"I need to know the name of that young woman we just saw, the one who tripped."

Edward shook his head and smiled. "Oh no, not another woman you're interested in, old boy? I thought you were staying faithful to Fleure these days."

I ignored his remark. "If there's to be a service in church on Sunday for these women, I'm going."

Eventually I even persuaded Edward and James to go to church with me. I saw the young woman again in the crowd and watched her stoic reaction to the reverend's remarks about remembering their religious duties. Most of the women were in tears, but she wasn't. I looked across at her and smiled, but she didn't appear to notice me. But I wasn't disheartened. I returned to the barracks alone after the service and spoke with the woman in charge.

"Do you have a list of the women passengers, ma'am? I need to know the name of the small young lady who tripped on the dockside when you first arrived."

"Oh, that was the hoity-toity one," she said. "On the ship she was always complaining about things, she was. She knew what she wanted, though, and most of the others were grateful to her. Her name is Jane Hopkins."

"Is she looking for a governess position?"

"Quite likely, sir. I have no idea what she wants to do."

That was enough for me. Now I had a plan for how I could get to know this woman.

Later, while we all waited for our lunch to be served at the Windsor, I turned to Edward. "How long will you be staying in Victoria?"

"Through the winter months, no doubt. Why?"

"James will need a governess, won't he? You said the schools here are not up to much."

"Uncle Gideon, I'm not a baby. I'm nearly eleven now. I don't need a governess."

"Hey, young man, all the best people started life with a governess. Ask your father."

"Did they, Father?"

"Possibly—but I'm wondering just what your uncle Gideon has in mind."

"I think I've found the perfect woman to be James's governess. Her name is Jane Hopkins. I hear some of the women from the *Tynemouth* are looking for governess positions."

"Ah—do you mean the mysterious lady who looks so young and probably has no qualifications—other than the fact that you seem fascinated with her?"

James began to laugh. "Uncle Gideon, have you fallen in love?"

"None of your business, young man! Right now, we must go down to the barracks and put your father's name on the board as a prospective employer. So as soon as we've finished eating, we'll go. Time's a-wasting."

It was raining again when we reached the barracks. I tacked Edward's notice up with the other postings, placing it lower down so she would see it first. And then I decided to place the two other governess positions way up high and leave only Edward's front and center, at eye level, so Jane Hopkins would see it first. I knew this was a little unfair, but I was sure, without a doubt, that fate would make Miss Jane Hopkins apply for our position. I just needed to make sure it happened. If Ma were alive she would understand.

That night, as I was falling asleep, it came to me in a flash. Da had told me long ago that I needed to find the right place in the world, the place where I was meant to be. Today I had found it.

I finally knew what had been missing in my life all along.

PART TWO

JANE – *The Governess*
(1862-1864)

CHAPTER 26

The night we docked in Esquimalt, Mrs. Robb came down to our quarters, her hands firmly on her hips. "You won't be able to disembark immediately. I'm afraid you have to stay aboard tonight."

Everyone groaned.

Early the next morning, after the other passengers left the vessel, we were allowed above deck. Circling us were men in small boats who pointed and called out to us. "Ah, the lovely bundle of crinolines has finally arrived!"

Mrs. Robb tutted and complained to Reverend Scott, who passed on her concerns to the captain, so he kept us aboard for a second night for our safety.

The men were still there in the morning, but finally, on September 19, the gunboat *HMS Forward* transported us from Esquimalt Harbour around to Victoria Harbour. Once we arrived, they rowed us ashore in smaller boats to the dockside. Buckets of soap and water awaited us so that we could do our laundry—in full view of the curious crowd gathered there to inspect us.

"Why do we have to wash our clothes in front of everyone?" Alice said.

What on earth were we supposed to do with wet clothes? Both Mrs. Robb and the Reverend Scott complained on our behalf to the captain, who came over to speak to us. "This is standard procedure, ladies. The harbour master requires you to do this in case you have brought disease or bugs with you on your clothing."

"Jesus Christ!" screamed Betty. "We're women, not pieces of meat or rotting vegetables. The only bugs around were already on your ship, not on us."

Nonetheless, we all obeyed orders and stood clutching our wet clothes before a welcoming committee of naval officials who finally arrived to escort us to the nearby marine barracks in James Bay. We would stay there until we found positions.

As if being forced to wash our clothes in front of an ogling crowd wasn't enough, one of the officials ordered us to march in file, two by two. I picked up my wet clothing, stuffed it into my valise, and mustered as much of my pride as I could. Pulling back my shoulders, I held up my chin and began the long walk through the milling crowds, who grew increasingly boisterous by the minute.

Walking like a lady was out of the question. I couldn't move without swaying, let alone march. I must have looked like a drunken sailor. The motion of the sea was still with me, and my stomach heaved with every step. The crowd closed in on us, and some of the men poked us and jeered in accents I'd never heard before.

Our situation was far worse than I had imagined. Why had I chosen to come to this awful place? When I put out my hand to push the crowds aside, I tripped and fell to the ground. Stumbling to my feet, I felt a large hand on my elbow, gently helping me up.

"My name is Captain Gideon McBride," he said in English, but with a strange brogue I didn't recognize. "And this is my friend, Edward Caldwell, and his son, James. I hope you're all right, miss."

I lifted my head, and through a blur of faces, I saw a tall man smiling down at me, his dark eyes filled with concern. He had a rugged look, reddish-brown hair, and a full beard. The other man with him was clean-shaven and slightly shorter. Both men were well dressed.

But I didn't want their pity. Mumbling my thanks, I regained my balance and moved on, my head held high.

When we reached the shelter of the James Bay Barracks, Mrs. Robb assigned us each a bed. The welcoming committee had prepared food for us on long tables, and while we ate, they passed around lists of available positions in New Westminster on the mainland and in Victoria. There were no positions for governesses. I was devastated.

"Now that the citizens of Victoria have had a chance to look you over, more positions will probably be added," Mrs. Robb said. "You'll find them on the notice board over there." She pointed to the wall behind us. I hoped she was right.

Although my first impression of Victoria by the harbour had not been the best, I had no desire to board yet another boat and travel to the mainland, to this place called New Westminster. I was determined to find a position in Victoria, at least to begin with.

After our meal, Alice and I joined a few of the others outside for some fresh air. The sun was shining now, and I could see beautiful, snow-capped mountains in the distance. I slowly began to feel more like myself.

* * *

Two days later, Mrs. Robb took us all to church, and we were forced to listen to another sermon by Reverend Scott. "Remember your religious duties," he said, "and at all times be a credit to your mothers, from whom you are forever separated."

Some of the women wept. Some laughed with scorn, but I sat sullenly on my uncomfortable, hard-backed chair, silently protesting that it was *my* mother who had separated from *me* a long time ago, not the other way around.

"Rely on providence for comfort whenever you might be beset by sin and temptation," he reminded us.

I walked back to the barracks with the other women, and it felt good to stretch my legs after months of being cramped inside the ship. Some women had already decided to leave for New Westminster that afternoon, and Alice was one of them.

"I'm applying for that job as a scullery maid in a big house on Royal Avenue in New Westminster, so I'll be going over there, Jane," she said.

"Remember, that means you have to travel on another ship, Alice!"

"But Mrs. Robb says it's only a short trip across the Strait. And the job sounds wonderful. There are no domestic positions like it here in Victoria."

"Well, good luck, Alice."

"Thank you, Jane," she said. "I will never forget your help. You gave me so much strength. Now, I can face anything." She flung herself into my arms.

Surprised, I mumbled, "Thank you, Alice."

But even as we bade those girls goodbye, I was thinking about my own future, and I was worried. I needed to find something quickly before my money ran out.

I glanced over at the notice board in the barracks once again. And that's when I spotted a new notice that had been placed low down on the board. It hadn't been there earlier. It appeared to be the only governess job available in Victoria:

Mr. Edward Caldwell requires a governess for his ten-year-old son, James. The applicant should be proficient in mathematics, literature, the arts, and music. Meet Mr. Caldwell at the Windsor Hotel on Government Street at 2 p.m. on Tuesday, September 23, for an interview.

Caldwell? I knew that name from somewhere.

And then, I remembered. The man called Captain McBride, who helped me when I fell on the dock, had introduced his friend to me as Mr. Edward Caldwell, and the boy with them was James. But what kind of captain was Captain McBride? He didn't wear a uniform like Philip Sinclair. The thought of another captain frightened me, but the two men had smiled warmly and looked pleasant enough—well-dressed, so probably wealthy.

I hastily wrote down the name and the address and told Mrs. Robb about my decision to interview for the job.

She smiled. "I'm relieved to hear that, Jane. I'll notify the gentleman that you'll be at the hotel on Tuesday for an interview. You are one of the last girls to make a decision. Some of the remaining girls are heading to the Cariboo. The gold miners up there are still looking for wives—if that appeals to you."

I shook my head. I had no wish to become the wife of a gold miner!

On Monday, Mrs. Robb kindly arranged accommodation for me at a boarding house on Government Street owned by a Mrs. Brady. Soon afterward, she left with her own family for a place called Nanaimo, farther up the island.

That night, I took a long bath at Mrs. Brady's and washed my hair until it shone. I was now alone in the new world, and it scared me.

I had to get this job tomorrow. If I didn't, I had no idea what I would do.

*   *   *

The next day, September 23, I somehow found the strength to make my way to the Windsor Hotel and begin the rest of my life.

I lifted my skirt to avoid the muddy puddles as I walked briskly along the wooden sidewalk bordering Government Street and easily found the Windsor Hotel. I marched through the open doors with a confidence I didn't feel. The aroma of cigar smoke and brandy in the foyer transported me back to the Sinclairs' beautiful library at Enderby House in London. I still missed her ladyship very much. But then Philip Sinclair's face flashed before me, and I shivered. *I must stop thinking about all that.*

While getting dressed that morning at the boardinghouse, I'd peered into the tiny mirror on my dresser and told myself I was a new person now, even though I didn't look it. I tried to recall Miss

Spring's appearance in exact detail so I could appear to be like a proper governess. She always wore her hair in a bun on top of her head, but when I copied that style, the mirror reflected back a pinched face that was far too pale and thin. I rubbed my cheeks to bring out some color, but dark circles under my eyes from no sleep the night before, coupled with how thin I'd become since I left England, made me look like a waif from a London slum.

But it was too late to change anything now. I had to have this job, and I would do anything to get it. I couldn't bear the thought of being a lowly domestic servant again. And I had no desire to head to the Cariboo to be the wife of a miner—or worse, a prostitute.

At the Windsor Hotel, I took a deep breath and walked over to the young man sitting at the desk. "I'm here to meet with Mr. Edward Caldwell," I said.

Almost immediately, a well-educated British voice from behind me said, "Ah, Miss Hopkins, I'm Edward Caldwell."

I turned. It was the clean-shaven gentleman I'd met at the harbour with the other taller, bearded man who had helped me up.

"It's good to see you again," he said, shaking my hand. "You remember my son, James?" He touched the shoulder of the golden-haired young lad standing beside him, who scowled at me and said nothing. Father and son looked alike; both fair, with a similar stocky build. But Mr. Caldwell had a pleasant smile on his face.

"I thought we could talk in the lounge over there." He indicated a table in the corner.

"Thank you, sir. I appreciate you seeing me."

After we sat down, Mr. Caldwell ordered tea from a passing waiter. A small chandelier hung above us, and red velvet chairs were scattered about. It was not nearly as grand as Enderby House, of course, but still impressive. My hands trembled from nerves, and I clenched them together tightly in my lap. But there was nothing I could do about my heart, which was beating so loudly I was sure he would hear it.

"Miss Hopkins, I want to start by saying how sorry I am for the unruly crowds when you first arrived. It wasn't a good welcome for you to our city."

No one had spoken so kindly to me before, except for Lady Sinclair. But the memory of that humiliating morning on the dockside still made my stomach turn, and all I could manage was a weak smile.

"Yes, well, I understand you have qualifications as a governess, Miss Hopkins. I have to admit that this might only be a temporary position while I stay in Victoria on business during the winter and spring months. My home is in New Westminster on the mainland, so for a few months, James will be out of school and in need of tutoring."

"I understand, sir." Even a few months would give me time to find my feet in this new land.

"I have a letter of reference from Lady Sinclair," I said, fumbling in my small pouch. "I worked as governess to her daughters."

My hand continued to shake as I unfolded the letter, and I hoped he didn't notice. Her ladyship had used their embossed Sinclair stationery, so the letter looked official. I'd read it so many times during the voyage, I knew it by heart. Thankfully she had not mentioned my exact position at Enderby House but had merely said I was a hard worker, listed my qualifications, and added that I'd make an excellent governess in the new world.

"But, Father, I told you and Uncle Gideon that I don't need a governess," James said gruffly.

"Nonsense! You can't let your studies lapse."

James narrowed his eyes at me. "At school I was learning geometry and algebra, and I was studying philosophy. I doubt you would be able to teach me those subjects."

"James, that's quite enough!" his father said.

I hesitated. "I also taught Lady Sinclair's daughters music and how to play the piano."

James threw up his hands. "Piano!" he spluttered. "Father ... really!"

"Please excuse my son's bad manners, Miss Hopkins. In what other subjects are you proficient?"

I thought back to my days at Field House and Mr. Lloyd's teachings. "Mathematics and geography, sir, as well as religious instruction."

"A perfect combination." He nodded. "Now, please tell me about your family."

"My parents were farmers and did well. They farmed land on an estate for the gentry. That allowed me to get an education and later to become a governess."

The lie came out so naturally, I almost believed it myself. "I was also Lady Sinclair's companion," I added for good measure.

As he scanned her ladyship's letter again, I looked up and saw the tall, red-headed man who had helped me up when I fell on the dock.

"Good afternoon, Ed," he said in a strange brogue.

He bowed slightly toward me and put out his hand. "We meet again, Miss Hopkins. Captain Gideon McBride. I'm happy to meet you here in more pleasant surroundings."

"Uncle Gideon, Father thinks I need a governess, but I thought you agreed with me when we talked before that I don't need one—especially not *her*." James pointed at me. "Please tell Father you understand."

"James!" His father placed his hand firmly on the boy's arm.

The captain ignored James's outburst as he shook my hand and sat down to join us. He gazed at me with piercing brown eyes, as though he could see right through me. Even if Mr. Caldwell believed my lies, surely this man would realize I was a fraud, despite trying to speak in an upper-class, well-educated way. At least I hadn't lied about my love and ability for music.

"Are you still staying at the military barracks in James Bay, Miss Hopkins?" the captain asked.

"No, sir. Yesterday I moved to Mrs. Brady's boardinghouse, a short distance from here."

"Excellent," he said. "Being close by, you could come here for James's lessons every morning. What do you think, Edward? Personally, I see no reason why Miss Hopkins couldn't start right away—that is, if you're satisfied with her ability to teach James."

Edward Caldwell cleared his throat. James muttered something under his breath, and his father leaned over and ordered him to go upstairs to his room. The boy glared at his father and stormed off.

"I'm so sorry for my son's rude behavior, Miss Hopkins. He assumed he would be allowed to avoid any form of learning for a few months, after we discovered the schools here in Victoria are still somewhat primitive."

I sympathized with the boy. To him, I must have seemed very inadequate as a teacher. He was tall for a ten-year-old, and I was small for a girl not quite eighteen.

"But your credentials seem admirable," Mr. Caldwell continued. "I'd be happy to hire you as governess for my son, at ten dollars a month."

"Plus the cost of Miss Hopkins's accommodation," added the Captain.

Mr. Caldwell frowned at him, obviously not sure about the extra money. But then he nodded and agreed to my accommodation being paid. But why was the Captain making all the decisions? He hadn't even heard what I could teach.

"That is very generous. Thank you, sir."

I could hardly believe my luck. I had very little money left from the small savings I'd brought with me—barely enough for a few more meals. The Emigration Society had only paid for the voyage and money for one week's rent at Mrs. Brady's, so after that I would be on my own.

"Will I now meet Mrs. Caldwell, sir?"

"James's mother died giving birth to him, I'm afraid," he said. "So we're just three bachelors, Gideon, James, and me."

My face grew hot. How stupid of me to assume there was a Mrs. Caldwell. I now felt an even greater kinship with James, as he was a motherless child and I knew how that felt.

But Mr. Caldwell merely smiled. "That was the reason I thought you would be more comfortable being interviewed here, in the lounge. But for James's lessons, I would like you to come to our suite upstairs, number two, every day at, say, nine o'clock in the morning and work with him until noon. Maybe you could start tomorrow?"

I almost went limp with relief. I had the job—even if the boy was insufferable.

"Thank you, sir. Yes, I can start tomorrow. Your son doesn't seem eager to learn music, so maybe I could begin with mathematics and then—"

"I'll leave his lesson planning up to you, Miss Hopkins," he said. "But I noticed you eyeing the piano over there. You must enjoy playing?"

"Oh, yes, sir."

"Perhaps Miss Hopkins would play for us now," the Captain said.

How did he know that my fingers were aching to touch those piano keys?

"I'd be happy to," I said.

The two men stood as I rose and made my way to the piano. I was so out of practice—surely I'd make a fool of myself. But the moment I sat down and my fingers touched the keys, the music poured from me once again. My spirits rose for the first time since I'd last played for her ladyship, so many months before. I now had an excellent job. I had my own room, and I didn't have to answer to anyone. My past was safely behind me.

When I stopped playing and looked around the room, I saw that some of the hotel staff had paused and were also listening. Everyone clapped, but Mr. Caldwell and the Captain clapped the loudest.

"Beautiful," the Captain said, walking over to me. "Where did you learn to play like that?"

"Thank you, sir. I ... er ... had lessons when I was a child, and I continued my studies later in London."

"I look forward to hearing you play again soon. And now, may I walk you back to your lodgings?"

"Thank you, sir, but there's no need. I walked here on my own."

"But the streets are full of ruffians and rogues. It isn't safe for a young woman to walk far alone. I'll take you safely back to Mrs. Brady's. I know exactly where it is."

"Thank you, sir. And, Mr. Caldwell, I'll be here promptly at nine o'clock tomorrow to start James's lessons."

He smiled and shook my hand, while looking at his friend, as though puzzled by his behavior.

"I will see you then, Miss Hopkins," he said.

I rose to leave.

Presumably the interview was over and I was now a governess.

CHAPTER 27: GIDEON

Hearing her voice while looking into those amazing green eyes again was nothing short of magical. She had moved with such grace over to the piano and played for us so beautifully.

But she looked flustered when I offered to walk her home and gently guided her outside. As she strutted along the wooden sidewalk, she reminded me of a peacock with its tail fully fanned out in order to keep her distance.

I was surprised when she suddenly said, "Where do you come from, Captain McBride? I've heard many different accents since I arrived. You're not from England, are you?"

"No, I'm from Scotland, lassie. I've been here four years. You'll hear a lot of this accent around here, I'm thinking. You'll also hear English and Irish, French, German, and even Italian. Victoria is made up of all kinds of newcomers, a cosmopolitan group. And what about you, Miss Hopkins? Where did you grow up in England?"

"In Oxfordshire, sir, on a farm."

"You must tell me all about it."

"There isn't much to tell."

"I love hearing about the old countries."

She hesitated before replying. "Well, perhaps another time, sir."

We walked on in silence.

"You are now safely home, Miss Hopkins," I said as we reached Mrs. Brady's front door.

"Thank you, sir."

"And you can stop calling me 'sir' all the time."

"But ..."

"No buts."

She opened her mouth to say something else, but I merely smiled down at her. I had intended to bid her goodbye, turn, and walk away without another word because of her standoffish attitude, but instead she somehow managed to have the last word. She spun around, entered the house and firmly closed the door in my face.

By God, she was a fiery little miss.

*   *   *

That night, after James had gone to bed, Ed and I talked in our suite at the Windsor about the contract for the land I'd purchased along the Selkirk Water. Originally the land was the preserve of the Songhees people, land they had not officially ceded to the colonial government. The government was now trying to delay the transfer of the property to me by inserting new clauses into the legal documents, making sure the Crown was covered at all levels.

"I have added your own conditions and I think the contract looks much better for you now, Gideon. It's a fair deal at a much better price," he said.

"What?"

"The contract, man. You asked me to draw up a new one. You should sign it and hand over the money. But I can see your mind is a million miles away. What's wrong?"

"Nothing, it's just that I haven't slept well since I first saw Miss Hopkins, and I can't think about anything else."

"Ah, I thought you would eventually get around to talking about the charming Miss Hopkins. Well, she seems qualified to teach James."

"I know—but that's not what I meant."

He laughed. "I didn't think it was."

He sipped his brandy and looked me straight in the eye. "I can see you're totally smitten with her, McBride, but slow down a bit.

She's very young, and this whole place must seem so strange to her. Remember how we felt when we first arrived. Don't overwhelm her."

"I don't intend to. If I could just bed her and get her out of my system, it would be fine, but I can't do that. My feelings for her are much more than that, and I simply don't understand it."

"You remind me of how I felt when I first met Gwendolyn, James's mother. I acted like a complete fool and came on too strongly at the beginning."

"Ed, I'm sorry if I reminded you of the past."

"Not at all, old boy. Those were happy days. I loved Gwen so much, and always will."

"What is so strange is that I've never had trouble being with women before—probably because it was usually only for pleasure. I'd never even had a real relationship with anyone and certainly never courted anyone. I was barely sixteen when I met Anya, as you know, and she was as innocent as I was and I had to make little effort. We were good friends, but I was never really in love with her, and then she was gone. Even with Fleure, our affair began with a mutual lustful attraction, which, for me, just grew into a friendship. I selfishly never bothered to find out how either of them had really felt about me."

Edward nodded.

"But with Jane, it's totally different. I want to get to know her better, and I want her to want me, too. Why am I even having these feelings and thoughts at all? It's so unlike me. Goddamn it, Ed, I've always been an adventurer, a gambler, a confirmed bachelor, but from the first moment I saw her, I wanted her."

"Well, I'm just warning you to take your time if you truly think you care about her. Be patient. It certainly worked out for me."

But patience was never one of my better qualities, so at noon the following day, after signing the new contract Ed had drawn up for me, I went with him to see how Miss Hopkins's first morning had gone with James.

"So, Miss Hopkins," Ed said, "how did my son behave today?"

She certainly looked flustered. Her face was flushed, and some wisps of hair had escaped from her tight bun. James, on the other hand, looked like he'd had more than enough learning for one day.

"Well, sir, I think we have both learned a lot," she said. "And we have discussed other places in the world. If James had an atlas we could possibly use that for a geography lesson tomorrow."

Edward said James didn't have one.

"I have a suggestion," I said impulsively. "Perhaps I could take Miss Hopkins to a bookstore and find one for him."

"An excellent idea," Ed said, and even James smiled. I knew that James had always enjoyed hearing tales from me about other places in the world.

"But first, may I take you to lunch, Miss Hopkins? The dining room here at the Windsor is excellent. Please say you'll join me. Afterwards we can walk to a bookstore."

"I ... er ... really don't think ..."

"It's quite all right, Miss Hopkins," Ed said. "Gideon will take good care of you. Go enjoy your lunch downstairs." I silently thanked him and whisked her out of the room before she could refuse. James started laughing before the door had even closed behind us. I could have wrung his neck.

*   *   *

The head waiter seated us at a small table by a window and handed us menus.

"What would you like to eat?" I asked.

"You can order for both of us. I'm sure I'll like everything."

When the waiter returned, I gave him our order and sat back in my chair, watching her.

Although she had appeared excited when she first glanced at the menu, she ate sparingly as each course arrived. She did sip all the consommé, but then just picked at the poached trout and the main course of roast beef and vegetables.

"I think it will take you a while to get used to eating good food again. I know what food at sea can taste like."

She simply nodded. "Yes."

"Are you enjoying Victoria so far?"

"Yes."

Her monosyllabic replies to everything I asked were driving me mad.

"After I left Scotland as a cabin boy, I worked for the Hudson's Bay Company in Rupert's Land before I headed west. The grub on board ship was pretty grim."

"Oh," she said, and then added, "Have you seen a lot of the world, Captain McBride?"

"Yes, I have, but I think I am finally settled. British Columbia is an exciting place and now definitely feels like home."

She didn't talk much during the entire meal, until the waiter returned with our final course—the plum pudding. This time she finished it off in quick order and then patted her full, enticing lips with her napkin. Her eyes began to sparkle.

"Ah, I see that went down well," I said.

Finally she smiled.

"Yes, I think I ate far too much, too quickly. It was so delicious."

"So in future I will know to only order plum pudding for you," I teased.

"But I'm sure I would gain far too much weight. I'm glad I made room for it, though."

"I think that rather portly gentleman over to your left has probably been eating far too much plum pudding all his life," I whispered as I leaned closer to her.

She glanced in his direction quickly and giggled. "I will let that be a warning."

My heart soared when she laughed. She finally seemed more relaxed. I realized she definitely had a fun-loving side, and I thanked the good Lord for plum pudding.

"Perhaps we should walk off some of our meal by heading to the bookstore now," I said, and she readily agreed. We left after I'd paid the bill.

We gazed in some shop windows along the way and then went inside a bookstore, where I purchased a few books for myself and an atlas for James.

As we wandered around inside the shop, I noticed how her eyes lit up with delight as she ran her hand over books on the shelves. I spotted a small book of poetry on a high shelf and reached for it.

"I've missed having books," she said. She obviously adored books as much as I did.

"Do you like poetry, Miss Hopkins?"

"Yes, I do."

"Well this is a collection of sonnets by Elizabeth Barrett Browning. I hear from my sisters in Scotland that her works are very popular. I would like to buy this for you."

"That is very kind of you, but I couldn't possibly accept such a gift, sir. It wouldn't be appropriate."

Maybe I had been too forward, so I added, "It would just be a 'welcome to Victoria' gift from the Caldwells and me. Would you accept it, then?"

"Well ..."

"Please say yes."

"I would love it, Captain McBride. Thank you."

Whenever we crossed the street on the way home, she allowed me to take her arm and help her step over the mud and horse dung left on the street. We laughed together about the terrible conditions.

"Some parts of the East End of London are like this," she said. "But not where I lived."

I thought she was about to tell me more, but she stopped.

"Yes, I've seen the same thing in parts of New York and San Francisco," I said, hoping she might tell me more.

But by then we were back at Mrs. Brady's and she simply thanked me and quickly disappeared inside. I hoped I had made some progress, because she had finally seemed to relax in my company.

Afterwards, as I strolled back to the Windsor Hotel, I asked myself again why Jane Hopkins consumed my thoughts as no other woman ever had. I crossed the street and this time hardly noticed when I stepped in a muddy puddle and a pile of horse dung.

She was beautiful, and I wanted her in a way I couldn't understand. I was familiar with feelings of lust and desire, but, as I'd told Ed, my feelings for her were much more than that. It was true I felt desire for her, but from the moment I first saw her, something else had happened to me that I simply couldn't explain.

I could only think that I must be falling in love with her—her inner beauty, her obvious courage, her smile, her determination, her innocence, and even her spark of defiance. In short, she had totally captivated me. Is this what my father felt when he first saw Ma?

As I reached the Windsor Hotel, I looked down at my boots as I scraped them on the mat at the door. They looked and smelled awful.

But for some reason, I felt really good.

CHAPTER 28: JANE

That first morning with James had gone very badly. I'd begun by trying to teach him mathematics, but he kept telling me over and over again that he was far beyond simple addition and subtraction. His nonstop complaints had given me a splitting headache. But I tried to speak to him as calmly as possible.

"Of course you are beyond that, James, so perhaps you should show me exactly what you *can* do and we'll proceed from there."

Although I had expected this behaviour from him, it had bothered me a lot because he might tell his father that he didn't like me and then I'd lose this job. I had to find something to interest him and make him change his mind.

"I have already done a little algebra."

"Good. Perhaps we could use that in problem-solving, James. In any event, we will persevere for the first hour today with arithmetic, and then continue with some geography. Do you enjoy learning about other places around the world?"

"Maybe ..."

"Then we must find an atlas and we can talk about some of those places. Perhaps you have even been to a few of them?"

He warmed to my gentler but firm approach and soon began to talk to me about where he had lived in London when he was younger. I told him I also had lived in London, and when I mentioned Belgrave Square, he said: "That is a very grand area!"

After our talk about places in the world, James had looked over at me and said, "I wasn't even going to have a governess at all—not until Uncle Gideon saw ... well, I've been told I am not to talk about that."

"Then perhaps you'd better not," I said, puzzled.

Whatever did he mean?

I was relieved when his father and Captain McBride came into the room at noon, and so thankful that I had thought of an atlas, which the Captain was kind enough to purchase on our walk. It seemed to be the incentive to stimulate his imagination and put us on a better course today. So our second lesson was a vast improvement on the day before.

"This atlas is fascinating," James said. "How large the world looks!"

"Yes, indeed. Look, here is London and here we are, on the far side of the world—thousands and thousands of miles away."

"And where is Scotland, where Uncle Gideon came from?"

I pointed it out on the map. "And here is Europe, James. See, the capital city in France is Paris, and here is Rome, the capital city in Italy. Those are very old cities, James, like London."

He kept nodding with delight. "And the oceans are so incredible, Miss Hopkins, bigger even than the continents."

He kept asking me more questions, and I tried to remember all that Mr. Lloyd had taught me about oceans and continents. I was very excited with his enthusiasm. Later I talked about the lives of all the great composers, a subject I felt more comfortable with. James was fascinated by the fact that Mr. Beethoven had composed such beautiful music even though he was deaf.

"I might like learning to play the piano after all," he suddenly said.

"That's wonderful, James." This was definitely progress.

The week continued well, but I didn't see Captain McBride again for a while. Mr. Caldwell said he had gone over to New Westminster on business. On that first Sunday it rained all morning, and the streets became a sea of mud again, almost reaching the high wooden sidewalks. I didn't venture outside until later in the day, when the sun finally appeared, and that's when I noticed the white-capped Olympic Mountains, which Mrs. Brady had told me were in Washington Territory. I hadn't realized the United States was that close.

When a rainbow crossed the sky in blazing colors, I was sure it was an omen of good things ahead.

*   *   *

I slowly began to feel at home in Victoria.

By the middle of October, Gideon and I were on first-name terms and had formed a friendship, but he was also away a lot. I had grown comfortable in his presence as he walked me home or we ate lunch together on many occasions.

One sunny Sunday morning in late October, after attending church with Mrs. Brady, I decided to go for a walk on my own and explore more of the city. Prior to that I had only seen what was on Government Street. Mrs. Brady had warned me on numerous occasions not to walk alone away from town, but I relished my newfound independence so much that I couldn't resist venturing farther afield that day.

I walked over the narrow bridge above the mud flats leading to James Bay because Mrs. Brady had told me the governor's house was over there and I wanted to see it.

She'd said that his house was very grand, but to me it appeared quite plain for a governor's residence. Compared to the elegant homes I'd seen in the West End of London, it looked almost modest. I think I saw the governor himself working in his garden. I recognized him from pictures I had seen of him in newspapers, and Gideon had told me he was a very large man who had helped him when he had first arrived in Victoria.

On my way home, I passed Mayor Thomas Harris, a fat, jolly man who was just leaving his butcher shop. He smiled at me.

"Good day, miss," he said, in a strong accent reminiscent of the East End of London. I smiled in return. The lady walking beside him, who I presumed to be his wife, had her nose in the air and did not acknowledge me. Mrs. Brady had told me that Mrs. Harris put on "airs" and fancied herself better than most people.

The following day, after my lesson with James, and feeling even more confident, I decided to walk westward along the trail leading to

Esquimalt. I immediately regretted going in that direction. I passed some vacant land inhabited by native Indians and saw some frightening sights. The natives were behind wire fences, and most looked very sickly. They stared back at me, their eyes hollow and vacant.

Suddenly, one of them began to walk closer to the wire. His face was pockmarked, and he began raising his fist and shouting at me in a language I didn't understand. I stepped backwards in alarm, thinking he might jump over the wire and attack me. I started running, my breath coming in restricted gasps of utter panic.

I kept running back toward town, remembering that Gideon had once told me of a recent smallpox epidemic that had killed off many native people. Some who had gone north went on spreading the disease as they fled. Those who stayed behind were still living in isolation on a small piece of land reserved for them, and most were obviously very ill.

Why on earth had I gone that way? Both Gideon and Mrs. Brady had warned me about walking alone. I hardly dared to look back in case the man was following me.

I was so shaken by what I'd seen that, as I approached Johnson Street and turned onto Government, I almost collided with a woman.

"My dear girl, I hope I haven't frightened you," she said gently as I started in alarm. She was dressed in an unusually vivid blue dress and matching hat.

"No—it was my fault. I was daydreaming. I'm sorry."

"Is something wrong?"

"Not really. I just walked too far and am regretting it. I saw some horrible things."

"Ah, you came from the direction of the Songhees Reserve, I think?"

She had a slight accent that was pleasing to the ear. Another one I'd never heard before. I nodded.

"It is not a good place to visit. There's still much sickness over there, and so those people live on their reserve and are isolated from us until something can be done about them."

"How awful. I was wrong to go there."

She smiled. "But naturally curious, I'm sure. Now, can I walk with you back to where you are staying?"

I shook my head. "No, I'm fine now, really. Thank you for your concern, Miss ...?"

"Madame," she replied. "Madame Harvey."

"I am pleased to meet you, madame. My name is Jane Hopkins and I'm a governess. I work for Mr. Edward Caldwell."

"Ah yes, of course. I've heard about you, and I've seen you from a distance as you come and go at the Windsor Hotel."

"Really?"

She smiled. "I've heard only good things about you, my dear, only good things."

"You know Mr. Caldwell?"

"Yes indeed." Something made me hesitate to ask exactly how she knew Edward Caldwell. It was something about her appearance that made me question her relationship with him, or perhaps even with Gideon McBride, so I refrained from asking more.

She was dressed in such bright colours, not typical of the women I'd seen in Victoria, who typically chose practical shades—grays, blacks, or light browns—for their clothes. Her bright blue dress, although very attractive, was perhaps more suited to a lady from—I hardly dared to think from where! I'd heard of and seen such women in London who stood on street corners or worked in brothels, and had actually met many aboard the *Tynemouth*. And here I was, talking to one on the street!

"Thank you for your kindness," I replied. "But I'm all right now, and I can find my way safely back to my lodgings from here."

"Yes, I see you are all right," she replied. "The colour has returned to your cheeks. I own the Western Star on Government Street, which I think is not far from where you are staying, so I would be happy to walk with you."

The Western Star. I had heard of it, and it seemed like a respectable hotel. And yet I'd also heard a rumour from Mrs. Brady, who knew everything, that it was connected to another trade. So, maybe I had been right about this woman. And how, in fact, did she know *where* I was staying? With these thoughts racing through my head, I refused her kind offer as best I could, bade her farewell and quickly walked on ahead.

"It was nice meeting you, Miss Hopkins," she said as I walked away.

I smiled but felt sure she was still watching me as I headed south towards Mrs. Brady's. She seemed nice, and I sensed a trace of sadness about her. Perhaps her life had been hard, like mine, and she had been forced into whatever it was she was doing to survive. Or perhaps I had completely misinterpreted her appearance and she was simply a kind lady who dressed rather colourfully.

I began to regret cutting our conversation short, thinking that perhaps I'd been somewhat rude. Despite my feelings, something made me refrain from mentioning her to either Edward Caldwell or Gideon. Perhaps I did not want to know what her connection was to either of these men.

In any event, a week later, while walking along Government Street, I noticed a sign in the window of the Western Star that read "Soon to be under New Ownership."

I assumed the kind lady in blue was leaving town, but I did not put any importance on it at the time.

CHAPTER 29: GIDEON

Whenever I left Victoria, I thought about Jane all the time. But I had taken Edward's advice and was trying to go slowly in my pursuit of her.

Usually, upon my return to Victoria, I immediately went to see her at noon after her lesson with James. But one day, it being a Saturday, I went to see her at the boarding house.

I waited in the parlour while Mrs. Brady went upstairs and knocked on her door to tell her I was there. The sight of her coming into the parlour made my heart skip a beat. She was so beautiful. I could barely restrain myself from taking her in my arms.

Instead, I stood patiently by the fireplace with my hands behind my back, concealing a parcel.

"I have something for you," I said as I handed it to her. "I found this in New Westminster at a music shop."

"Gideon, what have you done? Not another gift."

She ripped off the paper and gasped. "Oh, Gideon, thank you. What a wonderful surprise."

"This sheet music just arrived from London. I thought you might like it, for when you practice on the hotel piano—I'm sure they would allow it—and for when you possibly teach James one day."

She clapped her hands together in joy and fairly jumped in the air with excitement. "I couldn't have asked for anything more special. Thank you again, Gideon."

"One day, I'd like to buy you your own piano."

She blushed and bowed her head.

"I'm serious, Jane," I said, placing my finger under her chin to tilt it upwards. I desperately wanted to kiss her.

But she was startled and stepped backwards in alarm.

"Don't be afraid of me, Jane, please. I'd never harm you."

"I was just surprised by your touch."

I smiled. "Then I will not surprise you again. The next time I touch you, you will be fully informed before the event!" For some reason, my words made her laugh.

"We will take our courtship slowly, Jane, because in the end you *will* want me to touch you, I promise."

"Courtship? Is that what this is?"

I was encouraged by her question, because she was smiling flirtatiously as she asked.

"I think it most definitely is," I replied.

*   *   *

That night, when I took Jane home after enjoying a dinner at the Windsor Hotel together, I asked her a question I was becoming more and more curious about.

"How did you come to be on the *Tynemouth* sailing to the new world, Jane?" I said. I knew many of the women on board were destitute, uneducated, and had lived on the streets. None of which seemed true of Jane.

She looked up at me with those delicious green eyes, which always unsettled me in a perplexing way and made me want to linger in them forever.

After a long pause, she finally said, "There is not much to tell, Gideon. I just wanted a change."

"But you promised to tell me about life growing up on a farm, and you never did. Then you lived in London and seemed happy. So why leave? I grew up with fisher folk and we had little to do with farmers up in Scotland. So tell me all about your life."

"Oh, it was pleasant enough. My father worked hard, as did my mother. After they died and I was working for Lady Sinclair, she became like a mother to me. She was very kind, but, as I said, I wanted to see more of the world, and she arranged passage for me on the *Tynemouth*."

"But what of your childhood? And your own family?"

"I was an only child, but I did have many friends, and we played in the fields. I helped to feed the chickens and milk the cows. I don't really remember much else."

I tried to draw her out more, but it was obvious she didn't want to expand on those facts that really told me nothing. There didn't seem to be much love involved, and I wondered why.

"You know, Jane, families can also be formed later in life. I know that to be true, because when I left my family back in Scotland I never thought to have another, but then I met Edward and James, and Skiff—you will meet him one day soon."

I wondered why I had felt it necessary to avoid mentioning Fleure, who had also been part of my circle of friends.

"Skiff works for me at my shipping company in New Westminster, and there have been other friends along the way, and all those people became my family in the New World. One day, I also hope to start my own family, with a wife and children."

I hoped I had not exceeded the boundaries of our relationship too quickly. She was an independent little creature and I had no intention of pressuring her. Had she been hurt by someone? Although she seemed to like to hear my family stories, so full of love, I sensed she had never experienced that family closeness. There seemed to be a cold edge around her heart that I could not break through.

Although I was always busy with shipping business as my stern-wheelers continued to ply the Fraser River, and I had to make frequent trips over to New Westminster, whenever I was in Victoria I always made time for visits to the Caldwells on the days Jane was there and her lessons were about to end.

I realized I was like a lovesick young boy. I missed her when I was gone and couldn't wait to see her again when I returned.

We had at least become good friends over the weeks. I often took her to lunch or simply walked her back to her lodgings. Sometimes we would arrange to meet later for tea or dinner. I had never before experienced a proper courtship with a woman, and it felt good.

I had told her about my work, my love of the sea, about Victoria, and sometimes nostalgically about my home and family back in Scotland, but I remained puzzled by the fact that she said nothing about her own past unless I asked questions. I wanted to know everything about her, but I sensed a reticence in her behavior towards me.

And her brief description of her early life on a farm did not really explain how she came to be on the *Tynemouth*. And if she had enjoyed her life with the Sinclairs in London, what made her seek a new life on the other side of the world?

It made no sense.

* * *

One night I stopped in at the Western Star to visit Fleure. I felt guilty that I had ignored her of late.

I'd noticed a sign outside about new ownership. What on earth was going on? I was certainly not prepared for what she told me.

"I have sold this place, Gideon, and I'm moving back to San Francisco."

"My God, why? You are doing so well here, and I thought you loved Victoria, Fleure."

"Oh yes, I do, but I do miss San Francisco. Perhaps this was not the right decision for me."

"Really?" Why was it that women never seemed to be telling me the whole truth these days?

She poured me a drink at the bar. "Yes, really, Gideon. I also suspect that you will not miss me or even know I'm gone." She laughed. "You have become quite fascinated with a little English girl, I hear."

"I suppose Ed and James have been telling you stories."

"Are they true?"

I paused, reluctant to share my feelings. "Yes, I admit I find her very charming."

"Charming? I think perhaps it is more than that, my friend."

"Perhaps."

She laughed and patted my hand fondly. "Ah—men! They do not always admit to the obvious. But I wish you well, Gideon. Meanwhile, I will be back in San Francisco, thinking of you all. I will miss you and Ed, and especially James—but it must be."

"But why, Fleure? The Western Star is flourishing. Why do you need to leave? "

"It was the right time to sell, and I got a good price. And as I said, I do miss San Francisco."

She seemed determined, and there was no point in arguing with her. I would miss her. She had been a good friend, but selfishly, I realized it was probably for the best.

It might not be a good idea to have my future wife ever discover my past relationship with a saloon madam—as she well might if they were living in the same town.

CHAPTER 30: JANE

Before I knew it, Christmas was upon us.

Mrs. Brady's boarding house was decorated with greenery for the season. In fact, all the shops and businesses along Government Street were hung with garlands of holly and laurel, and some windows displayed decorated trees. Mayor Harris's butcher shop had large loins of beef hanging in the window, surrounding a boar's head with an apple in its mouth.

Mrs. Brady did her best to make all her boarders comfortable, and I was very happy living there. After I attended church with her on Christmas morning, Gideon called on me and invited me to join him and the Caldwells for a late lunch at the Windsor Hotel.

"Skiff will also be with us, Jane," he told me. I had met Skiff once before and we had got on well together, even though I was somewhat startled by his appearance when I'd first seen him.

"I admit I have never seen a person with his skin coloring, Gideon, but Skiff is so nice. I really like your friend."

I accepted Gideon's invitation for lunch, and after we had all dined, James gave me a gift of embroidered handkerchiefs, and I gave him a book by Mr. Charles Dickens. He had recently taken a great interest in the plight of the poor living in London, and he was thrilled with the small copy of the book called *Oliver Twist* I had found in the bookshop on Government Street. My own copy had comforted me on the voyage to Victoria.

"I was fortunate to find a bound copy, for it has apparently only recently been published in book form," I told him. "Previously it was only serialized in the London newspapers."

"I will treasure it always, Miss Hopkins," he said. "Thank you very much." I couldn't believe this was the same boy who had acted so badly towards me back in September.

"I'm delighted that James has taken such an interest in literature, Jane," said his father. This pleased me so much.

The three men then presented me with gifts, which I had not expected.

"Oh my goodness," I said in alarm. "I have nothing for you gentlemen."

They all laughed as I unwrapped Skiff's gift first.

"We don't need anything," Gideon said.

Skiff's present was a small painting of the *Sarah M* moored at Hope on the Fraser River.

"The Captain named this vessel for his ma back in Scotland," said Skiff. "I thought that you would like it, miss."

"Oh Skiff, I love it. And to think *you* painted it yourself. You have great talent." Skiff bowed his head in embarrassment and thanked me for the compliment.

Edward Caldwell's gift was a glass vase. "James has told me how you love to have flowers, Jane, so now you can always have flowers in your room."

"Thank you, Mr. Caldwell. You are very kind."

And then Gideon handed me a small box wrapped in gaily colored paper. Every eye in the room was on me, and I felt very uncomfortable. Beneath the wrapping was a carved wooden box with a lid inlaid with mother-of-pearl. I slowly lifted the lid and music played as a tiny dancer twirled inside. The music was a piece by Mr. Beethoven I often played, called *Fur Elise.*

"Oh Gideon ... it is ..." A tear trickled down my cheek. "I have never received anything so beautiful. Thank you so much."

I quickly wiped the tear away, as I felt so self-conscious. I had no desire to be vulnerable should the happiness of this day be ripped away from me.

As though sensing my embarrassment, Gideon changed the subject quickly. "Let's go into the lounge," he said, "and perhaps Jane will play for us so we can sing carols."

"It will be like that Christmas in San Francisco," said James. "I was just a small lad, but I still remember, Father, how we all sang those French carols Fleure taught me."

Suddenly, everyone started talking at once and we were soon singing carols together and enjoying the evening.

When Gideon took me back to Mrs. Brady's later, I told him that today had also been my birthday.

"Why didn't you tell us, Jane? It could have been a double celebration."

"The day was perfect anyway, Gideon. Thank you so much for my gift."

He smiled down at me. "Jane, you are so adorable. You smell of cinnamon and primroses and I want to touch you and so much more, but I am giving you fair warning this time. I am about to kiss you."

He first took my hand gently and raised it to his lips. "Please don't be afraid of me, Jane. I would never, ever harm you, although I sense that someone once did. Instead, I want you to feel joy when I hold you close and kiss you."

"Oh Gideon," was all I could say. Was I giving him permission? Perhaps so, because I liked it when he leaned in towards me, held my face between his hands and placed his lips gently on mine. But I could not imagine what the future might hold beyond that kiss.

We said goodnight and I went up to my room. I ran my finger across my lips trying to savor the moment as long as I could. The smell of pipe tobacco, mixed with the strong, salty sea-aroma cologne he always wore, lingered there.

Gideon had kissed me, and I admit I had liked it, but now I was even more confused. Being in his arms had felt safe, but was it what I truly wanted? Why had I allowed this to happen? I still craved my independence, and yet he made it feel so right to be there in his arms.

For a long time, I played with my music box before placing it on my dresser. I lay down on my bed, picked up Mrs. Browning's book of sonnets and started reading.

"How do I love thee, let me count the ways ..."

Is this what falling in love feels like? I decided not to think about it any longer that night and finally fell into a fitful sleep.

*   *   *

The days passed quickly, and soon spring was upon us.

Gideon had been very busy preparing for a new season of travellers who would need transport to the northern parts of the province, so it gave me time to think. He had only kissed me one more time, just before he left, but his intentions were becoming more and more obvious.

I also knew the Caldwells were now planning to return to New Westminster. I felt sad about this, because I had grown very fond of James and we now got along well. We were able to laugh together as we discussed his lessons, and I soon discovered he was a very bright young boy.

I sensed his knowledge on most subjects would soon far exceed my teaching capabilities. This, however, did not apply to his abilities at music, and there I was able to teach him a great deal. He began to enjoy playing the piano in the hotel lounge, and, although we started with simple scales and drills, we soon progressed to some short pieces, which James picked up with ease.

But I knew the day would come when my services would no longer be required and the Caldwells would return to New Westminster. I really wanted to stay in Victoria, but if I did, I would then need to search for another position. The thought was somewhat daunting.

One day in early March, Mr. Caldwell asked me to stay behind after our usual morning lesson. "I have something to discuss with you, Jane," he said. Even he now always used my first name. Life for a governess was far less formal in the new world.

"Yes, of course, Mr. Caldwell."

"James enjoys your lessons so much that I am reluctant to draw them to a close, even though I have to tell you that by the end of this month we will be moving back to our home in New Westminster. So I would like to ask you to come with us and continue teaching him, through the summer months at least, until September, when he will start a new school year over there. What do you think of that idea?"

I was overwhelmed. Not only would I have a few more months in this position, I would also be with people I liked and would not have to seek another position just yet. On the other hand, I did not fancy the prospect of leaving Victoria and especially of crossing over more water. My months at sea aboard the *Tynemouth* were still a nightmarish memory.

"I ... I am very honored ... but ..."

"Ah, I know, you want time to think about it. And have no fear that when this position does end, I would most certainly do all in my power to find another for you with high recommendations—either in New Westminster or back here in Victoria."

"Thank you. That is very kind, and I will give the matter careful consideration."

It seemed more than a little coincidental that two days later, when Gideon returned from his latest business trip up the Fraser River, he immediately sought me out at Mrs. Brady's with a strange request.

"Jane, I want you to be ready very early tomorrow morning for a surprise. I am hiring a carriage and driving you out to Beacon Hill. It is so beautiful right now, with yellow broom covering the hillside and the snow-capped mountains in the distance. We will take a picnic basket, which the hotel will prepare," he added.

"But Gideon, a picnic! It's still far too chilly." I laughed. "And I have some lessons to prepare for James for next week."

"No excuses! There will be time enough for lesson planning later. And we will take blankets to keep us warm."

"You seem to be so determined," I ventured. "But why tomorrow?"

"I am determined, Jane—more determined than I have ever been in my life. Please say you will be ready by ten o'clock. There is no time to waste. I have been patient long enough."

I tilted my head slightly and gazed into his dark brown eyes, which were smiling down at me in anticipation.

"Yes, Gideon, I will be ready, but really—a picnic in March?"

He was still laughing when he left, and that night I hardly slept because I'd hoped I wouldn't have to make a decision yet about my feelings for him.

But I kept wondering why he was so determined to take me on a picnic tomorrow, and at the same time dreading what it might well be about.

Suddenly I was facing things I did not want to face. I had come to the new world to start a new life, to be independent, and to better myself, *not* to find a husband. Could that be what he was implying? I had lied and connived myself into this position of independence, and I did not want that to change.

And yet I could not stop myself from remembering his crooked smile, his red-gold hair that curled at the nape, and the soft touch of his fingers on my skin. Wasn't that part of what I had always dreamed about? Becoming a lady in a big house and having servants? And how would I do that without a husband?

Gideon had always behaved like a perfect gentleman, treating me with great respect. I realized I must stop judging all men by my experience with Philip Sinclair, because I now knew that there were some good men in the world—and Gideon was one of them.

CHAPTER 31: GIDEON

Promptly at ten o'clock the next morning on that beautiful March morning, I drew up in a McBride's Transportation carriage outside Mrs. Brady's boardinghouse.

I jumped out, telling the driver to wait while I went inside. Jane was already in the parlor, dressed in a pretty beige woolen dress, which she usually wore for church. Her green eyes were sparkling.

"You look beautiful, Jane. Make sure you bring your cape, though—just in case."

She smiled at me. "Yes, I am well prepared. The sun is shining, but I'm sure it's still very chilly."

I linked her arm in mine as we stepped outside into the sunshine. As I helped her inside the carriage, I could see she was impressed.

"Gideon, this is a very elegant carriage. I love these plush red velvet seats and—the bouquet of snowdrops and primroses on the other seat is so pretty."

"The flowers are for you, my love," I said.

"Gideon, they are exquisite. Thank you."

I instructed the driver to head to Beacon Hill, where we were greeted by a sea of yellow daffodils mixed in with broom, covering the hillside in a blaze of brilliance. Across the Strait, the snow-capped Olympic Mountain Range stood majestically as a backdrop to this incredibly picturesque scene.

As the carriage drew to a halt by an oak tree, I helped Jane down and instructed the driver to return for us at noon.

I began to spread our blankets on the ground, and Jane started to laugh. "Gideon, this is ridiculous. It is much too cold for a picnic in March."

"But feel the sunshine, Jane. The first warmth of spring is always so special."

I pranced around like a happy child, laying out plates and opening up boxes containing cold chicken, fruit and more, which the hotel had prepared for me.

"Now, what shall we start with? Chicken? Bread? Some cheese? A little wine perhaps?"

She shook her head as I continued to cavort around, like a puppy wagging its tail at the pure joy of living.

"Gideon, you are so funny, but to satisfy you and to make you sit down, I will agree to eat some chicken and cheese, and even have a small glass of wine. This place is so lovely. It is almost magical." I was pleased she had acquired a taste for the occasional glass of wine whenever we dined together.

"Yes, my love, it is magical, which is why I chose it."

I finally sat down beside her and handed her a napkin with a chicken leg and a slice of cheese. I then opened the wine bottle and slowly began to pour us two glasses.

We fell into a comfortable silence as we gazed out across the water, watching the slight breeze make ripples on the sea. The blaze of yellow around us was startling and somewhat overpowering to the eye. The combination of that and perhaps the wine gave me the courage I needed.

"You are so beautiful, Jane. Since the first day I saw you, you know I have thought of little else."

"I fear you are seeing me through rose-coloured glasses."

"No, you truly are beautiful, inside and out, and you must know how I feel about you. I have made that far too obvious, I fear, even though I have also tried to be patient. I sensed you could not be rushed. I respect, and, yes, I love you far too much to spoil this, because what is happening between us is meant to be. It is our destiny, Jane."

"Gideon, you are talking nonsense. Destiny? Why, you hardly know me, nor I you."

"Then we must get to know more about one another, Jane, because I am about to ask you a question—and I'm warning you now, I will not take no for an answer."

"Oh?"

"Jane Hopkins, will you marry me, lass?" I took her hand in mine and then, much to my own amazement, knelt down on one knee. "I meant to do this properly, Jane. So, I'll ask you again, will you no' marry me?"

"Gideon, I don't know what to say. You are much older and more experienced than I am."

"I am twenty-seven and you ... you are ...?

"Just eighteen."

"Ha! Very little difference."

"Nine years!"

"So?"

"You have family and ..."

"Yes, and so do you. Even though your English family is gone, you now have me, and one day we will have our own children and a new family. As your husband, I will devote my life to making you happy. I know we will have a wonderful life together."

"Why did you have to ask me this question so suddenly and with such urgency, Gideon? We have only known one another for six months."

"Because I know the Caldwells want you to stay on as James's governess for a few more months, but as my wife you would not have to work. You would be Mrs. Gideon McBride and would have your own fine home in New Westminster and everything your heart desires."

She was silent for a moment, so I tilted my head towards her.

"Please look at me and say something, Jane."

"I'm thinking."

"Ah, a good sign. The lady is thinking. At least she has not said no."

"Gideon, I do want to continue teaching James for a while, which, I know, means moving to New Westminster as his governess. So I have to say no to your offer. I cannot marry you. It is far too soon."

"But why, Jane? Even if you continue to teach James until he goes back to school, we could still be married after that."

"But I cannot promise you that yet, Gideon."

I kissed her hand. "I will not give up, Jane. I can assure you of that. Maybe you need more time and I must prove my intentions are honorable."

"Maybe. Oh, Gideon, I just don't know."

I pulled her towards me and placed my lips on hers in a tender kiss. It was hard for me to restrain myself. I wanted so much more, and my body was responding to hers accordingly.

Although she didn't pull away, she seemed relieved that I went no further. Instead, we sat side by side together amidst that sea of yellow broom overlooking the ocean, and I vowed once again my undying love.

*　　*　　*

I still couldn't understand why Jane had turned me down, but I knew I wouldn't give up. Temporarily crestfallen, I buried myself in my work, hoping against hope that, given time, she would accept me. At the end of March, I crossed back over to New Westminster with Jane and the Caldwells.

"I'm already missing Victoria," I overheard her say to James as they stood by the ship's railing.

Maybe that would be something I could work on, I thought. If she loved Victoria, perhaps I could convince her that that was where we would live once we were married. I thought about the land I had purchased along the Gorge, for which Edward had negotiated a far better price for me. I had never talked to her about that, so I kept it at the back of my mind for now.

I walked to where she was standing on the deck with James. "It's not that far away, Jane. You will return one day, I'm sure. But look now at all these small islands. Aren't they charming?"

She nodded. "What are their names?"

When I told her the native names, she wanted to know what they all meant in English. I had noticed before how she always loved to learn. She was quick to pick up new things, and when I talked about my sternwheelers, I could see she had a definite aptitude for business.

"You will be intrigued by the Royal City of New Westminster, too. It was originally named Queensborough, but later Queen Victoria decreed that it should be called New Westminster."

"Ah, like Westminster in London," she said.

The town itself, other than a few small huts at the shoreline, could not be seen from the water as we drew closer.

"Once we climb that rise, you will see the town of New Westminster. The town site was laid out by the Royal Engineers."

As we disembarked and walked towards Royal Avenue, I explained to Jane that there was only one main street in town, and the Caldwells and I had adjoining houses there.

"Our houses were also built by the Royal Engineers in a Gothic style using California redwood throughout, and are similar in design."

"Tell me about them," she said.

"Well, each one has a large front parlor to the right of the entrance hall and a library or smoking room to the left. The dining room and kitchen are at the rear. There's a narrow flight of stairs leading to the upper floor, where there are three bedrooms, and a second, smaller flight leads to two more small rooms, which are the servants' quarters. Mrs. Finch, Edward's housekeeper, occupies one, and now the other will be yours at the Caldwells' house. You'll soon see it all for yourself."

We headed first to the Caldwells' house, where Mrs. Finch welcomed us and then took Jane upstairs to her room to settle her.

Mrs. Finch was a rotund lady with a superfluity of fat that made her appear cuddly rather than obese. She was constantly smiling, her red cheeks aglow, and I knew she would take Jane under her wing and make her feel comfortable. She was a warm, caring woman and in many ways reminded me of my own mother.

During the following months, I continued to be the perfect gentleman with Jane, but soon it must have been quite obvious to everyone that I absolutely adored her. I was already hatching a plan to make her accept my next proposal.

One night, as Edward and I had sat together smoking cigars on the front porch outside my house, I shared my thoughts with him.

"I know how you feel about her, Gideon, but please be cautious. She is somewhat fragile, I feel, despite that outward bravado she exhibits."

"I have been patient, Ed. Good God, I already made a fool of myself once, back in March, by proposing marriage."

"You did? What happened?"

"She turned me down flat."

He threw back his head and laughed. "Good for her! Just what you deserve, old chap. Remember, you have lived a pretty adventurous, wild life until now, but she is a delicate flower and has led a far different life."

"I'm hoping she will accept me despite all my faults."

The next day, I went over to Ed's house to discuss a legal issue. Mrs. Finch answered the door and invited me inside.

"Mr. Caldwell has left for his office, Captain, but should return shortly. I can make you some coffee while you wait." She returned to the kitchen and I went into the smoking room to wait. But just then, I overheard voices and realized Jane and James were talking in the parlor.

"I think my dad needs a wife, Miss Hopkins. I think he should marry you."

I heard her soft laugh. "Things don't work that way, James," she said.

"Yes, I know that. My father told me that he knew Uncle Gideon was completely smitten with you the moment he saw you, so he was not about to fight with his best friend over a woman."

"Well, I'm sure he had no intention of fighting for me anyway, James."

"Don't be too sure. I think my father cares for you a lot."

Their voices drifted away, leaving me bewildered. Did Ed care for Jane, too? Perhaps that was why he had told me to go slowly in my pursuit of her and why he was glad Jane had turned me down. Maybe, I considered, I should move my plan along before someone else steals Jane's heart, even my best friend.

So in June, I asked Jane to accompany Skiff and me on a day visit back to Victoria. I had decided to put my plan into action. I wanted to show her the land I had purchased the year before along the Gorge Arm waterway.

CHAPTER 32: JANE

In March I had turned down Gideon's proposal of marriage, and I soon began to doubt he would ever propose again, despite what he'd said.

I kept asking myself if I truly loved him. I felt sure that I did, but something inherent in my nature made me question my feelings. Inwardly my heart was full of joy and almost bursting that day when he'd asked me. I had wanted to dance on that hillside, hoping that at last I'd found love and was at peace. Surely I was safe from all the evils I'd left behind.

But the words would not yet come. I was too afraid to admit my feelings, in case this joy was also taken away from me. Would I ever be able to dismiss those losses I had suffered as a child? How could I ever forget how it felt to care about someone so much and then have that person leave and wrench away my happiness?

Worst of all, how could I accept Gideon's proposal if I didn't explain all my lies? If I told him the truth about my past, would he feel the same way about me?

So instead, on that March morning, I had simply allowed myself to be held momentarily in his tight embrace. And I prayed that one day I would be able to make the right decision—whatever that might be.

Gideon had accompanied us over to New Westminster when I left with the Caldwells at the end of March, and in the following weeks he behaved perfectly towards me. I began to think I was right and he would never ask me to marry him again.

But one day in June, he asked me to accompany him and Skiff over to Victoria for the day. At first I was reluctant, as I always hated the thought of crossing the water. However, as the weather was perfect that day, I eventually agreed.

The sailing was very smooth, and after a delightful lunch in town, we left Skiff. Gideon then hired a pony and trap and we headed north.

"I want to show you some land I own, Jane," he said.

I immediately fell in love with the surrounding countryside as we travelled along the narrow trail, bordered by wild roses growing in profusion on both sides.

To our left was the Gorge Arm of the Selkirk Water, a narrow waterway heading away from the harbour, and to our right, dense forest land. Finally, we reached the acreage Gideon had purchased. He helped me out of the trap and we stood for a moment in silence on the rise, gazing down the sloping hillside towards the water.

"This is the land I purchased last year," he said. "What do you think of it?"

"Gideon, this is magnificent! How many acres do you own?"

"Twenty-five. Do you really like it? The land stretches for quite a way in that direction—over to the other rise you see there, and beyond. Come, let's explore."

I saw his excitement as we started to walk. I began to feel an enormous sense of peace. I could not quite explain it, but for some reason I sensed I had finally come home. As we walked, he took my hand in his.

"What do you think about me building a house here, Jane?"

"Right here? But what about your New Westminster house?"

"There is much talk about the capital city being Victoria one day, and you love the city as much as I do."

"Yes, but surely your business is better run from New Westminster."

"Not necessarily. I can always work from here, too. I would keep the New Westminster house for when I'm over there. But this land is so peaceful—and perfect for a large mansion."

"I feel that peace, too."

He smiled down at me. "Then it's settled. I will build a house right here. But only on one condition—that this time you accept my marriage proposal. You can design the house exactly as you want it. Now, what kind of house is it to be?"

"Oh Gideon, what a question. I have no idea about houses. And it is your house, not mine."

"It will be *our* house, Jane, yours and mine. If you will only say yes to my proposal. "

I was silent for a long time.

"And I will buy you your very own piano, my love," he said.

"I think it will be a grand mansion, Gideon."

"And?"

"Are you sure you still want me?"

"Goodness, woman! Have I not made that abundantly clear by now?"

"Yes, Gideon."

"Yes, I have made it clear, or yes, you will marry me?"

"Both."

He was so taken aback that he simply stood there with his mouth wide open.

"Aren't you going to say anything, Gideon?"

"Oh Jane, there are a million things I could say." Instead, he lifted me in his arms and swung me round and round. "I love you, and I promise to make you the happiest woman in the world. Now, what sort of house are we going to have?"

"Perhaps like Enderby House in London, where the Sinclairs lived? We could include all that was so special in their mansion in London. We could have a great hall with black and white marble tiles and a staircase that rises up and then separates to the left and to the right, and it will be made of redwood, like the one in your New Westminster house. And we will have a large drawing room, with bay windows overlooking a rose garden, and you will have a smoking room. Upstairs, we will have many bedrooms. Oh, and another floor with a turret, where you could look out across to the harbour and watch the vessels coming and going. And there should be verandas, lots of verandas, circling the house, so that in the evenings we can sit and admire the garden."

"My, my! My little wife-to-be certainly *does* have lots of ideas," he said. "I love to see your enthusiasm."

"Oh Gideon, I'm so sorry. Have I gone too far?"

"Not at all. The house will have whatever you desire, my love. And the grounds will be magnificent, with rolling lawns down to the water. Rose gardens, Italian gardens, whatever your heart desires."

He squeezed my hand and kissed me more passionately.

I ran a short distance down the slope, looking back up to where he stood gazing down at me. "Gideon, this is the most perfect spot for a house. It will be ideal."

"It must be providence that I brought you here today, my love."

"That's it! That's it, Gideon!"

"What is *it*? Now what have you thought of?"

"The name of the house! *Providence*! We should call it Providence. You have always said that destiny brought us together, and now providence brought us here today. That will be the name of our home." He ran down to where I stood and kissed me again. It was settled. We were officially betrothed.

It was only much later that I realized that, although I had accepted Gideon's proposal and the idea of us building a house, I hadn't actually said I loved him.

CHAPTER 33: GIDEON

My plan had worked. This time she had accepted my proposal.

I had lured Jane back to Victoria, despite her dislike of crossing the water, with the promise of building us a house on the land I'd purchased the year before, along the Gorge Arm waterway. So as soon as we returned to New Westminster later that day, we went straight to Ed's house and told the Caldwells and Mrs. Finch that we were to be married.

Edward congratulated us and shook my hand, telling me what a lucky man I was.

James threw himself into Jane's arms. "I'm sorry I was so horrible to you when you first came to teach me, but I've really grown to love you, Miss Jane, and I'm so happy you are marrying Uncle Gideon."

"Thank you, James," Jane said as she wiped away a tear.

Mrs. Finch clucked around the room like a mother hen, her face beaming. "I'll make your wedding gown and trousseau, Miss Jane," she said. "We'll get started right away."

"Yes, you'd better hurry, Mrs. Finch," I said. "We plan to marry very soon, probably September?" I looked at Jane for confirmation.

"But we haven't talked of a date yet, and September is so soon," she said. "Maybe we should wait until next spring."

Why was she hesitating?

"We have waited too long as it is, my love. And Ed, we have decided to build a house on the land I purchased in Victoria the day I first met Jane."

"That's wonderful, old chap." Edward turned to Jane and raised an eyebrow. "Jane, are you absolutely sure you want to take on this rogue?"

She nodded, putting her arm through mine and smiling. "I'm fortunate that he wants to take *me* on, Edward."

In the weeks that followed, while Mrs. Finch organized numerous dress fittings for Jane, I made many trips over to Victoria to supervise the building of Providence.

But amidst all the turmoil and excitement, I constantly asked myself if she really loved me. Many times she appeared distant, as though she was worrying about something. Had I rushed her into this? Everything in this new land must be so strange for her, so maybe that was the problem. But still I felt it was more than that. Something else was wrong, but I couldn't quite put my finger on it. What was she so afraid of?

I tried to dismiss these thoughts by occupying myself with work. I also met with an architect named Gerald Wright, and together we worked on the house plans, embracing all that Jane had wanted in the design.

Whenever we discussed the house together, Jane seemed to come alive. I hoped she wasn't marrying me only because of what I could give her. But I didn't believe that, because she wasn't that kind of woman. It just seemed that what I was offering her was fulfilling all her childhood dreams. And who was I to question that? I loved her so much, I only wanted to give her everything and make her happy.

*   *   *

Edward accompanied me on one of my frequent trips across the Strait to inspect and supervise the house building. The redwood lumber had by then arrived in Victoria harbour from San Francisco and had been shipped up the Gorge waterway by barge to our property. It now stood piled up by the water's edge.

The house foundation had already been excavated, and large stones from a nearby quarry were being fashioned by two masons I'd hired. The whole area was buzzing with activity.

"Many of these labourers have just come up from San Francisco, Gid, especially the Chinese," Ed pointed out. "Do you plan on housing them somewhere while they work?"

I hadn't thought about that before, but it was a good point.

"Perhaps I should have a shack built down by the water, Ed. It could later be a boathouse, but meanwhile it would be somewhere for them to sleep and eat."

As Ed and I discussed this possibility, a young Chinese fellow walked over to us. He was slight of build, with a long pigtail hanging down his back.

"Thankee, Captain McBride, for giving me this job. I promise we build you beautiful house here. I like it here. Good place. It has good feng shui. Wind and water good for you in this place."

I smiled at him.

"I'm glad you like it. What's your name?"

"Ah Foo, siree."

"Well, Ah Foo, my friend and I were just discussing how we could house all the workers while you are here. How would you like to build a bunk house down by the water, with beds for you all? I would provide blankets and your food."

His face lit up, beaming from ear to ear. "Very good, Cap'n. We very happy with that idea. We come every day and work hard for you."

He went off to his fellow workers and told them in Cantonese what I'd said. He appeared to be the only one who spoke a little English, so I hoped they would understand the building foreman when he gave them instructions.

They all grinned and bowed to us, and we bowed back. From my experience in San Francisco working with the Chinese, I knew they were hard workers, and I felt sure they would build their place quickly and that our house would be erected with equal speed.

On subsequent visits, I was extremely pleased with the progress of the house, and to see four of the Chinese labourers already installed in their simple bunk house.

As the house continued to grow, I often spotted Ah Foo working alongside the others. Sometimes he waved at me, but mostly he was engrossed in his work. There was something mystical about him that made me notice him more than the others.

*   *   *

I was also busy making plans for our wedding. It was to take place at noon on September 5, 1863, at the home of Edward and James Caldwell, and the Reverend Matthew Bolton would be performing the ceremony.

During the weeks leading up to that day, I often felt overwhelmed with passion for Jane, but I had never stepped over the boundaries of propriety with her. We had kissed often and I had held her close to me, but my frustration about wanting more was beginning to show.

In normal circumstances, I would have been tempted to visit a whorehouse or saloon and relieve my frustration. It had been a year since I'd had sex with a woman and it was becoming harder and harder to stay faithful to Jane every day. But I loved her too much to spoil things now. We were so close to our wedding night, and I was sure I could wait. I wondered, selfishly, whether, if Fleure had still been in town, the temptation to visit her for a night of passion would have been too great. Perhaps it was better she had left Victoria and was now far away in San Francisco.

But one night towards the end of August, on a visit to Victoria just ten days before our wedding, I found myself walking along Government Street, heading towards the Western Star. I'd spent the day out at the building site, trying to keep busy so as to alleviate my frustrations that way—but it hadn't worked.

Since Fleure left, the Western Star had ceased to be a respectable hotel. It now advertised out front exactly what it was—a saloon where girls could be enjoyed by the hour. I stood at the swing doors for a long time before pushing them open and going in.

A brazen, overbearing woman wearing ghoulish makeup came up to me immediately.

"What can we do for you tonight, sir?" she said. "A drink? One of my girls?"

"Just a whisky."

She took me to the bar and poured me a drink.

"Now dearie, just you take a look over there. Pick any one of my girls for your pleasure upstairs. Aren't they all the most beautiful women you have ever seen anywhere?"

I looked to where she pointed. Suddenly I felt completely nauseated by what I was seeing—and wretched about being there at all.

What was I doing? I didn't belong here. What the hell was I thinking?

I drank the whisky down in one gulp and turned back to the madam as I threw a coin on the bar.

"As a matter of fact, madam, they are *not* the most beautiful girls. Thanks for the offer, but I've already found the most beautiful woman in the whole world, and I'm marrying her next week." With that I turned round and headed for the door.

I heard her mutter something behind my back about being insulted, but I didn't care. Outside, the crisp night air and later a tepid bath back at the Windsor Hotel made me feel invigorated.

And that night was when I realized just how much I truly loved Jane.

CHAPTER 34: JANE

The morning of our wedding, I woke to the sight of my pale ivory satin wedding dress, with its elegant hoopskirt, hanging in my bedroom. Was this really happening to me?

It would be the first hoopskirt I had ever worn, a fashionable style worn by ladies of the upper class. My dress had a bodice trimmed in duchess lace, and I would be carrying a shower bouquet of pink roses, which would be delivered later.

My trousseau consisted of two other gowns. Mrs. Finch's niece was a seamstress, and she had helped her in making these over the past weeks. One dress was of a light pink rattine; the other, a pale green and apricot wool dress trimmed in lace. Mrs. Finch had also made me two white crepe de chine nightdresses, which were exquisite. I knew I would be wearing one of those tonight. She had repeatedly told me how beautiful I would look for the Captain.

I had never imagined owning clothes like these. I had now achieved all my dreams. But at what cost? Did I deserve all this? When had I become that lying, deceitful person?

As I lay daydreaming, a tap came at the door and Mrs. Finch brought me in a tray of tea and toast and some fruit.

"You must keep up your strength today, Miss Jane." She smiled as she set the tray down and opened the drapes, letting in the sun.

I didn't feel like eating, but I managed to nibble on the toast as she chatted away, all the time thinking about the lies I had told Gideon and the Caldwells to get where I was today. How could I have been so deceitful? But what choice did I have?

Later, as Mrs. Finch helped me dress, she let out a gasp when she saw the scars on my back. "Oh dear God," she said. "What happened to your back?" This time my lips were ready with another lie.

"It was a terrible accident on the farm," I said. "I fell onto some wire and cut myself badly."

She tutted. "Oh, poor sweet. The scars look so painful."

I was on the point of tears, wondering if Gideon would also accept the lie so easily. But then, as I felt the softness of my undergarments touch my skin and I ran my hands over my satin wedding gown, the tears really came. I was thinking about how far I had come from the days at the orphanage and how much I had at stake by perpetuating these lies. Mrs. Finch simply assumed that I was an emotional bride as she kept fussing around me.

But, later that day, as I made my vows to love, honour and obey my husband, I also silently vowed I would be a good wife to Gideon despite the lies I'd told him. I prayed he would never discover the whole truth about my past. I doubted he would still want me if he knew everything about me.

After the short ceremony, we had a celebration party with a few neighbours and close friends, including Skiff. He brought with him a much younger black woman called Dulcie, whom he'd met on Salt Spring, one of the islands between Victoria and the mainland. He lived there on the island now, with a community of other black folk, but he still worked for Gideon in New Westminster and Victoria.

Dulcie was a friendly soul who appeared to adore Skiff, and the feeling was obviously mutual. They constantly gazed into each other's eyes, and Dulcie had her arm looped through Skiff's the whole time. Gideon joked that theirs would be the next wedding.

Everyone drank to our health and wished us well. I was now officially Mrs. Gideon McBride.

*   *   *

At nightfall, Gideon and I slipped away to his house next door, where we would live until Providence was finished. The apprehension

I felt earlier in the day returned with such force I thought I would faint. Would Gideon discover the truth? Would he know that I wasn't a virgin, that I'd been spoiled? Would he be disappointed in me?

He did not seem bothered at all as he whisked me away from the group of merrymakers and carried me through the entrance to our home. He very gently put me down in the hall and told me to close my eyes.

"I haven't given you your wedding present yet, my love," he whispered as he took my hand and led me into the parlor. "Now you can open your eyes."

My mouth opened, too, in amazement, for there by the window stood an upright mahogany piano.

"Oh, Gideon. What have you done?"

"I ordered it from Kirkham's in London. It came around the Horn and mercifully survived the journey. It is your very own piano, my love, just as I promised."

I thought then that I must have died and gone to heaven. How could I ever repay this man who had brought me such happiness and joy? He had made all my dreams come true. Everything I had ever wanted was now mine.

I ran over and touched the keys. Tears spilled down my cheeks. "It's beautiful. Oh, Gideon, it's magnificent! Thank you, thank you."

Putting his arms around me, he kissed me gently. "Tomorrow, you can play it to your heart's content, but now, my dear wife, we will retire to bed, and I hope tonight I will be able to bring you other joys and show you just how much I love you."

He picked me up with ease and practically ran up the flight of stairs to our bedroom. "You're as light as a feather, Mrs. McBride," he said as he laid me on the bed.

Mrs. McBride sounded so good. I was no longer Jane Hopkins. I had a husband, a house being built for me, and now a piano!

"Oh, my beautiful dress," I cried. "It will get wrinkled."

"Then we must take it off," he murmured. And he did. In mere seconds, I was lying on my back in only my undergarments, feeling rather foolish as I watched him hang up my dress so carefully. He then began to undress with alacrity until he stood completely naked before me, showing me his muscular body, so strong and firm.

"I love you, Jane," he whispered as he lay down beside me. "Never, ever, forget that. I will try not to hurt you, because I want this to be pleasurable for you as well as for me." He began to stroke my face and neck. His fingers played with the strings of my camisole, and his hands brushed my breasts. "You are so beautiful."

I turned slightly as his hands reached under my camisole and explored me further. I forgot for a moment the terrible secret I had carried with me for so long, but as he turned me slightly to kiss my shoulder I felt his hand caressing my back. He removed my camisole completely and I heard him gasp.

"Oh, my poor darling. What happened to your back?"

He had pulled the camisole down away from my scarred back, where Mrs. Creed had beaten me so long ago. The ridges of her leather whip, although long healed, must still be clearly visible embedded across my back. If I told Gideon the truth about being beaten, I would have to explain about the orphanage and Mrs. Creed—and everything else.

I turned to face him. "I know it's ugly, Gideon. I'm sorry."

"My darling, my poor sweet love. What happened?"

So I decided to tell him the same lie I'd told Mrs. Finch earlier. I couldn't believe how easily these lies slipped off my tongue.

"Oh, it was just an accident on the farm, Gideon, years ago. I fell backwards off a bale of hay onto some wire which we used to restrain the cows. It cut my back badly. I know it must look ugly."

He listened intently and I could not tell from his expression whether or not he believed me. When I stopped talking, he began to tenderly kiss me. He started slowly kissing my damaged back, taking time over each scar.

He was so gentle. "I hope my kisses erase all the pain you suffered," he whispered.

Then he kissed my shoulders, my neck, and, turning me over to face him, he kissed my lips. His lips moved down to my breasts, his tongue licking and sucking on each nipple, while his hands continued to explore my body lower down.

But I felt nothing but emptiness. My body didn't stir. I wanted to be aroused, as I assumed women were when touched at the core of their most secret place.

I tried. Oh dear Lord, how I tried. When he finally entered me and our bodies were joined together as man and wife, all I could think about was when my body had been violated by Philip Sinclair. I could still see his face above me and smell his sweat and the odor of whisky. I just lay beneath Gideon in terror, but he smiled at me and continued to hold me until he was completely spent and we fell asleep in each other's arms.

The next morning, I noticed there was no blood on the sheets, as there had been after my encounter with Philip Sinclair. Would that reveal to Gideon that I was no longer a virgin? Did blood only come the first time?

My thoughts were in turmoil, but I also doubted I would ever be able to fulfill his needs as a passionate wife should.

Nonetheless, that night of our wedding, I vowed I would try with my entire being. After all, I now had everything I had ever wanted. I had lied to make all those dreams come true, and it was now a lie I had to learn to live with.

* * *

By January of 1864, I had still seen no sign that I might be carrying a child, so I decided to talk to Mrs. Finch. I hoped I wasn't damaged internally by the violation of my body. I remember Lady Sinclair's physician saying that I had some scarring. What did that mean?

"Is there something wrong with me, Mrs. Finch?" I asked her one day. "I thought by now a baby would be on the way, and yet ..."

I desperately wanted to have a child. Gideon often talked about the family we would one day have and laughingly said that it was a good thing Providence had many bedrooms, because we would have numerous children to fill those rooms.

Gideon's passion for me was always obvious, so I thought there must be something wrong with me for not conceiving a baby. I knew little about the body's anatomy or the workings of a woman's menstrual cycle, which I always thought of as "the curse." No one, other than Rose at Field House, had ever talked to me about such mysteries, so I assumed that once my husband joined his body with mine, I would automatically find myself with child. I had feared that after I'd been violated by that odious man..

"Are you perhaps taking precautions?" Mrs. Finch said.

"Precautions? Oh, no ..." I stammered, my face growing hot. I hadn't the vaguest idea what such *precautions* might be.

"Yes, dear, like trying to prevent yourself from having a baby just yet. There are many new ways, so I hear, and after all, there is plenty of time, and you are still so young."

"No ... we are just ..." I blushed. "... just doing it, Mrs. Finch."

She smiled gently. "Of course, my dear. Well, give it time. These things happen in their own sweet time, you know. You've only been married a few months."

And so I tried to forget my concerns and continued to endure the rituals in our marriage bed. I feel a sense of guilt for thinking of it as endurance, because I was sure that I now loved Gideon with all my heart. It was simply that for some reason my body could not respond with passion the way it should. And even though I now felt this incredible love inside for Gideon, even my response to him in everyday life was often cold and emotionless.

What was wrong with me?

* * *

There was still much talk in political circles as to where the new capital city would be—Victoria or New Westminster. We favoured Victoria, because within a year our house should be finished and we would be moving back there.

Gideon and Edward often became embroiled in political discussions in Victoria about the future of the colony.

"Will you be all right on your own, Jane?" he asked me whenever he went away.

"Gideon, of course I'll be all right. I have Mrs. Finch and James to keep me company next door."

When Gideon was home in New Westminster, our evenings were often spent discussing business and political matters in the company of other men in our circle of friends. I loved to join these discussions, and Gideon allowed me to sit with the men, even though women were usually excluded from such matters.

"You, my sweet little Jane," he told me on more than one occasion, "are smarter and more knowledgeable than most men." We laughed together and it felt good.

During that time, we also often dined with the recently married Caroline and Peter O'Reilly. O'Reilly had been the Gold Commissioner in the Cariboo, and they were now living in New Westminster but intended to move back to Victoria one day. We also dined with Joseph and Julia Trutch, in-laws of the O'Reillys.

"These people seem very grand to me," I said. I purposely never talked about England when we were with them, in case they happened to know the Sinclairs.

Because Gideon's fleet continued to expand, he often left on even longer business trips. He frequently travelled up to Quesnel at the top of the Fraser, where he'd established another office. I felt safe while he was away, as Mrs. Finch was close by and James came over twice a week for piano lessons. James had by then returned to school in New Westminster. He had turned twelve and would soon be heading back east to a prestigious boarding school in Upper Canada. Edward was reluctant to part with him, but thought it best for his all-round education and character building.

That spring, we all made a trip over to Victoria to see the arrival of the new Governor, Arthur Kennedy. James Douglas had now stepped down, after almost twenty-one years of being the chief power figure, first as governor of the colony of Vancouver Island and then of British Columbia.

One night, we watched the grand parade as Governor Kennedy and his family drove through the streets of Victoria in a splendid carriage and horses, and later that evening we all gathered at the St. George Hotel to listen as the Governor was serenaded by the German Choral Society in a moving torchlight ceremony. Everyone now felt optimistic about the future of the colony. The new Governor's arrival seemed to herald an era of prosperity.

That same night, as we ate dinner together at the Windsor Hotel, we had more good news from Edward.

"I have also decided to build a house in Victoria," he told us. "It will be on the land I purchased in James Bay, so I will be near to you both at Providence."

"Oh, that's wonderful, Edward," we both chimed in.

"And I won't be so lonely while James is away at school. Mrs. Finch is coming too, as my housekeeper."

The next day, Gideon and I inspected the construction on our home and were delighted with the progress. We were told it would be finished by September, exactly one year since our wedding. I felt that life was indeed perfect.

So, despite my nervousness about the whole subject of pregnancy, the very next day I made an appointment with Dr. Helmcken, James Douglas's son-in-law. I said nothing to Gideon about it, but I'd heard good reports about him as a physician from Mrs. Finch and felt I could trust him. Many people referred to him lovingly as "Dr. Heal-My-Skin."

After examining me, he confirmed my hopes that I was indeed already with child, and the baby would arrive in early November. Being very ignorant about these matters, I accepted his assessment and practically ran all the way back to the Windsor Hotel to tell Gideon. He was ecstatic and insisted that I must rest often and that he would watch me constantly.

"I will not make any trips away from home until after the birth," he said.

"Oh, Gideon, it is still months away, and I have Mrs. Finch right next door in New Westminster."

I was now longing to get back to our house on Royal Avenue to tell her the news.

*   *   *

But one afternoon towards the end of May, I began to feel very ill.

The pains started in earnest while Mrs. Finch and I were having tea together. She laid me down on the couch and loosened my corset. Then, placing a cool rag across my forehead, she ran to the front door. I heard her yelling to someone in the street.

"Run immediately and fetch Dr. Belmont from down the road, and then go to Captain McBride's offices at the wharf—quickly."

After that, I remember very little else. I drifted in and out of consciousness. There was a wet sticky feeling between my legs, and for a moment I thought I was back at Field House and my curse had begun. But this was far worse. I sat up for a moment, looking down at the blood spreading like red ink and beginning to seep through my dress.

It was my baby. My baby was coming—but much too soon. I was losing it in a pool of blood now staining the couch and dripping onto the carpet. By the time Gideon and the doctor arrived moments later, our longed-for child was gone.

Gideon took me in his arms and sobbed, but I felt nothing. Nothing but emptiness once again engulfed me, as something very precious had been taken from me. Nothing Gideon, Mrs. Finch, or the Caldwells said to me later could console me.

"Dr. Belmont has assured us that there will be other babies, Jane," Gideon kept telling me, but it made little difference to how I felt. My heart was already broken in two. I told myself I was doomed to see all the most joyful things in my life taken away from me.

This was obviously going to be my punishment for lying.

PROVIDENCE
(1864–1869)

CHAPTER 35: GIDEON

On the 6th of September, 1864, we moved into Providence.

The house was well-designed, with many stylish rooms inside, and was surrounded with large verandas—just as Jane had wanted.

As we walked around inspecting everything on that first day, I thought back to when I was a lad living in a shack with my family in Scotland. The room we'd all slept in was about the same size as my smoking room alone in Providence.

Jane's eyes were wide with amazement. "I can't believe we are the owners of such an enormous mansion," she said.

And when we stood on our rear veranda and looked to the west, down towards the water, we both were again stunned by the exquisite view.

"By next year, we will have all that shrubbery cleared away and there will be green lawns all the way to the water's edge. Perhaps a rose garden by the following year. What do you think?"

"Oh yes," she sighed. "That sounds wonderful."

I was sure she was excited with the plans, so I continued. "And we will buy all the very best furnishings for the house—crystal chandeliers; a large oak dining table and comfortable sofas and chairs in the drawing room."

"Can we afford all that?"

"Yes, my darling, we can."

She smiled, but her beautiful eyes were still so sad. Where was that enthusiastic young woman who had cavorted around on this land as we'd planned the house. Would she—would we—ever be able to recapture that joy?

One day, as the leaves of autumn turned golden, we were sitting on the front porch enjoying the warmth of the early evening sunshine when a young Chinese man I recognized wandered up our driveway and bowed to us.

"I am Ah Foo," he said. "Remember me, Cap'n? I worked on house and now look for more work."

His pigtail bobbed up and down behind him as he spoke. "When I came off boat from Canton last year, you hired me to work here. But I can do many other things too. You need me now, yes?"

I stood up to greet him, bowing back in acknowledgment. "Yes, I remember you, Ah Foo. You were a hard worker. Can you also cook?"

"Oh yessee."

"But, Gideon," Jane said, "I do our cooking."

"I know, my love, but you are the mistress of this large house and you deserve to have someone do these things for you."

I turned back to Ah Foo. "Can you clean? And chop wood? And garden?"

"All those things I do."

"Ah Foo, this is my wife, Mrs. McBride."

"Pleased to meet you, Mrs. Cap. Your husband is good man. I call him Mister Cap and you Mrs. Cap. Okay?"

We both laughed. "That's fine, Ah Foo," I said. "Mister and Mrs. Cap we are. We don't have a houseboy, so we could certainly use one. When can you start?"

"I start now. Show me kitchen. I cook you first meal tonight."

Jane showed him the kitchen and the servant's room he would be sleeping in, and I arranged with him the wages he would receive if he did a good job. We told him we would hire him on a week's trial. I must admit it did feel good to actually have a servant living in the house, and I thought it would lighten the load for Jane and make her feel better.

Ah Foo turned out to be a treasure. The meals he conjured up for us in the kitchen were beyond belief. They were tasty and wholesome, and he served them to us with style. He made roast beef taste rich and juicy and prepared succulent vegetables. He more than passed his trial that first week. Not only could he turn out a meal of excellence for the two of us, but whenever we had company in the following weeks, he presented an equally magnificent dinner for any number of people.

"But if more than eight people for dinner, I need help with serving dishes," he informed us, and we readily agreed. He was an absolute treasure, so at that point we would have agreed to anything.

"His culinary and serving skills are equal to anything I saw in London," Jane said.

And his proficiency did not end in the kitchen. He kept our house spotless from top to bottom and resented any interference. There was never a speck of dust to be found anywhere. He merely listened to instructions and followed them to the letter, adding his own little embellishments along the way. He found amazing cleaning materials in Chinatown which he used at Providence making the house sparkle.

In the garden, he was also a marvel and could do just about anything required of him. Where, we often asked ourselves, had this incredible young man learned so many skills? And how had we been so lucky to have him come into our lives? I had always felt there was something special about him, and he soon became an integral part of our life.

We could not imagine Providence without him.

* * *

Jane spent a great deal of time over the coming year playing the piano that now stood in our drawing room. I loved to watch her, as playing seemed to help alleviate the sorrow she still felt about the loss of our baby. At other times she retreated into her shell and refused to discuss the matter whenever I brought it up.

Then, in the spring of 1865, Jane miscarried a second time, causing her to retreat even further into despair. I felt her pain as well as my own, but she would not allow me to comfort her, and it made me feel useless.

"My own mother suffered the loss of two babies before I was born," I told her, but it didn't help.

"So?" she snapped. "How does that help me now?"

We were, therefore, quite unable to enjoy the May Ball that year held at Carey Castle, the new official residence of the Governor. We were invited, along with Edward and many friends, and it was a very grand affair. We were now firmly established as part of the so-called elite circle of Victoria, but Jane took no joy in any of it.

The months went by, but Jane's sadness refused to go away, so when the Christmas season started that year, bringing with it the usual number of invitations to parties and balls, I was far from enthusiastic. Sometimes our house seemed like a morgue, and my frustration about Jane's attitude grew. We frequently argued about the most trivial of things.

After one very long and unpleasant day at work, I was still sitting in my office going over the books late into the evening. Something seemed wrong, but I couldn't quite put my finger on it.

"Jim, come in here for a moment," I called out.

My bookkeeper, Jim Benson, came in from the next room, looking worried. No doubt my obvious foul mood all day had upset everyone at McBride's.

"Jim, I talked to you about these discrepancies last week." I pointed to the ledger. "At the time, you said it was just an error in adding up the figures, but I think it must be more than that. More money appears to be missing this week. Do you know what happened? Did you lie to me last week?"

"I'm sorry, Captain. I, er ... I took some money out, but I intended to return it."

"Why did you steal, Jim? I pay you well enough."

"I gambled a bunch of money and lost it all. I had nothing left at the end of the week for my wife and children."

I understood the folly of gambling only too well, but I'd learned my lesson long ago.

"But, by God, man, why the hell didn't you tell me? I could have helped you out of the mess if you'd told me the truth."

He hung his head. "I was stupid, I know."

"How can I ever trust you again? You know I will have to fire you because of this, don't you? But I will pay you for the next two weeks to tide you over. But no more gambling, d'yer hear?"

He grabbed my hand. "I'm sorry, Captain. I was desperate."

"I understand—but that's no excuse, Jim. I will try and find another job for you somewhere else, though."

That was the best I could do, but I hated firing a man already in financial difficulties, and Jim had been a good bookkeeper. But I would never again feel confident while he was in my employ.

* * *

Later that evening, as Jane and I sat in the library before Ah Foo called us for a late supper, she sensed my mood. "Whatever is wrong?" she asked.

"It's Benson. I had to fire him!"

"Why? What happened?"

"It's a long story. He stole money from me."

"Jim? Are you sure?"

"Yes. He admitted it. He lost money gambling."

I poured myself a whisky and Jane a sherry. "I hate this kind of thing, Jane. I didn't want to fire him, but he lied—so I knew I could never trust him again."

As I handed her the glass, she looked up at me with a strange, anxious expression on her face. "Is that how you feel about all liars?" she said.

"Jane, let's talk about something else. I think perhaps we should hire a personal maid for you."

"Where did that come from? I don't need a maid. I'm perfectly capable of dressing myself and doing my own hair. I don't need to be pampered."

Her irritated response baffled me. She had told me once long ago that she had always dreamed of being a lady of importance, and yet now had dismissed my offer with disdain. Why had she changed?

"But all ladies in your class have personal maids."

"My class?"

"Jane, you have to accept that we are now part of the elite society in Victoria, and as such we must live up to those standards. We have many parties and balls to attend this season, so you will appreciate having help getting dressed and having your hair styled."

"Are you suggesting that I don't look good enough?" she snapped.

"Of course not, Jane."

"Well, we have Ah Foo as our houseboy, who does everything else. And I can easily dress myself. I always have."

"But wouldn't it be nice to have someone style your beautiful hair for you?"

After a long pause, she somewhat reluctantly agreed. "Well, I suppose I should have a personal maid. You're probably right, Gideon."

"I'll place an advertisement in the *Daily Colonist* for a maid to apply at my office, and then I'll send any good candidates up to Providence for you to interview them. It will give you something else to think about," I added.

She glared at me.

Two days later, a woman stopped by my office in answer to the advertisement.

"I'm from England," she told me, so I was convinced Jane would feel a connection to her. "I have a lot of experience, as I've worked for many important people, sir."

I was very busy that morning so had no time to study her credentials. I simply glanced at them quickly, because I knew nothing about servants in England anyway. "Well, you seem suitable, miss, but I would like you to meet my wife tomorrow and show her your references. We live up at Providence, along the Gorge waterway. I'll give you the directions."

A few days earlier an invitation had arrived from Julia and Joseph Trutch for a Christmas party at Fairfield House, and I had discussed it with Jane.

"I think this party might cheer you up, Jane, as I know you like Julia. So I accepted it for us."

"Yes. I feel empathy with Julia," Jane said. "Like me, she is unable to bear children. I am amazed at how she manages to remain so warm and serene. I feel sure her serenity is just masking her great inner sorrow."

I thought the timing might be perfect, as she would appreciate having a lady's maid help her prepare for this particular Christmas event. So, on the morning after I'd briefly interviewed the woman, I reminded Jane about it.

"Jane, don't forget that the woman who applied for the maid job is coming to meet you this morning at ten o'clock."

Then, without giving it another thought, I left for the office.

CHAPTER 36: JANE

I woke up that morning with a splitting headache and was in no mood to interview someone.

After Gideon left, I asked Ah Foo to bring up some hot water for a bath. I still relished being able to soak in a large tub in our dressing room. It felt so good to luxuriate in hot, clean water of my own instead of having to be the last one in line for a bath in cold, dirty water.

Afterward, I went down to the library, calling for Ah Foo to bring me some tea and toast. While I waited, I lay back in Gideon's chair with my feet up and closed my eyes.

The doctor had told me a few months ago that, because of my size, I might never be able to carry a baby to full term, but I had not mentioned this to Gideon because I didn't want to disappoint him yet again. Perhaps the doctor could be wrong.

A tap on the door disturbed my troubled thoughts.

"Lady to see you, Mrs. Cap. She come about job as maid. I will bring tea soon."

I knew I had to go through with this, as Gideon would be upset if I didn't find someone soon.

"All right, Ah Foo. Show her in," I said, without looking up. I heard him talking in the foyer, asking the woman's name, and then, "Mrs. Cap, Miss Molly Jenkins to see you."

I turned slowly.

"Cor blimey! If it ain't you, Janey," said a familiar, long-forgotten voice from my past.

She hadn't changed much, although she did look older. But I would have recognized that disdainful look anywhere.

"I beg your pardon." I stood as tall as I could to face her, my pulse racing with fear.

"Janey, it's me, Molly! Can't believe it's you. You look so bloody posh in those clothes. Do you work here too, and they supply clothes like that?"

"What on earth do you mean! I am *Mrs. McBride.* Ah Foo, please close the door." I could see his puzzled expression as he hovered there. "What are *you* doing here?"

"I've come about the job as personal maid to Mrs. McBride. Do you work for her, too?""

"I told you. I AM Mrs. McBride."

"Blimey, Janey! Is that so? Well, you've certainly come up in the world. You did right well for yourself. When I left the Sinclairs, I knew you'd come to Columbia on the west coast, so I thought I'd try my luck, too. What a voyage it was! But, God almighty, I never thought to see how well you'd done here. This house! Oooh, and that handsome husband! I met him yesterday. What a man you've landed! And just look at this place. It's as good as Enderby House or Noxley Manor. How'd you do it, Janey?"

"Molly, you are being very impertinent. I am no longer Jane Hopkins! My past is behind me now, so I certainly don't think it would be a good idea for you to work here and remind me of it."

"Well, now, that's funny, 'cos I was just thinking the opposite. Working here would be perfect for me."

"Well, I am not offering you the job!"

"Why's that? Your husband said you need a personal maid. And just think what fun we could have, reminiscing about the past."

"I do not think about the past any more, Molly, and I want you to leave my house right now. The job is not yours. I'm sure you'll soon find something else, perhaps over on the mainland."

She paced around the room, running her hand over various objects as she went. She smiled as she turned back to me.

"You seem worried, Janey. Are you afraid I might talk about your past? Could it be that perhaps your handsome husband and all your posh friends here don't know the truth about you? After all, you were only a scullery maid and then a personal maid in England. And you came from the orphanage where you'd been abandoned by your mother, who was a whore!"

"How dare you speak to me like that!"

"But it's true, Janey, and you know it. I'm guessing no one here knows about that, eh? And then of course, there was the rape ..."

"Get out! Go!" I screamed.

Instead, she sat down in the chair I had vacated moments earlier.

"Now, let's think about this seriously, Janey. This job would be perfect for me. A lovely house where I'll be working for a woman who I know is no better than me. A *lady's* maid I'd be, to the daughter of a whore ..."

"Stop! I told you to leave, and I meant it. Right now."

"Oh, I'll leave all right, Janey. For now, but I'll be back to see you in the morning. You can count on it. Think about my proposition overnight."

"Your proposition? What are you talking about?"

"You tell me the job is mine in the morning, and in return, I'll keep my silence. Your husband will never have to know the truth about you, 'cos I'm thinking he doesn't know it now, right? Fair's fair, don't you think? After all, you took away the best job from me with Lady Sinclair."

"I did no such thing!" I walked over to the bell to ring for Ah Foo—who probably had been hovering outside the door, because he appeared in an instant.

"Ah Foo, please show Miss Jenkins out."

She stood and smiled ominously at me. "See you in the morning, *Mrs. McBride*! Thank you so much for your time."

And with that she was gone and my life was in ruins. A few minutes later, Ah Foo returned with my tea and toast.

"I not like that one, Mrs. Cap. She no good ..."

Oh, Foo, if only you knew. But all I said was, "Thank you," and dismissed him with a wave of my hand.

However, I was sick with worry. What was I to do? I could not have Molly in my life again, as she would forever be able to hold that threat over my head.

I clenched my fists. I was perspiring profusely. Perhaps I could offer her coffee or tea in the morning and slip some poison in it. I was sure Ah Foo kept rat poison in the potting shed. She would become violently ill and collapse on the floor. She would die right there before me and would be taken away, and that would be the end of it.

Or, perhaps I could shoot her. Yes, Gideon kept guns locked in the glass case. I knew the key was in his drawer. But no, poison would be easier.

Oh my God, what was I thinking? Have I really sunk this low? Was I actually contemplating murder?

* * *

"I didn't hire her, Gideon," I told him later as we prepared for the evening ahead.

"Why? What was wrong with her?"

"Oh, everything. ... I promise I'll find someone suitable soon."

"I hope so, Jane."

It was a grand evening, and all of Victoria's high society was there. But my mind was in turmoil. The evening became worse when I noticed a strikingly tall woman with dark hair and deep blue eyes, wearing a dress of pale yellow chiffon draped around her curvaceous body. I would not normally have paid her much attention, except for the fact that she made a direct beeline towards Gideon and placed her arm through his.

"Oh, dear Captain McBride, I have heard so much about you from Julia, and I've wanted to meet you for so long," she said in a rather sickly sweet accent. "Please excuse us, Mrs. McBride. I must borrow your husband for a while and hear all about his darlin' little ferry boats on the Fraser. I'm from the South, you know, and now that that beastly war is over down there, I can at last travel freely again, and I have heard *so* much about the famous riverboat captain, Gideon McBride. Come, Captain, let's find a quiet corner and you can tell me about all your adventures."

Gideon smiled and shrugged at me, but still allowed himself to be led away to a corner of the room behind two large pillars.

I glared at him in response and gave her an equally black look, and then I heard Edward's calming voice in my ear. "Jane, my dear, your eyes are flashing, and I fear the green dragon of jealousy has reared its ugly head."

"Oh, Edward, I just took an instant dislike to her, that's all. Who *is* she anyway? And how dare she walk off with my husband—although he did not appear to be the least bit reluctant to go off with her."

"Ah, Jane … don't think such thoughts. She is just a terrible flirt and Gideon is simply having a bit of fun. Her name is Marybelle Winton, and her family comes from Georgia. She is an acquaintance of Julia's, I believe, but I don't think you have much to fear from her. She will not steal your loving husband away from you."

"Look at them! She is positively ogling him, and he's enjoying it! Men are *so* ridiculous."

"Well, come and dance with me, Jane, and let's make Gideon a bit jealous too, eh?" he said, grinning mischievously.

"No chance of that. He'd never be jealous of *you*, Edward. You're his friend and he trusts you … but I don't trust that woman … not one little bit!"

Edward waltzed me around the room, but my mind was not on dancing. The evening was ruined for me as I watched that creature flirt outrageously with my husband. He appeared to be enjoying it and didn't even seem aware of my irritation. In fact, he was obviously relishing her attention.

Eventually I could stand it no longer, so the next time he wandered over to me and stood by my side, I told him I wished to go home immediately. The *creature* had temporarily excused herself to powder her nose.

"But, my love, the night is young. Are you tired already?"

"No, Gideon, not really. But I *am* tired of that woman and her outrageous behavior."

"Woman? What woman?"

"Oh, for heaven's sake, Gideon! That creature, Marybelle what-ever-her-name-is. She has been monopolizing you all evening, and I refuse to be humiliated any longer. Please find my cloak. I will make our apologies to the Trutches. We are leaving now."

And with that I walked off in a huff and left him standing. Men are so blatantly dimwitted sometimes. Could he not see what that woman was after?

From the corner of my eye, I noticed she was once again heading his way, but fortunately Gideon followed me to the foyer, where we said our farewells to our hosts. I took some delight in noticing Miss Marybelle's disappointment as her prey disappeared from view.

CHAPTER 37: GIDEON

"Can you explain what I did wrong?" I asked her as we began to undress later. "Or are you never going to speak to me again?"

She retreated into the dressing room and did not reply until she'd finished her ablutions. Then, standing beside our bed and holding her head high, she said in a haughty voice, "Gideon, can you possibly imagine how humiliating it was for me to see you fawning over that woman and, what is more, enjoying the way she was flirting with you."

I began to laugh. "My dear, sweet little wife, I can assure you I was *not* fawning over Miss Marybelle Winton, even though she may well have been flirting with me."

"Oh, she was flirting with you all right. It was most embarrassing."

She removed her robe and climbed onto her side of the bed. "How could you allow such a thing to happen?"

"Jane, she was merely asking me about my business."

"And in what business of yours *exactly* do you suppose she was interested?" Sarcasm dripped from her lips.

I laughed again. "Do I detect a hint of jealousy, Mrs. McBride?"

"Jealousy! My foot! I was merely insulted that you would spend so much time talking with her, *and*, I might add, flirting with her, while I stood alone."

"Edward was with you, my dear. I didn't leave you alone."

"That is beside the point."

As I continued to laugh, she became more and more incensed. "How can you laugh at this when I am feeling so awful?"

I reached out across the bed to touch her, but she pulled away. "I'm so sorry, my darling. I didn't realize you were so upset."

"Well, I am. My head is aching and I feel terrible."

"But why, darling? It meant nothing."

"Nothing?" she began to scream. "Nothing? Oh, Gideon, if only you knew ..."

"Knew what?"

Suddenly she burst into tears. Her sobs became so intense that I ran around to her side of the bed to comfort her. "Jane, my darling, whatever's wrong?"

"I can't bear it any longer, Gideon. I'm just a terrible person. Today I actually contemplated murder! I must be like my mother."

"Murder? What on earth are you talking about?"

And then the words spilled from her in a deluge of sobs.

"I have lied and lied ever since I first met you, Gideon. Nothing I ever told you was true, and I can't bear it anymore. I knew you hated liars when you told me about Jim Benson lying to you, but you are married to a liar, too. I must tell you everything now, and if you turn me away, I will have to accept it. I was abandoned as a baby by a woman who was a prostitute, and I grew up in an orphanage, where I was beaten by Mrs. Creed. She was so cruel. Those are the marks on my back. It's true I worked for the Sinclairs, but I began there as a lowly scullery maid and then became a lady's maid. I was never a governess. It was all a lie to get the job with Edward and ... then today, that woman who applied for the job threatened me and ..."

"Threatened you? My God, what did she do? And who the hell is Mrs. Creed?"

"Mrs. Creed was the matron at the orphanage, and she was cruel and evil. The woman who applied for the job is Molly Jenkins. We worked together in service and she has threatened to tell you everything unless I give her the job."

"Jane, slow down, slow down. I have told you so many times how much I love you. I don't care where you came from or who your mother was. I just don't understand why you needed to lie to me about anything. Why couldn't you tell me all this before?"

"You would never have wanted me, Gideon. And I would never have got the job working for Edward as James's governess ..."

"I've always wanted you ... since the moment I first saw you. And you are not a fraud. You are an intelligent, strong woman and a gifted pianist."

"But Gideon ... it's even worse."

I put my arms around her.

"Nothing is so bad that you cannot tell me, my love."

"I was ... violated by Lady Sinclair's son! That's the real reason I left England and why Lady Sinclair helped me leave."

My whole body tensed. "My God."

I was so angry. Not with her—but for her. This must have been what had been weighing on her mind for so long.

I held her tightly for a while and then extinguished the candles and drew her down to the bed in my arms.

Finally I spoke. "I'm trying to think of a plan of how we can deal with that awful woman in the morning, Jane. I don't want you to think about it anymore. It's over."

"Deal with her? After all I have just told you about my past, that's all you're thinking about?"

"Nothing in your past changes my love for you, Jane. But remember, now that you have told me the truth, that woman has no power over you anymore."

"But I lied to you, Gideon—so many times. And I was attacked by that odious man. You have said nothing about that. What about my terrible past? You must hate me for all that."

I gently wiped the tears from her eyes and kissed her forehead.

"How could I possibly hate you, Jane? None of that matters one bit to me. Yes, I am disgusted that you were violated by that man but the rest ... is nothing. Tomorrow you can tell me the whole story. You know, you could have told me all this from the very beginning, and I would still adore you. As for tonight, well, I was enjoying myself tonight at the party. And I suppose men act a little ridiculously when a beautiful woman pays attention to them."

"Beautiful? Did you think she was beautiful?" she said.

"She was quite pleasing to the eye."

"Ha! You see, you admit it."

"But not nearly as pleasing as you."

"You merely say that to appease me."

"Perhaps, but it's still true. And now, I will show you exactly how much you please me and how very much I love you and only you."

We looked at each other, and suddenly we were kissing passionately. Before I knew exactly what was happening, Jane was returning my kisses with equal passion. Our love-making that night was powerful and intense, as she responded to my every touch, moaning with delight as we reached heights of desire we had never before both experienced together. Her body arched towards mine, begging me to satisfy her needs and fill her with my love.

Next morning, while she stayed in bed, I took her a breakfast tray of eggs, fruit and toast from Ah Foo's kitchen. She was smiling at me as I came back into our bedroom.

"Your breakfast is served, madam," I said. "You know, it occurs to me, my darling, we should perhaps argue more frequently."

"Argue? But Gideon, it was so much more than that."

I bent to kiss her tenderly. "Yes my love, it was, and I'm so glad you finally told me the truth. But don't you agree that making-up afterwards is well worth it?"

She put the tray to one side and reached up to me, drawing me down towards her.

"Yes, I certainly do," she said.

Her breakfast was temporarily forgotten.

CHAPTER 38: JANE

We made love again before eating breakfast. For the first time, I felt completely relaxed and unburdened by fear.

My husband still adored me in spite of everything. I'd told him the truth the night before and in even more detail, when we finally ate breakfast together.

"I have never discovered who my mother was, or why she abandoned me at the orphanage. It was only through what Mrs. Creed told me that I thought she might have been a prostitute, but I prefer to think she had just fallen on hard times."

"I'm sure that was it," he said.

"And it was through Mr. Lloyd, the reverend at St. Mary's Church, who secretly gave me music lessons, that I learnt how to play the piano. When Mrs. Creed discovered our secret, she beat me."

"What an evil woman she must have been."

I nodded.

"Finally, I discovered information about her which I could hold over her head."

I told him about how I'd discovered her in bed with Mr. Finch, and he laughed at my description of Mr. Finch falling out of bed.

"How fortunate it was that you saw them and could use the information to your advantage. What a clever ploy. So that was how you escaped her clutches and were able to leave the orphanage and go into service."

Telling him about Philip Sinclair was much harder. "He pursued me for months, and I was so scared to tell the Sinclairs, for fear of losing my job. Then he—he violated me, Gideon, in the worst possible way. I felt unclean, and I've wondered for so long if I'm still damaged and unable to have children because of it."

He hugged me close. "I'm sure that has nothing to do with it, my love. You have been able to conceive twice, and I'm sure one day you will be able to deliver a baby, so please don't worry. Whatever the future brings us, I will always love you." The relief of letting go of everything and hearing him say that was exhilarating.

And then, we began to plan how we would deal with Molly Jenkins.

* * *

She arrived mid-morning, and Ah Foo showed her into the library.

She already had a smug smile on her face. He closed the door and she walked boldly towards me.

"Good morning, Janey? How did you sleep?" Her impertinence was so irritating, but I refrained from showing my true feelings. Instead, I feigned a false expression of fear.

"Not too well," I said.

"Sorry to hear that. But once I have the job here, it will be so much fun reminiscing about the past. I can't wait to tell Tom and your little friend, Dory, my sister-in-law, how well you've done for yourself in the new world. They have two little ones now—a boy and a girl, you know. So, now let's get down to business. You must have made a decision. I'm sure the job is mine, right, Janey?"

"First, you can stop calling me *Janey*! I am Jane McBride, Mrs. McBride to you."

At that moment the door opened, and Gideon joined us, just as we had planned.

"Oh, Captain McBride. How nice to see you again. Your wife was just about to offer me the job as her personal maid."

"Was she indeed?" he said, walking towards me and placing an arm around my shoulder. "And what were you about to do if she did not give you the job?"

She looked perplexed. "I don't know what you mean, sir."

"Well then, let me explain. Yesterday, I understand you threatened my wife, saying you would expose her past to me and all our friends if she did not give you the job. Am I right so far?"

"Captain McBride, of course not. I simply knew your wife in England, and she does have quite a colourful past, I can assure you, but of course I would not dream of threatening her. I just ..."

"Just what, Miss Jenkins? You see, I already know everything about my wife's past, and in this house we do not tolerate blackmailers, so I suggest you turn around and be on your way immediately. There is *no* job available here for you, and if I ever find you are spreading false rumours about my wife's good name, I promise you will regret it."

"The rumours are not false. I bet she didn't tell you everything— like, her mother was a whore. Or that she was raped by the son of the house and she enjoyed it. She probably even gave herself to the Reverend in order to have piano lessons. Bet you didn't know that, either. She's nothing but trash!"

"Leave now," Gideon thundered at her, "before I call the constabulary and have you escorted to jail for blackmail!"

"Well, I never! I can't believe you would think I would blackmail her. I am just telling you the truth."

As I watched it all unfold, I suddenly felt superior, knowing that Gideon and I had planned this whole scenario together and he was on my side.

"You know, Molly," I said, "I once hoped we could have been friends, but you were always mean to me. It was such a pity. I wish you well in the new world, but I hope it's far, far away from here. I hear they are still looking for women for the miners up in the Cariboo, aren't they, Gideon?"

"Oh yes, Jane, and it's a delightful place, full of mosquitoes, too."

She began to shake as she turned towards the door. "God almighty, what a fuss about nothing! I meant no harm, honest I didn't."

"And remember, Miss Jenkins, if I hear of one piece of gossip you are spreading in town, you will be off to jail." Gideon opened the door to find Ah Foo standing there, grinning from ear to ear, obviously having eavesdropped on the whole conversation.

"I escort Miss Jenkins out now, sir!"

"Thank you, Ah Foo!"

And with that she was gone. Ah Foo actually slammed the front door behind her before returning to the library. "I told you, Mrs. Cap, that one no good. Good riddance, I say."

"Good riddance indeed, Ah Foo."

We all watched from the window as Molly ran down the driveway as though someone was in hot pursuit behind her. Gideon and I then looked at one another and doubled over with laughter.

"From now on, Jane, we deal with problems together, right?" he said. "There is nothing you cannot tell me. We will always work it out."

I fell into his strong arms, experiencing a peace I had never before known.

Ah Foo smiled and, with his usual wisdom, nodded his agreement. "Yes, we all family now," he muttered to himself, as he left the room, leaving us alone.

We were indeed a family now. So perhaps I didn't need to know who my mother was and why she had abandoned me, and maybe it didn't matter anyway. Maybe it was enough now for me to be here in this place, with my new family.

I so wanted that to be true.

CHAPTER 39: GIDEON

"The Signora is quite exquisite! Her petite figure ... her colouring ... and those eyes! *Bella! Bella!*"

The slimy little Italian artist was gazing at Jane in adoration, and the more he complimented her, the more irritating he became. A few weeks after the incident with Molly Jenkins, we had been introduced to him at a party given by the O'Reillys at Point Ellice house, where they now lived, near us along the Gorge waterway. The Italian artist had immediately tried to monopolize my wife.

"I must paint her!" he said, flapping his arms around in the air.

His overbearing manner was annoying me beyond belief. He was so flamboyant and excitable. He had recently arrived in Victoria from San Francisco and now owned a studio on Johnson Street, but he also painted portraits privately on commission.

I admit I was also a little jealous because of the attention he was paying Jane. I could now understand how annoyed she must have been when Marybelle Winton was fawning over me at Christmas.

"Oh please, Gideon, it would be such fun," she said. "Signor Raggozini, can you come to Providence, or should I come to your studio?"

"I prefer to paint my subjects in their own surroundings, Signora."

I could not believe this change in Jane. Everything was now fun for her. She was light-hearted and happy all the time, and when she wasn't playing the piano, she was singing as she went around the house.

At last she was enjoying being the lady of the house as she should, and we entertained a lot. We hired maids to help Ah Foo run the house and we held garden parties on our immaculate green lawns and had boating parties along the Gorge. The O'Reillys and the Grants were our near neighbors, and we all enjoyed those halcyon days of spring and summer that year.

So, this latest interest of hers in having her portrait painted made me agree, and I allowed Roberto Raggozini to come to Providence, but with one stipulation. He could only come when I was present. It took five sittings for the portrait to be completed, and I must say I was very impressed. His painting captured not only Jane's beauty, but also her spirit.

Signor Raggozzini also appeared to have no ulterior motive as far as my wife was concerned. It was just his way to fuss and compliment whenever he was around beautiful women, so I even consented to have my own portrait painted when Jane suggested it.

Of course, I had known the main reason for Jane's happiness since early March, when we found out she was pregnant again. She told me this wonderful news just before the first sitting for her portrait. I was stunned but incredibly excited.

"Dr. Helmcken has confirmed it, Gideon. I thought I would never be able to conceive again, but a miracle has happened. This time it will be all right, I just know it," she said with conviction. I was delighted by her optimism, and I felt the same way. I was sure our son or daughter would arrive safely in October as planned, and all would be well.

Nonetheless, at least a hundred times a day, I repeated to myself that this child *would* be born safely and would be healthy, because I knew that Jane could not take another disappointment. I prayed harder than I ever had during those months, and I pandered to Jane's every whim, making her rest every afternoon. The only exercise I allowed her was a short stroll around the garden with me in the evening when I returned from my office. Ah Foo was instructed to keep an eye on her at all other times, and this he did with his usual faithful and dogged resolve.

"Oh, Gideon," Jane said one day. "You fuss over me far too much. I have endured much, and I'm much stronger than you think." Of course I knew she was.

The two paintings were completed by the end of June, and Jane's was hung at the top of the staircase. She wanted mine alongside hers, but I said that her portrait should stand alone in Providence because the house had been built for her and she was its *chatelaine*.

"You're being ridiculous, Gideon. This house belongs to us both."

Finally we agreed to hang my portrait over the fireplace in the library, and somehow it seemed to fit better there anyway. We called it "the captain in his uniform in the smoking room."

"It's a man's room, and you are most definitely a man," Jane said, laughing.

Ever since the night she had confessed everything to me, she had become an insatiable, passionate woman, and I was certainly not complaining. We seemed to laugh a lot that year, and we especially enjoyed our beautiful home, in which Jane now took so much pride.

"Pride was always my downfall as a child," she confided. "Mrs. Creed told me that pride was a sin, but I don't care anymore."

"And neither should you," I said.

Earlier that year we had donated two acres of our land on the rise to the Anglican Church, so that a small community church and cemetery could be built there. It would be known as St. Luke's-on-the-Hill, and we felt joy at being involved in its building. Jane had been raised in the Church of England, and though my background had been Presbyterian, we agreed that the Anglican faith conformed well to our spiritual needs. We were especially pleased to learn that the Reverend Matthew Bolton, who had married us in New Westminster, would be the first Rector.

Although the baby was not due until the beginning of October, we tempted fate this time by transforming one of the bedrooms into a nursery.

"I want the walls painted blue, Ah Foo," Jane told him. "I am sure it will be a boy! And we must hire a nursemaid, Gideon."

"Of course, my love." Ah Foo and I exchanged a look of hope. If we lost this baby like the first two, I was sure Jane would not be able to bear it.

In August, Her Majesty the Queen gave royal assent to the British Columbia Act, which would finally unite the two colonies of Vancouver Island and British Columbia. It became official two months later.

At first we were devastated by the terms of the Act, which were not at all favourable to Victoria. In particular, our city lost the privilege of being a free port, and this was not good news for my shipping business.

"Victoria has been shortchanged in this latest decree from London," I said to Edward.

"I tend to agree with you, old boy, but you have many other businesses now, which will hopefully counteract this depressing state of affairs."

It was true. I now had numerous business interests in British Columbia, though the sea remained my first love. I had built up McBride's Transportation along the Fraser River, and that business was thriving. I was always on the lookout for new enterprises. Diversification was the key to success.

Despite this news and the consequent economic gloom hanging over the city, we refused to be downhearted as we awaited the birth of our child. And late on the evening of the 2nd day of October, Jane's labour pains began. For the next twenty-three hours, they continued in earnest and Jane suffered excruciating agony. Her screams echoed throughout the house, and I wondered why I had been so selfish as to put her through this.

We had by then hired Mary, a nursemaid who ministered to Jane with gentle care until Dr. Helmcken came. Mary was a cheerful soul with rosy red cheeks and a positive attitude, and she was always smiling, so she was just what Jane needed to console her when the pains became unbearable.

Finally, Dr. Helmcken arrived and examined Jane. He came to talk to me, where I waited on the landing.

"The labour is likely to be a very long one, and it will be hard on someone of your wife's stature and size," he said. But this time she had carried the baby to term, and at least he had not said she would lose the baby.

By the time our son arrived, shortly before midnight on October 3, 1866, I had almost worn a hole in the carpet from pacing back and forth, and Edward and James, who were downstairs in the library, had emptied an entire bottle of brandy between them. At fourteen years of age, James had been initiated into the world of alcohol because, as he told his father and me, he could not bear to hear Jane suffering.

"Will she die like my mother did?" he asked his father.

"No, of course not," said Edward, without much conviction.

But Caleb Angus McBride was born a healthy boy, and despite Jane's weakness and utter exhaustion, by the time he finally made his appearance, my heart overflowed with joy at the sight of him. I knelt at her bedside in awe, feeling both humble and proud.

"My darling, he is wonderful, and you were so brave. I felt every agonizing pain with you. I'm so proud of you."

"I cannot believe this tiny piece of humanity is a part of us, Gideon. Finally, we truly have a family."

Quite naturally, in my eyes, Caleb was the most handsome child God had ever created.

"I think he is quite remarkable," I said.

"I do too," she whispered as he suckled on her finger.

"But he's *so* tiny," said James, when the doctor finally allowed Jane to have other visitors.

"Oh, he'll grow," I said with paternal pride. "And soon he'll be running around and chasing you across the lawn out there, young man."

"He looks like a little angel," James added, obviously as awestruck as we were.

And that is exactly what he was—our angel.

CHAPTER 40: JANE

The night my son was born, God and I made a pact.

I felt convinced He had finally agreed that I had suffered enough for my past sins. After confessing all my lies to Gideon, God had given me Caleb as my reward.

My recovery was slow, but I followed doctor's orders and rested frequently. I had lost a great deal of blood during the delivery, so I remained pale and sickly-looking.

"Motherhood becomes you, Jane. You look beautiful," Gideon frequently told me, but I didn't believe him. I'd asked Mary to bring a mirror to me as I lay in bed, so I knew I looked ashen.

However, shortly before Christmas, when Caleb was eleven weeks old and I was feeling much stronger, we were able to have him christened at St. Luke's Church, with the Reverend Bolton officiating at the ceremony.

Ah Foo and Lum, our new assistant gardener, had previously decorated the church with laurel evergreens, and Mary had placed white satin bows around the altar and font. Caleb Angus McBride did not fully appreciate all their efforts. He cried throughout most of the ceremony!

The following May, the usual Queen's Birthday celebrations were held, with a regatta of gaily coloured boats passing our property along the Gorge Arm. There were fireworks later, and we sat on our veranda to watch them with Edward, James, Skiff, and Dulcie, the charming lady he had now married, while Mary kept an eye on Caleb in the nursery.

By then, Edward had moved into his house in James Bay, with Mrs. Finch as his housekeeper. James had now completed his first year at Upper Canada College but was home that May on school holidays. I always felt Edward might be lonely in his large house without his son, so I frequently introduced him to suitable ladies, but all to no avail. He seemed content to remain a solitary widower, despite the fact I wanted everyone to be as happy as Gideon and I and our beautiful son.

Edward, indeed, seemed perfectly happy with his own life. He was a born politician, and he and Gideon had many discussions in the library in the evenings about where the new capital city would be.

It was hinted that Governor Frederick Seymour would make an announcement about the capital city during the Queen's Birthday celebrations, but the holiday weekend came and went and the Governor stayed away from the celebrations, on the grounds of ill health.

On the following day, May 25, Victoria was finally proclaimed British Columbia's official capital city. We were all very surprised that the decision had been made in our favour but very excited by the news.

No sooner had that question been settled once and for all, when those in power began discussing the burning issue of whether or not British Columbia should join the Confederation and become a part of Canada. I sometimes thought that men just loved to talk—especially men in politics.

As for me, I now preferred the simple life, enjoying my son and our lovely home. I played the piano to Caleb now, and he seemed to enjoy the music. Even before he turned two years old, he was placing his fingers on the keys and saying, "Mama ... play ... pretty music ..."

To a certain extent, I suppose I neglected Gideon during those months. My whole world centered on my son.

Caleb grew so fast, and I doted on him. I loved to sit in my rocking chair on the veranda, singing to him as we both rocked gently back and forth. I could gaze across the lawn, admiring the work of Ah Foo and Lum. Between the two of them, they had transformed our acreage into a masterpiece of floral delights. They had planted two more dogwood trees, which delighted us in the spring, and I could smell the aroma of clematis, honeysuckle and jasmine. My rose garden was coming along nicely. I frequently had to pinch myself to believe that all this was mine.

My fear of Molly's threats, which were irrelevant now anyway, had come to nothing, and we heard she had left Victoria for the mainland and not returned. I had no desire to learn where she had ended up, just as I had never wanted to know where Alice from the *Tynemouth* was now. They were all a part of my past, which these days I rarely thought about.

On one particularly warm day, while walking across the lawn with Caleb in my arms, we saw Ah Foo working in the arbour by the boathouse. He called to us.

"Hi, Mrs. Cap. Hi, little young'un. Come to Foo. Come see Foo."

Caleb smiled and gurgled his delight at the sight of Ah Foo, whom he adored, so I placed him on the lawn to test his legs—and much to my amazement, he took a step on his own. And then another. Foo held out his arms.

"Come to Foo, little Cal. Come ..."

And, without more ado, my son took his first few steps. We laughed and clapped our hands before he promptly sat down with a plop. He was quite young to be walking, just eleven months then, but his legs were sturdy and he was anxious to be mobile. He performed again for Gideon later that day, and after that there was no holding him back. He soon became quite a handful for Mary. I suppose I made the situation worse because I tended to spoil him terribly.

The Queen's birthday in May of the following year brought with it the usual celebrations along the Arm. We spent Saturday with our neighbors, the O'Reillys, who had three children of their own now: Frank, Kathleen and baby Mary Augusta. We played croquet on the lawn, after which Ah Foo served us all a delightful picnic lunch.

On the Sunday, Gideon, Edward and James took Cal over to Esquimalt Harbour to see the arrival of a large vessel from China. James, who was now seventeen, was home again from Upper Canada College. He was still enjoying his studies and was talking of becoming a lawyer like his father, which of course filled Edward with pride. James had grown into a charming young man, and I felt some pride in helping to shape his character.

The men enjoyed their day together in town, but that evening, as Gideon and I dined alone at Providence, Ah Foo hovered around us, seemingly very agitated.

"What's wrong, Foo?" I asked.

"I hear talk today, Mrs. Cap. There is pox in the city again. Bad thing. They say a man aboard that ship from China bring it to Victoria."

"Oh my goodness! Gideon, could it be smallpox again?" I still remembered the horrible sight of the native people I had seen many years ago at their reserve on the outskirts of town.

Gideon looked equally concerned. "It sounds like it might be. I will make enquiries in the morning with the harbour master. If it's spreading in the city, we must take precautions. I think we should go over to New Westminster with Cal and stay there for a while. I'll find out something definite tomorrow, my love."

* * *

But the next day, the news was worse.

Smallpox was indeed spreading throughout the city, and the rumour Ah Foo had heard was true. Gideon thought it might be a good plan for us to leave immediately for the mainland.

That night, as we began making plans to leave the following morning, Cal developed a slight fever. Ah Foo rushed for the doctor, and I was petrified.

Dr. Helmcken soon arrived, by which time Cal's fever was even higher, and within a few hours he was experiencing all the classic symptoms of the dreaded smallpox disease.

"He will be fine once the fever breaks," Dr. Helmcken assured us. "We are waiting for the vaccine, too."

But, despite all our efforts, the fever refused to break, and the vaccine did not arrive. Within a few hours, a rash was also developing on his chest, and then it spread to his face and arms. Images flashed before my eyes of the pockmarked natives I'd seen on the reserve.

"How could this be happening?" I screamed. "He's so young. My baby—my poor baby."

We sat by his bed all night, bathing his head and body with cool, wet rags, but still the fever refused to break.

Suddenly, Caleb stopped crying and tossing in distress. Instead, he lay dormant and unresponsive for two more days. The doctor tried everything possible, but nothing worked.

And in the early hours of June 3, 1869, our beloved child was taken from us. My sorrow was quite simply too great to bear. I could no longer talk or scream or feel anything. I was numb with grief.

I sat in stony silence beside his crib as the doctor covered him with a sheet. I could not speak, because I knew that if I did, I would blame Gideon for taking him to the harbour that day. And I would blame that damnable man who had arrived on the ship from China and then mingled in the crowd. But most of all, I would blame God, who, once again, had seen fit to take something precious from me.

Then, from somewhere in the distance, I could hear a baying sound that grew louder and louder until it became deafening. I placed my hands over my ears to try to eradicate that mournful, plaintive wailing. Why didn't it stop? I couldn't bear it. Who was making that awful noise?

I tried to resist as the doctor placed an arm around my shoulder in an attempt to lead me from the room.

"Come, Mrs. McBride. You must leave him now. There is nothing more we can do. He is gone."

And that was when I realized where that wailing sound was coming from. It was me. I was screaming and I couldn't stop.

* * *

Two and a half years after Caleb's christening at St. Luke's Church-on-the-Hill, his funeral took place there. It was the church's first funeral, and his tiny body was the first placed in the cemetery and given up into God's hands. The date was June 7, 1869.

I refused to attend the funeral. Gideon had slept downstairs in the library the night before, but he came to our bedroom that morning to talk to me.

I still could not look at him, remembering how he had taken our son to town that day and exposed him to that deadly disease. I blamed him, and I blamed myself for not stopping him.

"I need you there with me this morning, Jane," he pleaded. "I *canna* do this thing alone."

I shook my head. "And I, Gideon, cannot do it at all. My son is dead, but I cannot bury him. It should not have happened."

"I know that, Jane," he cried. "I know!"

"Then you must take care of things alone."

He turned in despair, slamming the door behind him. And later I watched from the bedroom window as the solemn procession slowly climbed the hill.

Gideon walked in front, flanked on each side by Edward and James. Behind them walked Skiff, Dulcie, Ah Foo, Lum and Mary. I watched numerous carriages filled with our friends drive past, including the O'Reillys, the Grants, the Trutches and members of the Douglas family. I stared at that somber group of mourners, but I felt nothing.

I thought that if I stayed away, somehow it would make the whole thing unreal. I could pretend it hadn't happened; that it had simply been a bad dream, from which I would soon wake up. Caleb would call me and ask to go out in the garden to play.

I stayed in my room all morning. After it was over, everyone returned to the house. I could hear their voices, but I refused to go downstairs to see anyone, even Gideon.

Mary brought me some tea. "You must try and have something, Mrs. McBride," she said.

I said nothing, and eventually the tea went cold. I locked my door, drew the blinds and lay down on the bed. I hoped I would die. Only in death would I find relief from this unbearable pain and anguish.

They kept knocking on my door, and I kept telling them to go away. Voices—so many, I lost count of who they were. First, I think it was Mary again? Then Edward? And then James? But not Gideon. I had made it abundantly clear that I did not want to see him.

I wanted to cry, but no tears would come. I was hollow, empty, void of all emotion. If God was playing games with me, this was the cruelest of tricks. Why was He making me suffer this way? Was it because of my pride again? Had I tempted fate by showing pride in my beautiful house and way of life? And most especially in my handsome little boy?

My thoughts were in turmoil. One minute, I thought I was a child again at Field House and Mrs. Creed was reprimanding me for lying. I could hear her voice telling me I would be punished for my evil deeds. But this time, I hadn't lied, had I? I had confessed all my lies to Gideon and he had forgiven me. And I hadn't cheated. I hadn't sneaked away to play Mr. Lloyd's piano without permission. So why was I being punished?

All I had done was to love someone unconditionally. So that must be it. It was wrong to love too much. Once again, the object of my love had been taken from me. I vowed I would never love anyone like that again. Never—as long as I lived.

I remembered a story I had once read as a child by Hans Christian Andersen, called "The Snow Queen." It was about good versus evil and a mirror breaking with pieces of glass floating around and landing in people's hearts, turning their hearts into ice. Like the child in that story, a piece of glass must have now landed in my heart. The glass had frozen my heart and made it quite unable to mend.

It was morning again. Another night had passed without my sweet boy, but I was still alive. I stood up and walked to the window. I needed to look up the hill to the church to see if Caleb was really there somewhere. Or was he still in the nursery? Had it all been a dream?

And then my eye caught sight of Ah Foo in the garden down below. He was sitting on the ground, leaning against the big oak tree at the edge of the lawn, and he was sobbing woefully .

Poor Foo, I thought. *How I envy you. You can at least cry. Why can't I?*

CHAPTER 41: GIDEON

I could still hear her screams in my head on that terrible day. They echoed through the house until I could bear it no longer.

So I left the house and ran, having no idea where I was going. I eventually found myself down by the wharf, and for hours I sat there, watching the whaling boats and the steamers, but I found no comfort from those seagoing vessels and their seafaring sounds.

Every time something bad had happened in my life, I ran away. My father had died at sea and I ran away to join the Hudson's Bay Company. When Anya died, I ran out into the frozen wasteland and later moved away and headed west. When I'd gambled and lost everything, I ran from San Francisco and headed north. And now, my beloved son had died, and I was running again. Was I a coward who couldn't face up to the truth? Was I as bad as Jane, who had refused all comfort?

Death is a strange thing. I knew it was simply a part of life which we must accept, because one day we all die. I remember when my mother died in Scotland, feeling guilt as well as sorrow because I was not there beside her, where I should have been. But eventually I accepted it because she had lived a good, long life and had died in peace. Her death was a part of her life—simply a journey to another place.

But our little boy? Why him? He didn't even have a chance to live a life here. So where was the justice in that? How could I possibly accept that, when I felt only bitterness and rage? A child should not die before his parents. How did my mother bear it when Duncan died at sea, along with her husband?

I knew Jane blamed me for taking Caleb to the harbour that day. What must she be feeling now? She had suffered so much. She was abandoned as a baby. She had never known love until I met her. She had been beaten and raped, yet had courageously ventured alone on a long sea voyage to the other side of the world.

But then, even in her new life, she had continued to know sorrow—miscarrying two of our babies. And then, the unthinkable had happened. Our beloved son had also been taken from her.

I wanted to comfort her, but I also needed her to comfort me. In that moment, I felt such intense pain inside. I needed her forgiveness for taking Caleb to the harbour. I needed her arms around me, so that we could grieve together. But would she ever forgive me? And how could I ever forgive myself?

This time, I vowed I wouldn't run away from what needed to be done. So eventually I returned to the house and, with Edward's help, made plans for the funeral. Jane wanted no part of me, so I slept in a guest bedroom after that whenever I was home, which wasn't often. I spent a great deal of time at our house in New Westminster, because at Providence, Jane and I barely spoke to one another. She seemed unable to understand how I felt, and I, in turn, could find no way to comfort her.

Her coldness towards me eventually became an irritation, and soon I could no longer even sympathize with her. I began to hate her as much as she must hate me.

She continued to lock our bedroom door at night, and after a while I gave up trying to make her let me in. We rarely took our meals together, and when we did, we ate in silence, each of us living in our own tormented world of despair and sorrow. Ah Foo's constant chatter became just another irritation. Edward often called at Providence when I was home and told me he was very concerned about us both.

"This can't go on, old boy," he said one day. "You should be comforting one another in your sorrow, not drawing further apart. You need one another now, more than ever."

"Jane has made it abundantly clear that she does *not* need me," I said. "I should never have taken Caleb to town that day. Our son was too young, too susceptible to the dangers."

"Oh Gideon, how could you know there was smallpox on that ship! Or that some of the crew had already mingled in the crowd? You cannot keep blaming yourself. You might as well blame me and James. We all went that day. It was just a tragic turn of events that little Cal lost his life."

"Stop! I don't want to hear all that, man. Don't you see, Jane keeps blaming me, and she will never forgive me, and I doubt I will ever forgive myself."

"So you are just going to give up?"

"What else is there to do? She barely speaks to me, and she locks herself away in our bedroom or in the nursery, day after day."

"Give her time, old boy. Give her time. And give yourself time, too. Eventually the pain will lessen."

"Will it?"

I didn't see how it ever would.

*   *   *

I left again the next day and this time headed up the Fraser to Quesnel, where I had a business meeting to attend. I really had little interest in any new opportunities up there, but it was a chance to get away from the gloom of Providence. I intended to stay away for a month—at least until the snows came. Maybe Edward was right and we both needed more time and space away from each other.

But just two weeks later, while sitting in the Gold Commissioner's office in Quesnel and trying to concentrate on some business that I no longer took any interest in, I realized I could not stand this empty feeling inside me any longer. I abruptly excused myself from the meeting and caught the first stage out for New Westminster. The next morning, I sailed over to Victoria.

I walked from the harbour towards the house, feeling suddenly determined in my mission. I noticed Ah Foo down by the water attending to the boat ramp, so I was able to slip into the house unseen by him.

"Jane! Jane! Where are you?" I called as I climbed the stairs and headed to our bedroom. I had slammed the front door behind me so she would surely know it was not Ah Foo coming in. He always crept around the house very quietly and would no more think of slamming a door than of cooking a bad meal.

For once, our bedroom door was unlocked, but she wasn't inside, so I went down the hall towards the nursery.

"Are you in there, Jane? Answer me!" I shouted from outside the nursery door as I attempted to open it. But it was locked.

"Yes, I'm in here. What do you want?"

"Why is this door locked? Let me in."

"I don't wish to be disturbed."

"Open the door at once, Jane. It's high time you *were* disturbed. I've had enough of this nonsense, woman. You will open this damn door now and we will talk about this. Do you understand?" I had never spoken to her that way before, my voice so angry and full of threats. I heard her unlock the door and I burst in, almost knocking her over as I pushed past her and began pacing back and forth.

"I thought you were still in the north," she said. "Ah Foo told me you would be away for at least a month."

"I had intended to stay that long, but three days ago, while sitting in the Gold Commissioner's office, I realized I couldn't take this any longer."

"Take what?"

"Your attitude, Jane! It has gone on far too long."

"*My* attitude! How dare you speak to me like that!"

"Jane, I cannot live like this a moment longer. I caught the first stage out of there and arrived in New Westminster last night. We have to talk."

"About what?"

"About us, and what happened to our lives back in June."

"There is nothing to talk about."

"There is a great deal to talk about. Our son is dead and you are blaming me! I know I was wrong to take him to the harbour that day. I *know* it, Jane, and I keep blaming myself too."

"Stop it. Stop it. I don't want to talk about it." She put her hands over her ears in a helpless gesture.

"Oh no, don't do this to me again, Jane!" I grabbed her hands. "Please don't keep shutting me out. We will discuss it, d'yer understand? In all these last months you have never, to my knowledge, gone to church or even visited our son's grave. Am I right?"

"There's no point. He's not there."

"No, he's not, and he's not here in this room either, where I know you sit grieving, day in and day out. He is hopefully in heaven, Jane. You always believed in that stuff before."

"Well, I don't believe in that *stuff*, as you call it, anymore. There is no heaven and no God. Why are you doing this, Gideon?"

"Because I need you, Jane." I softened my voice. "I need you to comfort me, and I want to comfort you. We have to talk about it. I buried our son alone back in June, and I've not had one moment's peace since then."

"And you think I have? Everything I have ever loved has been taken from me, but this ... this was just too much, Gideon. He was my baby. My own flesh and blood. My little boy."

"He was *my* son, too!"

"But you had a family before me. You had parents and a brother and sisters. I had no one that belonged to me alone. No one who was a part of me."

"Caleb belonged to me, too, Jane. He was my flesh and blood also."

"Then why did you cause his death? Why did you kill our son?"

She had spoken the words I had told myself a million times, and we were both stunned into silence. She had told me what I already knew, but I couldn't bear to hear it from her lips. In that moment, I knew there could never be peace between us again if she truly felt that way. I had to get away from her—far, far away.

"If that is what you believe, I will leave you," I finally said. "I will go back to Scotland, and you can stay here alone in your ice palace, the house you wanted so much. You can live here like the queen you always wanted to be, relishing all the material things that meant so much to you. Your house, your two pianos, the jewels and fine clothes I gave you. And you can wallow in your misery forever, for all I care."

"Go then, go! Leave me alone. I hate you, Gideon. I will never forgive you for what you did."

"I'm sure you won't." I turned and walked towards the door. "I will be catching the earliest passage I can find for Scotland. Ah Foo will take care of you. "

"I don't need you or anyone else to take care of me. I've always had to take care of myself."

"We all need someone, Jane. Maybe one day you'll realize that. Meanwhile, I hope you will be happy in your chosen life."

I slammed the door behind me, thinking inwardly that I would never be happy again.

Two days later, I was heading for San Francisco aboard the *SS Jupiter* and sailing from there to Scotland and my old home.

PART THREE

Separation

(1869–1873)

CHAPTER 42: JANE

He was gone. Our marriage was over.

But it was better this way. I could no longer bear to look at Gideon. Now the house was silent and empty. Despite the roaring fires Ah Foo insisted on making in the drawing room and the library every day, I was always cold. I no longer wrote in my journals. There seemed no point, as there was nothing good to write about.

One day, I opened my last journal and stared at a blank page. Then I wrote: *hate, grief, despair, denial, sorrow.*

I studied the words for a long time before adding *pride, lies, punishment.*

What was I doing? I ripped out the page and threw it into the fire, and then flung the journal across the room. Momentarily, that senseless action made me feel better.

As we drew nearer to Christmas, many visitors called at Providence, but the only ones I agreed to see were Edward and James.

One day, when Edward called, I was sitting alone in the drawing room by the fire, staring into space, as Foo tapped gently on the door. "Mr. Caldwell here, Mrs. Cap," he said.

Edward walked over to me and kissed me on the cheek. He looked pretty grim as he sat down beside me on the sofa.

"I am so sorry that you have this great sadness in your life right now, my dear, but it will pass. You shouldn't be alone, and you should not have turned Gideon away. He loves you."

"Love? What is that? All I know is it is dangerous to care about anyone. I have proved that, over and over again. You were wise never to fall in love again, Edward. And if Gideon had truly loved me, he wouldn't have risked Caleb's life that day."

"Oh Jane, be reasonable. You can't blame him for that. He had no idea smallpox was about. We assumed it had been eradicated here in '62. Thankfully there has not been another outbreak—just a few random cases. We all went to the harbour that day, so are we all to blame? I told Gideon the same thing, because he blames himself."

"And so he should!"

"That is so unfair, my dear."

"Stop it!" I screamed. "I don't want to talk about it. Why did our beautiful boy have to be one of those 'random cases'? It makes no sense. So maybe I do blame you all. Maybe I blame the whole bloody world. I certainly blame the man who had smallpox and brought it back to our city and then was allowed to mingle in the crowd. I blame God for allowing this to happen. And I blame myself. Perhaps I did something to deserve this pain, but I don't want to discuss it with you or with anyone, anymore. I am not good company these days, Edward. It's best that you leave now."

He pulled away, his eyes opening wide in astonishment at my violent outburst. He had never heard me swear before. Rising with a sigh, he left me alone again. A few days later, he sent James to see me, but even the sight of James's dear face, now grown into young manhood, could not break through my pain. I turned him away also.

Caroline O'Reilly and Julia Trutch also called on occasion, but both were turned away at the door by Ah Foo at my instruction. Eventually they, too, gave up. I was beyond all comfort or reasoning. I lived one day at a time, a chatelaine in a cold ice palace. I hardly ate, so I lost weight. I merely existed in a dark place, with no interest in life.

When I couldn't sleep at night, I wandered around the house. My portrait at the top of the stairs reminded me of Gideon calling me the *Chatelaine of Providence*. How happy I'd been when that portrait was painted, because I was carrying Caleb inside my body. His presence did not show yet, but an inner glow of peace and happiness was apparent on my face. Roberto had captured my contentment and joy to perfection. But was I ever really that happy? Did it really happen, or was it all in my imagination?

No one but me was allowed into Caleb's nursery. "There are to be no changes," I told Ah Foo. I wanted it kept exactly as it was.

Mary had left us soon after Caleb's death to find another nursemaid position, so most days I sat alone in the rocking chair in the nursery. I let my eyes drift upwards to the ceiling and became mesmerized by a cobweb hanging from the ceiling. I buried my face in his clothes to savour the sweet scent of his baby aroma. Every night I slept with his favourite blanket in my arms. But still I couldn't cry.

Edward and James invited me to their house for Christmas dinner, and Mrs. Finch did her best to make things as happy as possible. Everyone tried to chat about happy things, but their voices wafted over my head. It seemed as though I was always somewhere else, far away, looking down on the scene.

Ah Foo had gone into Chinatown on Christmas day. In fact, he spent most of his time there these days, playing mah-jongg with his fellow countrymen. I'm sure he found Providence depressing, because I certainly did.

Soon after Christmas, a short letter arrived from Gideon, saying he was now in Scotland and staying with his sisters and their families in Rosehearty. The letter said little more, and I wondered why he had even bothered to write it.

Near the end of January 1870, I made a decision.

*   *   *

It came to me in a flash in the middle of the night, and I knew that it was the right thing to do. I was no good to anyone this way, and there was nothing I could ever do to change things and make them better. There was only one answer.

It was snowing lightly the following morning as I slipped out of the house early, without Ah Foo seeing me. I could hear him rattling some pots and pans in the kitchen. I didn't bother to put on my heavy boots, and so I felt the bitter cold on my feet, clad only in light slippers, as I ran quickly down the snow-covered lawn towards the water, almost slipping as I went. I finally reached the pebbled beach below.

The stones hurt my feet, but I didn't care. Soon, nothing would ever hurt me again. All the pain I had suffered since I was a child would be gone. Images flashed before my eyes—Dory and me sitting on a cold bench after her mother died; Mrs. Creed beating me within an inch of my life; scrubbing floors and emptying chamber pots; Philip Sinclair ripping at my underwear and violating me—so much pain. And then my two babies lost in a pool of blood. And Caleb—dear, sweet Caleb—feverish and covered in pockmarks before taking his last breath. These were images I would never be able to erase.

I gingerly made my way toward the steps leading up to the bridge further along the beach. The snow was coming down heavily now. I climbed the steps quickly and walked onto the bridge leading to Esquimalt.

Halfway across, I found the spot I was looking for. I had seen it many times before and had always steered Caleb away from it when we walked that way, because the railing was broken. As I suspected, it had not been repaired.

I stopped, shivering with anticipation and fear, as I gazed down into the murky water below. Soon I would be warm again, and I would see Caleb.

The swirling water was beckoning to me, so I took a step forward and prayed that it would be over quickly.

Then I felt a hand on my arm, pulling me back.

"That is not the answer, Miss Jane," a deep, gentle voice said. Where did it come from? Who was there? The softly falling snow must have muffled the sound of footsteps behind me.

"Go away," I said.

"No, Miss Jane, I won't leave you. You are cold and you are sad, but you have friends here who care about you." Skiff gently pulled me away from the edge, but I began to fight him fiercely.

"Please, Skiff. Leave me alone. I must do this."

"I know, I know." He put his big arms around me in a bear hug and began to rock me gently to and fro. When I finally stopped fighting him, I noticed that Ah Foo and Dulcie were also standing on the bridge.

Dulcie began to run toward us. She was covered in snow, but she took off her own cape and wrapped it around me. "Come home with us, Miss Jane. We'll take care of you."

"I want to die!" I screamed at her.

"That's not the answer, Miss Jane. We stopped by Providence this morning, and Ah Foo was in a big old panic. He said he saw you climbing the stairs to the bridge. At first, he thought he'd seen a ghost. My Skiff ran on ahead. Thank the good Lord he got to you in time."

"I want to die! Go away—all of you."

But Dulcie and Skiff held me up between them and began to walk me back along the bridge.

"We will never leave you, Miss Jane," Skiff said, and somewhere nearby Ah Foo was muttering to himself. "Bad thing you try to do, Mrs. Cap. Mr. Cap never forgive me if I let that happen."

And then everything faded to black.

CHAPTER 43: GIDEON

When the SS *Jupiter* docked in San Francisco Bay for a day to take on more supplies, I didn't go ashore. I couldn't risk running into someone I knew.

Seeing Fleure again would require too much explanation, and I was in no mood for more sympathetic compassion from anyone. So instead I enjoyed the company of a bottle of whisky in my cabin and wallowed in my own misery before passing out in a drunken haze.

A few hours later, I woke to the sounds and smells of the sea. We were moving again, and I felt comforted by the roll of the ocean.

For the next six weeks, the sturdy SS *Jupiter* took every battering the ocean threw at her. While other passengers were throwing up their breakfasts and dinners, I stood up on deck every day, invigorated by the mountainous waves as I held onto a mast while doing my best to forget everything and everyone back in Victoria.

By the time we reached Aberdeen, the captain and crew had decided I was quite mad. "It'll be a sad day when sailing ships are a thing of the past and only steamers ply the seas," I told them.

"Well we can't wait for the day when we have steamships with strong stabilizers," they retorted.

From Aberdeen, I took the new train into Fraserburgh and walked the rest of the way into Rosehearty. I had become interested in railway travel in Victoria, anticipating that a line from the east coast to the west in Canada would happen in the next decade. Edward and I had wanted to get in on the ground floor of rail travel, but now it held little interest for me. Still, I was impressed with the efficiency of the Scottish train service.

My sisters' two houses were high up on the bluff, away from the beach where our old bothy had once stood. That had long since been demolished, and now my sisters and their husbands lived in small cottages sitting side by side on the hillside.

My whole family ran towards me, and I felt overwhelmed by their display of love. Janet and her husband, Tom Ritchie, and their two sons, Jamie and Douglas, reached me first. By the look of my sister, a third bairn was on its way. Janet, always the most demonstrative of my two sisters, threw herself into my arms.

"Oh Gideon, Gideon, it is *so gud* to see you, brother. We knew the time the train would get into Fraserburgh, so we worked out how long it would take you to walk here."

Fiona was right behind her. She also hugged me close to her, and I shook hands with my two brothers-in-law, Tom Ritchie and Robbie Buchan. Fiona's two little girls, Clara and Anabel, smiled at me shyly, but the boys were more outgoing.

"Uncle Gideon, did you bring us some gold from Canada? We heard the streets are paved with it," said Jamie.

"Did you mine in the gold fields, Uncle Gideon?" asked Douglas.

"Now, now, boys," Janet said, sounding remarkably like our mother. "Let your uncle come inside and have some dinner before you bombard him with questions. Gideon, we have food and drink waiting for you. We are all so happy you are here. There will be time enough for some wee tales later."

They were all bonny children, but I was grateful Janet shushed them and took my arm. It still pained me to see other children so full of life. Not to be outdone, Fiona clung to my other arm, and Tom and Robbie steered all the children back to the house ahead of us.

"And why is Jane not with you, brother?" asked Janet, never one to beat around the bush. "After the tragedy you both suffered, she should be here."

I shook my head. "There is time for that later, sister. I will explain it all, but right now I just need to see your cottages and enjoy your good cooking."

Sure enough, a delicious roasted chicken was waiting for us on the stove, surrounded by potatoes, carrots, and green beans, along with warm homemade bread. What a relief she hadn't cooked fish!

We all sat around the table, one boy on either side of me, as we held hands and said grace. For a moment it felt like being back with Ma and Da. Janet's table was different, and there were new family members gathered around it, but the depth of love was the same.

"You will have the boys' bedroom," said Janet. "They will be sleeping next door in their aunt's cottage. The girls will be sharing with Fiona and Robbie."

"I don't want to put anyone out," I said, but Janet simply tutted at me.

"It's our pleasure, brother."

I remembered the days when Ma and Da, Duncan, Janet, Fiona and I had all shared one room, with a hanging blanket separating the sleeping areas. Times had definitely changed for the better in Rosehearty, and I was pleased that I'd helped in some way, sending money over in the early days.

But I also felt guilty when I thought of my own magnificent home back in Victoria, a mansion standing on a large acreage with only Jane now living there on her own. Could I have done more for my sisters, so they too would have had larger homes, with many separate bedrooms for all their children?

After we finished the first course, the boys asked their mother if they could show me their room, where I would be sleeping.

"Yes, boys, but be quick, because your aunt has prepared a special dessert for us," she said.

They each took one of my hands and led me to their room, chatting excitedly and eager to show it to me.

Once we returned to the living room, Fiona brought over two large apple pies, which we all shared. Afterwards, while my sisters cleared the table, Tom, Robbie and I enjoyed a shot of whisky and a cigar I had brought them from Aberdeen.

"We have great plans for the future, Gideon," Tom said. "Robbie and I intend to start a fish business in Fraserburgh and spend less time ourselves at sea."

"We are also investing in the new railroad, Gideon," Robbie said. "It's something you should consider putting money into, too. There is a great future in train travel."

Fiona returned after a while and spoke to us all. "All right now, that's enough business talk for tonight. You men go next door and put the children to bed, while Janet and I catch up with our long-lost brother."

The children protested, saying they wanted to hear all about Canada. I promised them tales galore the next day, knowing my sisters wanted to ask me a thousand questions tonight.

After the men left, Janet flung her arms around me again. "Oh Gideon, we are so sad for you and Jane. Losing your little Caleb—it's so unfair. But there will be more children, I feel sure."

"Hardly likely, with her in Victoria and me in Scotland," I said.

"But she will join you soon, right?"

"Not likely, Janet. She wanted me gone. Our marriage is finished."

"What nonsense is that!" Fiona said in disgust. "You should be together at this time. If she will not come here, then you must go back to her."

"You don't understand ... no one does. All she ever wanted in life was to have a family of her own, and I couldn't provide that for her. One day, I took Caleb to the harbour and there was smallpox around and ..." My eyes became moist so I looked away.

They both patted my hand gently. "We know, we know, brother," Janet said. "Your friend Edward wrote to us about all of it, but that wasn't your fault."

"Yes I asked him to contact you, as I couldn't find the words to write myself. Maybe it wasn't my fault—but for now, I want to stay here with you all for a while. I need time to think and plan. I don't know if I'll ever go back."

"Ah Gideon, of course you will. You love Jane so much, and I'm sure she loves you. But you should be grieving together and helping one another."

"She wants no part of me right now, and I'm not sure exactly what I want. But for now, I'm meant to be here at the Broch with you all."

"For now," Janet said with a smile.

And so we talked no more of it and they both left me alone, clucking like two mother hens as they went about cleaning the remainder of the dishes and glasses.

I was exhausted, so I said goodnight and escaped to my room, where I fell into a deep, peaceful sleep. I was home again in Scotland, and it felt good.

*   *   *

For the next few months, I worked alongside my brothers-in-law, mending nets and gutting fish again. I also went out to sea with them on occasion and helped them haul in their catches. I even looked forward to it, no longer bothered by the harshness of the fisherman's life.

I also played with my nieces and nephews without feeling my own incredible loss, and in June we welcomed the arrival of another Ritchie bairn. Janet gave birth to a third bonny lad, and much to my delight, they named him Gideon.

When I first saw her healthy son, I had a fleeting moment of intense pain, remembering Caleb when he was born, and then later on his deathbed. But I also felt joy for my sister and her husband. Perhaps there was still hope and joy in the world. *I must hold on to that*, I thought. Jamie and Dougie were intrigued with their new baby brother, but even more intrigued by my tales of gold fever, which I embellished every night for them— surely the right of every good uncle.

"My friend Ed and I ventured into the Cariboo," I told them. "Man, it was a wild and fearsome place back then, in the '50s. We panned for gold along the Fraser River while mosquitoes as big as eagles swarmed around us and tried to eat us alive."

Their eyes opened wide in awe. "But did you find any gold?" said Dougie, who was more interested in the magic yellow stuff than the size of the mosquitoes.

"We did indeed. We had to stake our claims at the commissioner's office, and then we returned to Victoria, where we found that other things, like running businesses, were far more profitable in a gold rush than mining for gold."

"Oh," they both said together, in obvious disappointment.

"And I bet those mosquitoes weren't as big as eagles, Uncle Gideon!" Jamie said.

"Pretty close, young man, pretty close."

I also told them about being a riverboat captain on the Fraser River, and they listened every night at bedtime in childish wonder.

"Uncle Gideon's stories are better than any books," the boys told their mother.

"Aye, they are that!" Janet agreed. "But I'm thinking they are a wee bit more exaggerated, too."

Fiona's little girls were too young to enjoy some of my wild tales. Instead, they wanted to hear about their aunt Jane and when she was coming to see them.

"Maybe one day," I said.

When I wasn't working alongside Tom and Robbie, I'd walk up to the Broch and sit on the rock where long ago I had talked to Ma about my plans for leaving Scotland. I still wore the talisman she had given me, and I could still hear her sweet voice telling me that destiny would always bring me home.

Was my being here again now what she had meant? At one time I believed I had found my destiny at Providence with Jane. Now, I wasn't so sure. Did she still hate me? And how did I feel about her? These were questions I turned over and over in my head as I fingered the talisman.

"Ah, so there you are," a voice interrupted my thoughts.

"Janet."

"And what are you doing up here, all alone and brooding, brother?"

"Thinking."

"They look like very painful thoughts."

"They are, because I feel so helpless. Although I gave Jane everything her heart desired, she was always haunted by her past. Even before we lost Caleb, she was never truly happy. She had suffered so much as a child, and for the longest time she lied to me about her childhood in the orphanage, the beatings she endured and—other things—because she thought she was unworthy of my love. Eventually she stopped lying and told me everything. She had been told that her mother was a prostitute and that was why she was left at the orphanage. After I said that none of that mattered to me, we were happy again for a while, and then our beloved Caleb was born. She finally felt she had someone who was part of her. But when he died—oh God, Janet, it was awful. Those unpleasant memories must have come rushing back to her, and she wouldn't let me comfort her. She blamed me—just as I blamed myself."

"Ah, poor wee lass. Such a terrible tragedy."

"We were so lucky, sister, to have had loving parents who cared for us. Even though we were poor, I realize now how very fortunate we were."

"Yes indeed." Janet was silent for a while, digesting all I had told her.

And then she said, "Have you ever thought that there might be one gift you could still give Jane that would bring her back to you?"

"What do you mean?"

"She always wanted to know her true roots and the family she came from, didn't she? Maybe you could find the truth for her."

"Yes, but if I found out more about her past, it might simply make things worse."

"Maybe—maybe not. Who knows? Think on it, brother. But now, come back to the house. I've brewed some strong tea, to which you can add a touch of Tom's best whisky."

So, arm in arm, we headed down the hill, and I soon completely forgot all about our conversation.

CHAPTER 44: JANE

The darkness had gone. I could now see a glimpse of light, and I was warm again.

My eyes hurt with the sudden brightness. Was I in heaven? If so, where was Caleb? I could hear a tapping sound close by. I turned my head slightly to see Dulcie sitting in a chair. She was knitting, her needles clicking to and fro. She smiled at me.

"Caleb? Where's Caleb?" I said.

"Ah, Miss Jane, you are waking up now. That's good."

"Where am I?" It was a strange room, with paintings on all the walls. Sunlight was filtering through a window. A blanket covered me and a roaring log fire was crackling nearby.

"You are in our house, Miss Jane. We brought you here yesterday morning. You've been asleep for a good long time."

"Yesterday?"

"Yes, you slept through the day and most of last night."

"Why did you bring me here?"

"Because I'm going to take care of you, Miss Jane, and soon you will feel better again."

"I want to die. I don't want to feel better. You took me away from the bridge. I remember now."

"You fainted, and Skiff and Ah Foo carried you here. You need rest now."

"No." I tried to sit up. I was dressed in a strange white nightgown that wasn't mine. "I want to get up. I need to relieve myself."

Dulcie came over to me and gently pushed me back against the pillows. "You can get up soon. There is a bucket for you beside the bed. Skiff has gone for another chair to place by the fire, and you can sit there with me. I will make you some tea now. And you need to eat something, so I've made some soup."

She began boiling a kettle on a stove in the corner. Was this small shack where they lived? Was I in their home on Salt Spring Island? Had I been sleeping in their bed? There appeared to be no other rooms and very little furniture, just the bed and two chairs. But there were many paintings on the walls, and I remembered that Skiff liked to paint. This collection must be all his artwork. Even in my confused state of mind, I could see it was quite exceptional.

"I want to leave here, Dulcie. Take me back home. I want to die."

"No, no, you don't, Miss Jane. Things will get better again, once you accept it all. I will help you."

"I will never accept it. No one can help me."

"You must eat some soup. It will make you stronger."

The door opened and Skiff came in carrying another old rocking chair, which he placed alongside the fireplace. He smiled at me. "I see you have finally woken up, Miss Jane. My Dulcie will take good care of you."

He then bent to kiss his wife and left us again while Dulcie helped me up so that I could use the bucket.

"Is this your bed I've been sleeping in?"

"Yes," Dulcie said. "I slept by the fire on blankets last night, and Skiff slept on a friend's boat in the harbour. But we're fine."

She wrapped another blanket around me and sat me in the rocking chair by the fire. "Why are you doing this, Dulcie? I told you to leave me alone."

"Eat some soup, Miss Jane, and then we will talk."

I sipped the soup slowly and drank the tea offered to me. It tasted good.

"Am I in your house on Salt Spring?"

"No, we are still in Victoria. This is our home now. We moved over here last June, to be near the captain to help him through this bad time—but then he went away. So now we help you, Miss Jane."

"But I don't need your help."

"Talk to me about your little boy, Miss Jane."

"No—no, please don't make me do that."

"When you are ready to talk about him, I promise it will help you. I only saw him a few times when we came to visit from Salt Spring Island."

"You don't have children of your own. How could you possibly understand what it's like to lose one?"

"I will try. Please tell me about him, because, you see, Skiff and I will never be able to have a child of our own."

"Why? You are still young." I thought that Dulcie was about my age, although Skiff was probably nearer fifty.

"Yes, I am young and could still have babies, but something real bad happened to Skiff as a young man, so it is not possible."

"What happened?"

"He was born a slave, Miss Jane, and his first master was a very cruel man. The male children born on the plantation were kept for breeding, later others were castrated if they were suspected of raping a white woman. Skiff was angry when he witnessed this happening to a friend of his so he got in a fight one day with the son of the slave master. He was punished by being tortured for hours and kicked violently in his reproductive area."

She smiled when she saw my shocked face. "Oh, he still has a penis and can still perform as a man, but he will never be able to father a child."

"How terrible, Dulcie. I'm so sorry. How can you bear it?"

"Because I love him, Miss Jane. I want no other man, so we are happy and have accepted this thing. You never get everything you want in life, but how lucky we are to have other things like love."

"You are braver than I am."

"No, I am not brave, because I am happy with my man and I love him dearly. He was lucky, though, because later he was sold by the first master to Master Skiffington, who was a good man. He paid wages to all his slaves and gave them all their freedom, long before the war began. Later, my Skiff left the plantation and went north and then headed west to San Francisco, where he met the captain. Eventually in 1858, they came to Victoria, as you know. The captain is a good man, too, Miss Jane. He never seemed to notice the colour of Skiff's skin. He was simply his friend."

The more she talked, the more comfortable I felt. I asked her about the paintings.

"Did Skiff paint all these?" I pointed to the walls.

"He did."

"He's so talented."

She nodded, smiling with pride.

By the third day with them, I even started to talk about Caleb.

"He was the most beautiful boy, Dulcie," I said. "He was like a little angel. He had such tiny fingers and such a sweet smile. He had begun to talk in longer sentences, and sometimes I can still hear his voice calling me, but I keep searching for his face in my mind because it is fading and becoming fainter. Why? I can't bear to never see his face or hold him in my arms again. I only have a few daguerreotypes of him. A photographer came to Providence after he was born and took them."

"But he will always be there in your heart, Miss Jane. He is around you all the time."

"You sound so wise. How do you know these things?"

"Because I have faith and I believe that the good Lord always takes care of us. There is a reason for everything that happens, even though we don't know what it is, and probably never will."

"God deserted me, Dulcie. He took my son away, and there was no reason for that. I need to see him again, not just feel him around me."

On the fourth day, Ah Foo brought over some of my clothes. I was relieved because, although Dulcie had washed and dried the dress I'd worn when I left Providence on that awful morning, it reminded me of that day and what I had tried to do.

I never wanted to wear it again, so the next day I asked Dulcie to burn it or give it away.

CHAPTER 45: GIDEON

In the middle of August, I received a letter from London from a man called Thomas Thurston, who owned a number of railroads in southern England. He wanted to meet me at his office in London the following week.

"I think I'll go and talk to him," I told Tom and Robbie.

"Good idea," Tom said, Robbie nodding in agreement. "It might be worth your while."

After saying my goodbyes to everyone, I took the train south from Edinburgh to London. I really liked this form of travel. It was quick and efficient. I could probably learn a lot from Thurston. He needed people to invest in the lines he was planning to build into southwest England. It certainly gave me something else to think about on the journey south.

I booked in at a nearby inn and later that afternoon walked to Thurston's office in Tilbury, near the London docks. His clerk told me he was waiting for me across the road at the Old Sea Shanty tavern, where he hoped I would join him for a drink and a meal. The clerk took me across, and after introducing us he left.

Thomas Thurston was a rotund little fellow with a very loud voice and a surprisingly strong handshake. Like all small men, he was somewhat cocky and a bit overbearing at first.

"Captain, it's a pleasure to meet you. I have heard much about McBride's Transportation, and I'm hoping you can invest with Thurston Travel to make us both some money."

No beating around the bush with this fellow. He laid it out straight away.

"I'm interested in hearing what you have to say," I said as we sat down. He ordered drinks and a pot pie for us both, and we talked pleasantly over the meal for the next thirty minutes. I suddenly missed Edward's wise counsel. He had always advised me on business matters like this.

Each time the tavern door opened, it brought in a welcome breeze from outside. It was a particularly hot August day, and the temperature inside was stifling. Once, when this happened, Thurston looked up in surprise and gestured to a tall, thin man who had come in.

"Ras, Ras, come over and join us," he gestured. "What on earth are you still doing here? I thought you had long since returned to the country."

"Thank you, Tom, but I don't want to intrude on you and your friend." The man walked with a cane and favoured his right leg.

"Nonsense, the captain would enjoy meeting you. But why are you still here in London?"

"Oh, there is still much work to be done here in the East End. Thankfully, I have not been summoned away just yet, so I hope to spend my last years here now."

"That's wonderful, Ras. Please sit down and join us. Captain McBride, allow me to introduce Erasmus Lloyd, a very dear friend of mine. Ras, this is the famous riverboat captain from western Canada. I am trying to persuade him to invest his money in our railroads, and he is anxious to learn things about our systems, which might be applied to a transcontinental line from east to west across Canada."

"Most ambitious," replied the stranger, extending his hand to shake mine. It was then that I noticed he was wearing a clerical collar.

"Yes, I'm a minister—hence the collar," he said, seeing my puzzled glance. "I used to be a rector in Oxfordshire but returned to London a few years ago. I was ordered back by the bishop to serve at St. Edward's here in the East End, which had once been my old home parish."

Before I had time to take this in, Thurston said, "Believe me, we were very happy to have Ras back with us after many years. Poor chap lost his wife and daughter back in the '40s and was sent down to some god-awful—excuse me, Ras—parish in Oxfordshire in the wilds. Thought they were going to send you back there again, but I'm glad you're still here."

The dark-complexioned man smiled. "It was Great Noxley, Tom, and actually, it was a pretty little village. St. Mary's was a wonderful church, but it was a sad time for me after I lost my beloved wife and daughter, so I didn't really do a good job there."

My mind was suddenly whirling with names that all sounded familiar. I had heard these names from Jane. *Oxfordshire, Great Noxley, Reverend Lloyd.*

"This may sound like a very strange question, Reverend Lloyd," I said, "but was there a place called Field House near your church?"

"Why, yes indeed—it was an orphanage. Why do you ask?"

"And did you know a child there called Jane Hopkins?"

"Jane?" There was a flash of recollection in his eyes. "Ah yes, a sweet child. She had so much talent. I've often thought of her. Do you know her?" He leaned forward, his eyes wide.

"Yes, Jane's my wife. We met after she arrived in Victoria aboard the *SS Tynemouth.*"

"Goodness me. What a coincidence! I heard she had left England. She reminded me of my own daughter, but I feel I failed her."

"Failed her? But didn't you teach her to play the piano? She was always so grateful to you for that."

He smiled. "I did indeed—until that wicked woman put a stop to it. At the time I was powerless to prevent it, but I should have done more. I should have spoken up, in view of what later transpired. I will regret that forever."

He had my attention now. "What happened later?" I knew the answer already from what Jane had told me, but maybe there was more.

"That woman, the matron at the Home, was not what she seemed. Eventually a new board of directors discovered all her evil deeds, like beating children such as little Jane, which I didn't know at the time.

She was also found to be stealing, so she was arrested by the constables and dismissed. By then, Jane had gone into service and I had left the parish, but I heard that Mrs. Creed was sent to prison and is in fact still serving time. I am so pleased to hear Jane's life ended happily with you. Does she still play the piano? And do you have children?"

"She still plays, but we lost our only son last year."

Tom Thurston had been looking pleased with himself until I said that. He was obviously delighted at having connected two strangers from different parts of the world, but my last words caused both men to pause and become silent.

"Poor Jane," the Reverend eventually said. "She had so much tragedy in her young life. And I was so wrapped up in my own grief that I failed her badly."

All at once, I heard my sister's voice in my head. *There is one gift you could give her, Gideon, which might bring her back to you?* Could I? Was it possible? Did I really want to try, after all that had happened between us?

"Reverend Lloyd, is Field House still operating?"

"No, it was closed down, I believe soon after I left Great Noxley."

"Would records still be there?"

"I can't help you on that score, but I imagine they would be held by the county still. But why, may I ask, are you so curious?"

"I need to know about Jane's parentage. She always wanted to know who her mother was and why she was abandoned in that terrible place."

Lloyd sighed, leaned back in his chair and lifted his glass of stout to his lips. "Captain McBride, like so many of those abandoned children, she was the child of a woman who was most probably of loose morals. I hate to say that, but it was what we all assumed."

"Assumed, but not proved," I insisted. "What about the Sinclairs, where she worked in service? Would they know?"

"It's possible—or at least they could perhaps assist you in searching the records."

All of a sudden, I knew exactly what I must do.

"Tom, could you please arrange a train ticket to Oxford for me in the morning, and have it delivered to my room at the Sailor's Inn?"

"Of course, Captain. Anything I can do to help. I wish you much luck, and you can try out our wonderful train service at the same time."

Thurston insisted I have another drink and stay a while, but I was anxious to make my plans, so I smiled, stood up and shook the hands of both men.

"Thank you both. Tonight has been most interesting and very rewarding. You might well have both been an answer to a prayer."

And as I made my way back to the Sailor's Inn, I marvelled at the ironies of life that had placed me in the path of a man who might hold the key to a door I desperately needed to open.

CHAPTER 46: JANE

On the fifth day, Dulcie suggested we go for a walk. The snow was beginning to melt by now, and the sun was even giving out some warmth. I took her hand as we walked around the harbour and passed other shacks and shanties similar to Dulcie's and Skiff's.

"If we were down south, Miss Jane, you would be frowned on for taking my hand. And I most likely would be whipped for taking such a liberty."

"Why, Dulcie?"

"Because you are white and I am black."

"But you are my friend. What difference does our skin colour make?"

She smiled and squeezed my hand tightly. "You and the captain are good people, Miss Jane, but you don't understand what it's like in America. Until Mr. Lincoln said different just a few years back, I would have been your slave."

"Goodness me. That's terrible. You told me about Skiff being given his freedom, though. What about you?"

"My daddy was enslaved, but he ran away to Canada years ago, when he was a young man. He met my mama here, and my brothers and sisters and I were all born here, so I suppose we are all free. But I still hear how hard it is for black folks down south. The war may have given them their freedom, but it didn't make white folk treat them any better."

I felt her sadness. "Being born black must be something like being born poor," I said.

"And even worse if you are poor *and* black. But since I met my Skiff and we settled on Salt Spring with others like us, life has been good."

"But you left Salt Spring and came back to Victoria to be here for my husband after our son died."

"He had been good to us, Miss Jane. It was the least we could do. He is Skiff's best friend."

We walked on a little farther, and I started to look around at my surroundings more closely.

"Why are there beggars sitting everywhere, Dulcie? Victoria is supposed to be a rich city with a good future, yet these folk are begging for money. Are there no jobs for them?"

"Skiff tells me that since the dominion of Canada was created in 1867, the government has refused to accept responsibility for the poor. There are no workhouses here to give the poor accommodation and food until they can find work."

I thought about what she was saying and realized how out of touch I had been since Caleb was born. He had been the center of my whole world at Providence, and I had never ventured far from home. I hadn't joined in Gideon's political discussions as I used to. And since Caleb died, my grief had consumed me.

"Who is responsible for these people?" I asked.

"I don't know, Miss Jane. Perhaps it is left up to charities and churches, but winter is always a time of hardship for many people. We are lucky because Skiff has a job with the Captain."

*   *   *

Eventually we left the harbour and walked away from town, across meadows leading to the forest. She steered me well away from Providence.

"I notice you've watched me knitting, Miss Jane. Would you like to learn?" she asked.

"Yes, perhaps, if you would teach me."

She readily agreed, and so that became our daily routine. Soon we had knitted many scarves of various sizes and colours. One day, we both walked into town again and handed them out to the poor people living on the streets. I purchased more yarn for Dulcie, and we continued our knitting marathons.

"I think I'll only ever be able to knit simple scarves, Dulcie."

"Oh no," she insisted. "Soon I will teach you other things. We can make socks and gloves."

I raised my eyebrows and shook my head, but somehow working my hands on the needles and creating something beautiful began to help me through those dark days. I constantly watched Dulcie and how contented she was with these simple things of life. I so admired her calm and wanted to be like her.

One night, Skiff returned to their shack and stayed overnight. When I awoke the next morning, I saw them both lying together on a pallet bed by the fire. They were still asleep, but his arms encircled her in a loving embrace. I had never seen a more peaceful and reverent scene. It made me long for Gideon beside me again, a quite unexpected feeling.

It was late April by then, and I decided it was time for me to leave and find a purpose again. But the thought of being without Dulcie by my side was beyond bearing. I no longer wanted to kill myself, but I still needed my friend. I realized that Gideon had been right. We do all need people in our lives.

So, as we ate breakfast, I told them my plan.

"I want to return to Providence," I said, "but I would like you both to come with me. I want to hire you both for the house. Skiff can help Ah Foo with outside jobs and the gardening, and you could be my companion, Dulcie."

"Ah, Miss Jane. I am happy to hear you feel ready to return to your home, but you know you are always welcome to stay here too, for as long as you need us."

"Keep your home here, Dulcie. Skiff can still use it as a place where he can come to paint."

"Bless you, Miss Jane," the big black man said, as a tear trickled down his cheek. "We would be honoured to work for you and the Captain at the big house, once you are ready to return. I am sure he will be back from Scotland soon, too."

I was sure that if there had been a letter from Gideon, Ah Foo would have brought it to me, but I had not heard anything more from him and felt he would never be returning. I didn't want to say that and spoil the moment, because finally I had begun to see a light at the end of a long, dark tunnel.

And so, on the first day of May, Ah Foo brought the carriage down to the harbour and we all went home together.

CHAPTER 47: GIDEON

As promised, my train ticket to Oxford from Paddington Station awaited me at the desk the next morning, and I was soon on my way.

Before I boarded the train, I had time to admire the elegance of the London station, which was built by Isambard Kingdom Brunel in 1854. Perhaps we needed stations like this across Canada to encourage people to travel by train, I thought.

Once I arrived at Oxford Station, I hired a carriage to Great Noxley, checked into an oak-beamed Inn called the Harp & Feather and headed to my room, with its sloping ceilings and comfortable feather bed. After washing the travel soot off my hands and face in a basin of warm water, I hired another carriage and headed to Noxley Manor.

It was a grand mansion at the end of a long driveway, and I imagined how Jane, at fifteen, must have been overwhelmed by such grandeur after years in an orphanage. But when I arrived at the front door, I was taken aback by the sight of a black wreath hanging on the door. Oh God, the house was in mourning. How could I possibly intrude?

Nonetheless, I had come this far and could not back away now. So I lifted the brass knocker and knocked loudly. The door was opened by a butler wearing a black armband.

"Can I help you, sir?"

"I wonder if I might have an audience with Lady Sinclair." That sounded like the right thing to say.

"Is she expecting you, sir?"

"No, I'm afraid not, but ..."

"Then Lady Sinclair is not accepting visitors right now."

"I do apologize for the intrusion, but this is very important. Is Lord Sinclair at home?"

"Lord Sinclair passed away two weeks ago, sir, and the family is in mourning. They are not accepting visitors right now unless by appointment."

"My sincere condolences, but ... could you please do me the favour of asking her ladyship if she would make a small exception. Tell her my name is Captain McBride, and I am the husband of Jane Hopkins."

He glared at me disdainfully. "I doubt that would make a difference, sir. Does her ladyship know you or your wife?"

"She did once know my wife, and this is of great importance. I have travelled a long way."

Before turning, he muttered, "Wait here." And then he closed the door in my face.

The minutes dragged by, and I began to think I had been dismissed and I should simply walk away. Just as I began to turn, the door opened again and the butler appeared.

"You are to wait in the drawing room, sir. Her ladyship will be with you shortly."

"Thank you," I replied in relief as I followed the man through the great hall before being ushered into a room to the right. I did not feel it was my place to sit on any of the elegant velvet chairs, so I began to pace up and down until the door opened again.

A tall woman dressed completely in black, her grey hair elegantly styled, walked towards me. "Captain McBride, please sit down and state your business quickly."

I wasn't sure whether I should shake her hand or bow. I chose the latter before taking the chair she indicated.

"My deepest condolences, Lady Sinclair, to you and your family. I had no idea about his lordship's passing, and I am so very sorry to intrude at this time."

"Thank you. Now, what business brings you here? You said you are Jane Hopkins's husband? Is that true? You have a Scottish accent, but you must be from Canada I think, because that is where she went."

"Yes, ma'am, that is correct. I met Jane when she arrived in Victoria aboard the *SS Tynemouth* years ago. I fell in love with her immediately, and we were happy—so happy."

"I am glad that Jane found happiness in the new world. She was a sweet young woman, and I remember how talented and bright she was. I have never forgotten her. I missed her greatly when she left England—but it was for the best."

"Lady Sinclair, I know about your son and what he did, but Jane and I eventually had no secrets and she told me everything—also all that she suffered at Field House. Last year, we lost our beloved two-year-old son, and it is a loss she has not been able to recover from. I am here now to ask a favour of you, because she always spoke highly of you, with respect and love."

"How kind. I am so sorry for your loss, Captain, but what is this favour?"

"Jane has always wanted to know the truth about her birth and who her mother was. Would you happen to have that information?"

She shook her head sadly. "Unfortunately I cannot help you. She was an orphan and I learnt she had been taught to play the piano by the church minister. She was very talented. I also heard that Field House was closed down a few years ago. Some gossip about the woman who ran it."

"Yes, the matron was Mrs. Creed. But would you have any idea where I might locate the records from Field House concerning the orphans there?"

She sighed. "Oh dear, I fear I am not of much help at all." She paused for a moment, as though thinking. "But wait, I have just thought of how you might find the records. My son-in-law, Giles Merryweather, is a solicitor in London. He is married to my eldest daughter, Penelope, and they are staying here with me right now. He's a bit of a pompous fellow, but he is an excellent solicitor. Let me talk with him, as I am sure he could assist you. They are out right now, but I will discuss the matter with him and get back to you soon. In fact, you are welcome to stay here with us."

"Thank you, Lady Sinclair, that is very kind, but I do already have accommodation at the Harp & Feather."

"Oh, that Irish place." She smiled. "I hear it is quite rowdy on occasion, so I hope the musical evenings there do not become too much for you. If so, you are welcome to come here. And rest assured, my son Philip is living in London."

"Thank you for your kind offer to stay, but I think it best if I stay at the inn. I would appreciate any help your son-in-law can give, though—but I do not want to impose on you any more at this sad time."

"I will do all I can to help you, Captain McBride." She stood up and I took my cue to leave. "I will send a message to you tomorrow if I find out anything from Giles."

We shook hands, and I made my departure with renewed hope that I might soon find my answer.

* * *

The next morning, a message from Giles Merryweather awaited me at the desk, asking me to meet with him at Noxley Manor at half past ten. I could hardly wait to get there.

Merryweather was indeed somewhat pompous and full of legalese, but he obviously knew his stuff and seemed pleased to have discovered some information for me.

"Captain McBride, although the old orphanage is now a school, I am told all the orphanage records are still kept there in the basement. Would you like me to accompany you there this morning? The school is willing to allow us access, and the custodian will meet us there."

"Thank you sir, I would be most grateful for your company."

We took off in his carriage for the short journey down the hill into the village. I again pictured Jane walking up that hill so many years ago after leaving Field House and going into service at the Sinclair estate. How scared she must have been.

Merryweather chatted away aimlessly as we rode along, but as we approached the old Field House, he said: "The building looks much the same as it once did on the outside, but I understand the interior has now been divided into classrooms. School is out for the summer holidays right now, but we are to meet with the custodian in the main hall."

But as we alighted from the carriage, the custodian came out to greet us. He was an excitable fellow, who was obviously thrilled to have someone visiting the school.

"The basement entrance is to your right, gentlemen. I will take you down and then leave you. If you find what you're looking for, please let me know, and I will make a note of anything you wish to remove."

We both thanked him and followed him down a dark staircase into the basement. I was anxious to begin, but I could immediately see it would be an enormous task. There were many boxes of files to wade through, but at least they were alphabetically marked. I went immediately to the one marked "H" and soon found some brief information about Jane.

"Jane Hopkins, arrived February 1846, aged six weeks. Parentage unknown. Bright student. Left Field House aged 15 to go into service as a scullery maid at Noxley Manor."

And that was it! "Damn it," I said to Merryweather. "There must be more! And even this is strange, because Jane was told she arrived in January that year and was just a few days old. Something is wrong here."

The custodian was still hovering by the door. He seemed reluctant to leave, as he was obviously curious. He pointed to an old desk over in the corner. "I believe that desk over there belonged to the matron," he said. "You could try that."

I went over to the desk and opened the three drawers on the right, all of which were empty.

Merryweather looked in and shook his head. "Nothing there, Captain."

But something seemed off. Then I realized what it was. "Look at this," I said. "The top two drawers are the same size, but the bottom one is shorter inside." I pulled it all the way out and then turned it around. "And this is why!"

At the back of the bottom drawer was another secret drawer, opening in reverse. I had seen that type of furniture before.

The custodian's eyes lit up, as did Merryweather's. I opened the secret drawer, and inside found an envelope, yellowed with age.

"What is it?" asked Merryweather.

"My God, it's a letter addressed to Jane!" It had already been opened, so I took out the paper inside and read the contents aloud to the two men.

We were all silent for a moment, and then Merryweather thumped me soundly on the back.

"I think you have found your answer, Captain McBride, and I'm sure you will be returning post haste to your wife with this information."

"Yes, indeed I will, but there is something else I must do first. Can you direct me to the prison where Creed is serving time?"

Merryweather looked alarmed. "Do you intend to confront her, Captain?"

"Not exactly. I just want to look her in the face and make sure she's suffering for her crimes the way she made my wife suffer. Her ruthless brutality to young children should not go unpunished."

Both men nodded. We then all shook hands, and I thanked them profusely for their help. Merryweather even offered to drive me in his carriage to the prison in Oxford Castle, on the outskirts of Oxford town.

I felt exhilarated that I would soon be confronting that evil woman who had inflicted so much unnecessary pain on Jane.

CHAPTER 48: JANE

After I returned to Providence in May of 1870, I gradually became stronger. With Dulcie's help, life slowly became a little easier and a little less painful.

Dulcie and Skiff moved into the servants' wing, she as my companion/maid and Skiff as gardener, assisting Ah Foo and Lum with all the outside work. That was a good thing, because over the past year the garden had become neglected. Even dear Ah Foo had lost interest in Providence since Gideon and I had gone our separate ways. Skiff also drove the carriage for me when I needed to go out.

I also became more aware of the rebirth of life, while spending time in the garden with Ah Foo. We planted seeds together and found new species of rose bushes for the rose garden. For some reason, I loved to get my hands dirty in the soil.

"My goodness, Miss Jane," Dulcie said one day as she came upon me sitting on the porch, sipping lemonade after gardening all morning. "Just look at your sweet hands. I will have to get some of my ointments to soften them again."

"My hands weren't always soft, Dulcie."

"Well, maybe not, but I'm sure you never worked like this before, Miss Jane."

"Oh Dulcie, if only you knew. I worked much harder than this when I was a child. Mostly my hands were red and raw from hours of scrubbing floors."

"What? But I thought you were a governess before you married the Captain."

"I was—but I meant long before that, Dulcie."

She looked at me strangely. I suppose to her I had always been "a lady." As I continued to sip my lemonade, I suddenly felt the urge to tell her everything about myself, just as I had told Gideon long ago. I remembered the relief after unburdening myself, and I needed that feeling again.

"I was an orphan," I began. "My mother abandoned me at a home for unwanted children. The matron at the home was very cruel. She worked all the orphans to the bone, and one day she beat me across my back. I almost died. Those are the scars you asked me about. I did not receive them from a farm accident, as I told you."

She took my hand in hers, and I saw a tear trickling down her face.

"After that, I went into service. I still worked hard, scrubbing floors and emptying chamber pots. But it became even worse ..."

"What happened, Miss Jane?"

"I was violated by his lordship's son."

"Oh, dear God. That is something I didn't know happened to white women. I thought it was just us."

She put her arms around me and hugged me tightly to her. I realized then why our friendship felt so special and unique. We were bound together forever in our understanding and compassion for each other. We had truly become kindred spirits.

"It was the reason I left England for good, Dulcie, and then I met the captain. But at first I lied to him about my past, for fear he wouldn't love me. When I finally had the courage to tell him, he said it made no difference. I was so foolish to lie. After we reconciled I conceived Caleb, having already lost two other babies. I thought that finally I'd found happiness."

"Ah, Miss Jane, and you will again. The Captain will return once he has worked through his own grief, I'm sure."

"You are so wise, Dulcie."

That night I wrote in my journal again, for the first time in a very long time. I poured out my heart on those pages, expressing all the pain I had felt. Now there was joy seeping back slowly into my heart.

I was finding peace but, more important, I had found a true friend.

*   *   *

The following week I purchased the shack Dulcie and Skiff had been renting down by the harbour and made them a gift of it, so that Skiff could still use it for painting or on the days he worked on repairs of McBride ships. It was now their own, rent-free, plus I paid them both a good wage for working at Providence. I felt Gideon would approve—though I don't know why his approval even mattered to me.

Some days I went down to Gideon's office, where Skiff and the remaining staff taught me more about the shipping and transportation business. They helped me keep McBride's Transportation going for Gideon—if he ever returned. The new bookkeeper ran everything smoothly and honestly. Skiff, with his limited education, made sure of that.

I never thought of Dulcie as my maid. To me, she was simply my companion and dearest friend. We continued to knit together, and I found it remarkably relaxing. We also walked together every day and learnt new things from each other. I taught her to read, something she had always wanted to do, but she taught me so much more in return. From her, I learnt how to be happy again with so little, and through her eyes and her relationship with Skiff, I learnt the meaning of true love.

By August, I was even allowing people to visit me again and was able to talk with Edward and James and others who called. I felt myself growing stronger daily. The year passed peacefully. I received a few letters from Gideon's sister, Janet, who informed me that I was welcome to come and visit them. I doubted I would ever do that. She told me that Gideon was a haunted man, and he needed me. But he didn't write or return to me, so I felt she was just trying to make me feel better. I wrote back to her with as little information about my life as possible, but assuring her that I was well.

We all spent Christmas at the Caldwells that year, and Mrs. Finch and Ah Foo prepared a splendid dinner of roast turkey, pork, carrots, potatoes and old-fashioned English plum pudding. I even managed to enjoy the company and the food.

And then, one day between Christmas and New Year's, I asked Skiff to send a message to Reverend Bolton, the rector at St. Mary's. I wanted him to call at Providence, because I had something to discuss with him.

He arrived early the next morning, as I had requested, and seemed surprised that I was up and about and obviously looking better than the last time he'd seen me. He had been one of the many callers at Providence after Caleb died and during the following months. I'm sure I had looked pretty appalling and grief-stricken on those occasions.

"Good morning, Reverend. Thank you for meeting with me. I will not keep you long, so will tell you immediately why I wanted to see you."

At that moment, Ah Foo came in with tea and biscuits, and while he served us I continued with my plan.

"It has come to my attention that there are a number of poor people in Victoria, many of whom have no prospect of ever finding work. I discussed this over Christmas with Mr. Caldwell and he told me that these people often end up in an asylum or, because they are forced to steal in order to survive, in prison. Is that correct?"

"I'm afraid that, sadly, that is often the case."

"Well, that must change. I have some ideas and wanted to discuss them with you, as I believe much charity work could be done through the church."

"We try our best, Mrs. McBride, but unfortunately many of the upper class who have the financial ability to help have a rather negative or condescending attitude towards the poor. They believe poverty results from a moral failing. Please don't take this as criticism of yourself or the Captain, but it is true of many people of means in Victoria."

I smiled. "I've never thought of myself as one of the 'elite' anyway, Reverend. Or one of the wealthy, for that matter."

"I can see their point, though," the Reverend continued. "This is a rich country, with many resources. They think that everyone should be able to make a good living off the land, and there should be no poverty. They don't understand that farming, for instance, is dependent on many things, such as weather conditions, as well as hard work. And, of course, many of the rich settlers arrived here with money already in their pockets."

"I agree, that is true. But my husband was not one of them. He worked hard to make his money here in British Columbia."

"Of course," he said. "But despite a willingness to work hard, there is still a great deal of poverty in our city."

"Well, I plan to do something about that."

"What did you have in mind, Mrs. McBride, and how can I help?"

"I intend to encourage other ladies of means in Victoria to help me set up charities to assist the poor until they find jobs. We can organize bazaars and bake sales at the church to raise money. I am happy to organize all this, if you approve. I'm sure we can find many other ways to raise funds, also. Not only can we help the poor who are unemployed, but we can help young women who are forced to work on the streets, or who were— er— taken advantage of, and become pregnant. We could set up a home for unwed mothers and their babies. What do you think?" I was amazed by my boldness to talk about these matters with a man.

"I am pleased to know you are willing to do this, Mrs. McBride. It's a wonderful idea, and I would be happy to assist you in any way I can."

"Excellent. Thank you, Reverend."

He cleared his throat before continuing. "Forgive me for mentioning this, Mrs. McBride, but may I say how very pleased I am to see you looking so well and enthusiastic about this idea. It's good to know you are feeling better now. The impulse to give to others is God's way of telling us we are on the right path to healing our own hearts again."

He shook my hand with sincerity as he stood up to leave, and I smiled at him.

"Yes, Reverend. I think I may finally be coming back to life."

And suddenly I remembered Lady Sinclair and all the charity work she did. Perhaps being rich did have its advantages, after all.

CHAPTER 49: GIDEON

As we drew nearer to the castle, Merryweather gave me a short history lesson.

"Oxford Castle dates back to Norman times," he said. "Most of the original wooden structure was replaced with stone in the late twelfth and early thirteenth centuries."

"It's certainly an impressive building. When did it become a prison?"

"It's been a prison since 1785, but there is now talk of it being expanded even more. We firmly believe that these prisons should be very unpleasant places, as a deterrent to crime. Once inside, prisoners are expected to pay for their crimes by doing hard labour."

"I agree. But I have heard that some of the crimes that bring men into English prisons are, well, trivial—like stealing a loaf of bread, for instance. Hardly a crime if you are starving."

"That's true. On the other hand, some crimes are horrendous. Inside, you will find a mixture of criminal humanity, from murderers to debtors, plus those who have committed much lesser crimes."

The grey stone building was austere on the outside and even more dismal once we went through the archway and knocked on an imposing inner door. Merryweather talked to the guard outside, who then left us to speak to the governor. I was impressed by the kind of power Merryweather had, as both a lawyer and a member of a prominent family.

We were soon ushered inside and through another door, which led down a long passageway, at the end of which was yet another barred and locked door. From there, a long set of stairs led downwards into a dungeon. For some reason, the clinking sound of keys and the echo of our footsteps on the stone floors made me smile. Behind all this security was the woman who had hurt Jane. God, how I hoped she was suffering.

The final door led into an area housing a number of small cells with bars. All around us were prisoners of various ages and appearance. Their shouts and moans echoed against the stone walls.

"Over there's the one you're looking for," the jailer said, pointing to the far cell. "Right bitch she is, too."

I gazed into a darkened cell, where a person with bended head sat on the floor in the corner, separating strands of rope. It was hard to tell if it was a man or a woman.

Merryweather whispered in my ear. "What she is doing is part of her hard labour punishment. It's called picking oakum. They have to do it for hours on end—until their fingers are red and raw."

I shuddered, but it was nothing compared to the scars she had inflicted on Jane's back.

"Mrs. Creed?"

No reply.

"Mrs. Creed, is that you?"

"Who wants to know?" the figure grunted.

"I want to talk to you."

She raised her head slowly. Her beady little eyes looked me up and down. She pushed her long, grey, unkempt hair out of her eyes, revealing a wrinkled, ugly face beneath. "And who the bleeding hell might you be?"

"Watch your language, Number 357," the jailor yelled.

"My name is Captain McBride, and I want to talk to you."

"Ooh, hoity-toity." She stood up slowly and began to walk toward the bars. "Handsome fella, ain't you? Bet I could do something for you for a price."

"Yes, you can tell me why you tortured my wife, Mrs. Creed, but there will be no price."

"What the hell are y'er talking about? I don't know y'er wife."

"You were the matron at Field House, right?"

"So what?"

"Do you remember Jane Hopkins?"

Her eyes opened wide.

"I see that you remember the name."

"Oh yes, she was one little madam, that one. She thought she was something special, she did."

"Why did you keep the letter her mother wrote to her, and where is the other letter?"

"Don't know nothing about any letters."

"But you kept the one that should have been given to her when she grew older, right?"

"Why do you want to know all this? Who the hell are you? The police?"

"I told you, Mrs. Creed. I am her husband."

"Bollocks! She could never have landed herself a gentleman like you, even though she always fancied herself as better than the rest of us."

"Why did you beat her?"

"She deserved it."

"For playing the piano?"

"She lied, she did. I couldn't let her get away with it."

"You are an evil woman, Mrs. Creed, and I am very glad to see you in this place, paying for your crimes."

"How dare you!" she screamed, trying to grab at me through the bars. As I stepped backwards, she hawked up a glob of spittle and aimed it straight for me. Thankfully, it missed my face and landed on my shoulder.

"I see you remember all this very clearly, so I will ask you again. WHY? Why did you find it necessary to harm an innocent child?"

"You don't know nothing about me, you being a gentleman. I had to claw my way up from the gutter. I was poor once too, and I had to fight every step of the way to get that comfortable job at Field House."

"By whoring and stealing?"

She screamed at me again, and I knew I'd hit a sore spot.

"So what, mister! So what? When her mother knocked on the door that day with the baby in the basket, I could see she was desperate, but she was also well-educated. She begged me to take care of her baby until she could return, and she left a letter. Oh yes, she cried her bleeding heart out, telling me how much she loved her child. From the beginning, I felt this baby was different. A few weeks later, a village girl came to tell me the mother had died, so I decided I had a right to read the letter and find out who she was. Imagine my surprise. Ha! I kept the letter in case I could use it to my advantage."

"And so you knew there was another letter she'd written, to a family called Sheridan?"

"Yes, and it drove me mad for years, trying to find it. I was getting close, mind, by asking around—but by then Jane had left and gone into service, and later I lost my job at Field House. Story of my life. You don't know what it's like to be poor."

"That's where you're wrong, Mrs. Creed. I know exactly what poverty is like. But the only way out of it is to work hard. That's what I did, and that's what Jane did, too."

"So why did you come here to torment me?"

I laughed. "Just to make sure you were suffering for what you did. It was a pleasure to meet you, and I will enjoy letting Jane know exactly where you are."

I turned as she tried to spit at me again. "Rubbish, that's what you are, mister, bloody rubbish."

"Oh and it will be my pleasure to continue the search for the other letter. My next stop will be finding the Sheridans. So easy to do when you have money and standing." I wasn't sure of that yet, but I wanted her to think I was.

As Merryweather and I walked away, she was still screaming foul language at me, which echoed along the castle walls. How ironic, I thought, that this witch was locked away in a castle dungeon while her victim was living in a palace on the far side of the world.

Later that night, Merryweather came to the inn and provided me with more documents he had found to confirm the truth of Jane's letter. He also had found an address in London for the family called Sheridan.

"My mother-in-law knows of the Sheridans," he said. "But she had no idea of their connection to Jane."

The mystery was slowly unravelling.

* * *

The next morning, I caught the train to London and hailed a hansom cab to the address in Kensington. It was a stylish area of fine homes, much as I suspected it would be.

A butler answered the door and I asked if I might talk with Lord or Lady Sheridan.

"His lordship passed away many years ago, sir," he replied.

"Oh, I am so sorry. Is Lady Sheridan at home?"

"I will see if she is accepting visitors. She is quite elderly and not in the best of health. Who may I say is calling?"

"My name is Captain Gideon McBride, but she won't know me. She would, however, have heard of my wife. Her name was Jane Hopkins."

He disappeared, and I waited patiently in the hall, listening to the ticking of a large clock keeping time with my heartbeat.

Eventually he returned. "Her ladyship will see you in the drawing room now, sir."

The lady who greeted me was seated by the window. She was dressed all in black, a somber look broken only by a white lace collar.

She reminded me of pictures I had seen of Queen Victoria, dressed in mourning since the passing of her Prince Consort.

"Thank you for seeing me," I began.

"Sit," she said with a determined voice, surprisingly strong for a woman so small. "Now, Captain ..."

"McBride."

"Captain McBride, what is this about a Jane Hopkins."

"Maybe you know the name Anne Hopkins better?" I wanted to edge into this gently. I needed her to co-operate, and I had no wish to upset her.

"What do you want?" She began to look frightened.

"I want nothing other than information, and perhaps a letter, if you still have it," I replied. "I want my wife to know who she really is. I'm not asking anything more, other than to tell you about her and what became of her."

She pressed a button by her side, and the butler appeared immediately, as though he had been listening outside the door.

"Creighton, please fetch me the small red box in my room. I think you know the one I mean."

"Yes, madam." He disappeared as quickly as he had appeared.

"My husband did not believe that woman, Anne Hopkins, you know. He dismissed it all, but I always had a feeling I should keep her letter. I have read it many times since my husband died, and now, if you are truly Jane's husband, you shall have it before I die. But first, you must tell me all about her. Leave nothing out."

And so I did. When she was truly convinced of my story, she handed me the other letter. I thanked her and told her that Jane would now know the whole story.

She sank back in her chair with a sigh. "It's always nice to have a happy ending. I am happy for her," she said as I thanked her.

"It's a pity she didn't have a happy ending earlier, but maybe you will meet her one day."

"Sadly, I doubt that, captain. I am a little old now for such a reunion. But you must give her my love and tell her how truly, truly sorry I am."

I said that I would and then bade her farewell.

That night, when I returned to my lodgings I wrote a brief note to Janet in Scotland.

Dear Janet, Remember you told me to find the gift Jane needed. I found it and will now be returning to Victoria. All the pieces of the puzzle now fit together. Thank you for everything. I promise to visit you again one day. Once I get back to Victoria I will write you a long letter and tell you everything.

I knew she would understand what I meant. I also contacted Tom Thurston, telling him I would be interested in investing in his company and the future of the railroad.

The next day, I booked a passage home, praying that Jane would still be there at Providence and would want to see me again—as much as I now wanted to see her.

CHAPTER 50: JANE

One morning in late February of 1871, while making a list of the charities I was working on and the people I still needed to contact, Ah Foo called to me from downstairs.

"Mrs. Cap, Mrs. Cap! Carriage coming up drive."

Oh drat, I thought. Who would be visiting this early in the day? And without an invitation? It couldn't be Edward, because Ah Foo knew his carriage and would have told me it was him. I looked out the window and saw a hired hack—one of McBride's— coming up the driveway. I would simply ask Ah Foo to tell whoever it was that I wasn't home. Even though I felt so much stronger these days and loved the charity work I was doing, I was still a little apprehensive about visitors—especially when I wasn't prepared. Dulcie had gone into town for me, so she wasn't here to offer her support.

But before I had a chance to call down to him, I heard his excited voice coming from the foyer.

"Mr. Cap, you home! God bless you. You return safe. Good thing you home at last. Very good thing."

Oh my God, it was Gideon. My heart skipped a beat. Was he really here after all this time?

My legs felt shaky as I stood up and descended the stairs from the turret into our bedroom. Then I walked along the corridor and stood on the landing for a moment, looking down into the hall. I wanted to savour this moment and look at him again before he saw me. I scrutinized his familiar curly hair brushing his collar as he removed his jacket and put down his valise, while Ah Foo hovered around him with excitement. Suddenly I longed to touch his familiar rugged face again.

He truly was there. "I call Mrs. Cap now ..."

"I'm here, Ah Foo." My voice cracked as I spoke. I tried as best I could to descend the stairs with a modicum of dignity. What was Gideon thinking as he looked up at me? Was he hating me still because of how I'd treated him? And how did I feel at seeing him again after so long?

He glanced up at me briefly and then looked away before I could study his expression.

"Thank you, Ah Foo," he said. "It is good to see you again. You may return to your work now. Mrs. Cap and I will be in the library." He had used Ah Foo's name for me. Did that mean something?

And without another word he walked into the library, obviously expecting me to follow. Ah Foo smiled and nodded as he disappeared with alacrity and I followed Gideon into the library. Gideon closed the door behind us.

"You're home," I said, stating the obvious.

"How are you, Jane? Were you in the nursery?" He sounded somewhat irritated and so formal and restrained.

"No, I was in the turret—working. I'm well—and you? You look tired. Would you like some refreshment? I can ring for Ah Foo." How ridiculous I sounded.

Without replying, he walked over and poured himself a shot of whisky. "This will do for now, and you might like a small brandy, I think." Without waiting for my reply, he poured it out and handed it to me, our hands touching briefly.

"Why do I need a brandy?"

"I have news for you, Jane."

Oh dear God, had he simply come back to tell me he intended to end our marriage for good?

"News? What kind of news?" I sipped my brandy, which tasted bitter as it burned my throat.

He reached inside an inner pocket of his jacket. "I have a letter here for you to read, Jane. You'd better sit down."

I obeyed as he handed me an envelope, addressed to me but with its seal already broken. As though reading my questioning eye, he said, "It had been opened before I found it. I will explain everything after you've read it."

Well, at least it wasn't a legal divorce paper, so I withdrew the creased paper, yellowed with age, from the envelope and slowly began to read.

> *January 6th, 1846*
> *My beloved child,*
>
> *Today I am heartbroken because of what I must do. I can no longer feed you or take care of you as I should so I must say goodbye to you for a while.*
>
> *You were born on Christmas Eve just two weeks ago, a beautiful daughter, and I called you Jane. Your father would have loved you just as I do.*

I paused, gasping before continuing. Was this really a letter from my mother?

> *But I must leave you today with the matron at Field House until I can come back for you. I promise you I will return as soon as I can. I have asked the matron to take care of you and have explained to her why I am unable to support you. I hope I can return for you before you even have to read this letter when you are older. If not, I have asked her to keep it for you and give it to you to read when you grow up.*
>
> *I am your mother, Anne Sheridan. My father, Samuel Hopkins (your grandfather), was the village apothecary. He was a self-taught scholar and if his parents had had the money he would have been able to study and become a surgeon. Instead he taught himself everything about the healing properties of various plants and substances and was able to make salves and tonics for his patients. He was a very*

knowledgeable man. He taught me to read and write as a child as he often did not have the money for my schooling.

We were not well off but we were comfortable, and we were a happy family until my mother, Jess, died of consumption one winter. My father blamed himself and thought he had failed her because his medicines could not save her life. He lost interest in everything after her death and his business suffered as a result. I had to find work as a dairymaid at Mr. Jarrod's farm in order to bring in some money. One year later, my father also died—perhaps of a broken heart. I lived on in our small cottage and worked as much and as hard as I could to survive.

One day, I met a gentleman walking through the village with his horse. He was on his way to the forge because his horse had lost a shoe while out riding. I happened to be delivering milk there, so we stopped to talk. His name was Richard Sheridan and he was visiting the Sinclair family at Noxley Manor. We were immediately attracted to one another. He was so kind to me, and he was very handsome.

We met frequently after that and our love for each other grew. He asked me to marry him, but of course our situations in life were very different. He said it did not matter to him because he loved me. So we were married secretly by a Justice of the Peace in Oxford and I officially became Anne Sheridan.

Two days later he headed back to London to tell his parents, Lord and Lady Sheridan, about me. He promised he would then return for me and we would move to London.

He left, but days and then weeks went by, and I heard nothing. Had he deserted me? Had I put my trust in a false lover? I would not believe it because I knew we had loved one another and we were married. It was not until weeks later that I learned from farmer Jarrod that on Richard's way back to London, while riding on the Oxford road, he was set upon by robbers. They stole his horse and shot him, leaving him to die on the roadside.

*My heart was broken, just as it is today. My love had died and
I was now alone. Then I discovered I was carrying our child—you.*

*I could only work for a few months, and soon my money ran out.
Even farmer Jarrod could not help me, as his farm was not doing well
and he could no longer afford to hire me. Now I have no food and no
one will hire me with a child to care for. I cannot pay anyone to watch
you. My milk has dried up, so I cannot even nurse you. I am desperate.*

*A while ago I wrote to Lord and Lady Sheridan, Richard's parents,
asking them for help but so far have heard nothing from them. I pray
that they will help me because you are their grandchild.*

*Please forgive me, Jane. I love you with all my heart, but this
is the only thing I can do to save your life. I pray they will be kind to
you at the Home. And I pray even harder that I will be able to come
for you soon, once I have found work and can bring you home to my
loving arms again.*

God bless and keep you safe always,
Your loving mother,
Anne (Hopkins) Sheridan.

My hand was shaking and my eyes were filled with tears—of both
sadness and of happiness—and I had a thousand questions. Was this
really a letter my mother had written to me? Was my father a gentleman
called Richard Sheridan, the son of a lord? Had Mrs. Creed kept this
letter from me—and where was the other letter she had written to
my grandparents, the Sheridans? I fired all these questions at Gideon.

He answered them as he handed me a second letter, the one
written by my mother to Lord and Lady Sheridan, my grandparents,
telling them about me.

"How did you find these, Gideon?"

"It's a long story I will explain to you when you have had time to
digest everything. I know it is a great deal to take in. But I assure you
it is all true. I have other documents here to prove it. The Sinclairs

were indeed acquainted with Lord and Lady Sheridan and their son, Richard, whom Lady Sinclair knew had been killed. But they did not know you were his daughter, of course."

"And my grandparents? The Sheridans? Why did they not come for me?"

"Apparently Lord Sheridan did not believe your mother's story and thought she was only looking for money."

"So how did you find the letter she wrote to them?"

"Lady Sheridan had kept it and gave it to me when I found her. At some level, she always had believed your mother. I will explain everything to you later—when you're ready."

"All that time ... oh, Gideon, Mrs. Creed told me my mother was a prostitute, a woman of loose morals. Instead, my mother really had just fallen on hard times, and she loved me and intended to return for me. And my father was a gentleman and the son of a lord. It was just the way I imagined it as a child. I had told Dory that, and I so hoped it was true. God, how I hate that Creed woman. She knew the truth all the time."

"She was a wicked woman, Jane, but I have more news about her. She was dismissed from Field House about two years after you left to go into service because she was found stealing, and the local constables took her away. She is still in prison in Oxford. I saw her there."

"What? You saw her? In prison? Oh, what delicious justice! But why did my mother not come for me later? She promised in this letter that she would come for me soon."

"Jane, I'm sorry, but she died a few months after leaving you there. A village girl came to the home to tell Creed. Your mother contracted consumption, like her own mother, and she did not recover. I have the papers for you confirming her death, as well as your parents' marriage certificate and your birth certificate. It's all true."

"So Mrs. Creed also knew my mother had died but did not bother to tell me later *or* show me this letter! My background would explain why she always wanted to torment me. She was jealous!"

"That appears to be the case. But at least now you know the truth."

He turned and began to walk towards the door before adding: "I hope this gives you the information you've always wanted. You now know your true roots, Jane. Perhaps it will give you some peace again. Once you have had time to think it over, I will come back and tell you how I discovered it all."

He looked so dejected and exhausted. I could not let him leave. "Gideon, please don't go. Please tell me why. Why did you do this for me? And how? I thought you were still in Scotland, visiting your sisters. I thought that maybe you would stay there and never come back here."

"I thought so too, Jane. There seemed no point. Our marriage is over. You've made that abundantly clear. But then a strange and incredible meeting happened and made me want to do this."

"And you've returned and brought me this news. Why?"

He stared at me with intensity for a moment. Then, in one purposeful stride, he came back towards me.

Placing his hands on my shoulders, he said, "Don't you understand yet, Jane? I realized after that meeting that I still love you, damn it. I would do anything in the world to make you happy. I told you that when we first met, and I meant it then and I mean it now. "

"But I thought I wasn't worthy of your love, Gideon. You gave me everything. Even a beautiful son—and when we lost him, I thought our marriage was over, too. But I've come to realize that this house, my piano, all my jewelry, my beautiful clothes—they all mean nothing without you. Oh Gideon, I'm so sorry. I have missed you so much."

"Do you mean that, Jane? Do you really mean that?"

"I have had so much time to think. I was very cruel to you. I blamed you for everything. But you? You must have forgiven me to have given me this incredible gift. You found out the truth about who I am."

"Jane, it never mattered to me who you are or where you came from, but I know it mattered to you. I loved you when you told me you thought your mother was a prostitute. I loved you when you considered yourself of no value because you were violated. I loved you when you felt you had to lie to me. None of that mattered to me. You were abused in the worst possible way, and I was angry, but I never stopped loving you. It was *you* I loved, and I still do. I always will."

He pulled me into his arms and kissed me gently on the lips and gradually with more passion.

I finally caught my breath, revelling in being held by him again. "Oh Gideon, I love you too." I paused. "Can you do one more thing for me?"

"Of course."

"Although I have gone to the church many times since you left, I have never gone to the cemetery. But I want to see our son's grave now—with you. Will you please take me, Gideon?"

"Of course—if you mean it."

"Yes. I mean it. I've never had the courage to go alone, but now ... now that you are with me ..."

He took my hand as we left the library and helped me on with my cape in the hall. A blast of cold air met us as he opened the front door and we walked together down the driveway. I looked back once and saw Ah Foo, Skiff and Dulcie smiling from a window.

Gideon and I did not speak again until we reached the trail heading north towards St. Luke's-on-the-Hill. I was out of breath by then and feeling the cold, despite my cape. "All the time you were away, I could not face coming here."

He did not reply until we passed under the lychegate leading to the cemetery.

"And now?" he whispered.

"It's time."

He led the way, and when we reached Caleb's grave, we both knelt down in front of the small gold-embossed tablet, surrounded by bluebells and crocuses already shooting up through the cold earth.

His voice cracked as he spoke. "Read it, Jane. Read what it says."

CALEB ANGUS McBRIDE
October 3rd, 1866 – June 3rd, 1869

Beloved Infant Son of Jane and Gideon McBride
  Abiding forever with the Angels
  I read it silently to myself, and then I read it aloud.
  "Now, d'yer see, Jane. He's dead. Our dear, sweet boy is dead. Only God knows the answer as to why. I don't, and neither do you. But we are still alive, and somehow we have to go on living."
  "I know, Gideon, but I simply couldn't face it."
  His voice was gentler when he spoke next. "I understand only too well, Jane, because I couldn't either. But you are a strong woman. You have overcome so much. You now know the truth about your past, and together we can make some kind of future—if you will allow it. Perhaps we will be blessed with more children, but, even if we're not, we still have each other. I cannot go on alone any longer. It doesn't make any sense. For the longest time I've blamed myself, just as you have blamed me, but then I realized that no one was to blame. This tragedy happened. There must be a reason why, but please, Jane, please help me understand it. I need you."
  He bowed his head, and suddenly he was sobbing violently. I stared at him in horror. I could not believe that Gideon, who had always been so strong, was weeping so bitterly. Without realizing what I was doing, I placed a hand on his arm and then my arm went around his shoulders as I drew him into my embrace.
  I allowed him to release his grief before speaking.
  "I too have felt so empty, Gideon, for so long. I could not let anyone inside my heart again, even you. But now I need you, too."
  He looked up, wiping his face with the back of his hand. "Jane, you were always in my heart, as I hoped I was in yours, but our son is now in heaven."
  "Do you think so, Gideon? Do you really think he is at peace?"

"Just as he would want us to be."

"Will we ever find peace, Gideon?"

"We will never forget him ... but we *must* find peace ... together."

I nodded as I ran my other hand gently over the small stone tablet. "Did you decide on the wording?"

"Yes."

"I'm sorry I didn't help you, but you chose well. The words are beautiful."

And then, finally, all the emotions I had stored inside me for so long exploded in one violent outburst of weeping which I could no longer hold back. At last I was able to shed tears, and with our arms tight around each other, we finally grieved together for our son.

* * *

Later that night, as we comforted each other in bed, I told him all that had happened since he left. I told him about my decision to bring Dulcie and Skiff into the house, my friendship with Dulcie, how I could now knit, and how I was helping the poor and organizing charities with Reverend Bolton. I even told him about trying to kill myself on that terrible day, because now there were to be no secrets between us.

In turn, he told me the whole story of how he had fortuitously met Mr. Lloyd that day in London and had then gone to Noxley Manor and eventually found the letter from my mother at Field House.

And as I listened, I finally understood the meaning of real love.

I marveled at Gideon's persistence and all that he had done for me in the name of love—just as he promised he always would.

EPILOGUE

I visited Caleb's grave every week after that, taking flowers from our garden whenever I could.

Sometimes I sat on the grass beside his grave talking to him. Sometimes I just sat in silence, enjoying the peace. Perhaps others might think this a morbid ritual, but I knew in my heart it was not. I had passed beyond the initial stage of grief and denial. I had moved on and dealt with my pain, and I had allowed my husband and my friends back into my heart.

Gideon moved back into our bedroom, and we made our peace as husband and wife. The sorrow never completely left us, but we moved on and began our new life together.

On April 1 that year, British Columbia entered Confederation, and, while the terms were being hammered out, we experienced the last days of colonial rule. At midnight on July 19, 1871, British Columbia became a province of Canada, and it was a momentous day in history. Church bells rang out around the city and gunfire exploded. That evening, we joined our friends along the Arm to watch a fireworks display. Governor Musgrave stepped down as our last governor, and on August 14, our old friend Joseph Trutch was sworn in as British Columbia's first Lieutenant-Governor.

Since the beginning of April, I had been sure that I was once again with child, and this fact was confirmed by our new doctor, John Ralph, in July, just as we were celebrating a new beginning for British Columbia. Dr. Ralph had taken over some of Dr. Helmcken's patients while he was involved in his political career. It seemed appropriate to both Gideon and me that our child would be born in that very momentous year.

And, on a cold, blustery December day, after a heavy snowfall that Dr. Ralph was barely able to get through, our daughter was born at Providence. We named her Sarah Anne, for Gideon's mother and for mine. For some reason, my labour was less painful this time, and her arrival came sooner than we expected. She was obviously in a hurry to come into the world, and was a fiery little soul from the moment she uttered her first cry. Her head was covered in dark red curls, which lightened as the days passed into a burnished auburn, a mixture of her father's colour and mine.

Sarah was strong and healthy and soon became the apple of her father's eye. He spoilt her terribly, just as I had spoilt Caleb, but I did not object. I was more content this time to sit back and watch his joy, fearing perhaps to give too much of my own heart to this child. I sensed inwardly that she would be strong-willed and feisty, and would perhaps not need me as much as Caleb would have. In any case, I argued my feelings this way, because happiness, joy and love are fleeting, and I could not bear to lose any of those three gifts ever again.

I went against doctor's orders, and before Sarah had her first birthday, I was with child again, even though by then Mrs. Finch had told me ways women could avoid pregnancy. I wanted to give Gideon a large family and fill Providence with children and laughter.

On the last day of May in the year 1873, when the weather was unbearably hot and humid, I gave birth to twin sons. It was an agonizing experience, and this time I was in labour for almost two days. The boys were very sickly and only weighed seven pounds between them, and we feared they might not survive.

Meanwhile, we had the boys christened Albert James and Edward Gideon, but from the very beginning they were known simply as Bertie and Teddy.

Dr. Ralph told me, quite definitely, that we should now use precautionary methods to avoid any more pregnancies. The twins' delivery had almost cost me my life, and another birth must be avoided at all costs. Gideon was simply relieved that I had survived and we now had a beautiful daughter and two sons, even though the boys were so small and seemed hardly able to survive. We prayed for them constantly. Slowly our prayers were answered and they grew more robust. We were content with our family of three children.

Our free-spirited daughter, Sarah, was the leader from the very beginning. She was strong-willed and temperamental and soon became quite a handful, so we hired Angelina, a Portuguese nanny, to help with our three children. She turned out to be almost as temperamental and difficult to deal with as Sarah and had even more tantrums. She did, however, have a wide repertoire of Portuguese songs, which she sang to the children and which, quite magically, seemed to calm everyone down. Gideon and I laughed a great deal at Angelina's erratic behaviour, and Providence was once again full of life, vitality and happiness.

Our servants' quarters were replete because Mary also returned, this time as my personal maid. Dulcie was now simply my beloved companion. She and Skiff would always be part of our family.

Mary often helped Angelina with the children, a fact that Angelina considered an insult to her own capabilities, though she gladly accepted the assistance. Our children were all growing bigger and stronger, and the future of Providence looked bright. But I soon learned that life never remains static for long.

Sarah's ardent, passionate nature was destined to almost destroy our family in the years to come.

THE END

THE McBRIDE CHRONICLES continue in *Destiny* (book 2 in the series), which tells the stories of Jane and Gideon's children and grandchildren.

ACKNOWLDGEMENTS:

It has always been my firm belief that a book is not written by one person alone. Certainly this has been the case with *Providence*, the first in the McBride Chronicles series. And a mighty book series such as this family saga has an incredibly long journey of discovery to travel before reaching its final destination.

My original idea for a family saga set in the early years of British Columbia's frontier days began long ago. Once I had completed the first, second and then the third draft of a very long manuscript titled *House of Tomorrow*, I decided to develop that manuscript into two or more books. This involved so much more work and research than I had anticipated, but eventually the manuscript turned into a much better and more professional version of itself—and became a series. I would like to acknowledge Sandra Jonas for helping with this process.

The fictitious story of Jane Hopkins and the family dynasty she and Gideon McBride create in British Columbia, Canada, had been on the "back burner" of my mind for many years, inspired by events over a lifetime of experience and my growing love for the history of Canada, my adopted country.

First, I acknowledge and thank my late uncle, Rob Stofer, who long ago back in England, gave me some old books from his rare book collection. One small book caught my attention and must have planted the seed of an idea in my imaginative, nine-year-old mind. Many years later, it became the inspiration for this series.

To my parents—Jimmy and Nora Stofer—who always believed that one day this story would be told, even when I lost faith many times. I wish they were here today to see that dreams do indeed come true, but I have a feeling they know and are celebrating this achievement with me today.

Although my characters are formed from a composite of memories, events and significant times in my own life, the characters in Providence and the other books in the *McBride Chronicles* series are most definitely all fictitious and simply figments of my imagination. Any similarities to real people are purely coincidental.

I want to thank all my friends who have always encouraged my writing and later as I moved from nonfiction and true crime to fiction– especially my late friend Colleen Manuel in England, who bravely fought a battle with cancer to the end; Gerri Laundy, my Canadian soul sister; Shirley Sanders, who read some of my very early attempts at fiction in England and told me she enjoyed them (even if she didn't—thank you, Shirl!); and my sisterhood of authors and friends here in Canada: Nancy Lewthwaite, Joan Neudecker, Susan Calder-Heaps, Carol Paton, Doris Fancourt-Smith and Ann Herbert.

I also want to thank Terry Stofer and editor Therese Laviolette, who both read the original manuscript when it was still called *House of Tomorrow* and told me not to give up; and my friend (and hairdresser) Marcy, who has been on this writing journey with me forever.

And I particularly want to thank Hancock House Publishers in Vancouver for accepting my debut into fiction after I had previously published over twenty non-fiction and true crime books, and especially their editor Doreen Martens, who was such a pleasure to work with as she smoothed out the rough patches and made *Providence* even better.

And every day I give thanks to my own family—my son Matt and his family (Sara, Finlay and Harry); my daughter Kate and her family, (Jason, Andrew and the spirit of Robbie); my sister, Sheila, and niece, Lisa, in England (and their families), and my chosen daughter Sarah and her beloved daughters in heaven, Chloe and Aubrey, who I hope would be proud of their Nanna Vee because I didn't give up. You darling girls will always be my inspirational angels.

And to the one person who has always believed in me and has stood by me through the good times and the bad—my husband, David.

When all is said and done, I guess I must be pretty lucky.

ABOUT THE AUTHOR

Valerie Green was born in England and studied journalism, short-story writing and English literature at the Regent Institute of Journalism in London. She aspired to being a writer since she was a child and has always been passionate about history.

Before immigrating to Canada in 1968, Valerie's employment included a short stint at the War Office for MI5, as well as legal secretarial work and freelance writing. Her writing career is extensive and includes writing a weekly history column for the Saanich News for nineteen years, a monthly column for the Seaside Times in Sidney, BC, numerous articles for the Victoria Times Colonist, as well as authoring and editing over 20 books on local and regional history, mysteries and social issues. Two of her most recent books were Vanished – The Michael Dunahee Story and Dunmora, both also published by Hancock House.

Now semi-retired, Valerie continues to freelance for a number of news-papers and magazines. In addition, she has served on the board of the Saanich Arts, Culture & Heritage Committee, and the Saanich Heritage Foundation and has volunteered with the Luther Court Society. She is a member of the Professional Writers of Canada (PWAC), the Federation of BC Writers, the Writers' Union of Canada, and the Hallmark Society of Victoria. She lives with her husband in Saanich, BC on Vancouver Island, and is the proud grandmother of two young boys.

Visit her website at:
www.valeriegreenauthor.com